Turning
Tables

Turning Tables

Heather and Rose MacDowell

The Dial Press

TURNING TABLES
A Dial Press Book / April 2008

Published by The Dial Press
A Division of Random House, Inc.
New York, New York

Book design by Virginia Norey

The Dial Press is a registered trademark of Random House, Inc.,
and the colophon is a trademark of Random House, Inc.

LIBRARY OF CONGRESS CATALOGING-IN-PUBLICATION DATA
MacDowell, Heather.
Turning tables / Heather and Rose MacDowell.
p.   cm.
"A Dial Press book"—T.p. verso.
ISBN 978-0-385-33856-1 (hardcover)
1. Waitresses—Fiction. 2. Upper East Side (New York, N.Y.)—
Fiction. 3. Restaurants—New York (State)—New York—Fiction.
4. Chick lit. I. MacDowell, Rose. II. Title.
PS3613.A27145T87 2008
813'.6—dc22   2007026697

Printed in the United States of America
Published simultaneously in Canada

www.dialpress.com

BVG 10 9 8 7 6 5 4 3 2 1

To the many chefs we've known and not always loved. Some were terrifying, most were difficult, but all inspired in us a love of food, and taught us that cooking, like writing, is one tough, rewarding job.

Turning
Tables

chapter 1

I'm going to kill Harold.

While I'm at it, maybe I'll kill my father, too. They're the ones who got me into this mess. If it weren't for them, I wouldn't be standing in a swank twenty-table dining room, wondering if the wineglasses are going to shatter.

"Whoever puts wilted flowers on a table is crazy! Should go to an asylum!"

My new boss, Gina, paces back and forth in stilettos and tight jeans, waving a limp white bloom. "How many languages I have to tell you in?" she shouts in a heavy Italian accent. "What did I do to deserve this?"

I stand frozen in a line of waiters, asking myself the same thing. What exactly *did* I do? Oh, that's right. Four months after being laid off, I let Harold, my father's golf buddy and one of the biggest liquor distributors in the state, talk me into taking a job at a "hot spot" called Roulette. "The owners are customers of mine, real sweethearts. And your dad tells me you can practically run a restaurant single-handedly."

Single-handedly? Did my father really think that a former marketing manager could wait tables at one of the best restaurants in Manhattan? Did he honestly believe that a college summer serving chowder prepared me for *this*?

"Answer me!" Gina shrieks.

I jump. Somebody answer her. Please.

"The florist has really been slipping lately," says Cato, the waiter who's been assigned to train me. With his blond crew cut and *Queen for a Day* T-shirt, he looks like he should be dancing on a bar downtown instead of serving pricy food on the Upper East Side.

"I don't care! Is your job to choose what goes on the table!"

"It won't happen again, we promise," says Ron. His deeply lined face and humble manner say "waiter for life."

Gina tosses the flower onto the scrolled carpeting. "I can't run a business with promises. In my country, is different. A waiter spends his own money before he gives dead plants to a guest. I turn my back for one lousy minute and what happens? Everything goes to shit!"

I step closer to Cato, hoping to make myself invisible, but catch Gina's attention instead. "Ah," she says, leaning forward to get a look at me. She's older than I thought, probably in her early forties. "You must be the new girl. The one Harold sent us."

"Erin Edwards," I say, my voice shaking. "Nice to meet you."

She smiles and extends a skeletal hand. "Gina Runyan. You know Harold and Brenda a long time, I hear."

"Most of my life. I used to house-sit for them when I was younger." I don't mention that their cat ate Cheetos on my watch or that I hosted a three-day party for my senior class while Harold and his wife bicycled around County Clare.

"For other people we make two interviews and a background check, but Harold brought us Ramon, our best prep cook, and he says we'll be happy with you the same way."

"He does?"

Gina tilts her head and her waist-length dark hair swings out to one side. "What size you are?"

"Uh . . . six, usually."

"You look more like eight to me. We give you a nice uniform. I hope it fits."

Eight? "I'll try to squeeze into it."

"Is not easy being a woman, I know." Gina gestures to Cato. "This shirt you wear. You have a mirror at home? Purple is no good on you."

Cato's cool expression doesn't change. "You're right. I look better in earth tones."

Everyone waits in silence while Gina moves from table to table, scrutinizing each centerpiece. Finally allowing myself to breathe, I glance around the dining room and notice for the first time the cathedral ceiling, huge multi-colored chandelier, red velvet banquettes, walls covered in striped silver silk. It looks like three different designers ran wild and went way over budget.

"Mama!" Gina sets down the last crystal vase as a frail little boy runs into the dining room. He wears a navy blue school uniform and carries an overstuffed backpack.

"Nino!" she says, throwing out her arms. "How was your kindergarten today?"

He drops the backpack and flings himself against her narrow thighs. "Okay."

"Just okay? We pay a lot to get you in that school. You must like it." She turns his head with her hands. "Say hello to Erin. She starts working tonight."

"Hi," he says in a small voice.

"Hello there. How are you?"

He studies me with suspicious brown eyes. "Daddy says boys make more money than girls."

"Hush now!" Gina snaps. She gives me an apologetic

smile. "He doesn't know what he says. Come on, Nino. You want a soda and some ice cream?" She takes his hand and pulls him toward a lounge filled with smoky glass tables and black leather club chairs.

"What, I don't get any ice cream?" a waiter named Derek says when she's out of earshot. He has a wrestler's build and a deep, penetrating voice. One of his pant legs is rolled up, revealing a calf streaked with bicycle grease.

Jane, the only woman on the crew, grabs the wilted flower off the floor. "That's it. Feed the kid sugar so he's too wired to notice that Mom's psycho."

"Welcome to the family, Erin," Cato says. "Come on. Let's get you that uniform."

I trot to keep up as he leads me to the back of the dining room and down a slate-floored hallway. "So, what do you know about Roulette?" he says over his shoulder.

"Not much. Just what Harold told me." He doesn't need to know about the anxious hours I spent on Google, where I discovered that:

Roulette's chef was first in his class at CIA, and cut his teeth at Le Bernardin under the late Gilbert Le Coze....He combines French technique, a modernist edge, and an endless imagination, making New American food new again.... The wine cellar includes such treasures as a 1971 Pétrus Pomerol that orbited Earth on the Soyuz spacecraft....

"We're one of the top five reservations in the city right now," Cato says. "That means no slow nights and no empty tables. I hope you're ready to work."

With a tower of bills sitting on my coffee table? "Absolutely. As much as I can." Anything to hang on to the rent-stabilized one bedroom I used to take for granted.

"That's what I like to hear."

He pushes open a pair of swinging doors and we step into the kitchen. "This," he says, "is the center of our little universe." I stop, momentarily stunned by acres of glittering white tile and stainless steel. The room throbs with the metal-on-metal clang of pots hitting burners, the drone of exhaust fans, and the clamor of male voices. At least a dozen cooks work at massive, steaming stoves; racks of well-scrubbed pans dangle from the ceiling. Taped to one wall is a sign: *Live as though your every act were to become universal law.*

"Guys, I want you to meet Erin," Cato shouts.

They glance over and I give them a little wave that I instantly regret. "Hi."

Cato starts reeling off names and positions, as if words like *garde-manger* and *poissonier* were actually in my vocabulary. I try to make up sayings in my head so I won't forget anybody, but give up after "Lorenzo the sauce guy" and "hope-he's-single Phil," a grill cook with thick, bristly brown hair and blue eyes. Strange that I never thought of white double-breasted jackets as hot until this very moment.

"Carl won't be here until the staff meeting at five," Cato tells me.

"Carl. The chef?"

"Chef, commandant, demigod, take your pick. I prefer 'food fascist,' but what you call him is totally up to you."

We start up a steep flight of stairs at the back of the kitchen. Each step is lined with slip-proof tape, and the walls are scuffed and splashed with what looks like dried coffee. "You haven't met Steve, have you?" Cato asks.

"Not yet."

"Then get ready. He's the grumpiest rich guy you'll ever meet." We turn at the top of the stairs and stop at a partially closed door marked "Office." Cato knocks twice. "Steve?"

A muffled groan comes from inside. "Yup!"

The first thing I see is a fleshy bare back, followed by a towel-covered rump, hairy legs, and brown loafers. Steve is lying on a massage table, his face pointed at the floor. The masseur, a muscular man in drawstring pants and Birkenstocks, looks irritated. "Can't it wait? He's finally starting to relax."

"Just need to introduce Erin," Cato says.

Steve raises his head and turns a slack cheek toward me. "Hi," he says, straining to sound friendly. "I forgot you were coming today. Cato showing you around?"

"He sure is," I say. "Your restaurant is beautiful."

"Better be. Cost enough to decorate. We have my wife to thank for that." He slides over an inch and settles down heavily. "I'll talk to you more in a bit. Right now, I need Alex to work last night's party of twenty out of my shoulders."

Cato guides me out of the office. "Sorry. I forgot Thursday was massage day." He takes me to the end of the hall and ducks under a low doorway. "Well, here it is. The last frontier. I keep meaning to bring in some plants to liven up the place, but I've been so busy with acting classes and all."

A row of metal lockers fills one wall of the cramped room, which is made even smaller by a slanted ceiling. Several chairs with blown-out seams are scattered around an old card table. A dented silver candlestick holds open the only window, letting in humid September air and traffic noise from Madison Avenue. The place reeks of sweat and cigarette smoke.

Cato opens a narrow closet and pulls out a slim black skirt and a white shirt with ruched sides. "Armani," he says, handing them to me. "Ruin 'em and you're out six hundred bucks."

"Six hundred?"

"What'd you expect, J. Crew? I've only been here a year and I'm already on shirt number three." He feels around the top shelf, then tosses me a package of black tights. "Here's a starter pair. You'll be putting them through heavy rotation, so you'd better stock up."

"I will," I say, planning to quit long before they wear out.

He takes a dark gray suit and pale-blue silk tie from a locker and drapes them over the back of a chair. "I'll look the other way if you want," he says, unzipping his jeans. "Otherwise just go ahead and strip. That's what the rest of us do."

We change in awkward silence. Uh-oh. I guess I *am* a size eight. When I turn around, Cato is no longer a would-be actor with a side job, but a polished, professional waiter. Even his crew cut seems stylish instead of funky. He punches in for both of us, then hesitates, frowning at my ballet flats. "You brought different shoes, I hope."

I look down. "Why? I'm supposed to wear black ones, right?"

"Yeah, but you know how it is when service starts. Stuff falls all over, the kitchen floor gets slippery . . . If you're not wearing rubber soles, you get airmailed."

"I've never had a problem with them before, but . . . okay. I'll wear different shoes tomorrow."

"Good. See you downstairs."

After he leaves, I stand in my uniform in front of the smeared full-length mirror. This is *not* how I pictured myself looking at twenty-eight. The glass is warped, making my small chin disappear and my hazel eyes seem farther apart. Even my hair is different—more red than light brown. Considering what I'm about to do, it seems fitting that I hardly recognize myself.

Maybe this is some kind of karma. My restaurant etiquette was never the best, even when I was earning a lot of money and eating out three nights a week. I made a habit of changing tables, leaving fifteen percent to the penny, and booking multiple reservations before choosing one at the last minute. Though I wouldn't have admitted it, I felt a little superior to waiters, never dreaming that I'd end up becoming one. I was too smart for restaurant work, too confident that another marketing company would snap me up. I turned down three jobs because the salaries were low and the positions beneath me. That was more than two months ago.

What an idiot I was. It would have been humbling to work as an assistant again, but at least I'd be wearing my own clothes.

"You used to have such promise," I mutter. "Look at you now."

Fold corners to center line . . . turn over and rotate one-quarter turn . . .

After forty-five minutes of polishing silverware, scrubbing baseboards, and steaming wineglasses with a portable humidifier, I'm folding napkins into peaked shapes called bishop's mitres. Despite Cato's detailed lesson, I've produced some very unholy results. How could I have eaten out so many times and never noticed the napkins? Have they always been this complicated? If I can't even fold napkins, how will I ever learn to wait tables?

. . . bring bottom edge up to top edge . . .

I slowly work through a mound of linen while the other waiters triple-check their sections. They squint at the tables from every possible angle, micro-adjusting spoons and sliding wineglasses a millimeter to the left. Ron stares at a red-and-white abstract painting, closes one eye, then taps on the upper corner. "There. That's better."

Six napkins down, dozens and dozens to go. "They were

fighting earlier," Jane says behind me. "Gina wants her mother to come live with them, but Steve won't budge."

Cato snickers. "Ten bucks she moves in by October."

"Think they'll end up getting divorced?"

"Gina wouldn't dare offend the pope."

"Knock it off," Ron says. "Their personal life is none of our business."

"That's why it's so interesting," Cato answers.

I hear a faint ring and glance up to see Derek pulling a cell phone from his trouser pocket. He snaps it open and ducks around the corner. "Gimme a break," he says. "Maybe if I get two more jobs and sell a kidney I'll be able to afford commercial space in Manhattan. Try again."

"That guy's insane," Jane says. She has blunt, eye-skimming bangs and skin that looks like it's never seen the sun.

"He's the only waiter I know who's dumb enough to want to open a restaurant and stubborn enough to make it happen," Cato says. He leans over my shoulder and surveys my progress. "Better pick it up or you'll be folding napkins until you hit menopause. Here, pass me some of those."

I push a pile of linen in his direction and shift from foot to foot. After only an hour on the job, my arches are throbbing. I start to lower myself into one of the velvet-cushioned chairs, but Cato reaches out and swoops me back up to a standing position. "Uh-uh. We don't sit down when Gina's here. *Ever.*"

"No leaning, either, unless you're off the clock," Ron adds, grabbing some napkins and heading for the lounge.

As we fold, Cato points out various employees and describes their functions and personalities. "Omar, head busboy, sends all his money back to Veracruz. . . . Kimberly, also known as Stepford Hostess. Answers to 'Mario Testino at table two.' . . . Alain, our French lady-killer bartender. He's the fantasy of half the women on the East Side, single, married, or status unknown. . . . Chen and Luis, our food runners. Chen taught economics in China."

That's a relief, I think. At least I'm not the only one working below my pay grade.

"His pal Luis has the worst temper this side of the Pecos. . . . The guy with the little black glasses is Geoffrey, our sommelier. He has a genius IQ and can give you vintage statistics for the past hundred years. The cocktail waitress gets here at six. The lounge is her turf, so watch out or she'll steal your Riesling."

"I could use help leveling tables in here," Ron calls.

"Sorry, man, I'm trying to get a wicked stain out of the rug," Derek says from under the front window.

Cato rolls his eyes. "This place would fall apart without me. Think you can finish the napkins on your own, Erin?"

I tell him what any waiter burdened with the new kid wants to hear: "I can handle it."

"Great. Stick them in the cabinet under the wait station and meet us in the kitchen for the staff meeting in ten minutes. Whatever you do, don't be late."

"I won't be." But as soon as he's out of sight, I start to wonder if I'll be done by morning. The napkins seem to multiply as I fold them, and for every good one there are two that are lopsided or deformed. *Bring the corners together, tuck one into the other* . . . damn bishops. I glance at my watch. Approximately thirty napkins divided by seven minutes is . . . impossible. I'll have to go faster.

One by one the waiters leave the dining room and walk toward the kitchen. I fold as if the place is on fire, and with only ninety seconds to spare I scoop the napkins into my arms and look around wildly for a mahogany hutch. It was near the kitchen, wasn't it? I run into the hallway, pinning the hats with my chin. Maybe it's behind that door. I stumble inside and find Steve, wearing a white terry-cloth robe and plastic sandals. He's sitting in what appears to be a private dining room, a balloon glass of red wine and the *Robb Report* on the table in front of him. "What the hell are you doing?" he asks.

"Trying to find the wait station," I say, horrified.

"You went right by it." His voice is tinged with irritation. "It's ten steps to your left."

"Thanks. Sorry."

"Close the door on your way out."

I free one arm and shut the door too hard, nearly dropping my entire load. Racing back the way I came, I see Cato, Jane, and Ron striding into the kitchen with Derek on their heels. I locate the hutch, yank open the cabinet, and start madly piling in napkins. Maybe it's the fact that half of them have collapsed, but they're not stacking well. At all.

"Come on, come on," I mutter, abandoning hope and stuffing them in pell-mell. I push the cabinet closed, get to my feet, and sprint toward the kitchen. As I round the corner I look back and see a crushed bishop's mitre lying on its side in the middle of the hallway, where Steve is sure to find it. But there's nothing I can do about it now.

I shove open the swinging doors and burst into the kitchen, arriving out of breath and—oh shit. Late.

chapter 2

A tall, solidly built man stands in the middle of the kitchen. His face is craggy and almost handsome, and his large features are weathered from the sun. He wears black-and-white checked pants, leather clogs with worn heels, and a starched chef's jacket with the words *Carl Corbett* stitched across the breast in dark blue.

"From now on, we'll be storing the salmon on their bellies in crushed ice," he says as I join the other waiters. "This mimics the swimming position and puts less stress on the muscle, so the texture stays firm. Please pass this information on to guests."

"That's Alaskan salmon, right, Chef?" Ron asks.

Carl briefly closes his eyes, as if the question were too painful to bear. "Ron, how long have you worked here?"

"Since we opened. Eighteen months ago."

"Have I ever served salmon in early September that wasn't hook-and-line-caught in Alaska?"

"Uh . . . not that I remember."

"If I decide to, I'll let you know."

Ron swallows. "Sorry. I was just trying to be thorough."

"While we're wasting my time, does anyone else have a pointless question?" Carl raises his eyebrows and looks around. I avoid his gaze by dropping my eyes to his calloused hands, where barely healed burns vie for space with cuts, scratches, and blood blisters. One of his thumbnails is completely black.

"No? Then let's move on. Cato, anything from last night's service you'd like to bring up?"

"Table sixteen, second seating," Cato says, his voice crisp and businesslike. "Peter and Laura Galbraith. They raved about the sturgeon sashimi and made another reservation for next month. We might want to send out an extra course when they come back."

"I'll make sure we do. Jane, you look tired. What's going on?"

"The usual," she says. "Nursing school during the day and Roulette at night."

"That boyfriend of yours must get awfully lonely."

Jane's face goes white. "Julian and I are fine. Don't worry, I can handle my schedule."

"If you could handle it, you wouldn't look like you'd spent the last twelve hours emptying bedpans. Start taking naps. Now, do you have anything to add to Cato's comments?"

She takes a shaky breath. "The O'Connells asked for your whole sea bass recipe so they can serve it at their daughter's bridal shower."

"I'll send it to them. Ron, any updates?"

"I'd just like to say that the energy in the dining room was amazing. Everybody was really fired up about the new tasting menu."

"Wait until I add roasted langoustines and pig's trotters," Carl says. "They'll be doing backflips."

Since I have nothing to report about last night except that I drank a few too many vodkas with my friend Rachel, I'm hoping Carl will pass me over. But as soon as his deep-set brown eyes settle on me, I know I won't be so lucky.

"So, you're Miss Edwards," he says. He gives me a quick head-to-toe appraisal, as if trying to gauge my serving ability on looks alone. "I hear you're pals with our favorite liquor distributor and annual wine-tasting emcee."

I laugh uncomfortably. "Well, not *pals,* exactly. Harold's an old family friend."

"We should all have friends like Harold to pull strings for us. Right, guys?" He turns to his cooks, who respond with a chorus of *yeah*s and *damn right*s.

Carl pivots back to me, his expression serious. "Tell me something, Erin. Are you in the habit of being late?"

"Actually, I'm not. I got turned around in the hallway and—"

He holds up his hand. "I expect you to be on time to these meetings, every afternoon, no exceptions. Is that going to be a problem for you?"

A young, acne-scarred cook looks up from chopping shallots. I can tell from his suppressed grin that I'm the evening's entertainment. "Not at all."

"Glad to hear it. Then we won't need to have this talk again, will we?"

The waiters visibly relax as Carl takes a clipboard off the wall and skims over a sheet of paper. I feel embarrassed yet strangely exhilarated, as if I were teetering on the edge of a cliff. It isn't attraction, but something disturbingly close— a sudden craving for Carl's approval. From the awestruck faces around me, I can tell he inspires this reaction in everybody.

He raises his head. "Cato, question: are you in charge of Erin's training?"

"Yes, I am."

"Her mistakes are your mistakes. Remember that."

"I will, Chef."

He sniffs and sets the clipboard aside. "Marty!" he shouts to a man I vaguely remember as the sous chef. "Let's have the first special."

Marty, who sports rimless glasses and a graying goatee, comes out from behind the row of stoves and stainless steel shelving that Cato referred to as "the line." He carries two oversized white plates, each holding a precarious arrangement of food that looks more like modern architecture than sustenance. On one plate, a rectangle of pearly fish balances on top of colorful, thinly layered vegetables; on the other, two pieces of beef form a tepee over barely wilted greens and a pool of bright pink sauce.

Carl clears his throat. "The fish special this evening is roasted monkfish with crispy shallots, mâche emulsion, and an eggplant and Black Zebra tomato napoleon. The grill selection is a ten-ounce rib eye. It's organic, free-range, slaughtered humanely, and dry-aged at high altitude. We'll be serving it with a Jerusalem artichoke gratin and red bell pepper jus. Both specials are forty-two dollars."

We furiously take notes as he dips his index finger into the pink sauce and touches it to his tongue. "These are the best peppers we've had all summer."

"I ordered two more cases this morning," Marty says.

"Good. Start thinking about a cold soup." We stand with our pens raised like reporters at a press conference, waiting for him to continue. "The salad tonight is Hirabara Farms greens with fresh sugar peas, Villa Stabbia olive oil, and a splash of seventy-five-year-old balsamic vinegar. Charge sixteen dollars for it." He takes a frilly piece of frisée from the plate, pops it into his mouth, and finishes with a direct order: "Sell the sole. Dover, same preparation as last night. We only have fourteen of them, so watch the board. Any questions?" He looks at each of us, then claps his hands loudly.

"Wake up, folks! The shift hasn't even started and you're comatose! Take NoDoz, get religion, whatever you have to do to make our guests happy. Thank you all."

My notes, complete with question marks, underlines, and scribbled-out words, are graffiti compared to Derek's orderly shorthand, which I inspect over his arm. He stares at me as if I'm trying to cheat. "Need something?"

"Just making sure I got everything, that's all."

I'm copying his spelling of Hirabara when the pastry chef, a stocky woman in her thirties with a long blond braid, comes over and gives me a floury handshake. "Betsy Lowe. The affirmative action member of the kitchen."

"She won the National Pastry Competition," Derek tells me. "It's kind of like *Iron Chef* except everything's fourteen feet high and filled with live goldfish and shit."

"I only won because the best cake collapsed," Betsy says. "I warned the guy his chocolate sailboat looked shaky, but he didn't listen."

She gives us a short dissertation on the quark-level components of tonight's gingerbread pudding ("spiced with Costa Rican blue-ring ginger and steamed in a Teflon-free mold") and instructs us to offer it with either honey whipped cream or bourbon-vanilla sauce. She leaves us with a miniature pudding to taste and encourages us to "have fun out there."

Jane pulls five forks from her skirt pocket, hands them around, and digs into the fish. "Make the most of it," she whispers to me. "We get a staff meal too, but it's usually just pasta and we hardly have time to eat it."

I pick at a corner of perfectly square onion tart while avoiding Derek's probing utensil. I feel oddly like an inmate, crowding around the table and sharing my meal with uniformed strangers under bright lights. Though my first bite is only a sliver of pastry and filling, the flavor is layered and offbeat, different from anything I've ever tasted. It takes a rare talent to surprise someone who's been eating— and eating out—her entire life, and every bite is both a revelation and a message: Carl isn't just a scary chef with a popular restaurant. He's a genius.

I stuff in my last delicious bite of bow-ties marinara as Ron chews and pops an antacid. "Did Cato fill you in on the guest mood evaluation?" he asks.

I swallow. "The what?"

"The guest mood evaluation," he says as if I'm hard of hearing. "We assign every guest a number between one and ten depending on their mood when they get here, then write it on the white marker board by the pickup window. Anyone who rates under seven is 'critical.' Our last sous chef came up with it. He used to be an EMT."

I want to laugh, but Ron looks so earnest I don't dare. "What an interesting system."

"We take unhappy guests seriously here," he says. "Their mood score needs to go up at least three points before they leave."

"How do you do it? Free drinks? Dessert on the house?"

"Sometimes, but our main weapon is the smile."

"You just . . . smile at them?"

"Of course," he says, his round face a little too close to mine. "We also send out good feelings. We walk by the table as often as possible and radiate positive energy. It's amazing how well it works. We can usually turn a six into an eight or nine on vibes alone. I guarantee somebody in the restaurant will be miserable tonight, and you'll see what I mean."

I hand my plate to the dishwasher and follow Ron to the lounge, where Steve is waiting with the reservation book in hand. He's showered, changed into a beige wool suit, and combed back what's left of his hair. His high forehead is dotted with sweat.

"Cato, I'm seating Dr. Benitz in your section at seven thirty," he says. "He's getting sued for malpractice again—I hear the woman's nose is a mess—make him your priority at all times. Erin, I assume you can find your way around the restaurant by now. Please make every effort to behave like a seasoned member of the staff. Jane, Bill and Nancy Garske are arriving at nine. I thought I recognized the name, so I did a quick Internet search and I was right on the money. He owns three casinos in St. Maarten. Keep him happy. Ron, you have a fiftieth-birthday party in the private dining room. Gigi Harrison, big in commercial real estate. Talk to Betsy about the cake."

"Will do, sir," says Ron.

Derek peers over Steve's shoulder. "Can I look at the book?"

"What for?" Steve says, pulling it closer.

"I want to see who I'm getting."

"You'll see who you're getting when they sit down. I always tell you when you have a VIP coming in. Tonight you don't."

"Okay, it's just that I've had a lot of boring deuces lately."

"If you need a challenge, talk to Carl about a prep position," Steve says. He reaches into his pocket and pulls out my runaway bishop's mitre, which is now just a limp, wrinkled piece of linen. "Erin, I believe you left this on the floor."

I frown as if I've never seen it before. "I must have dropped it on my way to the kitchen."

"Our guests are either well-connected or they spend days on the phone and online trying to get a table two months in advance. Somebody actually sold their Saturday reservation on eBay for five hundred bucks. These things don't happen because we leave napkins on the floor for people to trip over."

"I'm really sorry."

"Please be more careful in the future." He looks at Cato. "I'd like Erin to be your runner tonight."

Runner. What do runners do again? Bring food to the table? Oh, God. I'm not even *close* to ready.

Cato nods. "Good idea."

"Isn't it a little soon?" I say.

"You can't learn just by watching," Steve tells me. "If you run food, you'll know the menu by the end of the night."

I feel a touch on my back and turn to see Gina, in a vampish red dress and bow-tied heels. The fine lines around her eyes are filled with concealer. "Bad posture makes even a pretty girl ugly. No slumping here, okay? And Cato, you don't train her by standing around. *Andiamo.*"

"You heard the lady, Erin," Cato says. "Let's go."

He leads me from section to section, rattling off table numbers ("There's no table thirteen—Gina's superstitious.") and quizzing me on everything from the specials to the responsibilities of each cook. But when the first diners hit the door at six thirty my thoughts switch from porcini reduction and mood evaluations to something much more important: social self-preservation. Please, God, don't let me see anyone I've slept with.

I stand against the side wall, imitating the other waiters—mute, ramrod straight, hands behind my back. Ron scores the first guests of the evening, a couple with deep suntans and bitter expressions. "Well, aren't they warm and fuzzy," Jane mutters.

Ron looks offended. "They could be coming from a funeral for all you know."

"Oh, please," Cato whispers. "They probably just lost at doubles."

After his initial visit to the table, Ron designates his grumpy couple a five and writes "Critical—upstairs neighbor renovating" on the whiteboard in the kitchen.

"Carl might send them an extra course and a glass of champagne, or ask Betsy to make a miniature jackhammer out of marzipan and garnish their dessert with it," he tells me. "The little touches let people know we care."

Next on my educational tour is the computer in the lounge, where Cato introduces me to dozens of mysterious codes. "Three-letter codes are for wine and liquor," he says, tapping lighted buttons on the screen. "Four-letter codes are appetizers. Four-letter codes made of consonants only are—"

He glances over the top of the monitor. "Oh, *fuck* me. The Wallers are back. Third time this month."

"Again?" Alain says, rattling a cocktail shaker back and forth. "They don't have a stove?"

"Great. They're sitting in my section, too."

I turn to see Steve leading an older couple to a corner booth. The man is short, with a graying comb-over and a slight limp. His plump wife brings up the rear in a purple tunic and slacks.

"Ivan and Elaine," Cato says. "Antiques dealers who never rate over a seven, no matter what we do. She likes to invent her own menu, and he always wants four ice cubes in his drink, the air-conditioning turned up, and two extra napkins. I never hear them talk to each other about anything but food."

"Ivan buys a little vase for a hundred euros in Aix, then sells it in his store for a thousand dollars," Alain says. "He's not so honest, I think."

"How'd he get the limp?" I ask.

"He claims he fell into a ravine on a buying trip to Morocco," Cato replies, "but he probably just slipped in the tub after a few too many. All right. Let's shoot smiles at Ron's people, then we'll tangle with the Wallers."

Now that half the tables are filled, my first step into the dining room feels like walking onstage. I'm both conspicuous and unimportant, an extra who could ruin the show with one false move. "Gina's watching, so show them your choppers," Cato says as we approach Ron's twosome, who are picking miserably at a basket of Betsy's black sesame flatbread. I grin at them and am surprised when they smile back.

"See that?" Cato whispers after we pass by. "It works every time."

In the few seconds it takes us to get to the Wallers' booth, Cato assumes a different personality. His expression goes from natural and animated to vacant and peaceful, with just a trace of contempt. "Good evening and welcome back. How nice to see you both again."

"Hi, Cato," Mr. Waller answers, hardly looking up.

"I'm starving," says his wife.

"So order," her husband answers. "That's why he's here." He glances at me and frowns. "Who are you?"

"Erin's a new addition to our staff," Cato says smoothly. "She'll be observing tonight."

Mr. Waller seems bothered by this, as if Steve should have consulted him before making changes to the place where he spends so much time and money. "Erin," he repeats. "Is that Irish?"

"Scottish, actually," I say. "I think."

"Are you married?"

"Not yet."

"Native New Yorker?"

"Does Long Island count?"

"To some people, I guess. You don't commute, do you?"

"No, I live in the city now."

"Alone?"

"Usually."

He rears back a little. "I see."

Cato tries to regain control of the conversation. "Same wine as always, Mrs. Waller?"

"Colder this time."

Cato doesn't miss a beat. "I'll have Alain put it on ice for you."

"Okay, but not for too long. My new crown is sensitive." She touches her tongue to one of her back teeth and pushes her menu across the table. "Give me the pigeon, well done, no vegetables, with the blood orange relish that comes on the bass."

"Excellent. For you, Mr. Waller?"

"I'll have what I had on Monday, hot as hell. And don't forget my napkins."

Without verifying a single detail, Cato repeats back Monday's appetizer and main course and trots to the lounge to punch it into the computer.

"You must have a photographic memory," I say.

"Don't be too impressed. He's ordered the same thing for the past two weeks. Some people get off on monotony."

After bringing the Wallers' drinks, Cato takes me to the kitchen, which is exploding with noise and activity. Orders flow in, giving the room the tense, urgent atmosphere of a field hospital. Phil and Lorenzo step around each other in a steamy two-square-foot area, peeling meat off the flame-shooting grill, poking tongs into sizzling pans, but somehow never colliding. Another cook whistles constantly as he arranges plates, stopping only to bark in Spanish at a man with dark bags under his eyes. Carl, his face blotchy from heat, peers over everyone's shoulder, reading the order tickets hanging in front of him, tasting and touching everything that goes out. He seems to be everywhere at once.

"Nice, Lorenzo," he says, licking sauce off a spoon. "Being Italian hasn't hurt your demi-glace. Phil, this isn't an extension school art class where anything goes. For the fifth fucking time, I want your grill marks to be dark caramel brown, not black. Should I brand it on your forehead or will you remember?"

"I'll remember, Chef."

"Cato, let me know when Dr. Benitz gets here. I'm going to make him an amuse bouche so mind-blowing, he'll smile all night."

Next to the list of table numbers on the board, Cato writes "Wallers—six. Bickering, dental work."

I'm turning to follow him out of the kitchen, when I step into a greasy spot next to the trash can. My shoe slips and I suck in a breath, instinctively reaching for Cato's arm, but he's too far away. With nothing to hold on to, I lose my balance and the ground pulls out from under me.

The last thing I see before I hit the floor is Carl's stunned face, gaping at me from behind the line.

chapter 3

"Erin!" Cato cries.

From my position on the floor, all I can see are Chen's shins and Marty's wide shoulders looming over me. "Wipe out!" he bellows. "Penguin down!"

I hear laughter travel around the kitchen, then Carl's voice. "Let's hope she's this impressive out in the dining room."

Ashamed, disoriented, tailbone radiating pain, I struggle to sit up and recover my shattered dignity. "I'm fine," I croak. "Nothing broken. Cracked, maybe, but..."

Cato reaches for my hands as Gina bursts through the swinging doors, nearly running into Chen. He steps back, lifts his plates above his head, and shoots through the opening before the doors close again.

"Dr. Benitz is here!" Gina cries. She peers down at me and squints. "What's happening? What are you doing?"

"Cato's trainee is showing us how graceful she is," Carl says.

"It was just a little accident," Cato says, looking as horrified for himself as he is for me. He yanks me to my feet and tries to divert attention by laying blame. "This floor is a safety hazard. Somebody get a mop before we have a fatality." Enrique the dishwasher comes running over with a rag.

"An important table is waiting," Gina says. "Can you walk?"

"I think so." Phil the grill guy watches with a look of half-amused sympathy as I brush off my skirt.

Carl wipes the rim of a plate and sets it in the window. "Ice skates don't cut it in my kitchen, Erin. If you can't stay upright, go home."

"My other shoes are being resoled," I lie. "I pick them up first thing tomorrow."

Gina pats my shoulder. "She'll change them and everything will be okay. Harold says she is a very good worker."

"How heartwarming," Carl says, then screams, "Firing two quail, one salmon, and a filet rare!"

Gina claps her hands twice. "Come on, waiters! The doctor wants to see you!"

"Well!" Cato says brightly. "I think we're finished here. Erin?" He turns me by the elbow and steers me through the kitchen doors. "I've been in a lot of crappy plays," he mutters, "but I've never seen a pratfall like that one. Well done."

Far from the brittle, white-haired man I'd expected, Dr. Benitz is in his early forties and doesn't seem the least bit disturbed by his legal troubles. Sitting across from him is his blond wife, a notoriously spoiled heiress who, according to Jane, "just adopted a baby from Zimbabwe to upgrade her image. Did you see the picture of her in *Vogue,* walking around the orphanage in four-inch heels?"

"Jamaican, British, what's the difference?" Dr. Benitz is saying as Cato and I approach the table. "It's not like we're giving her power of attorney."

"Why don't we hire a Mormon nanny, then, if it doesn't matter to you?" Mrs. Benitz says.

"Good evening," Cato says, the faintest hint of amusement in his voice.

Dr. Benitz flips a few pages of the wine list before glancing up. "How's the fish tonight?"

"Flown in this morning, sir," Cato says crisply. "If you're interested in seafood, I suggest the wild salmon."

"Why?"

"It has a firm texture and rich flavor that goes perfectly with Chef's caramelized ginger-shallot broth."

"Interesting. Let's hear about the lobster."

This is the beginning of a ten-minute dance that is less a customer-waiter exchange than a subtle negotiation between adversaries. "Where do the blood oranges in the relish come from?" asks the doctor, clearly enjoying the challenge.

Cato looks as if he might yawn. "Andalusia, Spain, by way of 737."

"You don't happen to know who makes this china, do you?"

"Chef had it designed exclusively for Roulette by Arte Italica. If you turn it over, you'll see his signature. Of course, I wouldn't recommend doing that with a full plate." Cato laughs lightly.

"My mother would love a set. Can you arrange that?"

"Just leave me her address and she'll have it by Monday morning. Unless she'd prefer afternoon delivery."

"Do any of the ingredients come from countries that use child labor?" the doctor says, gazing over the freesia at his wife. "Martina needs to know before we order."

No matter what the question, Cato uses a combination of charm, knowledge, and subtle maneuvering to keep the upper hand. "That's why I memorize the menu," he tells me when we're away from the table. "Not to make Gina happy, not to make money. To put assholes in their place."

As his section fills up and guests flood the foyer, Cato becomes as edgy and all-seeing as an air traffic controller. "Main courses for table four will be ready in a few minutes," he says. "Chen and Luis are busy with Ron's ten-top, so if you can take those out for me . . . Bring the cocktails to table seven. . . . Make sure Omar's cleared five. . . . Got it? Then come find me. And keep your eyes open for anybody with *the look*."

"What look?"

"Like they want something but haven't figured out what it is yet." He starts to turn away, then turns back. "And wipe that panic off your face. You act like you've never seen a busy dining room before."

He disappears into the packed lounge, where Alain is pouring a pale-green cocktail for a woman in a sequined tank top. She leans forward, hair falling into the mixed nuts, trying to outshine the other well-groomed groupies who press against the bar. Alain whispers something in her ear, then grins broadly. She rewards him by laying several bills next to her glass.

Paralyzed, I press my back against the wall and listen to Ron detailing the specials to a group of businessmen. When he gets to the word *emulsion* he makes two fists and rapidly rolls them over each other, which, as I recall from Girl Scouts, is actually sign language for "take the bus." Derek, no longer the loud slob who hogged the specials and bolted the staff meal, glides across the room with a martini-laden tray as Jane smiles over a party of six. Geoffrey frowns with concentration as he uncorks and pours a bottle of red wine for three women who clearly don't need more alcohol.

As much as I'd like to observe all night, it's only a matter of time before Gina or Steve spots me lurking by an urn filled with white peonies. Replaying my conversation with

Cato, I move toward the kitchen with what I hope looks like purpose.

"Marty's expediting tonight. He's usually pretty cool, as long as you do what he says. And don't crowd Luis. You've never seen a runner so territorial."

"Sure. No problem."

But "no problem" quickly becomes "God help me" when I walk through the swinging doors and into barely controlled chaos. "Behind you!" Omar squeezes by me and dumps mussel shells and meat bones into a giant trash can, splashing my skirt in the process. "You don't want to stand there, okay?" The dishwasher sloshes like a drive-through car wash while clouds of steam and garlic-scented smoke shoot up from the stoves. "*Quiero el* sea bass *ahora!*" Carl shouts to José as he polishes the edge of a plate with a towel. "You told me your cousin knew his shit! I don't care who he cooked for before! He can't even handle the basics!"

Marty rips three tickets off the little printer in front of him. "We're taking it up the tail now," he says, his words just audible over the hum of exhaust fans.

Luis paces behind him, peering over his shoulder at every plate that comes out. "Table twenty, table twenty," he mutters, giving me a cold glare that says, "Stay the hell away from my order."

I check the ticket Cato gave me. *1 pigeon, 1 salmon.* Easy enough, but how will I know which ones are mine?

"Luis!" Marty says. "Here you go, my man. Duck, trio of veal, sea bass. Table twenty."

"Gracias, *cabrón.*" Luis takes his plates and disappears into the dining room. I stand beside Marty, hoping my presence will be enough to result in the right plates with the right food, but he doesn't even notice me. From what I can tell, expediting involves screaming out orders, staring intently at the tickets hanging in front of the heat lamps, and gulping mouthfuls of soda from a large plastic tumbler. What does "three halibut all day" mean? And why won't anyone look in my direction? Phil grills with his back to me while Carl bends over a plate, squirting red sauce from a plastic squeeze bottle. One dish comes up, then two. "Excuse me, Marty, are those mine?" I ask.

No answer.

"Marty?"

"Need a *coconut* soufflé, Betsy, *on* the fly!" he shouts.

"Yeah, I heard you the third time," she says from her station.

More tickets roll out of the printer. Am I invisible or what? I can't stand here forever while the Wallers go hungry. If I'm going to get my food, I'll have to project. *"Marty!"* My voice rings through the kitchen.

"What the fuck?" he says.

Carl whirls around, his eyes narrowed, a sizzling skillet in his hand. "Erin, get over here." He gestures for me to step closer and leans forward so the tip of his nose is tinted orange by the heat lamps. "Waitstaff *never* yell in my kitchen. Understand me? I don't care if you're code blue and Sid Vicious just sat down at table eight. My cooks are busting their asses to put money in your pocket, so stop distracting them. I assume you came in here for a reason. What was it?"

I try to sound confident but stammer instead. "The— entrées for table four?"

He drops the skillet over a flame with a sharp bang. "You're late again, Erin. Chen picked up the plates three minutes ago. My food doesn't hang around while cute girls with family connections learn the ropes. If you're not waiting for something, *get out.*"

"Now I'm really in deep shit," Cato says, setting two kir royales on a tray. "Jesus, Erin. You violate the first rule of kitchen etiquette and you're surprised when Carl flips out?"

"Sorry, I don't put up with that from anybody," I say.

"Are you kidding? You've waited tables in this town. You know how chefs are."

I've told so many lies tonight, what's one more? "Of course, but this is ridiculous. I mean, haven't you guys ever done sensitivity training?"

Cato laughs. "I don't know who you've worked for, but Carl isn't sensitive to anything but his food and the guests. If you want a job here, you'll have to deal with it."

The cocktail waitress reaches between us and grabs two lime wedges. "I guess I don't have a choice," I say as she vanishes back into the martini-swilling throng.

"Nope. Chefs aren't big on free will." Cato gives my arm a quick rub. "There's a table waiting to hear specials. Shall we?"

From the second we step back into the dining room, I don't have time to think about anything except staying afloat. The next three hours zip by in a blur of finger-scorching plates, confusing orders, and muttered instructions. "Serve from the left, clear from the right," Cato says. "You served from the right on table two and that doesn't fly here. Always put seating positions in the computer so runners know where plates go. But you should already have this stuff down cold."

I carry a guinea hen and a rib eye to table three while trying to emulate Luis and Chen: confident stride, aura of knowledge. I've helped create marketing campaigns for Fortune 500 companies, for Christ's sake. I can get a couple of plates to the right table.

"Not table six!" Cato hisses in my ear. "Table one. Over there by the urn."

"Oh! Sorry, I got confused."

"Next time, double-check your ticket. The last thing you need right now is another screwup."

Gina takes over the task of scolding me while Cato enters a detailed order into the computer. "Smile," she says. "Don't touch your hair. You need powder, your nose is shiny. You look scared. Why are you scared?" Between the loud voices, piped-in Duke Ellington, and nonstop nitpicking, I'm completely dazed and of no help to Cato, who manages to control a full section of tables while I trail after him like a dead appendage. We circle the room, making sure that glasses are filled, plates are cleared, and everybody's ecstatic about the food. " 'Good' isn't enough for Carl," Cato tells me. " 'Fine' is unacceptable. He wants them to say it's divine, or the best thing they've ever tasted. If they don't, we give them so much free food they change their minds."

"Is everything to your liking?" he asks guest after guest. "How are you enjoying the foie gras / duck breast / ris de veau?"

"This steak is sublime," moans one woman, while another sniffs, "The last salmon I had was better, but what do you expect—I was in British Columbia."

"Would you prefer another preparation?" Cato asks, leaning close and wrinkling his forehead to show concern. "Carl can make it with a wonderful horseradish crust, or steam it with Meyer lemon and green papaya. Or I'd be delighted to bring you something else . . . ?"

"No. Really, it's fine."

"I swear, some people come here just to be spoiled brats," Cato says when we're back in the lounge. "If she doesn't want the food, why's she inhaling it? Now we have to comp her entrée and baby her all the way through dessert. She's a peon in the real world, but in here, she gets to act like Kimora Lee Simmons."

By the time the restaurant begins to clear out around midnight, my face hurts from smiling and I've heard the word *delicious* at least two dozen times in three different languages. I've asked Cato countless questions ("Where's position one on table four again?") but have already forgotten the answers. He leads me to the wait station and takes a pilfered pomegranate mojito from the cabinet. "Here, drink this," he says. "Make it snappy before somebody sees."

I suck several swallows through the thin straw. "Thanks. That tastes great."

"Alain squeezes his own juice. Carl wants everything to be made in-house." Cato guzzles from the glass and hands it back to me. "So, tell me, Miss Sensitivity Training. Where have you worked before?"

"As in restaurants?" Fuck. What was that purposely vague answer I practiced again? "Um...a few places on Long Island, and one downtown."

"Yeah? What's it called?"

I hesitate. "You probably haven't heard of it."

"Try me."

"It's a . . . little seafood place near Wall Street."

"Casual?"

"Pretty nice. We did a good lunch business. Lots of boring talk about hedge funds and mergers."

He nods but doesn't look entirely satisfied. "Why'd you leave?"

"No reason, really. I just wanted to have some time to—" think fast, Erin—"take courses and stuff."

"Oh, yeah? I do that too," he says. "If I didn't fill my days with acting classes and auditions, I couldn't handle wearing this suit every night." He tucks the drink back into the cabinet. "Okay. Let's drop the doctor's check and get him out of here before he talks me into pec implants."

As we round the corner, Carl emerges from the kitchen

in a fresh chef's jacket, a bushy rosemary sprig sprouting from his buttonhole. He strides jauntily into the dining room, his presence expanding like helium. Everyone turns, electrified, forks in midair. I catch snatches of praise as he stops at various tables. "...thrilled that you finally came uptown"..."never eaten anything even close"..."read the review in"..."drove here from Providence just to..."

Back rigid, Carl braces a hand on the edge of the Wallers' booth. "Steve tells me you're writing a cookbook," Mr. Waller says. "Got a title yet?"

"It's called *Corbett Takes France*. I blow the dust off a hundred traditional French recipes and give them a new twist. We'll be selling signed copies here in a few months. Each one comes with a DVD so the home cook can learn my more advanced techniques." Carl's eyes are already on the table where Dr. Benitz and his wife sit ignoring their bill. "Great to see you both..." He sprinkles some hellos around section two, then swaggers over to the doctor. "Lou! How's the beauty business treating you?" Standing behind Cato one banquette over, I listen as Carl switches into a different kind of charm.

"What is it?" he says as he leans over to kiss Martina on the cheek. "Pilates? Why do you look so fantastic?"

"Giardia. I got infected when I was in Africa and lost thirty pounds. The trick is going to be keeping it off."

"That's too bad. I was hoping you'd say it was the foie gras." Carl chuckles.

"Which was a revelation, by the way," says the doctor. "I might need a triple bypass tomorrow, but it was incredible. Thank you."

"My pleasure. How was everything else?"

"Wonderful, as usual. And our waiter was a kick. Brighter than most med students and a heck of a lot more useful."

"Good old Cato. He doesn't miss much. So what do you

say we meet for golf one morning when you're not making somebody gorgeous?"

"Sounds great. Just give me a call."

On his way past the wait station, Carl stops and claps Cato on the back. "I was just talking to the Benitzes," he says. "Apparently you made quite an impression."

"I do my best to keep the guests happy, Chef," Cato says.

"They should be talking about the food, not the servers. Save your showing off for the stage and let our guests enjoy what they came here for."

Cato's cheeks turn pink. "Of course, Chef. I understand."

"By the way, how's the acting coming along? Famous yet?"

"I have a few auditions coming up."

"Terrific, good for you," Carl says with a final pat. "I'll be sending a plate of mignardises to the Benitzes in a minute. Make sure you bring them a half bottle of Sauternes on me."

chapter 4

At the end of the night, Cato and I go over closing duties, which include sterilizing the door handles, grooming the velvet upholstery with a brass brush, and hydrating the Italian olive wood breadbaskets with almond oil. I'm scrubbing the espresso machine at the wait station when Geoffrey appears beside me. Despite a hectic night, he looks cool and unruffled. The only sign that he worked a full shift is a tiny red spot on his shirt.

"You'll want to familiarize yourself with this," he says, holding out a foot-thick wine list. "Please take it home for the night."

"Of course," I hear myself saying. "I was going to ask if that would be okay."

"Each one was hand-bound in Scotland, so be careful with it. If I were you, I'd concentrate on burgundy first. It's very popular with our guests."

"I'll do that."

He touches the counter to make sure it's dry, then sets down the list. "If Harold vouched for you, you must know your stuff. I look forward to hearing your thoughts at our next wine class."

"I imagine I'll have a lot of them."

"Tomorrow I'll show you the cellar," he says, square chin

high. "We received a *Wine Spectator* award for excellence four months after opening."

"Harassing the waitstaff again?" Cato says, walking toward us with a lowball glass in his hand.

Geoffrey smiles. "Just making sure there are no gaps in her training."

"Don't worry. She'll be game-ready by Monday."

"Great. Then good night."

As soon as Geoffrey is out of sight, Cato sets his drink on the wine list. "These things make perfect coasters. Little big for the end table, but really absorbent."

I laugh. "If that stains, he's going to blame me."

"You're right. Sorry."

He deems the espresso machine shiny enough to see his pores in and takes me to the bar, where Ron stands with a glass of red wine. I order vodka on the rocks and the three of us take our drinks up to the changing room. The second I sit at the card table, I begin to ache. And it isn't just my tailbone. I hit my head on a drawer at the wait station and took Derek's elbow in the back. My stomach is so painfully empty that the first sip of vodka goes straight to my head.

Cato lights a Salem. "We tip out a lot here," he says. "The busboys, runners, Alain, Stepford Hostess...it's a hefty chunk of change, but the more the waiters give away, the less Steve has to pay everybody."

Ron pulls on the knot of his tie and cracks his neck. "At least you're not slaving in the kitchen. Those guys make peanuts compared to us."

"Boo-hoo," Cato says, stuffing envelopes with money. "I'd like to see them walk a mile in my Bruno Maglis. The first time some lady whined about her gimlet, they'd run to the little boys' room in tears. Now be quiet. You're throwing off my count."

"I'm just saying, we've got it easy," Ron says.

"I guess that's why I have flat feet and a thing for Ativan." Cato slides a twenty across the table at me. "Here. This is for your help tonight."

"Thanks." I suppose I should be grateful. Two bucks an hour is a fortune compared to what I've made combing through employment Web sites and waiting for the phone to ring.

"Nobody gave me a dime when I trained," Ron says.

Cato takes a drag of his cigarette. "I'm surprised you can remember back that far."

The banter ends abruptly as Steve comes into the room. He peers around like a parent hunting for contraband, then pulls up a battered chair and sits beside me. "How'd your shift go?"

Beautifully, if you don't count bruising my backside, spilling a gin and tonic all over the bar, and lightly peppering at least two sleeves. "Pretty well, I think."

He glances at his lap and scratches what appears to be a small patch of eczema on his forehead. When he looks at me again, I can tell he's going to give it to me straight. "From what I saw, you've got a lot of work ahead of you. I've been in this business for twenty years. I've been a maître d', a manager, and an owner, and I've made and lost a lot of money. I've seen hundreds of waiters come and go. I can tell when somebody has natural talent. You don't."

I can't believe it. He's going to fire me already.

I feel Cato and Ron staring at me, waiting for my response. "I just need a few more days to learn your system."

"I'm not saying you can't succeed here," Steve goes on. "But whatever experience you had before isn't cutting it. You're going to have to put in more effort than somebody like Ron, who has service in his bones."

"He took some professional waiter's course," Cato says. "Technical college with aprons. He paid big bucks to learn how to push bottled water."

"What do you know about it?" Ron says. "For your information, that was the most demanding week of my life. The final exam was so hard, one guy passed out."

Steve waves a hand between them. "Am I talking to either of you? Quit bickering and wrap it up so you're not on the clock all night."

Cato stubs out his cigarette and goes back to counting tips. Ron stacks a large wad of cash, folds it inside a computer printout, and slides it into a red vinyl bag marked *House*.

"Listen, Erin, this isn't just about taking orders and getting plates to the right people," Steve says. "You need to lose the shy schoolgirl bit. It makes people feel like nobody's in charge. They want to stop thinking when they walk in here, and they can't do that if you're nervous."

"Right. I understand."

He scrapes his chair back and stands up. "Good. See you tomorrow. Cato, what was your check average tonight?"

"$592.50."

"Ron?"

"$574 and change."

"Are you guys bothering to sell anything or are you letting people order well drinks and risotto? Ron, the next time the Kapinskis come in, charge them twenty-four dollars a martini. They drop in twice a month for appetizers and split a main course and then camp out at their table half the night. They're going to start paying for it."

Ron looks shocked. "Aren't they going to notice?"

"The way they drink? If they give you a hard time about it, just tell them Alain is making them doubles because they're special customers."

"I don't know. They're nice people and they always ask for me."

"Getting attached to guests won't keep me in business. Tomorrow, I want to see better numbers from all of you." He walks out and clatters down the stairs while I sit there, too stunned to move.

"Don't let it bother you," Cato says. "He was all over me when I first started. Remember, Ron? He told me to tone down the fairy act, right in front of the cooks."

"You *were* wearing eyeliner," Ron reminds him.

"Anyway, the kitchen staff's been on me ever since. Lucky thing I have a thick hide for that kind of stuff."

"They're kidding," Ron insists.

Cato tosses a thin pile of money in front of him. "Yeah, well, this may come as a surprise to you, but Aunt Betty isn't my real name."

I crack a smile, forgetting for a second that I'm now a person who gets scolded in public for being inept. On the first day of my last job, I walked in radiating competence and energy, even though my résumé was fabricated and my clothes were cheap knockoffs. What I didn't know, I hid behind dedication and a good attitude. Here, I'm the staff liability. If I don't prove myself in a hurry, I'll be eighty-sixed along with the spit-roasted grouse.

Ron counts his tips, turning over a ten-dollar bill as if it's mislabeled. "Three hundred and ten dollars? Is that all we made tonight?"

Cato shrugs. "You're the one who brought in eighteen percent, my friend. If we didn't pool, you'd be going hungry."

"I save my money, Cato. I could quit tomorrow and I wouldn't go hungry for three years."

"Sounds like you need to splurge on some six-hundred-thread-count sheets."

Ron drains his glass. "Speaking of sheets, I'd better head

home to the wife. If I'm later than one, she gets ornery." He carefully hangs up his uniform and goes downstairs with tip envelopes for Derek and Jane.

"I guess I'll change too," I say. I start to stand but Cato reaches out and grabs my wrist.

"Wait."

As soon as I look at him, I know what he's going to say. "You haven't done this for a while, have you?"

"What? Of course I have." God, listen to me. I've never been a very good liar. I never had much reason to be.

"Come on, sweetie. This is Cato Poole you're talking to. I've been waiting tables since grunge was big."

"I just need a refresher course."

"No such thing. Either you know what you're doing or you don't."

My mouth goes dry as I realize I'm out of excuses. He looks at me expectantly, eyebrows raised. "Okay, you're right," I admit. "I haven't been waiting tables, I've been working at a marketing firm. The company went under and I couldn't find another job, so Harold helped me out. But I *have* worked in a restaurant before, honestly. It was pretty casual, though, and it was . . . eight years ago."

Cato drops his head back. "*Eight years* ago? Shit! Does Harold know that?"

"Not exactly. My father exaggerated my experience. I don't think he realized what he was getting me into."

"If Steve or Gina—if *Carl* finds out you're— Christ, why didn't I figure it out before? All I had to do was look at your shoes."

I shift gingerly on my sore right flank. "Oh, yeah. My shoes."

"Do you even know anything about food?"

"A little. I mean, I've eaten out a lot, but I never paid much attention to the details."

He rubs his temples. "What a disaster. The guy you're replacing was a top-notch waiter. It's not like people won't notice the difference."

"I'll go tell Steve it was all a mistake," I say. "I never should have let it get this far."

"Now, hold up. Let me think for a second." Cato lights another Salem and studies the ceiling. A minute later, his face relaxes and he breaks into laughter. "Wouldn't it be a riot?"

"A riot? What are you talking about?"

"I'm talking about trying to save your ass."

"And how are you going to do that?"

"With a little ingenuity and a whole lot of balls." He points his cigarette at me. "It's a good thing I like you, because if I didn't, I wouldn't even *consider* taking this kind of chance."

"I don't want you getting fired because of me."

"That makes two of us. I can't do poor. If I go home with less than three hundred a night, I bitch like an old lady on a fixed income." He blows smoke toward the window and says, "Listen. What if I teach you everything I've learned, from the time I was humping chicken at Popeye's to right now?"

"Forget it. You can't turn somebody into a good waitress overnight."

"Maybe not, but I see good raw material in you, Erin. Do what I tell you and five days from now, you won't even know yourself."

I belt back the watery remnants of my vodka. The thought of going home without a job frightens me even more than Steve and Gina. "Okay. Let's say we go through with it. Where do we start?"

"Well, first, we need to fill in the missing pieces of your background. If Carl asked who the chef was at your last job, what would you say?"

"Cato, this is insane."

"Look at me. If you're going to pass as a professional waiter, you'll have to carry yourself like one while I do my damnedest to whip you into shape. What's your alma mater?"

I exhale slowly. "NYU."

"Okay. You started out at a steakhouse in your junior year. After that, you worked at Babbo, but your last job was Spice Market. You were there for a year, but you quit to travel around Europe with a friend. You worked four doubles a week and your manager was Barry."

"Barry? Is that a real person?"

"Dated a friend of mine. Left for D.C. a few months ago. Do you know who the chef is?"

"Jean-Georges something?"

"Vongerichten. All I've heard about him is he's French and he married his hostess. The rest you'll have to improvise. If anybody asks you what he was like, say he was opening his tenth restaurant and wasn't around much. Just don't say he was nice. *No* chef is nice. Everybody will know you're full of it."

I shake my head. "How am I going to remember all this?"

"Easy. Just rehearse it until you start to believe it. I'll e-mail you a study guide in the morning. Make it your bible from now on."

chapter 5

I jerk awake the next day at noon and sit straight up in bed. Evidence of my new life lies scattered around the bedroom like clues from a crime scene: A sauce-smeared ballet flat. A crumpled seating chart for table six. An open wine list showing selections from the Loire Valley. Next to me on the comforter is one of Cato's coveted Uniball pens, which somehow made it into my skirt pocket last night. I'm so stiff I can hardly move.

When I finally stumble into the kitchen and turn on my laptop, I find two "thank you for your résumé, but..." messages and an e-mail from Cato entitled "Roulette for Dummies." I scroll through the ten-page attachment, wondering if it wouldn't have been easier to fake it as a news anchor. Over a breakfast of leftover pad thai and coffee, I begin my education.

Hey, Recruit!

Welcome to boot camp with pop quizzes and gourmet snacks. We have only four days left until your big debut, so every minute counts. You've made a crazy decision to start at the top (Ivanka Trump says hello), and if you want to stay there, you'll have to surrender your life to me. It won't be easy. Roulette is sort of like a foreign country—the locals are nasty and the guys in charge are looking for reasons to deport you. My job is to teach you the language so you can get by without making anybody suspicious. And who knows? Once you get the hang of it, you might even start to have fun. If not, you'll at least make some serious money. Some basics to learn ASAP:

1. *Soup is considered a beverage and should be served and cleared from the right like other beverages.*
2. *A cocktail is never more full than when it's dropped.*
3. *Never ask "why" (try not to even think it). Say "Of course" or "I'll attend to it immediately."*
4. *The handle of a teacup is called "the ear" and should be placed at the four o'clock position to the right of the guest.*

DO: Treat the busboys like a rich old aunt. If you're nice to them, you stand to make a lot more money.

DON'T: Check your tip in view of the dining room. Get mad later, in private.

DO: Channel your inner psych nurse and use a soothing voice with rude guests.

DON'T: Be honest if anyone asks how you like working at Roulette. You love what you do and plan to stay forever. Right?

NEVER: Refold a guest's napkin and put it back on the table. Replace the used napkin with a fresh one.

ALWAYS: Thank your lucky stars. You could be selling ladies' shoes at JC Penney or trimming trees in Oklahoma in December. Trust me, I've done both.

After forty-five minutes of cramming service etiquette, I prepare to venture out into the muggy afternoon. I'm due back at Roulette at four o'clock, and I still have to buy the mandatory rubber-soled shoes.

Bzzzzt.

The sound of the door buzzer blasts through my apartment. "Who the hell . . . ?" I glance out my living room window, but all I see are some schoolchildren on the corner of Twenty-fifth and First. Could it be my ex-boyfriend, Chris, wanting to rekindle what a year ago was smothering the life out of him? Or maybe it's Jay, the Nader-worshipping, newsboy-cap-wearing editor of a men's magazine. After meeting at a party, we dated for six rocky weeks, during which he suggested a threesome, argued that men were better at science than women, and in one extremely awkward moment, sobbed about his need to be accepted for who he was. Please, please don't let it be him.

Bzzzzt.

I know—it's Frank, the jovial, barbell-lifting young CEO of the software start-up in my old office building. A mutual late night at work last winter led to a kiss in the stairwell, which led to a daily e-mail flirtation that culminated in an offer of elopement to Vegas the day I packed up my desk. "Chapel of the Roses, ten P.M. Saturday? We'll *make* it work!"

The frantic buzzing stops, and a few seconds later, my phone rings. It's not one of my feared ex-lovers, but Rachel, my closest friend since we interned at the same ad agency after college. Six years, five jobs, and many men later, we still talk almost every day. "Why aren't you answering the buzzer?" she asks. "I know you're home."

"How?"

"How do you think? You just answered the phone."

"Christ. Hang on."

A minute later I hear her footsteps in the hallway and she knocks on the already open door. She wears a black vintage dress and flip-flops and her long auburn hair is frizzy from the humidity. Over her shoulder is a large nylon bag. "Didn't you get my voice mail?" she asks, stepping inside.

"What voice mail?"

"If you'd gotten it, you wouldn't be asking."

"I haven't had time to check my messages," I say. "I've been busy pretending to be someone I'm not."

She drops her bag onto a chair with a clinking thump. "I guess that means you went through with it."

"What do you mean, *went through with it*? You make it sound like I married the town drunk. The job's only temporary, for God's sake."

"It's also *way* out of your skill set. You should be marketing the place, not pitching the food."

"That's what I love about you," I say. "Your amazing ability to put things in perspective. Coffee?"

"Wow, one night and you're already a service pro," she says, taking a mug from my cabinet. "How'd it go, by the way? Obviously, you survived."

"If you call walking thirty-five miles and cleaning the kitchen floor with my ass surviving. The guy who's training me figured out I don't know anything, but luckily he decided to make me his personal improvement project."

"Sounds like an interesting start. I can't wait to stop by and watch you in action."

"Don't do it, Rachel. If you see me in uniform, you'll never get the image out of your mind."

"Come on, it's one of the best restaurants in Manhattan," she says. "Most waiters would kill to be in your shoes."

"Let them kill me, then. They'd be doing me a favor."

She puts an arm around me. "You'll be out of there in a month. Six weeks tops."

"Think so?"

"You're the one who said it was temporary," she reminds me.

"Oh, right. Fine then, six weeks."

"Hey, if it makes you feel better, I just had the craziest

shoot of my life. Two mastiffs who got spooked by the flash and took out a bookcase."

Since quitting her job as a graphic designer for an advertising firm, Rachel has turned to her real interest—pet photography. The Polaroids she used to take of her boyfriend asleep with his mouth open evolved into black-and-whites of pigeons and stray cats, then finally became a paying job when a coworker saw a portrait of her tabbies, Tolstoy and Dottie. Word of mouth and an ad posted at the vet's office brought her enough business to make it full-time.

"But I'm not here to complain," she says, reaching into her bag. "I'm here to spark your maternal instinct."

"How do you know I have one?"

"I don't, but I'm hopeful." She pulls out a bruised apple, a string of colored condoms, and three rolls of film before producing a small jar of water. Floating in the water is something blue and bullet-shaped.

I peer more closely at it. "What the hell is that?"

She sets the jar on the counter. "This, my dear waitress, is a Japanese fighting fish. The guy across the hall from me is moving to Florida and Tekka here needs a new home."

"Oooh, no," I say. "I can hardly take care of myself these days. Look around."

She glances at the high-heeled sandal in the bathroom doorway, the bags of recycling leaning against the kitchen wall, and the sink filled with yesterday's dishes. "You're going to get mice," she warns.

"See? The last thing I need is a pet to keep track of."

Rachel holds up the jar, where the fish hovers, perfectly still. "He's not technically a pet, Erin. His life span is so short he'll probably be in the sewer system by Halloween." She pulls a yellow can of fish food from her bag. "He can live in a bowl but he'd be happier in a tank. I'll help you shop for one."

"No, you won't, because I'm not adopting him. Why don't you take him if he means that much to you?"

"I have my hands full with Tolstoy and Dottie. Besides, I don't want to come home and find the tank on its side, water all over, Dottie not hungry for dinner..."

"Isn't there somebody else you can dump him on? I'm overwhelmed as it is."

"Which is exactly why you need something on your end table besides a dirty wineglass. Am I making sense?"

The fish drifts slowly to the top of the jar and his little round head breaks the surface of the water. "I don't know," I mutter, starting to weaken. "Maybe. But never again, I mean it."

"This is a special circumstance," she promises a bit too lightly. "A one-time deal."

I take the jar from her. "What do I do now? I feel like I just came home with a baby."

"Okay, and what do babies do?"

"Let's see. Cry?"

"*Eat*," she says, pushing the fish food can across the counter at me. "Just don't overfeed him or he'll explode before you have a chance to bond."

◆

I float into Roulette on an inch of new Vibram and find Cato already waiting for me in the lounge. "Go put on your uniform and make it quick," he says. "We have a month of training to do in two hours."

"On my way," I say, scurrying down the hallway.

When I return to the dining room, Cato parks me in front of a tray of wet silverware and hands me a small towel. "You were too slow yesterday. No piece should take more than three seconds to pick up, polish, and put down."

"Three seconds," I say, buffing furiously. "That's not much time to get rid of these water spots."

"First rule of service—do what you're told, even if it's impossible. You'll figure out a way to get it done."

"That doesn't make sense."

"Which brings us to the second rule—there's no logic in this business. So stop looking for it and polish that spoon."

By six thirty, I've graduated from the complexities of sidework and the hidden meaning of specials to what Cato calls "Introduction to Guest Management." We watch while Kimberly, our gangly, snub-nosed hostess, seats the first customers.

"This is the time to start thinking about who people want you to be," Cato mutters. "The lobster-bib crowd might be satisfied with fast service and hot food, but here you have to be part of their fantasy. If they're in the mood to celebrate, you should be upbeat and smiley. If they're mauling each other, push aphrodisiacs like the caviar mousse and oysters with champagne cream. Sometimes you get these weirdos who need a friend for a few hours, so you chat like you give a shit how their custody battle is going or which third-rate publisher is putting out their memoir. Just don't get sucked into any personal dramas. I played marriage counselor once and ended up getting stiffed."

"What if you can't tell *what* they want?"

"Then you're not paying attention. It's all about controlling the guest's experience, and that means adapting to every table. When I'm talking to guests, I'm not me anymore. I'm a green Midwesterner, Colin Cowie, whoever they want me to be."

"I don't know, Cato. I'm not an actor."

"Neither is Derek and he never pulls in less than twenty percent. His skills are all right, but it's the local-boy Brooklyn accent that charms the pants off everybody. Get into character and see what happens. Seriously, I've met waiters whose income went up thirty percent when they put on French accents or dyed their hair gray. People don't just tip for service. They tip because they like you, or because you make them laugh, or because they're afraid not to."

"Maybe I'll masquerade as someone who should be here."

"Good idea. And don't be afraid to suggest entrées and give your opinion, but never ask guests if they have questions."

"Why not? I thought I was supposed to help them decide."

"Wrong. You're here to help them *spend money.* Say they're on the fence about dessert. You tell them the satsuma mandarin tart is Betsy's signature dessert, and that if they don't taste it, they'll be missing out. Now they think they're fools if they don't try it, so they order one to share and you just made fifteen bucks for the house and three for yourself. Takes a little practice, but you'll get it. I won't let up until you do."

By the end of the shift, Cato's relentless coaching ("Become *one* with the sweetbreads, Erin") has elevated me from off-the-street amateur to run-of-the-mill flunky. I even survive a late-night tour of the wine cellar, during which Geoffrey corrects my pronunciation of everything except "zinfandel" and "chardonnay" and proclaims me "even worse than Derek was. And Derek drinks Rolling Rock."

The next day, Cato promotes me to the lounge so I can road-test my new skills. The cocktail waitress tosses me a few tables and for one seemingly endless night, I experience a downscale version of the dining room, complete with pickup lines ("I've never written poetry before, but looking at you is making me reconsider") and plenty of pointed criticism:

"You should smile more."

"Speak up. We can hardly hear you."

"Miss? Our nuts have been empty for ten minutes."

Though my best tips come from older couples waiting to be seated for dinner, I also become familiar with the "group tip," aka the forty cents left over after each person has thrown cash onto the table to cover their own drink. When I complain to Cato, he gives my shoulders a quick squeeze and says, "Oh, honey, that's nothing. Go be a gay waiter in Oklahoma City and then talk to me."

I'm learning that the best way to stay out of trouble is to pretend I'm hitting the beaches at Normandy—move fast, keep my eyes open, and expect to be shoved aside or sacrificed for the good of my unit at any moment. By the time I walk into Roulette on Tuesday, my usual surge of panic and adrenaline has been replaced by a steady stream of low-level anxiety. Maybe I'll get through this week without any major mishaps. A few more days of practice and I might even be able to call myself a subadequate waiter.

Unfortunately, my confidence doesn't last long.

"Erin!" Gina calls as I walk past the lounge. She sits at a table with an espresso in front of her and a sailor-suited Nino on her lap.

"Hi, Gina. Hello, Nino. How are you?"

He presses his cheek against his mother's paisley silk-clad shoulder. "He is tired," Gina answers. "Too much play date. Too much fighting with a boy who won't share his Nintendo."

"Uh-oh," I say in a sympathetic tone.

"Don't worry," Gina tells him. "Your grandma will come soon and make you happy again. Won't that be nice?"

"Well, I'd better go change," I say. "Cheer up, Nino."

Gina raises a finger. "Wait, I want to say something. You take your own section tonight, okay? Is time."

"My own...what?" My face gets hot. "How many tables?"

She shrugs. "Three or four. I don't make up my mind yet."

I may be down to my last forty dollars and desperate to make real tips, but I'm not ready to be in charge of that many hungry strangers. "I thought Cato said I'd be training for at least a week."

"Jane is serving a private party, so I need you to help. You're new, but without her, what can I do? I watch you since you started. You work hard, you have a big smile, people like you. You know your opening and closing side-work?"

"I think so."

"What about the computer?"

"I still have a few codes to memorize, but I'm doing all right." Except for my battered left foot, that is, which has been accumulating moleskin and Band-Aids since I started wearing my new Made in Norway shoes.

"Then maybe you are ready. My husband isn't sure about you, but I say we won't know until we watch you on the floor alone."

"Shouldn't I work in the lounge for a few more days?"

She shakes her head. "Listen to me. In Italy we have a saying. I translate it to English for you." She looks up at the ceiling and back at me. " 'Move your legs or the duck will run you over.' You understand what that means?"

"No. Not really."

"Sometimes you must do things you don't want to do, but in the end it's better. Better for me, too, because I see you work and decide if you're good for my restaurant. No more hiding behind Cato." She reaches over Nino and picks up her espresso. "Another thing. We have many VIPs tonight and I can't say every table will be easy."

"I'm going to get eaten alive out there."

Cato tosses his backpack into his locker. "You should be proud of yourself, sweetie. This means you're actually conning Gina. Of course, she made me take tables my second night and I cruised right through it, but I had the advantage of eleven years in the biz."

I find my time card in the rack—Steve has spelled my name "Eron"—and punch in. "What if I can't keep up? Or somebody asks a question I can't answer? What am I going to do?"

"Exactly what you've been doing," Cato says, pulling off his T-shirt and revealing a slender white torso. "Lie, smile, and lean on me."

"I can't lean on you. Steve's going to be watching my every move."

"Make that *Gina*. Steve's too distracted by the restaurant opening on Lexington."

"What restaurant?"

"Capers. Rick Holland's new place."

"He's opening another one? My God, he's taking over the city."

Cato nods. "Like cancer. He got the whole thing finished in four months. Pisses Carl off no end."

"Why? Because it's three blocks away?"

"Worse than that. Those guys have a rivalry going back fifteen years." He beckons me closer and lowers his voice. "I don't know the whole story, but they apprenticed in the same restaurant in Provence, and I guess they got into it over how to roast a rabbit or something. Carl needed stitches on his forehead and Rick threw out his shoulder. There was a girl involved, too, some American who was over there studying. She came back here with Carl and they ended up getting married. They split up recently, though, real nasty. He was after Kimberly before his divorce was even final."

"Kimberly—the *hostess*?"

"Of course. Chefs and hostesses are the oldest hook-up in the history of restaurants. Anyway, Rick and Carl have been stealing each other's line cooks for years. Segundo was one of Rick's top guys until Carl offered him better pay."

"Uh-oh. Sounds like it could get bloody."

"Damn right." Cato buttons his white shirt. "Believe me, Carl'll torch Madison Avenue before he lets Holland take customers away from Roulette."

Downstairs, I make coffee, fill shakers with gray sea salt (throwing a pinch over my shoulder for luck), and obsessively arrange my little three-table section. But nothing can distract me from the nightmare scenarios running through my head, most of which involve mangling the specials in front of a bunch of snickering stockbrokers or waiting on a table of women I went to college with. As I contemplate bribing Alain for a belt of Jamaican rum, Steve strides into the dining room, a roll of double-sided masking tape in one hand and a small headlamp in the other. "Gather round, people," he says, gesturing us over. "I came in this afternoon and wasn't happy with the state of the dining room. This carpet needs serious attention."

Ron squints at the floor. "Mmm, I see what you mean. Definitely a weak spot."

"I'd like you to walk around and pick up every speck of lint," Steve says. "Erin, put on the headlamp and get under the tables so you don't miss anything. Staff meeting in half an hour." He hands the tape to Cato and the lamp to me, then disappears toward the kitchen.

Cato sits on the nearest chair, crosses an ankle over his knee, and applies a strip of tape to the sole of his shoe. "Apparently, I really *will* do anything for money," he says, passing the tape to Jane. "Want some help with that lamp, Erin?"

I hand it to him and let him strap it over my hair. "You look dazzling," he says. "Very miner-chic."

Ron finishes taping his wingtips and stands up. "I'll take sections two and three," he says, lurching stiff-legged across the restaurant.

I bend down and peer under a four-top. "I don't know, Cato. I'm not seeing anything."

"It's not about reality. It's about paranoia."

"What are those things glued under the chairs?"

"Huh? Oh, they're ten-Euro coins. Gina hired some feng shui guy to come in the day the restaurant opened. She was supposed to use Chinese money, but there was no way she was going for that. A priest showed up too. Geoffrey told me he lit incense and threw holy water around." Cato's right foot comes into my field of vision and starts tapping the rug. "Okay, you've been under there long enough. Watch your head on the way out."

Twenty tables later, all I have for my sciatic trouble are a 1986 penny and one silver sequin. Jane lifts her leg and examines several loose threads dangling from the bottom of her shoe. "That's it?" she says. "No acrylic nails? No bra inserts?"

"Anybody need an attorney named Bruce?" Ron asks, holding up a bent business card.

Cato plucks it from his fingers. "If he's muscular and under forty, I need him."

"And the code for I'm totally out of my element is . . ." I'm quizzing myself at the computer when Alain walks into the lounge with a case of beer. His sleeves are rolled up and the muscles on his arms stand out. "Congratulations," he says. "You made it through the first week."

"No one's more surprised than I am."

"Many waiters I know, they train for a few days and never come back. In this country, people want to be treated like babies. In France, you expect the boss to be hard. You don't respect him if he isn't."

"Maybe the French have thicker skins."

"Something like that. I've been in America six years and I'm afraid I'm getting soft." He laughs. "Oh well, I came here for my wife, that's it. My father thought I would be an electrician in his business, then I said, 'Bye, I met a woman at the flea market and I'm leaving for New York.'"

"Do you ever go back to visit?"

"Every June. Gina knows how it is to miss your country, so she's okay about it."

Footsteps echo through the foyer and Steve breezes in, patting his hair into place. He wears chinos, loafers without socks, and a navy blazer that's tight around the shoulders. "Hi, everybody." He glances over at my tables. "Erin, make sure your place settings are symmetrical or my wife will get out her ruler. You don't want that."

He takes a seat at the bar, where Alain is unloading the beer into a lowboy refrigerator. "My lunch didn't settle too well. Why don't you give me a Moretti."

"A tall cold one—coming up," Alain says, opening a bottle and filling a frosted glass.

As Steve takes a gulp, Carl comes into the lounge. "Here it is," he says, holding out a black paper folder.

Steve grabs it from him and opens it. "How'd you get this?"

"Had Patrick go in and ask to see a menu. When the hostess answered the phone he took it with him."

There's a short, tense silence. I try to act engrossed in the computer sign-in process. "This was the big secret?" Steve says. "They just kept it under wraps to generate publicity. Looks like another fusion joint to me."

Carl snorts. "North African or some such thing."

"He's charging a fortune, too. Forty-five dollars for chicken livers with rose-petal jam."

"Rose petals?" Carl scoffs. "That's great for idiots who know nothing about food, but it won't win any Michelin stars. People will go once, that's it."

Steve puts down his beer. "He draws them in somehow."

"Yeah, with gimmicks and flash," Carl says, his voice tight. "He's always done what's trendy—that's how he stays in business. People like his pretty-boy image and his line of pots and pans, but he's no chef. He'll be lucky to last a year up here."

"He's on his third wife, too," Steve adds. "Some TV actress nobody's ever heard of. Wedding cost almost a million bucks—can you imagine?"

"The fool's already paying double alimony," Carl says with obvious delight. "You'd think he'd have learned his lesson by now."

"Men never learn when it comes to women," says Alain.

Steve laughs. "Yeah. I'm living proof."

chapter 6

The Holland incursion is the topic of choice as we set up the dining room. "This has nothing to do with food," Jane says, smoothing a tablecloth over a four-top. "It's a dick thing, pure and simple."

Cato laughs. "It's always a dick thing with you, isn't it, Jane?"

"Uh-uh. That's *your* specialty."

Ron holds a water glass up to the light. "If we lose regulars it won't just be Carl's problem. We'll all feel it in the wallet."

"But Capers sounds so different," I say. "I don't see why we'd lose regulars."

"Half the time people don't care where they're eating," Ron answers. "They just want to be seen at the hot new restaurant. I already heard Carl talking about tweaking the menu. 'Preemptive strike,' he called it."

"These guys aren't quitting until somebody goes down," Cato says. "Kind of like Monster Trucks. Without the trucks."

At five o'clock we file into the kitchen and stand silent and alert while Carl marches around, peering into pans and snarling orders. "Lorenzo, your station may pass muster in Naples, but in Manhattan, it looks like a public toilet. Leather clogs only, Patrick. Wear Crocs in my restaurant again and I'll chop you into pieces and mail you to Del Posto. Don't read into what I say, Phil. It's not that complicated."

Phil swallows. "I just need to know if—"

"If what? If I can lend you money again? Buy you a beer? Let you take my car to Queens and bring it back with a broken taillight?"

"No, and I really appreciate all that, but I wasn't sure if you wanted the venison to be an app or—"

"I want it to be the most incredible app that's ever come out of this kitchen. Whether or not you get it right will show me if you've been listening or just standing around jerking off!"

Phil glances at me with shame in his eyes. I give him an understanding smile as Carl slams a pan on the counter and vanishes into the walk-in, presumably to cool off. Phil smiles back and mouths, "Hey."

After a staff meeting that is a bizarre combination of happy (Phil stares at me) and harrowing (Carl asks me to recite the ingredients in the squab terrine "as if you were talking to Frank Bruni, not that he knows shit about anything but politics"), Carl pulls a hardbound book from the bottom shelf of the prep table. "Before you sample the specials, I'd like to share a quote from Nietzsche." He reads to himself for a minute, then nods slowly. " 'In heaven, all of the interesting people are missing.' Let's carry that thought with us as we go about our work tonight."

Derek leans over. "Who's Nietzsche?" he whispers. "Is he in the restaurant business?"

We've barely finished inhaling our turkey tetrazzini when Gina walks through the kitchen in a full metallic-blue skirt and a tight black top that dips below her shoulder blades. "Your first table comes in an hour," she says to me. "Cheap ones—tourists from Canada with little children. Sorry, but you don't get to choose."

Steve thumps down the stairs behind her, waving a piece of paper. "I got the lowdown on your VIP, Ron. His IPO was this morning. He'll be spending other people's money, so push the Le Pin. Remember, folks: mandatory wine class, two thirty Friday afternoon."

With only half an hour until service, Cato pulls me aside and gives me a pre-service briefing at the wait station. "If you forget something, wing it. I realize you're panicking right now, but your section is small and I'll be keeping an eye on you. By the way, I had to let Jane in on our little secret."

"Oh no, Cato. Why?"

"Because when you wait tables together, you know each other better than an old married couple. She had a feeling something was up, and I couldn't lie to her."

"She's not going to tell Steve, is she?"

"Are you kidding? Nothing gives her greater pleasure than screwing the management with a smile on her face. Once a week she walks out of here with a purse full of coffee beans and peppercorns."

Luis, scowling, goes by with a stack of linens. *"Hola,"* Cato says. "Hi, gorgeous."

Luis mutters something under his breath that sounds like, "I'd kill you if it wouldn't get me deported."

"Te amo, baby," Cato calls. "You set me on fire..." He nudges me. "I'm going to break him down one of these days. He's going to fall for me. Just you watch."

Gina wasn't lying. Not only are my first customers from a country with dubious tipping practices, but most of them are under ten years old: two wound-up little boys stuffed into camel blazers and their sullen younger sister. Their mother herds them across the dining room, widening her eyes and pointing at everything. Their father, wearing corduroy slacks and a striped button-down, brings up the rear. While the rest of his family sits, he stands by his chair, head tipped back, examining the map of the world painted on the ceiling. He appears to be wondering why Italy is larger than Africa.

Gina beckons me from the lounge with a crooked index finger. "Look at those brats," she says. "Don't let them bother anybody, okay? I mean it. Keep them quiet."

With this albatross around my neck, I approach the table. Both parents smile expectantly and I hear myself speak as if from across the room. "Good evening, and welcome to Roulette." I'm repeating Cato's spiel word for word, but something is missing: the warm, heartfelt tone that makes it sound like I mean what I'm saying. "May I offer you something to drink?"

Though the parents order prosecco immediately, the children tell me their names (Charlie, Evan, and Haley), their hamster's name (Lucky), and what games they played on the plane before they finally ask for lemonades, "extra lemony."

"This is why I will never have kids," Alain complains midway through squeezing a pound of lemons, a task two women on barstools appear to find fascinating. "Always asking for silly things."

"And taking way too long to do it."

Cato comes up beside me and gently turns me toward the dining room. "See that guy in your section?" I follow his gaze to table six, where an attractive wavy-haired man in a black crewneck sweater and gray trousers is sitting down. A petite, freckled blonde wearing a strand of huge pearls takes the chair beside him.

"That's Daniel Fratelli," Cato says.

"Who's he?"

"You tell me. It's time to start using those people-reading skills I've been teaching you."

I stare across the room as Daniel unfolds his napkin and spreads it over his thighs. "Oh, God," I say.

"Try to look past the devastating exterior if you can."

"Sorry." I refocus my attention, noticing his squared shoulders, his quick "thank you" as Omar fills his water glass, the way he leaves his menu unopened and glances around the room. "He seems a little tense."

"Okay. What else?"

His date says something and he closes his eyes briefly, then reaches out and spins the tiny salt shaker with his thumb and forefinger. "That woman's annoying him and he's trying not to let it show. How am I doing?"

"Not bad. What does he do for a living?"

"Let's see . . . real estate?"

Cato groans. "Is he wearing a chunky gold watch? I didn't think so."

"Finance?"

"He'd be loosening an Hermès tie and flagging us for a mojito."

"Help me out here, Cato."

"He's a *producer.*"

"For what? Broadway shows?"

"Jesus, you're highbrow. For the news show *Flashback.*"

"That junk? Him?"

Cato feigns shock. "*That junk* is good, wholesome entertainment. And it was on the brink of cancellation until he came along."

"So he's a TV hotshot. That means he's difficult and demanding."

"He just knows what he wants. And when he gets it, he's a hell of a tipper. He's also pretty cool once you get to know him. He got me a bit part on a soap last year."

"You're kidding. Which one?"

"*Forever and a Day.* I played a wedding guest who set fire

to the bride's dress with kerosene and a match. They had fire extinguishers and an ambulance standing by."

I stifle a laugh. "You're making that up."

"Swear to God. I posted it on YouTube and got fifty thousand hits the first week. Check it out when you have a chance. The best part's when the bride throws her flaming bouquet into the . . ." He trails off as Steve marches into the lounge and shoots me a glare.

"What is this, a Fuckups Anonymous meeting? One of our best regulars has been waiting in your section for over a minute."

"I was just giving her some background on his likes and dislikes," Cato says.

"Well, talk faster. I want to see a drink on that table in thirty seconds. In fact, bring over a couple of Chopin martinis, on me, so we can get this thing back on track." He turns abruptly and walks toward the end of the bar. "Hey, Jerry! Just you and the boys tonight?"

"I thought you said he was going to be distracted," I mutter to Cato.

"Sorry. Even us veterans blow it once in a while." He pushes a loose strand of hair back from my face. "Good luck. If you need anything, I'm just a meltdown away."

While Alain loads my tray with lemonades, I watch Daniel reading his menu. His ankles are crossed and his strong, straight nose is illuminated by the reddish glow from the wall sconce. He's exactly the kind of person I don't want to wait on—a handsome, successful man for whom everything has gone right. I should be the woman sitting with him, not the one waiting on second-graders and wearing the ugliest shoes in the room. He looks up and his eyes rove the restaurant, finally landing on the bar, then on me. I smile quickly, letting myself imagine for an instant that someone like him could notice me.

Not in this uniform. Never.

After delivering drinks and a halting rendition of the specials to my Canadians, I leave Mom and Dad to siphon a dinner order from their kids and bring martinis to Daniel and his date. "Compliments of Steve," I say, setting down the brimming glasses. I'm so self-conscious I feel naked.

"Thank you," Daniel says. "Tell him to stop by when he has a chance."

"I will."

He narrows his eyes. "I haven't seen you here before. Are you new?"

"I started a few days ago."

"This is our favorite spot, so you'll probably be waiting on us a lot."

"Great." I swallow and struggle to collect my thoughts. Okay, specials first, send Geoffrey over to sell the big-ticket cabernet, then—

"AaaAAaaahhh!"

I gasp as a piercing howl erupts not four feet away. Gina's head appears instantly from around a column, gold earrings swinging, eyebrows low and flat. Glancing over, I see little Haley squirming in her chair, red-faced, explosive, a danger to everyone's pleasant evening. And to my job.

"I'm not half-asleep anymore," Daniel says, putting the tip of his finger in his ear and shaking it. "That's good, at least."

His date peers over the top of her menu. "Why did they bring their children to a place like this?"

Daniel shrugs. "I don't know, Sonia. Maybe they're tired of eating at Chuck E. Cheese."

"Is that racket going to go on all night?" She looks at me, clearly expecting a promise that it won't.

"She's just hungry," I say, with more confidence than I feel. "I'm sure she'll settle down."

"I hope so."

If I were sitting with a man like Daniel, Haley and her brothers could establish a tyrannical government that controlled half the restaurant and I wouldn't even notice. I wonder where he and Sonia are going after dinner. Helicopter ride to view the skyline, with a swing over midtown to see his office from the air? No, too flashy. They'll probably just retreat to a quiet lounge, where he'll mesmerize Sonia with tales of his world travels and rapid rise through the cutthroat world of television. Oh, Cato, how could you let me wait on this man?

"I have a question about the smoked fluke," Sonia says.

"Of course." Shit. Have I had the fluke?

"Is it salty? I hate waking up puffy in the morning."

I scramble through my memory, trying to remember the dozens of dishes I've tasted since I've been at Roulette. I should know this, but I don't. What am I going to say? That the fluke is just right? What if I'm wrong and she sends it back? My heart begins to pound as the silence becomes embarrassing.

My eyes connect with Daniel's and I see that he knows I'm stuck. I can't tell whether he's amused, irritated, or an awful combination of both. I open my mouth to say something, anything, but he speaks just in time. "Get it, Sonia. If you don't like it, you can always order something else."

"Okay. Fine," she says.

At that moment, Haley lets out another penetrating scream.

"Oh, boy," Daniel says.

Several guests swivel in their seats. "Would you excuse me for a moment?" I say in the calmest voice I can muster. "I'll be right back."

I rush to the table, where Mom is attempting to distract her daughter with an emergency copy of *Madeleine*. A giant tear rolls down Haley's face and onto the front of her white dress. "Let me see if I can find something fun to play with," I say.

"Thank you so much," says her mother. "Anything will do."

Gina follows me to the wait station, which I begin scouring for anything remotely entertaining. "Is all my fault," she says, letting out a defeated breath. "I let them come because I am nice and this is what happens."

"Does Nino have a toy she could play with?" I echo from inside the cabinet.

"In the office, maybe, but I don't want that one touching his things."

I pull out some tarnished napkin rings, an old calculator, and a bent birthday card addressed to someone named Lauren. "Then these had better do the trick."

Gina tosses in her burgundy lip gloss for good measure. "Give her what she wants," she hisses. "Any more crying and people will stop coming to Roulette. I will be on the street with my suitcase! Understand? Not a peep."

After decorating the tablecloth with their appetizers, Charlie and Evan shed their blazers and attempt to construct a fort using their napkins and a mysteriously empty pepper shaker. Haley, having exhausted the joys of playing with junk, stares silently at the tattered birthday card.

"We should have left them at the hotel," I hear the father say.

"With a stranger?" protests the mother, peeling the lip gloss wand off the tablecloth. "Those people don't care. God knows what might have happened."

"It couldn't have been worse than what's happened here. We ordered her an eighteen-dollar bowl of soup she didn't touch."

"I've been looking forward to this meal for a long time. Let's try to have fun, please. If that's possible."

Chen lays down the parents' entrées while I set a half order of penne with duck sausage in front of Haley. Her face crumples. "I don't want it."

"Yes, you do," says her father.

"I don't!" the girl shrieks. Chen, grating Reggiano at point-blank range, winces.

Sonia looks up from the half-eaten fluke she pronounced "not as bad as I thought it would be" and rolls her eyes. Daniel says something to her, but she just chews furiously.

Haley's mother throws up her hands. "Well, now I've lost my appetite. We go to a nice place for the first time in months, and I can't even eat in peace."

Gina glares at me from the podium and points toward the door. I scan my other tables, which appear to be momentarily under control. "Please enjoy your dinner," I tell Haley's mother. "I'll take Haley . . . on a little tour!"

"That's very kind of you, but . . ."

"Just for a few minutes. What do you say, Haley?"

The girl glances between her mother and my outstretched hand. "Can I, Mommy?"

Her mother sighs. "Okay. But behave, please. And you'll need to eat everything on your plate when you get back."

"I will," she says, slipping her hand into mine. Gina pauses in her conversation with a guest in Ron's section and gives me a covert thumbs-up.

After quick stops at the wait station and the ladies' room (the door of which bears a drastically thinner version of Botticelli's Venus), we begin our return trip to Haley's tepid pasta. But she drags her feet. She's not ready to sit down yet, and I sense another tantrum building. "Okay. We'll swing by the kitchen and then it's time to eat." I lead her to the double doors, through which we hear a steady murmur of activity. "Everyone's busy, so we can't go in. But if you don't make a sound, I'll give you a peek."

She nods, her lips clamped tight. I lift her up until her head is level with the window. "See? That's where they made your dinner tonight." Carl steps out from behind the line to confer with Marty. "And that's Chef," I say. " 'Chef' means he's the boss."

Carl turns and looks right at us. "Uh-oh, time to go." I let Haley slide to the floor, but he's already coming our way. The doors fly open and he strides out, not glaring and aggravated, but grinning broadly.

"Hi there, princess." He crouches down and chucks Haley under the chin. "What's your name?"

She stares at him with round eyes. "This is Haley," I answer. "We're tracing our penne to the source."

He laughs and wraps an arm around Haley's thin pink legs. "Well, you're not going to find it out here, silly!" he says, hoisting her six feet into the air. "Come on in!" She seems both thrilled and terrified as he carries her to the bright world on the other side of the doors.

"Hey, Betsy," I hear José call. "Why don't you grab some vanilla custard and meet me in the alley?"

"Sure, *maricón,* but only if you wear that little pink dress," she replies.

Several cooks laugh. "I got your custard right here," Patrick says. He grabs a squeeze bottle, sticks it between his legs, and moans loudly as the white contents drip onto the floor. But everyone falls silent the second they see Haley riding into the kitchen on Carl's shoulder. Patrick yanks a side towel off the counter and hurriedly wipes the floor.

"Betcha can't count how many stoves I have," Carl is saying as the doors flap shut.

I take this opportunity to pour more wine for Daniel and Sonia and assure Haley's parents that their daughter is getting the education of her young life. They finally appear to be relaxing—Mom snaps a picture of each plate, then she and Dad taste each other's entrées while the boys pulverize a semolina herb biscuit with their fists. All four look up in astonishment as the chef himself walks into the dining room, signature rosemary sprig in place, the smiling Haley still in his arms. She points to her mother and Carl gently sets her down in her chair.

"Enjoying our fine city, folks?" he asks.

He chats with Haley's parents about heli-skiing in the Bugaboos while Chen replaces the girl's cold pasta with a fresh bowl. She's polite and well-behaved through dessert, and though she skips outside without saying good-bye, her father slips me an extra fifty. "This is our first night in New York. Thanks for making it a memorable one."

Daniel and Sonia decline my offer of coffee and dessert, as they "were supposed to be at a party an hour ago." Sonia lays her coral-smeared napkin on the table and walks toward the bathroom.

"It got so quiet in here I thought I'd died," Daniel says as I present the check. "What happened?"

"I tried some good old-fashioned babysitting. Sorry if she disturbed you."

He pulls his wallet from his back pocket. "She disturbed my *dinner*. Disturbing me takes more than a few tears from a five-year-old." He slides his credit card into the leather folder and hands it to me. "Here you go. And if anyone else asks, the fluke is excellent. Not too salty at all."

I back away, blushing. "Okay. Thank you. Thanks very much."

After he and Sonia leave arm in arm, Cato comes up and puts a hand on my back. "How'd it go?"

"I can't believe it," I say, showing him Daniel's credit card slip. "After all that, he left me thirty percent."

Cato lets out a long, low whistle. "That's generous even for him."

"What did I do?"

"I don't know, but whatever it was, he liked it."

chapter 7

"You made two hundred dollars in one *night*?" my father blares into the phone. "All right, let's hear it. Did Harold do good or what?"

I reach up and pull my shirt off the shower rod, where I left it to dry late last night. "Good is one word for it."

He chuckles. "Enjoy the freedom while you can. Before you know it, you'll be back at an office sending half your paycheck to the government." He holds the phone away from his mouth. "Anne! She made two hundred bucks last night!"

"Is that how she should be using her mind?" I hear my mother answer.

"Tell her I don't have a choice, Dad," I say. "New York has too many marketing geniuses."

"She says she's having a great time and not to worry!"

I toss my shirt over a kitchen chair and plug in the iron. "It's waitressing, not a summer in Nantucket. Why aren't you at work, by the way?"

"Your mother needed help getting ready for the barbecue on Sunday. I just finished mowing the lawn and now I'm heading out to buy ice and potato chips. Sure beats doing the accounts for Fremont Dry Cleaners. You've never seen books so screwy. No wonder they got audited."

The all-important yearly barbecue. How could I have forgotten? And now that he's reminded me, how will I get out of it? Past barbecues have always involved discussions about my promising future with people who greet me by saying, "Erin! Made a million dollars yet?" "You might have to celebrate without me," I say. "I'm probably working that day."

"Really?" My father sounds disappointed. "This would be the first barbecue you've missed since you went to Martha's Vineyard with what's-his-name. You know, your secretary."

"That was three years ago, Dad, and he was an intern, not my secretary. Do we have to discuss things I wish I hadn't done?"

"I'm just wondering, was it worth missing a family barbecue for?"

"I get the point. If I have Sunday night off, I'll come."

"That's my Erin. Here, your brother's grabbing the phone out of my hand."

Nate immediately puts on the pressure. "Don't you even *think* about backing out on Sunday."

"Sorry, I'm no longer in charge of my weekends."

He groans. "You're going to leave me alone with those boring old geezers?"

"If you didn't want to be alone with boring old geezers, you shouldn't have moved back home."

"I'm recovering from college," he argues. "If I'd known Dad was going to have me doing all these chores, I'd have stayed in Cambridge. This morning he made me install a firewall on the computer at his office, then I had to sweep the entire parking lot. Meanwhile, he sleeps in and takes the day off. I'm totaled."

"Come off it, Nate. You're talking to somebody who hasn't sat down in four days."

"Then it sounds like you need a break."

I hesitate, wavering between guilt and the fear of being put on the spot by boring old geezers. Unfortunately, guilt wins out. "All right. I'll see if I can get somebody to cover for me."

"Great. And invite some friends. The more people under fifty, the better."

"There's a grill cook I'd like to bring, but he works twice as many hours as I do."

"Just try to make it, okay? I'm depending on you."

My father gets back on the phone. "Please call your brother if any dishwashing jobs open up. There's nothing like minimum wage and a little dirt to make a twenty-three-year-old face his future."

I slide my warm shirt onto a hanger. "Sorry, Dad. I wouldn't do that to my worst enemy."

✦

When I walk into Roulette that afternoon, I find Cato slouched on one of the banquettes, listening to music. The table in front of him is covered with wine bottles, glasses, and baskets of sliced baguette. Without the usual white linen covering, the table is just a battered circle of plywood draped with felt-backed vinyl—not nearly as elegant as it looks hidden under silver and crystal. In the center is a large brass spittoon.

I hear the tinny twang of country-western guitars as Cato pulls off his headphones. "Sit here," he says, patting the spot next to him. "We can sneak sips together. No way in hell am I spitting out a hundred-dollar Barolo. Where I come from, Mateus is top-shelf."

Jane, Ron, and Derek arrive a few minutes later, looking stressed out, just showered, and fired up, respectively. Jane pronounces herself "ready to ditch this whole nursing thing if I don't get a good night's sleep," and Derek gives us the scoop on a run-down space in Williamsburg that is the perfect spot for his own restaurant.

"The rent's pretty reasonable. All it needs is a floor, furniture, and a new kitchen. I met a couple of cooks who are dying to get out of Asia de Cuba, so if I can scrape seventy-five thousand together, I'm on my way." He's describing his dream menu (lobster frites, Kobe beef burger with Camembert) when Geoffrey strides in from the lounge, already suited up for service, a notebook under his arm. His thin lips are pursed and he has the air of a professor who can't wait to show his students how much he knows.

"We have an hour to cover Tuscany," he says, grabbing the bottle closest to him and slicing off the foil cap with his corkscrew knife. "Let's get started." After passing around copies of a regional map, he name-drops grape varietals and spouts words like *denomination* and *aromatized* while I struggle to retain key bits of information.

"The same grape grown half a mile away will exhibit a different *terroir,*" he says. "Add weather and the winemaker's own style and the combinations are endless."

He pours half an inch of white wine into each glass and passes them around the table. Then, just as I'd feared, he calls on the least knowledgeable person in the room. "Erin, how would you describe the Vernaccia?"

Since I normally determine the quality of a wine by its price, I ask, "How much does this bottle cost? Retail, I mean."

"That doesn't matter right now. Just tell me what comes to mind when you drink it."

This is what I get for teasing my father about his ten-bottle "wine cellar" next to the antifreeze in the garage. I take a large sip and, forgetting to spit, swallow. With everyone's eyes on me, I can hardly taste the wine, let alone describe it. "Very nice."

"What do you mean by nice?"

I cast around desperately for something to say. "It's . . . refreshing."

"When guests ask you about a wine, they expect you to be more specific. And so do I."

Cato gives my knee an encouraging squeeze under the table. Backed into a corner, I throw out the only wine term I know. "Fruity?"

"You're not concentrating," Geoffrey says, adjusting his glasses. "If you're going to work here, you'll have to learn to think with your tongue."

"Okay . . ." I try again, sniffing, swirling, and sloshing the wine around in my mouth as instructed.

"Racy?" Geoffrey prompts.

"I guess you could say that."

"Remember the terms I mentioned. Is it flinty? Herbaceous? Flowery?"

"All three!"

He rolls his eyes. "You'll be lucky to sell bottled water."

While the other waiters start their sidework, Geoffrey makes me stay after class so he can force-feed me sips of "tobacco" and "leather."

"I taste butter," I say with sudden confidence.

He winces. "Using white wine terms to describe red wine should be punishable by law."

"This is forty dollars a glass?" I ask as a mouthful of Chianti rushes into my bloodstream.

"It's all about what the market will bear. These grapes were grown on a patch of hillside that's been owned by the same family since Caligula was in power. People don't mind paying for that." Producing a white napkin and a waiter's corkscrew, he tutors me in the art of presenting, opening, and pouring a bottle of wine. "Turn the label this way so I can see it," he says. "Not toward the *wall,* Erin. Now it's aimed at the floor. Are you listening?"

"I'm just a little rusty," I say.

He sniffs. "Remind me to ask Harold what he sees in you."

Pop! Geoffrey claps his hands over his ears. "Quietly, please. We don't want to give the guests heart attacks."

"Sounding good, Erin," Cato calls from the lounge. "Keep swallowing."

The last time I was this tipsy in the afternoon, I made out with a guy named Seamus at Ryan's Irish Pub. I'm so oblivious that when Jane says, "It's your turn to wait on Gina and Steve," I assume she's talking to someone else. I look up from polishing spoons to see her smiling at me. "Are you with us, Erin?"

"Sorry?"

"Gina and Steve are having dinner here tonight and they'll be sitting in your section. We all have to take turns waiting on them. This time they asked for you."

If I were any less drunk, I'd panic. "Are you sure I'm ready for that?"

"Don't worry," Cato says, "they usually don't eat until after ten. You'll be nice and alert by then. Speaking of which, I need a can of Red Bull and a slap. Jane, would you do the honors?"

She reaches across the table and gives him a smack on the jaw. He blinks a few times. "Much better. Ron? Little backhand to clear the cobwebs?"

"I don't need one," he says, though his flushed face suggests otherwise. "Maybe somebody can start sobering up by getting us more flatware."

"I'll do it," I say. Now that Gina and Steve will be evaluating me up close, I need to be as awake as possible. I chart an unsteady course across the dining room to the kitchen, which is almost unbearably bright to someone who just imbibed ten different kinds of grapes.

Where is everybody? There isn't a cook in sight. Suddenly I hear a distant slam and a yelp, followed by the thunder of footsteps as Patrick pounds down from the office in his clogs, checked pants, and chef's jacket. On his heels are Carl, Phil, and four other cooks, all of them breathing hard and laughing.

Patrick stops at the prep table and spins around, chest heaving, holding out a whisk like a switchblade. "Anybody comes near me, I'll truss your nuts. I mean it!"

"Give it up, Patty," Marty says, approaching him slowly. He holds out a greasy fistful of butter.

"I got him covered on this side," says José, blocking off one end of the line.

His eyes never leaving Patrick, Carl opens a low refrigerator, pulls out a plastic container, and peels off the lid. "You poor bastard. Look at you, cornered like a rat. I'll teach you to last a year in my kitchen."

"Oh, yeah? Fuck that." Patrick hurls the whisk toward Phil, hitting him in the shoulder.

"Get him! He's heading for the basement!" Phil cries, and they all take off, jumping on Patrick just as he reaches the stairs.

I watch, flattened against the door, while they drag him, half-giggling, half-shrieking, to the dishwasher's station, where they strip off his jacket and dump sauce and olive oil over his head. Enrique the dishwasher stands to one side, a confused half-smile on his face.

"Congratulations, you little shit!" Carl shouts, pouring demi-glace in Patrick's hair.

Marty grabs the giant sprayer and hoses him down. "Couldn't even dice brunoise when he showed up, the jackass!"

Patrick sputters and struggles, then finally goes limp. Red-cheeked and disheveled, he grins and wipes béarnaise from his eyes. "Hi, Erin," he says.

Steve appears at the bottom of the stairs. "Who took my stapler?"

"I was about to pierce Patrick's eyebrow, but I think he's suffered enough," Carl says, laughing. He wrestles the stapler out of his pants pocket and throws it in a perfect arc across the room.

Steve catches it out of the air. "No rough stuff. I don't want to be hearing from a lawyer tomorrow."

"Patty likes it painful. Don't you, Patty?" Marty punches him on the thigh.

"Get off me, you assholes," Patrick says. "I have work to do."

My image of Carl the stern dictator dissolves as he yanks off Patrick's clogs, puts them on an empty rack, and sends them through the dishwasher. "Your feet stink," he says.

"Not so good," says Enrique as the smell of steamed leather fills the room.

The cooks straighten their jackets, wipe their arms, and straggle one by one to their stations. Patrick, standing at the sink in his socks, rinses the goop out his hair. "Your demi-glace is a little runny, Marty," he says. "I'd reduce it some more, if I were you."

As soon as he puts on his wet shoes and goes back behind the line, the kitchen is once again all business. The conversation is clipped and even the usual jokey epithets have a serious ring to them: "I told you before, cocksucker, don't touch my parsley."

I smile at Enrique and reach for a huge tray of clean flatware. "It's heavy, miss," he says. "Be careful."

"Okay." I hoist the tray, which is dripping wet and weighs a good forty pounds. As I turn to go, I glance across the kitchen and catch Phil's eye. He's carrying an enormous spatula and his jacket is spattered with water and green stains, giving him a "half culinary genius, half food-fighting punk" look that sets my blood churning.

With my eyes still on him, I step off the rubber mat and stumble, nearly dropping the tray. I grab the edge again, only to wrench my thumb. "Ouch!" Reflexes dulled by too much *terroir*, I lose my hold. Completely.

The tray comes down with a deafening crash on the edge of the sink. Instinct tells me to get out of the way of flying knives, and as I step backward I see Carl, Phil, and the rest of the cooks, their faces twisted with surprise as flatware rains down on the floor and every nearby surface. Just when the worst seems to be over, a single fork goes skidding over the metal counter, which is scattered with dirty dishes and utensils. With astounding speed, it glides across a puddle of pink soap and careens into thin air. It's heading right for Carl. Please, God. No.

By some act of fate, the fork just misses his arm and ricochets off the wall. Then, with a sickening *ker-plunk*, it plunges into an enormous, bubbling pot. Lorenzo peers in after it. "My bisque. I spent four hours making that."

For a second, I almost expect everyone to laugh, to see me as just one of the boys, clowning around and making a mess. But all I get is a long, ominous silence. Carl glares first at the silver carnage, then at me. "Did you blow Harold to get in here, or what?"

I open my mouth to protest, but he holds up a hand. "You've done enough damage. Don't make it any worse."

The first person to move is Enrique, who drops to his knees and begins to gather the scattered utensils. I bend down to help. He flashes me an understanding glance from under his dark brows, then uses both rubber-gloved hands to dragnet the flatware across the wet floor. When I stand to deposit my second load into the tray, I see Lorenzo pulling out my dripping fork with a pair of tongs.

"I put them through again," Enrique says, sliding the full tray into the dishwasher and closing the metal door.

"Thanks. I'll wait," I tell him.

"No, you won't," Carl says, pointing toward the door. "Enrique will bring them out. Now leave. I can't stand the sight of you."

chapter 8

It's only seven thirty and the night already seems endless. Despite having just half a section, I've managed to lose a drink ticket and recite the specials to the same party twice. A man at table ten holds out the check cover I returned to him thirty seconds ago. "Ma'am, you gave us the wrong credit card." After my performance in the kitchen, I feel self-conscious and accident-prone. Cato and Jane won't stop teasing me ("Hey, Erin! Fork you!"), and soon I'll be testing my shaky skills on my bosses. I have to get it together immediately.

"Table seven just flagged me for a drink order," Derek says, catching up to me in the lounge.

"I'm sorry. I'll be right there."

He hands me the ticket. "Too late. I shouldn't have to pick up the slack while you screw around on the computer."

"I'm not screwing around," I say, my heart picking up speed. "I'm busy."

"So's everybody else. This isn't some shithole, you know. You have to pull your weight."

Every time I turn around, Steve is spying on me from the perimeter of the room and Gina is at my shoulder, correcting me. "Why are you not running?" She gestures toward the front of the dining room, where Cato is speed walking between tables. "That is why we hire you. You must do the *hustle*, okay? Fast-fast all the time!" Her heavy gold charm bracelet jingles at her wrist.

"Fast-fast," I say, nodding. "Okay."

By the time she and Steve sit down for dinner, I'm getting a second wind born of pure anxiety. Approaching the table, I realize I'm in the awkward position of having to pretend I don't know them in order to maintain the proper level of formality. I'm just saying "Good evening" when Gina interrupts me.

"You're too far away."

I lean in, not sure what she means. "Excuse me?"

She gestures for me to come closer. "From the table, Erin. From the table."

"Step up a few inches," Steve says. "If you're too far back, you have no authority over your guests. And you're bending your knee."

I glance down at my legs, which, except for one small bump, are hidden by my skirt. "You're right. I wasn't aware of it."

"This isn't a casual place," says Gina. "You can't stand like you do at home. And smile, okay? You look depressed."

I grin widely and struggle to recall what I was saying before this unexpected detour. Steve flaps open his napkin. "Let's hear the specials."

The second the words *licorice-simmered turbot* leave my mouth, his eyes get wide. "*Licorice?* Jesus. Is that because of this Rick Holland thing?"

"I don't know. Carl didn't say."

"All right, I'll have braised greens and the lamb shoulder. He knows how I like it done."

"And for you, Gina?" I ask, scribbling down his order.

"What's so difficult about lamb?" she answers. "You don't need to write it."

"You should have no trouble remembering an order for a deuce," says Steve.

I drop my hand to my side. Lamb shoulder, I think. Lamb shoulder and greens.

"I'll have tuna," Gina says. "Plain. Seared for forty seconds, no more. And don't let Lorenzo cook it, his mother is from Palermo. It will taste like sardines."

Steve snorts. "Oh, come on. That's your imagination."

"I taste Palermo in everything he touches," Gina insists. "Ugh."

"We lifted him from Bellavitae," Steve tells me proudly. "He was stuck making bruschetta, pulling in two-fifty a week. He's a real talent."

"No more talk about Lorenzo or I lose my appetite," Gina says. "I want some vegetables, too, Erin. Eggplant, spinach, whatever. I won't eat much anyway."

"You should at least try." Steve seems concerned and frustrated, as if she were a finicky child. "You can't survive on espresso and cigarettes."

She looks at him, doe-eyed. "I'll eat, okay? For you." To me she says, "Now, tell Geoffrey to get us a bottle of Brunello. And bring some mineral water, no gas, and take this bread, we don't eat it."

Head reeling with commands, I dump the bread at the wait station, put Geoffrey on the trail of the Brunello, and go to fetch the mineral water. "The agent tells me it's a shack," a familiar voice is saying as I enter the lounge. "By Bridgehampton standards, anyway."

It's Daniel Fratelli. The producer.

He sits alone in khaki pants and a faded blue button-down, a pint of dark beer in front of him. He's eating the Hawaiian escolar from the bar menu and talking to Alain and Cato. Looking at the side of his face, I almost forget that I'm waiting on my bosses and don't have time to lust after out-of-my-league regulars who already have girl-friends.

"The house itself isn't great," he says to Alain. "It's all about the view."

"Does it come with any land?" Alain asks.

"About half an acre, with some pine trees and a pond."

"Sounds pretty sweet," Cato says from the computer.

"With some work it could be."

"Acqua Panna, please," I practically whisper to Alain.

At the sound of my voice, Daniel glances over. "Hello. How are you?" I say.

He nods and goes back to his sandwich. Just when I think our exchange is over, he says, "Any misbehavers in there tonight?"

I give him what I pray is a professional smile. "None under twenty-one so far."

"That's too bad. You seemed to have found your calling."

"Erin grew up on Long Island, if you need advice about buying out there," Cato pipes up. "Her parents live in East Quogue."

I fight the urge to reach out and pinch him. Yes, they live in East Quogue, in a three-bedroom ranch with aluminum windows. What do I know about waterfront mansions, or the men who can afford them?

"How do they like it?" Daniel asks.

Rather than mentioning the commune at the end of the street or the elderly neighbor who gardens in a Speedo, I say, "Oh, they love it. They've been in the same house for twenty years."

He wipes his mouth with his napkin and pushes his plate across the bar. "I'm driving that way tomorrow to meet with my real estate agent and see some friends. They're probably hoping I make an offer so they can have their guest room back."

"You're going to your parents' barbecue tomorrow, right, Erin?" Cato asks.

I hesitate. "I don't know yet."

"You told me you'd already packed."

"I did," I say coolly. "Just in case."

He grins and I get the feeling he's about to say something he shouldn't. *Alain, hurry up with that water.*

"Maybe you two can ride out together," Cato says, shrugging as if the thought had just occurred to him. "I mean, since you're both going in the same direction."

I widen my eyes at him. What is he *doing*? Daniel doesn't want to drive a waitress to Long Island, and I don't want to spend an hour and a half with a wealthy customer who knows more about the menu than I do.

"I'm taking the jitney," I say. "We're probably leaving at different times, anyway."

"Are we?" Daniel says. "I'll be hitting the road around ten."

"What time's your reservation, Erin?" Cato asks.

"It's . . . at ten."

Alain sets the bottle of water on my tray as I fumble with slices of lemon. Daniel stares at the rows of illuminated bottles behind the bar. He seems to be wondering if it would just be easier to give in and take me along for the ride.

"I don't mind a passenger if you decide to go tomorrow," he says.

"Thanks a lot, but I'm fine on the jitney."

"No, you're not," Cato says.

"Yes, I am," I say. "I've been taking it for years."

"That's a pretty lukewarm recommendation," Daniel says. "Ever done the Long Island Expressway in a convertible?"

"Never," Cato answers for me.

"A convertible?" I say.

"Not just any convertible," Daniel says. "A classic."

"As a matter of fact, I haven't," I admit.

He slides his business card toward me. "We'll have to remedy that. Write down your address and I'll pick you up in the morning."

✦

"After I dropped the silverware, I had to wait on Gina and Steve. No tip, of course."

"Nothing?" Rachel says. "Not even five bucks?"

We're at a Soho bar that features bamboo floors, a blandly attractive clientele, and an eco-hip drink list complete with organic liquor and all-natural mixers. It's my first night out since I started at Roulette, and I'm celebrating nine days of not being fired.

"Three hours of charity work, can you believe it? Jane told me all the waiters get the same treatment."

"Oh, well. At least you have tomorrow off."

"Right, and I get to spend it at my parents' barbecue. Thanks to Cato, I'm hitching a ride with a *customer*."

Rachel lifts her snifter of small-batch tequila. "A sexy one, I hope."

"I guess you could call him that, he's just . . . too serious for me. Besides, he's a television producer."

"So?"

"Successful producers and unlucky waitresses don't mix."

"At least he won't be threatened by your accomplishments," she says brightly.

"How consoling."

"Look, Erin, you're not *really* a waitress. It's just what you happen to be doing at the moment."

"The moment is all that matters. Besides," I say, not sure whether I'm trying to convince her or myself, "I'm more attracted to that cook I told you about."

"The one with the nice ass?"

"And the most *amazing* blue eyes. We've hardly said a word to each other, but that's going to change, even if I have to trap him in the walk-in." I take a sip of sauvignon blanc, which, thanks to Geoffrey, I analyze (do I taste wet flagstones?) before allowing myself to enjoy it. "Which reminds me, are you still seeing the guy with the four-year-old?"

"I am, and his name is Brian, and the sex is fantastic. But we don't really talk. It's 'Hi, let's fuck, I've got to pick up Olivia, see you Friday.'"

I lean back in my chair. "Sounds like it's working fine. Why ruin a good thing with communication?"

"This isn't like you, Erin. Don't you usually make them wait a month or something before you give in?"

"I've been reconsidering that strategy lately. It seems kind of fussy for somebody who handles raw meat."

"A cook," Rachel says dreamily. "Imagine having a boyfriend who could whip you up four-course dinners."

"And after dinner, we could consume each other."

She swirls her straw through her nearly empty drink. "Speaking of adorable things you sleep with . . ."

"What are you talking about?"

"Forget it," she says. "There's just this dog, that's all."

I put down my glass. "Absolutely not."

"I haven't said anything yet!"

"If you think I'm a pushover because I took Tekka, you're wrong. I've already done my good deed. Not to mention I blew half a night's tips on a tank and supplies. I couldn't afford another pet if I wanted to."

"Dogs are cheap," Rachel says, waving her hand dismissively. "This one's a nine-year-old Jack Russell whose owner just died. She left him with a woman from the camera shop near my apartment. She can't keep him either, and you know where that leaves me."

"No, where does that leave you?"

"Looking for a foster home."

"What's wrong with your place?"

"Two hostile cats and a landlord who doesn't allow dogs. *Your* landlord, however—"

"Already thinks Tekka's tank is going to flood the apartment below mine."

She reaches out and grabs my hand. "Please, just for a week. He doesn't even bark. He sleeps all the time, he loves everybody, and his name is Rocket."

I scowl at the ceiling. "I knew this was going to happen."

"Believe me, I didn't plan it. One minute I was buying film, the next I was begging some stranger not to put a dog to sleep."

Why, *why* did she have to say that? "Is he really going to be put to sleep?"

"Not if I can help it. Come on, Erin. You like dogs."

"From a distance. When they aren't invading my apartment and costing money I don't have."

"I wouldn't be asking if I weren't desperate. Remember, it's only for a week. That should give me plenty of time to find him a permanent home."

I imagine a growling old mutt, fur-covered furniture, and the smell of canned food. Then I picture an innocent little dog being led to the death chamber, a victim of circumstances he'll never understand. "Oh, God. As if I don't have enough to worry about."

Rachel brightens. "So you'll do it?"

"A week, that's all," I say. "And on one condition."

"Name it."

"Bring the dog food and buy me another drink."

chapter 9

I can still taste the wine when my alarm goes off the next morning.

After hitting the snooze button twice, I roll into a sitting position and open one eye. I never should have let Rachel drag me to another bar, and then another. I feel a flash of "got drunk and got married" regret—did I really *agree* to foster Rocket? Focusing my scratchy eyes on the clock, I realize that I have just forty-five minutes to resurrect myself before a near-stranger shows up to drive me to the barbecue. I trample last night's clothes and stagger to the bathroom, where the mirror reveals a pasty mug-shot version of my face. One shower, two cups of coffee, and three outfit changes later, the buzzer rings and I step into heels far too high for the occasion.

"Good morning," Daniel says as I emerge from my building in jeans and dark sunglasses, a bottle of aspirin rattling in my purse. He wears shorts and a polo shirt and is sitting on top of the front seat of an ancient silver convertible riddled with rust holes. Bright sunlight glints off the cracked side mirror. *This* is what he calls a classic?

"Morning," I croak.

He slides down behind the wheel, which is wrapped in black electrical tape. Suddenly he looks less like a sophisticated producer with a trophy girlfriend and more like a regular guy with a really ugly car. "So, what do you think?" he asks.

"Of what?"

"My Austin-Healey. I've been restoring it on weekends and I'm finally making progress."

I try to look impressed. "You got it running," I say, eyeing the crooked front hubcap. "That's something."

He leans over and shoves my door open. "The latch sticks. If I don't give it a shot of WD-40 every so often, it gets angry."

I climb in and clip the fraying lap belt, praying it won't snap before we get through the Queens Midtown Tunnel. "All set?" Daniel asks, starting the engine. The noise of the motor is so loud even I can't hear my response. "I'll take that as a yes!" he shouts, and slams the gearshift into first.

As we roar through the streets of Manhattan, people on the sidewalk and at outdoor cafés look up to see where all the racket is coming from. We may be following a Harley and a city bus, but all eyes are on the fossilized clunker with the loose muffler.

"So, Cato tells me you're a producer!" I say through my swirling, still-damp hair. "*Flashback,* right?"

"Right. Ever watch it?"

"I don't have much time now that I'm working nights."

"Not getting your tabloid TV fix, huh?" he says, turning on a blinker that sounds like a cheap clock. "That's a shame."

"I wouldn't call *Flashback* tabloid. It's just a little... slick."

"We prefer the word *polished,*" he says, narrowly making it through a yellow light.

"It does have a nicer ring to it."

"Three focus groups thought the same thing. But enough

about what I do all day. I want to know how you ended up at Roulette."

While he rides the bumper of the car in front of us, I give him a well-rehearsed, pared-down account of my journey from marketing to fine dining. By the time I finish with "Waitressing is temporary. I'm just waiting for the right job offer," I'm halfway to hypothermia. The wind chill makes it feel like November, most of my lipstick is somewhere in my hair, but my hangover is miraculously cured.

"I've seen people trying to make it in show business who get stuck in restaurants for years," Daniel says. "Every time you talk to them, they say they're on the verge of a break-through."

"Good thing I'm not in show business."

He glances over. "Are you cold?"

Coming from him, it almost feels like a personal question. "Maybe a little."

"I think there's a sweater back here somewhere..." He leans toward me and gropes around on the floor behind my seat. I stare rigidly ahead as his hair brushes my shoulder. "Put this on."

"Thanks," I say, yanking on a musty-smelling wool pullover with a Christmas tree on the front.

"You look festive." He pulls a knob and a thin stream of hot air begins to incinerate my foot. "That better?" I give him a thumbs-up and lean my head against the crumbling headrest. Though I expect sporadic small talk for the rest of the trip, Daniel is soon telling me about his search for the perfect house (a rambling fixer-upper with original mold-ings), his real estate agent (a redhead in her fifties who calls him "lovey"), and how he'd like to shoot a documentary of the whole experience. "That used to be my goal, before real-ity intervened. To make movies about the ordinary things people go through."

"What's stopping you?" I ask.

"If I quit the network, there'd be no house to buy. No subject for the documentary."

"Ironic."

"Yup, but that's how it works."

We pull onto the road that leads to my parents' house and I suddenly feel critical of everything I see. Why don't the Taylors take in their recycling bin? Did the O'Sheas really ruin their yard with that ridiculous cherub statue? Doesn't anybody in this neighborhood have any taste?

I point to the boxwood hedge my father can never get square enough. "We're right up here on your left."

"Okay." He turns into the gravel driveway, where the bumper sticker on my father's Buick *(Annoy a Liberal— Work Hard and Be Happy)* duels with the one on my mother's Prius *(Annoy a Conservative—Think for Yourself)*.

"Must make for interesting election years," Daniel says, turning off the engine.

"And stimulating barbecues." I pull off his sweater and push back my tangled hair. "Well...thanks a lot for the ride." Now what? I should probably invite him in, just to be polite. Not that he'll accept. He may have a beat-up car, but he's not the kind of man who eats budget cuts of meat that have been marinated in salad dressing and cooked until black. "You're welcome to have lunch with us. I know you're going to meet your friends, though, so—"

"They're all at the beach, and I'm not meeting the agent until four."

"Oh, well..."

He looks toward the back of the house, where a belch of grill smoke rises into the air. My father likes to start the coals early so he can get them good and hot before people arrive. "It won't be anything special," I say.

"That's okay. I was going to find a clam shack or something, but homemade barbecue sounds better if you have an extra plate."

Oh, God. Now he'll have to meet the whole crowd. "Sure!" I say, using all my strength to push open the passenger door. "Let's go inside!"

"Erin?" My mother steps onto the porch, which is cluttered with long-dead potted plants and oversized wicker chairs. She wears white capris and a sleeveless denim blouse and her light brown bob swings against her cheeks. "What was all that noise?"

Daniel smiles. "My muffler's on back order."

"Hi, Mom!" I say, walking up the front steps. "This is Daniel Fratelli."

"Ah, yes, hello." She peers at the trail of gray exhaust hanging over the driveway. "I'm Anne. You make quite an entrance."

"I've been accused of that before."

"We're going to fortify him with some unhealthy food before he goes house hunting," I say, opening the screen door.

"Well, Daniel, you'll have to talk to my friend Naomi when she gets here. She knows the market better than anybody."

"Great." He follows me into the living room, which looks even tackier than I remembered. The ice-blue carpet clashes with the flowered wallpaper and the overstuffed furniture is dated and tired.

My father comes toward me in red chinos and one of his Duke University T-shirts. "Well, if it isn't our very own short-order technologist!" he says, kissing me on the temple. "You brought one of your waiter friends with you. Terrific. Dennis Edwards." He thrusts a hand toward Daniel.

I feel the blood drain from my face. "This is Daniel, a customer at the restaurant. We drove out together."

"No problem!" Dad says, covering his faux pas with a

joke. "We'll let you in for free this time, but next time you'll have to pay. So . . . are you two seeing each other?"

"Dad. My God."

"Republicans aren't known for their tact," my mother says from the kitchen.

He shrugs. "Well, what kind of customer drives you all the way out here unless he's got ulterior motives?"

"The kind who's going to eat something and then go meet with a real-estate agent."

"Don't worry," Daniel tells my father. "The only designs I have are on a shingled three-bedroom with a deck and a water view."

"That's a refreshing change. Anyway, you must have quite the corporate expense account if you're a regular at Roulette, huh, Daniel?"

"The network only pays for business dinners, unfortunately. The rest comes straight out of my pocket."

"The network? You're an actor?"

"I'm a producer for *Flashback,* the television show."

My father's eyes light up. "No kidding?" He looks at me and then back at Daniel. "You know, this could be kismet. I've been an accountant for almost forty years. I worked hard at it and put my kids through college with a little help from Sallie Mae, but now I wonder if I shouldn't go into directing."

I envision my father in a director's chair, bellowing through a bullhorn with a scarf around his neck. "What are you talking about, Dad? Since when?"

"Since he started ripping on every DVD we rent, saying he could do better," my brother says.

I introduce Daniel to Nate, who has dressed up for company by wearing a threadbare striped button-down shirt, cargo pants, and duct-taped sneakers. His hair is growing out and he looks like he shaved with a blunt razor last week.

"So, you're that cook I've been hearing about," Nate says, holding a bottle of beer in one hand and a bunch of mini-pretzels in the other. "I thought they never let you out of the kitchen. Hey, what do you think of taking over the grill while you're here? My dad cremates everything he comes in contact with."

"The grill? Already?" Daniel's face is deadpan. "But, Erin, you hardly know me."

"Nate," I say through clenched teeth. "You've got the wrong guy."

"Wha...? Uh-oh," he says quietly, and swigs his beer.

I turn back to my father, grateful for a distraction. "Isn't this movie stuff a little out of the blue?"

"Let's not panic," Dad replies. "I've just been jotting down some screenplay ideas, that's all. Mind if I run them by you, Daniel? You can help me put the chicken on."

"Dad, no," I say, stepping between them. "Please."

"I'll do anything for a good meal," Daniel says over the top of my head. He takes the beer Nate offers him and the grill brush from my father. "You say you've got chicken out there? Breasts or legs?"

"Wings," Nate says. "Two hundred of 'em."

"Then we'd better get started."

"So then they find the judge dead in his car," my father is saying through the thick smoke rising off the chicken. "And the defendant—*poof!*—gets on a single-engine bush plane and disappears into the mountains."

Daniel flips a wing over with a pair of tongs. "Forever? You mean the story ends there? That's heavy."

"You like it?" My father leans back and sets his empty beer bottle on the brick patio wall. "Go ahead, tear it apart. I can take it. I do people's taxes for a living, and believe me, you have to be tough. Nobody likes being told what they can and can't write off. Know what I mean? It's an ego blow."

"Sure, I see it all the time. Nielsen ratings in the toilet? Call the producer bad names."

"Daniel?" I say from the back door, where I've been listening in amazement. "He's not too much for you, is he?"

"What, me?" my father says, pointing at himself. "I'm just an old man spinning a yarn."

Daniel waves the tongs in the smoky air. "Remember, I'm used to dealing with TV writers. The kind who take themselves way too seriously."

"Get back inside and take care of our guests," my father commands me. "You're in the service business now. So serve."

"But there are only four people here."

"So? Did your mother mix the Bloody Marys?"

"Ages ago. Daniel, don't let him work you to death. And Dad, please, no more pitches. One is enough."

"Yeah, yeah." He grabs the barbecue sauce and a brush off the picnic table and turns back to Daniel. "Anyway, I've been thinking about this horror plot, real bloodbath but with a nice social message. Tell me if it's been done before, because I don't know *how* it could have gone unwritten all these years..."

I step inside just as the front door flies open and five middle-aged men charge into the house. "Watch out, here comes the opposition," says my mother. "Where's my backup? Damn Democrats are always late for everything."

"Erin!" one of the men booms. It's Walt Babcock, one of my father's oldest friends.

I take a gulp of beer. "Great to see you, Mr. Babcock. Ready for some chicken?"

He pats the stomach straining against his navy golf shirt. "Darn right."

"Hi, Erin. Word around the neighborhood is you're changing careers." This comes from John Neuwirth, Dad's business partner. Even on a Sunday, he's dressed to crunch numbers in black slacks and a crisp broadcloth shirt.

"Don't believe everything you hear," I answer.

"Your dad tells us you're in the hospitality industry now," Walt says.

"For the moment, yes."

"Interesting. In what capacity?"

I give Nate a pleading look. "She's a higher-up," my brother says, using one of my father's euphemisms.

"Super!" Walt bellows, swiping a sweating Bloody Mary off the dining room table. "If you have to be in the army, you might as well be a general, right?"

Mom walks by with a large bowl of paprika-flecked potato salad. "Don't tell me your father's pestering Daniel with his film ideas," she says, glancing out the window.

"That's exactly what he's doing," I answer. "How long has he been like this?"

She lowers her voice. "A few months. Since he started listening to our Henry Mancini records and stopping at boat dealers 'just to browse.' I don't know what he's going through, but I wish he'd get over it. I already have one lost kid under my roof."

"I wonder what's happening to him. He's too old for a midlife crisis."

She licks mayonnaise off her pinkie. "You want my opinion? He's facing his final twenty years and realizing he's spent most of his life pressing buttons on a calculator. He's never used the right side of his brain."

I think of my upbeat, optimistic father, going to work

carrying the same plastic travel mug every morning since I was nine. All this time I thought he was content, someone who didn't aspire to more because he had everything he wanted. "Good enough for me," he'd say of his office with its rickety desk chairs and antiquated phone system. He loved fixing broken appliances in his spare time, and was happy to vacation at an old cabin in Vermont while his friends and neighbors went to Europe. Maybe all of it was "good enough" because it was the best he could do.

I sit at the picnic table between Daniel and Mom's friend Naomi, listening as she tries to convince him that she's the only person from here to Montauk who can find him the perfect house. "Not that Shelley isn't a fine agent, but she isn't aggressive enough. If you see a house you like and it isn't for sale, I'll ring the doorbell and tell them I've got a buyer. I keep showing up until they give in."

"I'm just starting to look," he says, raising a forkful of Walt's "famous" blue-cheese coleslaw. "But if things don't work out with Shelley, I'll be sure to give you a call."

"Sorry," I mutter when she goes back for more potato salad. "Ever since you got here, it's been one sales spiel after another."

Daniel shrugs. "Just a normal day at the office for me."

He doesn't seem to notice that he's at the sort of house where the olives are canned, the picnic table splintered, and the company decidedly middle-class. He works the barbecue like a pro, listening attentively to Walt's boring golf stories and complimenting Naomi's cheese enchiladas. He tells Nate about going to Asia after college to escape his father, who wanted him to join his investment company, and reassures me about my drunken decision to take Rocket. "When I got Fritz five years ago, it was totally overwhelming. I'd come home to this puppy bouncing off the walls the way all Labs do, then he'd howl at night and wake me up. Every weekend I had to run him around the park for miles. I didn't date for four months."

"Oh, my God. I hope Rocket's easier than that."

"He's older, so he probably will be. And who knows? You might keep him. Once you've had a dog, you can never go back. Though Sonia wishes I would."

I stiffen at the sound of his girlfriend's name. "She doesn't like Fritz?"

"She doesn't like anything that jumps on her. And even though I've tried to train him, Fritz jumps on *everybody*."

When John Neuwirth snares Daniel in a conversation about what happened to all the good sitcoms, Nate slides onto the bench beside me. "You're totally in love with that guy," he mutters.

"I already told you, I like the cook at work."

"Nothing wrong with seeing two people at once. And Daniel isn't some bigheaded producer or anything. He's cool."

"He's a lot friendlier here than at the restaurant."

"Hmm," Nate says. "I wonder why."

"Keep your voice down. He has a girlfriend."

"Oh, yeah? Then why's he eyeing my sister over the relish?"

I fight to keep from smiling. "Shut up. You're giving me heartburn."

"Even Mom said so."

"Said what?"

"That he's into you. She also said he needs to take his car to a body shop."

"Who wants cherry pie?" John Neuwirth asks, getting to his feet. "Fresh baked by Pillsbury. I brought four of them, so go crazy."

"Erin, can I cut you a piece?" Daniel asks.

"Sure. Why stop now?"

John leans over and cups his hand to his mouth. "Good catch, Erin. I'll be checking my mail for an invitation."

Everyone gathers for a game of "horseshoes, no rules" while Daniel drops his cherry-smeared paper plate into the trash can and says good-bye to my parents.

"Good luck with your house search," Mom says, shaking his hand.

"We'll have to get you out here again," says my father. "Next time *you* can lull *me* to sleep."

"Keep writing," Daniel calls. He pulls his keys from his pocket as I lead him through the side gate. We walk across the driveway and hesitate next to his car, smiling awkwardly at each other. "So . . ." he says.

"So, thanks again for the ride," I say, suddenly wishing I were going with him.

"My pleasure."

"You were really nice to indulge my father. I had no idea he was going to corner you like that."

"I enjoyed myself," Daniel says.

I shake my head, not quite believing him. "We're an interesting family, that's for sure."

"Nothing wrong with interesting."

Honk honk!

I whirl around to see Harold Pancratz's old black Cadillac bouncing up the driveway. "Perfect timing," I mutter.

"What was that?"

"Nothing. Just a couple of party crashers."

Harold rolls to a stop, toots his horn to the rhythm of "Shave and a Haircut, Two Bits," then climbs out and opens the door for his wife. "Afternoon!" he shouts.

"Hi, Harold. Hi, Brenda," I call, forcing enthusiasm into my voice. I introduce Daniel ("a friend from Roulette"), who immediately wins Harold over with three words I hope he doesn't mean. "Car's a beauty."

Harold beams. "Got a fine machine there yourself. Bit of rust, though. That's the trouble when you buy foreign."

"Sorry we're late," Brenda says, showing us a platter of tiny quiches. "My egg whites wouldn't peak, but things turned out okay in the end."

"They look great. Too bad I have to get going," Daniel says.

"Here, take one for the road." Brenda picks up a quiche and drops it into his bare palm.

Before I can get Daniel safely behind the wheel and down the driveway, Harold turns to me with shining eyes. "I'm so proud of you, Erin."

"You are? For what?"

To my horror, he grabs me by the shoulders and gives me a suffocating hug. The cigar in his shirt pocket presses into my chin. "Steve had nothing but praise for you when we talked yesterday," he says, his short black beard scraping my forehead. "It sounds like you've distinguished yourself in a very short period of time, young lady."

I pull back, rumpled and humiliated. "I have?"

"You bet. Are you happy at Roulette? Are they as good to you as I said they'd be?"

"Uh . . . absolutely. Even better."

Daniel buries me deeper by saying, "She has a lot of talent, especially with little customers who flip out."

"I knew she'd be a hit," Harold says, his dark eyes crinkling at the corners. "That's why I staked my reputation on her."

"Okay!" I blurt. "Anybody for chicken?"

"Go give this to Anne, hon," Brenda says, handing her

husband the platter. "I want to catch up with Erin for a minute."

Daniel yanks open his driver's-side door. "Well, I'd better get going. Nice to meet you both." He holds the quiche in his teeth as he fires up the car and drives off in a cloud of burning motor oil. I'm preparing to stare after him for the rest of the afternoon when Brenda grabs my hand and pulls me toward the porch swing. "Now that we're alone, let's have a little girl talk."

We sit down and she starts us swaying with a push of her foot. I expect her to quiz me about "that gorgeous doll with the British jalopy" or where I bought my shoes, but she lowers her voice and says, "I've been dying to ask what you think of Carl."

"Carl Corbett?"

She lays a plump hand over her heart. "He's a genius, isn't he? I mean, have you ever tasted better food?"

"It's amazing, all right."

"I'm sure you've seen the way women stare at him. Gina said his wife left him last year because she couldn't compete with the restaurant anymore. If you ask me, no one could."

"Actually, I hear he's seeing Kimberly, one of the hostesses. She can't be more than twenty-three, and she's as tall as he is."

"Be careful, Erin. He'll be asking for your number next."

I laugh. "He isn't very nice to me, to be honest."

"Nice doesn't come with the territory, my dear. But what magnetism. Try to resist him and he'll draw you in anyway."

"I don't think so, Brenda."

"That's what they all say," she replies, patting my knee. "Then they taste his pan-seared red mullet."

chapter 10

"Rocket, no!"

The following Tuesday, I race across the kitchen, drop to my knees, and nab Rocket as he raises his leg to one of my chairs. He whimpers and struggles in my arms, then finally relaxes when he realizes I'm not letting go. "Why didn't you do that ten minutes ago in the park?" He blinks at me, his gray eyebrows slanted outward in an expression of confused remorse. A fragment of dried leaf sticks to his folded ear, evidence of the hour he just spent crushing flowers and rolling in dirt.

"Remember our agreement," I say in the firm voice Rachel recommended for infractions. "You behave and you can stay here until next week, okay? Now let's get you outside before you have an accident."

Sunlight burns through the mid-morning mist as we circle the block. Now that I'm walking a beast of my own, dogs and their owners seem to be everywhere, and what started as a chore soon becomes an opportunity to socialize.

"Annabelle, cut it out," a white-haired man in jogging clothes says after his huge mutt growls at Rocket.

"Don't worry—this little guy's fiercer than he looks," I tell him.

"Isn't he adorable," says a woman with a Chihuahua. Though she wears a trim plaid suit, her dog shows off a studded collar. "Jack Russell, right?"

I smile proudly, as if I'd raised Rocket from birth. "And he's got the bark to prove it."

She stops and we spend the next few minutes discussing everything from names to temperament to eating habits ("What he can't eat, he turns into a chew toy," I say) while the dogs yap and dance around each other. "See you next time," the woman calls as we go in opposite directions.

Now that I'm no longer part of the eight-to-five world, there's something comforting about suddenly belonging to a new group: those who are slaves to their dogs.

Rachel drops by at noon to give Rocket a rubber starfish toy and to "see how our arrangement is coming along."

"It changes hourly," I tell her. "One thing's for sure—he needs a lot more exercise than he's getting."

"Here, maybe this will help." She hands me a shiny blue business card. "Best dog-walking service in town. Highly recommended by two of my clients."

"Dogopolis," I say, turning the card over in my hand. "Over seven hundred and forty-two served."

"They're expensive, but Rocket will be in a much better mood when you come home from work. Where is the little powder keg, anyway?"

I lead her to the bedroom, where Rocket, having finally exhausted himself, is curled up on the slipcovered chair.

"He looks so peaceful," she whispers.

"That's because he's spent the past four days wreaking havoc. He broke into the garbage, drank out of the fish tank, pissed off my landlord . . . I got a knock on the door and a nasty lecture at eight thirty this morning. Half of it was in Greek, but the gist was 'Shut that thing up or I'll change your locks.'"

"Really? Nick's usually such a nice guy."

"Rocket ended all that."

She strokes him between the ears. "Then it's a good thing we're getting him out of here."

"We are?" I ask, frowning.

"As soon as I can make the arrangements. A groomer I know is interested in taking him."

"Really?" I sit down on the bed. "When?"

"This weekend, if I can talk her into it. She already has two dogs and a cat, so it's a square footage issue."

"This weekend? That's so soon."

"Yeah. I thought you'd be overjoyed."

"I am, it's just that . . . well, he's kind of like my adorable, infuriating roommate. When he's not going after something, he's sweet and affectionate."

"Wait a minute. You *like* him?"

"Sometimes," I say, shrugging. "When he's good. And . . . when he's bad but really sorry."

Rachel shakes her head quickly. "I'm getting mixed messages here. If you want to keep him, you'll have to make up your mind. Are you sure you're ready for the responsibility of a dog? An old dog who might not be around much longer?"

"Probably not. I don't know."

"You've got forty-eight hours to decide. After that, he's up for grabs."

"Shhh. He'll hear you. Animals pick up on that kind of thing."

"Wow," she says. "He's got you sitting up and begging already."

"Shouldn't it be the other way around?"

She laughs and sits beside me. "I didn't come by just to

check on Rocket. I want to hear about your trip to Long Island with the producer."

"We had a nice conversation and a couple of chicken wings before he went to his friend's house. That's all."

"That's all?"

"It's not going anywhere, trust me. I'd be dating the cook by now, but hooking up at the restaurant isn't easy. I can hardly flirt under that kind of pressure."

"Speaking of pressure..." She checks her watch. "I have to go. I'm photographing an iguana in Yonkers in two hours."

"A *lizard*?"

She stands up and sets Rocket's toy on the arm of the chair. "Dogs, cats, and birds may pay the bills, but exotics keep things interesting."

✦

"Loyalty. Without it, we're not a team."

It's almost eleven at night and Carl has called Cato, Jane, and me into the kitchen for an impromptu meeting. "True loyalty extends outside the walls of this restaurant."

The cooks are scrubbing the stoves and walls behind him. Phil, the only man hot enough to interrupt my mental replay of everything Daniel did and said at the barbecue, stands on a stepladder scouring the ceiling. He stops to push the hair off his forehead with his wrist and we lock eyes over his Brillo pad. He's wearing blue rubber gloves and a puka shell necklace, igniting a "surfing janitor" fantasy I never knew I had.

"We can't beat our competitors if we don't know what they're serving the average guest," Carl continues. "I'm too well known to go anywhere and expect a typical meal, and my cooks might be recognized. That's why I'm sending the three of you on a mission. Right now." He hesitates. "Paid, of course."

Though we're drained and disheveled after hours on our feet, no one objects. Carl is giving an order we don't dare disobey.

"What's the assignment?" Cato asks.

"You're going to infiltrate Rick Holland's restaurant. I made a reservation for you under the name of MacArthur."

"As in Douglas?" Cato asks.

"That's right. Now, listen. I want you to eat as much as you possibly can. I expect a report on everything—the specials, the way the food tastes, the service. Holland should be there tonight, so he'll probably come into the dining room. *Watch his every move.* Take notes. Give me information on the guests, too. Famous faces, what people order, anything else you can find out."

He hands Jane a wad of cash. "This should cover it, and I've included a hundred-dollar bill for each of you to keep. Remember, this is *la guerre.* War. No pretty-boy hummus peddler calls my food 'pablum for the Zagat crowd' without getting napalmed in return."

"*Zagat crowd?*" Jane repeats.

Carl nods somberly. "This is a small community. He had to know he was firing the first shot. Now, you'd better get going. They stop serving in an hour and you've got a lot of eating to do. Ron and Derek will close up."

We change into street clothes and, jumpy as pilots on our first sortie, head down the block to Capers. From the understated beige exterior, it could be any other elegant restaurant on the Upper East Side, but inside we find wrought-iron lanterns, tapestry-swathed booths, and pseudo-Moorish architecture. "Am I the only one having an LSD moment?" Cato murmurs.

On the wall by the podium is a framed article proclaiming Holland, with his blue-black hair and hooded eyes, New York's Sexiest Chef. Beside it is a magazine cover with a mug-shot-style photo and the words "Who Is Killing the Great Chefs of Manhattan? Ask This Man."

We follow a caftan-garbed hostess through the narrow alley between tables. The clientele is younger and more downtown than Roulette's, and the air smells like the Latin quarter of some foreign city. We squeeze in at a four-top in the center of the room.

"What's a Smith and Wesson?" Cato says, peering at the cocktail menu. "Vodka...Kahlua...hmm, maybe not. Might make me belligerent."

"Relaxed but lively," I say. "That's what I'm aiming for."

We order drinks, then spend fifteen minutes deciding what to eat. "We have to get one of everything," Jane says.

"Uh, Janey dear, there are...wait a second...forty-two items here," Cato says.

"Carl said to get a good overview," I remind him.

"Critics go back to the same place over and over again," Jane says. "We have only one shot."

Cato studies the menu. "Okay, I have it all figured out. We'll order every third item, and whatever we can't finish, we'll take home and evaluate tomorrow while we're recovering from our hangovers." He samples a drink containing oolong tea and rum and pronounces it "the new absinthe. Just prop me up if I fall over."

"Holland at twelve o'clock," I say. He wears immaculate chef's whites and a diamond stud in his left ear. Glass of white wine in hand, he stops at the table next to us and starts chatting with a sweet-faced brunette and her paunchy gray-haired companion.

"Laurie! Harv! How was dinner?"

"Fan*tas*tic," she answers.

Holland puts a hand on her shoulder. "You're not reviewing me, are you? Go easy, I've been open only a few weeks." He laughs.

Cato eyes the woman as if he knows her. "Correct me if I'm wrong, but isn't that . . . ?"

"Laurie Pearson," Jane says.

"Who's Laurie Pearson?" I ask.

Cato lowers his voice. "Food writer with baggage. She was going to be head critic at the *Herald* until she got too cozy with one of the chefs she was reviewing."

"What do you mean, 'cozy'?"

"A suite at Trump Tower when hubby was out of town. That doesn't sound like objective reporting to me."

"Her editors weren't too pleased, especially since she expensed the whole thing," Jane says, running a finger down her frosty glass. "Now she's writing a column called 'The Budget Epicure.'"

"Yeah, tips for the bon vivant without a pot to piss in," Cato says. "I read it every week, and the only thing I've learned is that fried egg sandwiches taste better when you light candles and drink a fruity rosé."

I sneak another look. "Who's the old man with her?"

"Um . . . Phil Donahue," Jane guesses.

"Checking out the ass of every waitress and going on about the history of the lychee nut?" Cato says. "Probably just another lonely foodie."

"Impressive," says our waiter as he jots down the third page of our order. Like the rest of the waitstaff, he wears a tight black shirt with French cuffs and is blessed with a near-perfect face. "You must be hungry."

"We smoked some high-octane pot before we came," Cato replies.

The waiter gives him a knowing smile. "You'll appreciate the food even more, then."

As he retreats toward the kitchen, Cato leans forward. "I

give him an A for service so far. Knowledgeable, sweet, not too pushy. Agreed?"

Jane and I nod. "What about atmosphere?" I ask.

"Love it," says Cato. "A little whorehouse, a little Arabian Nights."

Jane looks at the old kilims hanging on the walls in place of art. "A bit busy," she says, scrawling in her notepad. "I give it a B plus. How about the cocktails?"

"Original bordering on bizarre," I say, raising my ginger–passion fruit martini.

"Anything that makes me sound more interesting gets my vote," says Cato.

Our wine arrives on the arm of a young sommelier so warm and unassuming she makes Geoffrey seem frozen in amber. "I think you'll enjoy this," she says, pouring some for me to taste. We click glasses of Pouilly-Fuissé ("To my fellow agents," says Cato) and the waiters begin to file out of the kitchen with our food. The clean flavors Carl prefers have been replaced by heady spices—curry, coriander, and cumin. I sip my wine, pull in my chair, and prepare to hate everything.

Jane squints at the almond-crusted yellowfin with cucumber salad. "Admit it. This is just as pretty as what comes out of Carl's kitchen."

I fork some tiger-prawn tagine onto my plate. "He won't be happy to hear that. We'll have to say it looked pretentious or something."

Cato and I watch as Jane takes the first bite of citrus-grilled octopus. She chews slowly, swallows, and shakes her head. "Oh, shit. We're in trouble."

"What?" we ask together.

"This is good. *Really* good."

I taste a warm, lemony prawn. "How are we going to break it to Carl? He'll fire us."

"You're right," Cato says around a mouthful of cucumber salad. "We'll have to say it in a way that's semi-honest. Like it's unique but too eccentric for most people."

"What if it gets glowing reviews?"

Jane smirks. "Carl probably won't believe them."

"Oh my God, my tongue is climaxing," Cato says. "Are we really getting paid for this?"

By the time Jane and I fight over the last bite of chocolate soup with tropical fruit, we've crowned Capers our favorite new restaurant.

"Carl can cook, but this guy has *vision,* you know?" Cato says.

I put down my spoon. "Screw semi-honest. We're going to have to lie."

"Having a good time?"

We lift our heads simultaneously, like three deer hearing a boot step. Standing over us is the toothy, smiling Rick Holland. "Yes! Thank you!" I say.

"Best food I've had in a long time," Jane says, displaying none of the loyalty Carl lectured us about.

"That's what I like to hear," Holland says. He looks at each of us. "You're from Roulette, aren't you?"

Cato's face drains. "I had no idea we were that famous."

"Word gets around."

"We just wanted to have a late bite somewhere," Jane says.

"Enjoy working for Corbett, do you?"

"Absolutely," I say.

"The money's excellent," Cato adds. "Food's great too."

A shadow passes over Holland's blue eyes as he no doubt recalls wrestling with Carl in a French country kitchen. "I hear Carl has a lot of turnover."

"No more than any other restaurant," Jane says.

Holland grins, as if she's confirmed his suspicion and

sincere hope that his enemy has a constant, low-level mutiny on his hands. "Well, tell him he can send his staff over to my place anytime. You're always welcome. And so is he."

"Thanks," Jane says, shooting me a sidelong glance.

"We'll let him know," says Cato.

A few minutes later, three glasses of reserve port arrive at our table. "Sometimes it's better not to tell people what they can't handle," I say.

"Carl doesn't need to hear about this," Jane agrees.

Cato lifts his glass. "Cheers to that."

✦

"Crowded at *midnight*?" Carl barks when we report back the following afternoon. Citing "morale reasons," he's pulled us into the walk-in, out of earshot of the cooks.

"It thinned out pretty quickly after that," Cato rushes to say.

"Was Holland on the floor?"

"The entire time we were there," I say.

Carl snorts. "Classic. He always was more interested in schmoozing than cooking. Who did he talk to?"

"Just about everybody."

His eyes get huge. "Including *you*? He didn't know who you were, did he?"

"God, no."

"Of course not," Jane says. "He hardly said two words to us."

"All right, what about the food?"

Cato describes the yellowfin and the spices as "a prescription for Maalox at four in the morning, in my opinion. Laurie Pearson was there, but that's no big deal because she's been blacklisted. Right, Jane?"

Jane nods. "Her credibility is shot."

But no matter how we dilute the truth, Carl takes it as a slight and a challenge. "I'm not going to be outcooked by some corporate commodity," he says, his breath exploding in frosty puffs. "If we were talking about Keller or Ducasse, I could see giving up a little ground out of respect, but Holland? Mr. Four-hundred-dollar Haircut? Mr. *Zagat Crowd*?" His voice rings through the small space.

"The quail broth had too many mushrooms," Jane says quietly.

"How was it otherwise?"

"Um, pretty good."

Carl's mouth twitches at one corner. "Thank you, that'll be all. Specials in five minutes." He stares at us, then whispers fiercely, *"Vive la guerre,"* before walking out and letting the door swing shut behind him.

✦

I've lost track of how much money I've made since I started taking tables two weeks ago, but I know it rivals my former salary. I've paid rent and bills with plenty to spare, and what's left over feels almost unreal, a treasure that magically renews itself at midnight. As part of the credit card generation, I've rarely carried more than cab fare. But now, after many brief transactions that involve satisfying someone else's primal instinct, I have almost four thousand dollars in large bills in my underwear drawer.

I secure a handful of cash with a rubber band and go downtown, determined to make up for all the snapped fingers and special requests ("I'd like everything chopped into bite-sized pieces. Yes, even the bok choy"). Before I know it, I've dropped two shifts' earnings on a cashmere throw, a bag of Yemeni coffee beans, two bottles of wine, and a throw pillow that was hand-embroidered in Provence. I have the blind sense of stuffing myself with whatever I want, of bingeing after a long period of deprivation. *That looks good, I'll take it. Another helping? Yes, please. I deserve it.*

A cool October wind is picking up as I yank my bags through the door of a small housewares boutique. Surely I can manage to carry one more thing before I head home and collapse. As I contemplate adding a cobalt-blue hand-blown vase to my haul, my cell phone rings. I struggle to dig it out of my purse, and see a number I don't recognize flashing on the screen.

"Hello?"

"Erin!" says an unmistakable female voice.

I hesitate. *"Gina?"*

"Your plans change today!"

"My plans?" I suddenly feel as if Gina were in charge, not only of my job, but of my destiny.

"The wedding reception at Roulette tonight. Is easy and we don't need you."

"Oh! Okay..."

"You and Cato go to work a private party instead. He says you do parties for Harold, so I send you both to my friend's apartment."

Cato, you're a dead man. "Uh, what kind of party did you say?"

"Dinner," Gina says loudly. "Twenty people, something like that. You wear black pants and do what they tell you, okay? Six o'clock you meet Cato at the corner of Seventy-sixth and Fifth. Make me proud!"

chapter 11

I meet Cato a few hours later in front of a vault-like gray building on Fifth Avenue. His hair is freshly gelled and he's leaning against the wall, smoking a cigarette. "Before you say anything, I'm doing you a favor," he says.

I glare at him. "Somehow I doubt that."

"Hey, I thought you'd be *happy* to get away from Roulette."

"I am, but couldn't you have given me a little warning?"

"What for?" he says. "You'll make the same money in half the time. You should have heard the way Derek begged me to take him instead. I had to beat him back with a barstool."

"Well, thanks for thinking of me, but they're expecting somebody who knows what they're doing."

He snorts. "That never stopped you before."

"Maybe it should have."

"Listen," he says, stepping on his cigarette. "Have you ever served your uncle Stu a sandwich on Super Bowl Sunday? This is a lot like that, only with snootier people. Get 'em tipsy, get 'em full, and get out of the way. I swear, there's not much more to it than that."

"I hope you're right."

"I haven't steered you wrong yet, have I? When you walk out of here with three bills, you'll thank me. Now, let's go have some fun."

He grabs my hand and pulls me into the cool, hushed lobby. After calling upstairs, the doorman escorts us to the elevator and waits until the doors close. "You look amazing, by the way," Cato says, taking in my red lipstick and long earrings, a gift from Nate. "Remember, we're serving at this party, not going as guests."

I examine my reflection in the mirrored wall. "I'm in lust, so I need to look good twenty-four hours a day."

"Daniel and Phil. I had no idea you were so versatile."

"Who said anything about Daniel?"

"Come on, honey. Ever since that barbecue, you've been a bundle of pheromones."

"Phil checked out my butt yesterday," I say. "That's all you're picking up."

"Just watch it. I know he's a hottie, but he's gone through a hostess and a female prep cook since last December. The prep cook ran out in tears one day and never came back. I'm telling you, the guy's trouble."

"Don't worry, Cato. I can take care of myself."

"Maybe," he says. "But Phil's one of Carl's boys, which means he's faithful to the kitchen. Trust me, anybody who looks like that is trailing broken hearts. That's why I always go for the plain ones—so I can feel like a prize."

I smile. "Ingenious."

"It's a short-lived thrill, but I'd rather feel cute for a few hours than ordinary all the time."

The elevator slows as we near the top floor. "Who are we working for tonight, anyway?"

"Frank and Patti Porter. She's one of those professional socialites and he's a bigwig at SSB Television. That's why I volunteered for this gig, so I can network between courses.

If I don't start making connections, I'll be doing bit parts and walk-ons until I'm back in diapers."

"Isn't it weird waiting on people in their own house?"

"Not really. I've worked a million of these things and they're cake compared to a night with Carl."

The elevator slides open, revealing a large round foyer with marble floors, glossy yellow walls, and a stained-glass dome skylight. A noseless Roman bust stares at us from a carved wooden table in the center of the room. "Just another twelve-million-dollar penthouse on the Upper East Side," Cato sighs. "Whatever happened to homey?"

"Wow," I say. "You mean we just . . . walk in?"

He yanks me out of the elevator. "Like you own the joint."

We hear the swish of fabric, then a high-pitched "Hello there!" Coming down the hallway toward us is a bronze-haired, dewy-skinned woman in her late forties wearing a flowing silk pantsuit and gold jewelry. "Thank you so much for coming. I'm Patti and you two are saving my life. How wonderful of Gina and Steve to spare you." She stops abruptly and examines a tabletop. "Oh no, not today. How many times have I asked her to dust in straight lines? Rosalinda!"

A heavyset Hispanic woman in a maid's uniform and black stockings runs into the room. "Yes, ma'am?"

Patti points to the table. "We discussed this, remember? The foyer is where first impressions are made."

Rosalinda whips a white cloth from her apron pocket and begins to polish the already gleaming wood. "I'm sorry, Mrs. Patti."

"Please check the entire apartment ASAP. Mantels and everything. *Muchas gracias.*" Patti turns to us again. "Ready to get started? Come with me."

Trailing her through an endless series of lacquered rooms,

I have the sense of being on a movie set, or in a famous artist's home that is now open to the public. Everything looks antique but perfectly new, as if it were bought two hundred years ago and covered with sheets until this morning. "You must love working for Gina," she says as we walk past black-and-beige striped sofas, Japanese screens, and enormous oil paintings. "Isn't she wonderful? We met last year at a benefit for Venice's canals and just *clicked*."

"She's a sweetheart, all right," Cato says, smiling at me over his shoulder.

"My eighty-year-old father fell in love with her. He just adores feisty women," Patti says, leading us into a kitchen that is two-thirds the size of Roulette's, with tall arched windows overlooking the park. There are two dishwashers, two refrigerators, four ovens, and a chef in a spotless white jacket standing at a twelve-burner stainless steel stove, a toque over his wavy gray hair.

"My God," I whisper to Cato. "Can you believe this place?"

"I'm so ready to marry up," he whispers back.

"You're professionals, so I'm sure you know the drill," Patti says. "Direct your questions to Rosalinda or my chef, Yves, and please remember that tonight is very important to me. Nothing puts your strengths and weaknesses on display like a dinner party."

Rosalinda shows us to the dining room, where we set two tables of ten with hand-painted china, and crystal so heavy it must be more expensive than my yearly rent. "Just picture paper plates and jelly jars and you won't break anything," Cato says. "It's one of those mental tricks, like imagining the audience in their underwear."

When we return to the kitchen for wineglasses, we find Patti and Yves in a tussle over the evening's dessert.

"But it doesn't go with the flowers!" she cries.

"I'm sorry, madame, there is nothing I can do."

"Mud! It looks like mud!"

"But, madame, this is how chocolate soufflé is supposed to look."

"Can't you make it..." She makes whipping motions with her manicured hands. "Paler? Poofier?"

Yves purses his lips. "You asked for soufflé and that is what I made."

"Please, Yves. It has to match the arrangements. I paid..." She rolls her eyes to the ceiling. "I can't even bring myself to say it. A king's *ransom* for those orchids."

"I am not an interior decorator! I do not make my food to coordinate wis' the walls!"

Patti's tone changes from cajoling to stern. "Listen to me, Yves. I give you a pretty long leash around here. When I want something done *my* way, which is not very often, then I want it done. Okay?"

He sighs loudly, a clear sign of surrender. "Okay, I will start over with lemon, but do not blame me if—"

She lifts her chin victoriously and pats his arm. "I wouldn't dream of it. Now," she says, turning to us, "the guests will be arriving shortly and you should both look as if you're having the time of your lives! Nobody likes dreary faces."

"I drown in soufflés," Yves mutters, grabbing a tray of eggs from one of the refrigerators.

A thick-necked man with salt-and-pepper hair appears in the doorway and kisses Patti on the forehead. This must be Frank Porter, media mogul extraordinaire. "Hello, all," he says. "I don't know who some of you are, but welcome, have a good time, and let's get everyone out the door by eleven at the latest!"

As the doorbell rings and guests begin to file in, Cato and I load silver trays with champagne and hors d'oeuvres and ferry them to one of several professionally mismatched living areas. A grand piano sits in one corner like a giant knickknack that never gets played. "Here we go," Cato says. "Put on your service face, baby."

With a smile that is part cheerleader, part politician on the campaign trail, I plunge into the crowd, muttering, "Salmon blintz? Prawn?" and dodging air kisses. Our host perches on the arm of a chair, trading handshakes and cheek-pecks and flirting outrageously with every non-uniformed female in the room. If his wife notices, she doesn't show it. She has another, more pressing matter on her mind.

"Uh, Erin, was it? Can we chat a moment, please?"

"Sure." Tray held high, I follow her outside the living room door.

"I need to ask you a favor," Patti says. Her voice is low, her face open and trusting. She's about to take me into her confidence, and I nod solemnly to show that I'm ready and willing to help.

"Of course. Anything."

She sighs. "Your earrings are interesting, but frankly, they're very large and distracting. They just don't *go*."

I touch the silver and onyx hoops Nate bought for me in Guatemala two years ago. "Go?" I suddenly feel like a big, ugly couch.

"With the décor, dear. They're a bit bohemian. And my style, obviously, is more classic."

"Oh. I see."

"When you get a minute I'd appreciate it if you could remove them."

Since I no longer question bizarre or humiliating requests, I smile and say, "I'll be happy to."

Her face relaxes. "Terrific! Thank you for understanding. Oh—there's my daughter and she's got champagne."

Patti hurries toward a laughing girl in a tight pink dress and tall wedge sandals. No more than fourteen, she's munching a mini lobster roll and conversing with a grown man as if she's been practicing party etiquette all her life. She ignores her mother's shoulder tapping until the object of her attention excuses himself. "What?" she snaps as I duck behind a potted tree and yank out my earrings. Without a pocket to put them in, I have no choice but to hold them in one hand and balance my tray with the other. "Mother, don't you know it's rude to interrupt?"

"This is an adults' party, Edie, and you have history homework to do."

"No, I don't," she insists.

"Look at me when I'm talking to you. There are three decent schools in Manhattan and you've blown through two of them. Do you want to end up in a boarding school in the backwoods of Vermont somewhere? Because that's what will happen if your grades don't improve." Patti points toward the door. "Homework. Now." She spots a friend and instantly replaces her smile. "Sonia!"

Sonia? I nearly drop my phyllo-wrapped shellfish at the sight of Daniel's girlfriend, standing two feet away in jeweled high-heeled sandals and a black dress that ends in a ruffle just above her knees. Her silver-blond hair is pulled back in a careless ponytail that conveys absolute confidence.

Daniel's here. He has to be.

"Sorry I'm late, Aunt Patti," Sonia says. "I had to go visit Gran again. You've seen how she gets if she's alone for even five minutes."

"I don't understand it," Patti says. "She has so many friends there. Lord knows Frank and your mother pay enough for the place. You'd think she could at least *act* happy."

"She hasn't been happy since 1995. First it was her thyroid, now it's her back."

"Nonsense. She can run circles around all of us. The last time we visited we couldn't get her to sit down. She's no more sick than we are."

"It's all in her imagination." Sonia lets out a short laugh. "She's probably going to hang on for another twenty years. Oh my God, do I sound awful?"

Patti lowers her voice. "Not at *all*. It's natural to feel put-upon now and then, and don't let anybody make you feel guilty about it. Did you eat while you were there?"

"No. I lose my appetite when I'm around wheelchairs."

"Poor thing. You must be about to keel over."

"Between work and visiting Gran every week, I can't remember when I've been so exhausted."

"Here ... have some of Yves's hors d'oeuvres," Patti says, grabbing me by the sleeve. "He really topped himself tonight. These shrimp are outrageous."

Sonia examines my tray without seeming to notice that it's held up by a human being, let alone one who waited on her ten days ago.

"And these are ..." Patti prompts.

"Grilled prawns wrapped in phyllo dough and brushed with lemon olive oil," I say.

"Like I said, Sonia, to die for," Patti adds.

"Well, I haven't washed my hands yet," Sonia says, taking a cocktail napkin and gingerly wrapping it around a shrimp. "Who knows what bacteria is floating around that place?"

Patti declines my tray with an almost imperceptible shake of the head. "I know exactly what you mean. These days, I feel like taking an antibiotic every time I step outside. Let's go get you a drink, take your mind off things."

"Wait a second, come back with those," Sonia says as I move toward the next group of guests. She reaches out and snatches two more shrimp. "These *are* good, Patti. Suddenly I'm starving." They link arms and drift toward the other side of the room.

I've just lost my last prawn to an older man who keeps winking at me when a voice says, "Excuse me, got any more of those salmon things?"

I swallow hard and turn to see a smiling, champagne-brandishing Daniel. "You certainly get around," he says.

"What are you doing here?" I ask, dropping my earrings among the toothpicks and crumpled napkins on my tray.

"I work for Frank Porter. And evidently, so do you." He tosses a blintz in his mouth and chews. "Not bad. It isn't an Edwards chicken wing, but it'll do."

"My father would be happy to hear you say that."

I suddenly have an image of my parents walking into the party—my father wearing white sneakers and shorts, my mother in her cherry-print sundress and carrying a ten-dollar bottle of wine—too straightforward and simple to act nonchalant. "Holy *cow*," I can hear my father saying to Mr. Porter, "is that painting original or just a really good print?"

"Did you have luck finding a house?" I ask.

"Not yet," Daniel says. "The place I liked got snapped up by a guy who's going to tear it down."

"Maybe it's time to put Naomi on the case. She'll have you in a house before the owners even know they're selling."

"If I don't find anything in a month or two, I'll give her a call." He finishes his champagne and sets the glass on my empty tray. "What's with the earrings? Did somebody trade them for extra shrimp?"

"Actually, they're mine. Patti thinks they're too loud."

"Why are you carrying them on your tray?"

"I don't have a pocket."

He reaches out, grabs the earrings, and slips them into the front pocket of his shirt. "You do now," he says.

After serving tureens of roasted yellow pepper soup, Cato and I circle each table, offering crème fraîche and chopped parsley. Daniel sits across the orchid arrangement from Sonia, who unfolds her brocade napkin and says, "You read that script, didn't you, Dan? The one by the Mexican drug dealer? What did you think?"

He squints. "I thought it was a little self-conscious. I had trouble getting into it."

"It was edgy," she says. "You didn't understand the story."

"Listen to him, Sonia," her uncle says. "You have to be quite a writer to make a heroin-trafficker appealing, especially when he spends half the film transporting illegal aliens."

"But he really lived this stuff. I think we need to start taking chances and producing grittier shows. Most of what we do is so mainstream."

"I admire your passion," Frank says, "and I'm all for gritty. But glamorizing crime doesn't fly, not with thirty-two-year-old white women from Missouri. Those are the viewers we're talking about here. When you've been at this as long as Daniel has, you'll be able to pick out in three minutes what's marketable to the Fox crowd."

She rolls her eyes. "The Fox crowd."

"You're not going to make her spend the next five years reading scripts, Frank," Patti says.

"Maybe just one or two," he says, putting his arm around his niece. "She's got to pay her dues like any other gorgeous girl from a good family, doesn't she?"

"That's right," Daniel teases. "Time to start breaking rocks like the rest of us."

"In that case, I'm hitting you up for a raise," she says to her uncle, then kisses him on the cheek.

"Parsley?" I ask Sonia.

It takes her a few seconds to realize I've spoken. "Any dairy in this soup?" she replies. I can tell from her blank expression that she still has no memory of me.

"I don't think so."

"If you could go to the kitchen and find out, that would be helpful," Sonia says. "And no, I don't want parsley, thanks."

"Isn't she horrible?" Cato says after I cheerfully deliver the bad news to Sonia (heavy cream, butter). "Exactly the sort of rich bitch I love to hate. And wish I'd been born as."

"I might not have done this if I'd known she was going to be here."

He smirks. "With Daniel on the guest list? Sure you would have."

"All zis talk gives me a migraine," Yves says. He pours an inch of sherry into a glass and takes a swallow. "Why must waiters always be saying something?"

"Sorry, Yves. Stress release," Cato says. "Keeps us from swan-diving off the fire escape." He leans closer to me. "Every time Sonia comes into Roulette, Luis crosses himself. Thinks she's the hottest thing since Rosario Dawson. It *kills* me."

"I can't figure out what Daniel's doing with her," I say quietly. "He's much more down-to-earth than she is. At least, I thought he was."

"Rich people breed worse than rednecks. It doesn't matter how nice he is or how enlightened he seems. In the end, the wealthy stick together."

"Have you seen his *car*?"

"No, but I've heard about it. The car is his hobby, Erin. He's not going to marry it."

"I thought maybe it meant something."

"Yeah, that the poor side of town can be amusing when you don't have to live there."

After dessert, the party moves to the library, where Cato and I glide from couch to fireplace to wing chair, offering digestifs, espresso shortbread, and chocolates. I affect "the murmur," a voice that is barely audible but relates such crucial information as "truffle" and "Calvados." Sonia and Daniel share a tiny flowered love seat, his arm engulfing her tanned shoulders. I hand him a snifter at the exact moment she kisses the corner of his mouth. " 'ank you," he says.

"Let's go to Harbour Island next weekend," she tells him. "I want to see the hotel India designed."

He sips his brandy. "Shouldn't we wait until hurricane season's over?"

"Why? Storms are romantic."

I stand at the edge of the room with my hands behind my back, aware that I'm making a sickening amount of cash for very little effort but feeling miserable anyway. I watch as Cato turns refilling Mr. Porter's cognac into an opportunity to beg for acting work. "... wrote that I brought fresh life to the character of Orlando," he's saying.

"I'm sure you did," Mr. Porter says.

"I'm open to anything, but stage work or a spot on a daytime drama is my short-term goal."

Mr. Porter yawns. "It's good to have goals."

By eleven thirty, the guests have started to leave and Cato and I are helping Rosalinda restore the kitchen to its pre-party condition. "Mr. Porter told me to go through my agent and fetch him another cigar," Cato grumbles as we dry wineglasses. "And I'm in this business why?"

"I'm sorry, Cato. What would cheer you up? Anything?"

"I don't know. I'll probably meet up with some people from work. Why don't you come? We can drink hard stuff and come on to strangers."

"Sounds like a great time, but I have to walk Rocket."

"Meet us when you're finished walking him. We'll save a seat and some cheap bourbon for ya."

"Where are you going?"

"Reactor 6. It's a dive bar on Avenue B with nuclear décor. Trust me, it's impossible not to enjoy yourself in the shadow of a papier-mâché mushroom cloud. It gives the words 'live for today' a whole new meaning."

I smile and set my last glass on the marble countertop. "Can I invite my friend Rachel?"

"Honey, any friend of yours is a dance partner of mine."

Patti comes into the kitchen with a pair of envelopes. "You two were godsends," she says, handing one to each of us. "Absolute jewels. Thank you so much. Everything went perfectly except for the soufflé, and that's not your fault. Have you seen Yves?"

We shake our heads, though we both saw him slip out the service door an hour ago.

chapter 12

Rachel and I hold up our drinks and squeeze into a concrete booth at Reactor 6. Cold war posters decorate a bunker-inspired room where flashy gay men, tattooed hipsters, and bored-looking college kids compete for spots on fifties-era sofas. Techno music vibrates the floor. "When did you decide?" Rachel asks.

"I didn't decide. I gave in."

"You understand what this means, don't you?"

"Uh, I think it means I have a dog."

"And you'll be taking care of him for as long as you both shall live."

I sip my nameless white wine. "Why are you lecturing me *now*? I thought this was what you wanted."

"Just making sure you've read the fine print. Are you ready for six A.M. walks against your will? Accidents? Shedding?"

"All of the above. I know what I'm getting into."

Jane emerges from the crowd carrying a tall pink drink and slides in beside me. I'm introducing her to Rachel when Phil walks in wearing a battered leather jacket, chef's pants, and red high-tops. He joins Alain and Cato at the bar and scans the room. His eyes find me and he gives me a meaningful smile, immediately erasing my memory of Daniel's hand on Sonia's bare knee.

"What do you think of Phil?" I ask Jane.

She squints through the dry ice haze meant to represent radioactive fallout. "Good fling material. Why?"

"Because we've been flirting since the day I started."

"Be careful," she says. "Carl's like a coach who doesn't want anyone distracting his players."

"I'm not going to distract him. I might rip his clothes off, but that won't keep him from cooking, will it?"

"If Carl finds out, one of you will have to go. And it won't be his protégé."

Rachel turns to Jane. "She's just doing this because of what happened with that Daniel guy."

"Word's already out," Jane says. "I heard the short version from Cato."

"Hey," I break in. "I thought it would be nice to get to know somebody I work with every day, that's all."

"Uh-huh," Jane says.

"Whatever you say," Rachel adds.

Ten minutes later, Phil and I are sharing a beer and a barstool and having our first conversation that doesn't revolve around what other people are eating. I learn that he's two years younger than I am, has never been west of Ohio, and came tonight only because Alain told him I might be here. "We never get a chance to talk at the restaurant, so I figured I'd track you down," he says.

"It's probably better to meet someplace else, anyway."

"Yeah, it's kind of weird for me, though. Cooks don't usually hang out with waiters."

"Just with prep cooks and hostesses, huh?"

He looks at me like he doesn't get the joke. "We don't have a lot in common, you know? Cooking's a life you can't understand unless you're part of it. It takes a lot of mojo to work the line sixty hours a week, and you don't make shit unless you're in a top position or you've got an ownership stake, the way Carl does. You have to keep coming up with new ideas, too. Like, Carl just had this guy at Lockheed Martin make a pouch that gives air any taste you want."

"*Air?*"

Phil nods. "Makes what you're eating more intense. And that's just the beginning. Carl's working on pushing flavor molecules together to make food nobody's ever had before."

"I guess that explains the new liquid carpaccio."

"Crazy, huh? Carl made us all sign nondisclosure agreements so nobody could rip off his inventions. He's even applying for patents."

"Patents? For food?"

"Got to protect yourself these days."

I finish off the beer and set the bottle on the bar. "What do you say we forget about Roulette for one night and just dance?"

"To this rave crap?" he says, pointing a thumb toward the DJ.

"It isn't stopping anybody else."

Soon we're in a sweaty dance-floor clutch. Phil's damp hair brushes my face as the crowd forces us closer together. "I like watching you do sidework," he breathes into my ear. "You always look so serious."

"That's because I don't know what I'm doing," I whisper.

He tightens his arms around my back. "Do you know what you're doing to me right now?"

After two songs we leave the dance floor and hold hands under the table while Rachel and Alain talk classic cocktails. There's a forbidden thrill in hooking up with someone from Carl's side, as if I'm trespassing on private property. I almost expect to hear a voice through a bullhorn instructing me to "drop the cheap chardonnay and step away from the line cook." Phil's thigh touches mine, and for the first time since my three-day dalliance with the communications director at my old company, I realize I won't be spending the night in my own bed.

Cato was absolutely right when he suggested coming here. I love that guy—where is he? I spot him swinging Jane around the dance floor, clearing away people for three feet in every direction. "Want to get out of here?" Phil asks into my hair.

I drain my drink. "Call me tomorrow," I say to Rachel.

She smiles knowingly. "Are you sure you'll be home by then?"

Phil and Alain shake hands and Alain winks at me. I have a vague sense that everyone at work will find out about this, but so what? I'll worry about it later. Phil puts his hands on my hips and follows me through the mob. The second we get outside I spin around and kiss him, and when he says, "I live a couple of blocks from here," I say, "Lead the way."

We walk to a shabby apartment building and up a flight of carpeted stairs. "Don't be surprised if Patrick and Kevin are home," he says, unlocking the door.

"Patrick from Roulette?"

"Yeah. Kevin's an assistant pastry chef at Esca. They usually come in before I do."

But the place is dark and quiet. Phil flips on an overhead light in the living room, illuminating a couch covered with a Mexican blanket, a stereo with enormous speakers, and a TV on a crate advertising canned tomatoes. Even with two tiny bedrooms and a sleeping alcove, the entire apartment can't be more than five hundred square feet.

"How do three people fit in here?" I ask. "Carl should give you a raise."

"He did a few months ago," Phil says defensively. "Believe it or not, twenty-nine grand is good in this town."

"Oh. I didn't know that," I say, grateful for the waitressing income that allows me to keep my roomy one-bedroom.

"I'm on the eighteen-year repayment plan with my culinary school loans. Sounds like forever, but when you figure how long it takes to pay off a house, it doesn't seem so bad."

Phil opens the refrigerator in the cramped kitchen and grabs two bottles of Bud Light—not my first choice, but I'm past caring. As I sip, I calculate the varieties of alcohol I've mixed times the number of drinks I've had and figure it equals two extra hours in bed tomorrow. But I'm not going to think that far ahead. Phil is taking me to his miniature rectangle of a bedroom, where there's a lamp with no shade and an open box of muesli on the dresser. The second he shuts the door, I surrender to lust-induced insanity and start unbuttoning my blouse.

"Come here," he says, sitting on the unmade futon and fumbling with his pants. "You've been giving me woodies for weeks." He pulls his sweater over his head, revealing the lean, muscular torso and hard arms of an endurance athlete. I sit next to him and he breaks into a sheepish smile. "Carl would kill us for this."

I lean toward him. "Tomorrow, maybe. But not tonight."

Boom.

I jerk awake just after four A.M. In the dim light from the street lamp outside the window, I see Phil lying flat on his back, the sheet down around his knees. Beads of sweat shine on his bare chest.

Are my pants on? I sit up and feel my legs. Not a stitch. I'm sticky, thirsty, and have a foggy recollection of Phil twisting me into a position I don't think there's a name for yet. After starting on the bed, we moved to the windowsill, the desk, and finally, the orange-and-brown braided rug. I touch my scraped left thigh and smile.

"...music on," a male voice says from the living room. I hear a cough, then footsteps and the sound of the stereo thudding. Oh no. Phil's roommates are back and it sounds like they've brought friends.

"...the woman Carl's been screwing." It's Patrick.

"Which one?" asks someone else.

"He's all over the map. Some are barely legal and some are grandmothers. The Puerto Rican one, remember her? Had to be forty-five at least."

"She was hot. My grandmother doesn't look like that."

"Ten more years and I'll be doing the same thing," Patrick says. "Perks of being a chef."

"If you can still get it up."

How many guys are out there, anyway? Four? Five? I want to go home, and I'll have to walk through an apartment full of strangers to do it.

"Phil," I whisper. "I'm leaving now." No response. I nudge him gently and he rolls toward me.

"Ready for more?" he murmurs.

"I would be, but your roommates are home."

He wraps his arms around my hips. "So? Ignore 'em."

"I can't. I think I'd better go."

"No," he says softly. "Stay where you are, okay? Just give me a second to wake up..." His arms slide slowly away from me as he falls asleep again.

"Time to get *hammered*!" somebody yells. Great. Get me out of here.

I slip on my shirt and pants, find my handbag slung over the bedpost, and feel around on the floor so I don't leave anything behind. All I have to do now is walk out and run for the exit. It'll be mortifying but quick. Besides, what's my option? Waiting for hours until everybody passes out? Phil cooking us all pancakes in the morning?

I reach up to make sure I didn't lose my earrings in the sheets. *Where the . . . ?* Then I remember—they're still in Daniel's pocket. I finally managed to put him out of my mind and here he is again, just when I don't want to think about him.

Curtis Mayfield blasts through the apartment as I put my bag over my shoulder and estimate how long it will take to cross the living room. If I'm really hauling, five seconds. Anyway, who cares what they think? I'm sure Patrick has slept with people he barely knows. Who's he to judge?

With that small boost of courage, I open the door and my eyes contract from the bright light. As if to announce my arrival, the music stops abruptly. There's no going back now. I raise my chin and stride into the living room. A guy at the stereo stares at me as three more glance up from making blender drinks in the kitchen. I look straight ahead and keep right on moving.

"Erin?" Patrick says. "What are you doing here?"

"You know that chick?" someone asks.

Blond dreadlocks pop up over the edge of the Formica counter. "Where do you guys keep your triple sec?"

Patrick's surprise turns to amusement. "Did we wake you, Erin? Hey, want a kamikaze? They're really good. I make them with Southern Comfort."

I rip open the front door and march down the hallway. "Fuck, fuck, fuck," I mutter. Their loud laughter follows me down the stairs and into the street, which seems darker than it was a few hours ago, with bits of paper on the sidewalk and a smell of urine in the doorways. Where am I? This is not a neighborhood I should be wandering around in in the middle of the night. I'm still carrying the cash I made at the Porters' dinner party—three hundred and fifty dollars minus a few rounds of drinks. I grip my bag and stay close to the curb, searching the horizon for an available cab. Ten minutes later I see a taxi half a block away. "Hey!" I scream, breaking into a run. I reach for the door handle, clamber inside, and blurt my address.

"You're lucky I saw you," says the driver.

I lean my head against the back of the seat. "If only everyone else hadn't."

It has never, ever felt so good to be home.

I take Rocket out for a five-minute walk, stuff my clothes into the laundry bag, and put on my robe. While brushing my teeth, I see myself in the mirror as I must have looked to Phil's roommates—smeared mascara, bloodshot eyes, and a telltale hickey on my jawbone. If I weren't so tired, I might actually feel humiliated. It isn't until I'm turning off the lights that I notice the flashing button on my answering machine.

You have one new message.

I press play and out comes the voice I least expect. *"Erin, hello. Carl Corbett calling. I'd like you to be at the restaurant an hour early tomorrow. It's going to be one of the most important nights of your life and you'll need to get a head start on your sidework. Have I piqued your interest? Excellent. Sleep well."*

◆

"I got the same message," Cato says the next afternoon. "Only mine said it was going to be like a premiere at the Gershwin."

"What's going on?" Jane says, snapping open a tablecloth. "When I got home last night, Julian said a man called for me after midnight and told him something cryptic about preparing for graduation day."

Ron digs a dead candle out of a crystal votive with a knife. "My wife and I were asleep and Carl rings up about preparing for year zero. I couldn't get a straight answer out of him. I went to the office as soon as I got here, but Steve isn't answering the door."

"Classic management tactic," Derek grumbles. "Make us work harder, then keep us in the dark."

"I'm sure we'll find out what's happening at five," I say, my voice raspy from lack of sleep. "Carl can't keep it a secret forever."

"Did you see the list of extra sidework?" Cato asks. "Spot-clean walls. Polish toilets. I shit you not."

"Somebody A-list must be coming in," Jane says. "Did Phil mention anything to you, Erin?"

"Not that I remember. To tell the truth, the whole night's a little hazy."

"Sweet hickey, by the way," Cato says. "Very ninth-grade dance."

We turn in unison as heels echo across the lounge and stop at the entrance to the dining room. It's Gina, wearing a sleeveless black dress encrusted with hundreds of crystal beads. Nino stands at her side in a pin-striped suit, lollipop in his mouth, a tiny gangster ready to rumble.

"Do I hear talking?" she asks. "I want no talking from now on."

For several seconds no one says a word. Finally Derek speaks up. "We were just wondering why Carl called us in early."

"What is the matter with you?" she says, tapping her temple with her fingertips. "You are stupid? Evelyn Harker eats here tonight!"

"Who's Evelyn Harker?" I ask.

"The reviewer for *Manhattan Today*," Derek answers.

"How do we know she's coming?"

"My source called me last night," Gina says. "Carl is so nervous he didn't sleep. He stays in the kitchen working and the cooks come at six o'clock this morning."

I imagine poor Phil being jingled out of bed in the half-dark. He must be worse off than I am.

"Ron, you have a hair like this." Gina makes a zigzag sign above her eyebrow. "Go now and fix it. Everyone must be perfect!" Ron ducks his head and disappears into the men's room.

Gina pulls Nino along as she inspects each table, then stands back and studies the room. "Table nine," she says at last. "We seat her there."

Cato's section, thank God. Jane's face goes slack with relief while poor Cato turns pale. Derek looks like he's been robbed of his opportunity to shine.

"Remember, Kay-*tow*," Gina says. "I told you what happened to my waitress who gave Harker a bad service. Good review, good business. Bad review"—she jerks her thumb across her throat—"Roulette is finished and so are you!"

Nino takes his lollipop out of his mouth. "Waiters make Mommy mad."

Gina smiles down at him. "I am not mad, Nino. I am Italian. We are passionate people." She grabs his wrist and tugs him toward the kitchen with a departing threat: "I'll be back in a minute, so get busy!"

Cato puts a hand over his eyes and whispers, "Pass me some drugs. I don't care what they are, just give them here."

"Calm down," I say. "You'll be brilliant."

"Two months after Harker reviewed Sybarite, they shut down permanently," Jane says. "The chef went to a Zen retreat in California and no one's heard from him since."

"Why did I ever leave Oklahoma?" Cato moans. "Why didn't I settle down with a nice guy and open a B and B?"

Nino appears at my feet and thrusts out a worn magazine. "Mommy said you have to read this now."

I take the copy of *Manhattan Today* out of his hand. As he skips back toward the kitchen, I skim the cover and see that the magazine is a year old. With Cato and Jane looking over my shoulder, I search the table of contents, flip to page thirty, and start reading aloud.

This week, Evelyn Harker travels to the Upper East Side, where she discovers that, sometimes, getting one's entrée is the most challenging part of dining out...

CORBETT GETS INTO THE GAME
by Evelyn Harker

Rising star Carl Corbett, having blazed his way through some of New York's most important kitchens, finally has his own venue on the Upper East Side. It's an exciting step for the thirty-eight-year-old chef, whose reputation as an enfant terrible is remarkable even in a profession where histrionics are par for the course. "I'm obsessed with excellence," he explains. "It's not enough that people enjoy my food. I want them to be changed by it."

Get ready for a change, Madison Avenue. Philadelphia-born Corbett has joined forces with Steve and Gina Runyan and opened the cleverly named Roulette. Mrs. Runyan, a native of Italy, assigned herself the task of interior design, and on the strength of just one high-school art class, created a look that is best described as European flair meets American excess. About her lack of formal training, she says simply, "Michelangelo runs through the blood of every Italian." One wonders what the Old Master might have thought of the peacock-feathered wall sconces or the Swarovski crystals embedded in the plaster columns, but then, what would he have thought of New York?

On our first visit, my companion and I are shown to a private, though noisy, corner near the lounge (see page 74 for my manifesto on restaurant acoustics). As we munch on a warm rosemary baguette, our server explains the evening's additions to the menu in a deflated monotone, making even sautéed loup de mer with celery essence sound tedious. But Geoffrey Gold, the übersommelier Roulette lured away from Café NoNo, positively sparkles as he decants the '97 Château Frederic. Boasting aromas of plum and saddle leather, there's nothing shy about this wine. My only complaint is the three-hundred-dollar price tag, a markup so steep it practically requires supplemental oxygen and crampons.

Unfortunately, even fine Bordeaux can't disguise dismal service. Our waitress visits with friends in the lounge before attending to us, a delay that throws off the timing of our entire meal. It takes forty minutes for our appetizers to arrive, during which we consume all of the bread and consider starting on the linen. But we're glad we waited. Chef Corbett describes his cooking style as "American food for the new millennium," and I can see what he means when I bite into the roasted squab leg topped with a decadent slab of seared foie gras. My companion is over the moon with his velouté of white asparagus: a rich, intensely perfumed soup he coins "haute Campbell's." It begs for a side of salted lavash with truffle oil, but our server is at the next table showing her ankle tattoo to a group of Japanese businessmen. We're hoping she'll redeem herself by being punctual with our entrées, but she appears to have either forgotten them or been squired off to a hostess club in Tokyo. We're considering running out on the check, when a polite young man appears with our dinner, prompting "There is a God" from my sullen companion.

One bite and the evening is saved. The chef counters the neglectful service by riveting us with plancha-crisped black cod with olive butter and pattypan squash. My companion revels in *his choice of canard de Corbett, pan-seared breast of Moulard duckling rubbed with garlic and single-estate cocoa and dashed with Armagnac. On a second visit, we're equally impressed by the Tasmanian sea trout, a rich fish scented with preserved ginger and Szechuan peppercorns. Another standout is the saddle of wild Scottish hare with melted black currant jelly. Wonderfully gamy and tender, it is a luxurious addition to a late fall menu.*

Desserts aren't quite as successful. Pastry chef Betsy Lowe's Chocolate Remorse is divine—an all-butter tartlet surrounds a rich ganache center shot through with crushed espresso beans. But my bread pudding is leaden, pure gravity, as if it had an iron core. Though the lime blood-orange custard is a luscious blend of bitter and sweet, the spun sugar accents are surprisingly sharp. Think of biting into a hatpin.

Save for the dessert missteps and the abominable service, the Runyans and Carl Corbett may be onto something here— a prestigious address, an eye-popping atmosphere, and dishes that inspire diners to wonder: What's next?

"Well, girls," Cato says. "I think we're about to find out."

chapter 13

By five o'clock, Gina's Harker hysteria has spread to the kitchen. Carl, hollow-eyed and drawn from thirty-six hours on his clogs, refuses to acknowledge the waiters standing in formation in front of him, choosing instead to scream at all twelve of his cooks. He's especially tough on the wan, unshaven Phil.

"Where's your head been all day?" he demands. "For Christ's sake, look at you! You're a vegetable on the most important night of my career!"

He hurls a towel onto the prep counter, then turns to give me a long stare. Shit. He knows what happened last night, I can tell. But who told him? If only I'd listened to Jane. If only I could rewind the past eighteen hours and take Phil to my place instead.

"I'll pull it together," Phil says. "I think I just...got a virus or something."

Carl doesn't move his eyes from my face. "A virus my ass. Your dick is the problem. Frankly, I thought you had better taste." He gives me a slight smile. "I had you pegged for a breast man."

I stop breathing as disbelief turns to boiling fury. Phil swallows and studies the floor.

"I got a whole *crew* of stupid fucks," Carl snaps, sweeping his arm through the air. "Which one of you wants out of here tonight? Huh? Who's gonna be the first to go? Come on! Let's hear it!"

José stifles a sneeze and Carl wheels around. "Was that a yes?" he asks.

"What?"

Carl reaches out and grabs him by the collar. "Ready to quit?"

"Of course not, Chef. I—"

"Want to go back to making soul food in Harlem?" Carl says, pulling José up onto the toes of his clogs. "Catfish and black-eyed peas? Fifty-cent WINGS?"

"No, Chef! I like it here!"

Carl puts his face an inch from José's before shoving him backward against the grill. "Then keep your mouth shut."

José straightens his jacket while the rest of the cooks stand in head-hanging silence. Carl stomps around muttering "Useless idiots," then snatches his clipboard off the wall with such force that the nail pops out and rolls under a stove. Finally, when he's red-faced and heaving, he barks, "Get your goddamn stations in order," and steps out from behind the line. "All right, waiters. Let's talk about how to blow away the most important critic in New York."

He glares at each of us in turn, then says, "Tonight is going to be like Christmas with the family."

No one says anything. I don't dare look at Phil for fear I'll explode.

"Remember your crappy childhoods? Remember the disappointment you felt when you opened the last box and found a fucking savings bond? Remember how your mother smiled while your father got plastered and the tree caught fire and the turkey came out half-frozen? Remember how she kept saying it was the best Christmas ever until you actually started to believe it? Do you know what she was doing?" He takes a deep, shaking breath. "She was maintaining an *illusion,* people. She was propping up Christmas so you little brats wouldn't fall apart. Do you understand what I'm trying to tell you?"

The entire group, the entire kitchen, is silent. I glance at Ron, whose face is rigid with terror.

"DREAMS!" Carl shouts, shattering my last intact nerve. "It's about three hours when real life stands outside the door! Your job is to make sure Timmy gets his two-wheeler and the tree stays up! Everyone in this restaurant has to click for the fantasy to operate. If somebody's unhappy at table seven, it will affect Harker's experience. And Harker's experience"—his voice drops to a whisper—"determines all of our futures."

I'm combing the changing room for an extra pen and trying to will my heart rate back to normal when the office door opens down the hall. "Go!" I hear Gina say. "I hope you die alone."

Steve snorts. "You'd like that, wouldn't you? Then you could blow it all."

"All of what? We are almost on the sidewalk! Nino and I will go live in Penn Station!"

"God forbid you should have to mother him yourself. This is the third night in a row you've called Bridget to come pick him up. If you spent more time with your son, we could ship the nanny back to Dublin and save ourselves a fortune."

"And leave you here alone? Americans know nothing about running a restaurant. This business *lives* because of me."

I move closer to the door, listening intently so I can report back to Cato and Jane.

Steve sighs. "You'd still be writing specials on a blackboard if I hadn't taken you out of that ratty little guinea town. And this is how you repay me? We're smothering in bills!" He pauses. "I never should have bought you that goddamned apartment. What's the point of a three-million-dollar view when you're too afraid of heights to enjoy it?"

"Is your stupid car," Gina says. "Two hundred a week in gas and broken half the time!"

"I asked you not to bring up the Hummer."

"Is not like I bring up your mother."

"Oh, yes, it is," Steve insists.

"No, is not."

"Yes, it is."

"You think I care about your car when you leave my mama all alone in Roccasecca? She can't live in a big house by herself! She will get sick and forget to eat!"

Steve laughs. "That woman could wrestle a cow to the ground."

Gina sucks in a breath. "You say my mother is a *contadina*? A farmer?"

"Well, isn't she? What else do you call somebody who has a bunch of chickens running around?"

"Listen to me," Gina hisses. "She comes here to live or I go and take Nino with me. You don't see him until your deathbed."

"How do you expect me to support somebody else? If your mother spends half the money you do, we'll have to move to Queens!"

"So make her go to work. Then call yourself a man."

"I'm a man, all right."

"Ha! A cheap fool is what you are."

"I'm more man than you can handle, and I'll prove it right now."

"Let me go."

There's a loud slap, then a cry and a quick scuffle. What's happening in there? After a few seconds of silence, the door clicks shut. I walk cautiously down the hall on the balls of my feet as rustling noises and low groans come from inside the office. Oh, my God. They're not . . . *doing* it, are they? A belt buckle jingles and a piece of furniture thumps against the wall. My stomach turns when Gina's voice reaches my ears. "Not on the chair, Stevie. Come here."

I hear a sheaf of paper hit the carpet, then a short gasp. As I sneak past the office, the floor begins to creak rhythmically. I don't stop running until I get to the wait station.

"That's the most disgusting thing I've ever heard," Jane says. "Come on, give us details."

I glance around, then say out of the side of my mouth, "I think they kept their shoes on."

Jane suppresses a laugh. "How long were they at it?"

"I don't know. They were just getting started when I left."

"Steve probably didn't last thirty seconds," Cato says. "Gina's too intimidating up close."

"She's better from the back," I answer.

"Good point," Jane adds. "Maybe he turned her around."

A few minutes later, Gina comes downstairs, flushed and blinking. She surveys the dining room and instructs us not to stare at anyone who comes in the door, as she's convinced our eyes will telegraph that we were tipped off by her sources at *Manhattan Today*.

"Only Gina could be *more* uptight after sex," Cato whispers.

"How would you feel if you'd just had a quickie with Steve?" Jane asks.

He gives it some thought. "Very used."

"When's Harker supposed to be here?" I ask. "The suspense is terrible."

"All they said was to be on the lookout for a woman in a navy-blue dress with a male companion."

Jane sneaks a mint. "That's ridiculous. You just described half of New York."

We go quiet when a middle-aged woman in a blue skirt walks up to the podium on the arm of a much younger man. He wears a turtleneck sweater and cuffed trousers and has sideburns to his jaw. "Avert your eyes, everybody," I say. "This could be our gal."

"Her hair's too black and shiny," Cato agrees. "That's definitely a wig."

"It's only seven thirty," Jane says. "Reviewers always eat late."

I nod. "Right. She's trying to throw us off her trail."

Gina charges past us, trailing the scent of Campari. "Is her!" she hisses. "Don't breathe!" She elbows Kimberly out of the way and takes Harker and her escort to Cato's section herself.

"How do we know that's her?" Jane asks.

"You can tell," Cato laments. "She just *looks* critical."

We watch as she stops, shakes her head, and says something to Gina. "What's going on?" I ask.

Harker points to the table farthest from the kitchen, a cramped deuce we call "quarantine." Ordinarily, Gina wouldn't let the mayor change tables, but Evelyn Harker is another matter. "Of course, of course," we hear her say as she leads the way across the dining room.

"That's your section, Erin," Cato says. He sounds both relieved and horrified.

I grab his arm. "You'll still wait on her, won't you? I'm not qualified. Gina wouldn't let me..."

Gina snaps her fingers at me from across the dining room. I close my eyes just long enough to see my life flashing by.

Carl lobs a pot against the wall when Gina gives him the news. After a deafening clang, the kitchen goes silent.

"Don't worry," Gina tells him. "She do *fine*."

"She *don't* do fine!" Carl shouts. "She shouldn't go near the woman!"

For once, Carl and I agree. "Actually, Gina," I pipe up, "Cato's been here a lot longer than I have, and I think he would—"

"Is better this way," she says, raising a hand to silence me. "We give her our best server at a bad table and she'll see we know who she is. We'll be in trouble for bribery. She'll say the food is good only for her!"

"Cato *wants* to do it," I lie.

"No," she says. "Is your section. Patti Porter talks to me about you the other night. She says you learn fast and are sweet to everybody. Anyway, is business. Is not up to me."

"Have Ron wait on her, then," Carl says. "Or Jane."

"Erin," Gina insists.

"Jane."

"Erin."

I can't believe what I'm hearing. It's as if she wants me to wait on Harker just to prove who's in charge. Carl claws his fingers through his hair. "Fucking ridiculous! All my years of work in *her* hands!"

Gina rolls her eyes. "So *dramatic*. You need to relax. You'll get a heart attack and fall down dead in the road like my poor father."

"Whatever," he says, throwing a pile of chopped onions into a pan. "I hope that bitch chokes."

"You cook nice for her!" Gina warns.

Carl grabs the pan and tosses the onions into the air with a quick snap of his wrist. "Who are you kidding? I *made* this restaurant, remember?"

Gina waves her hand at him dismissively. On her way out of the kitchen, she stops in front of me and smiles. "See? I always get my way." She reaches out to straighten my collar, then pats my cheek. "Don't let me down."

When I hesitate, she claps twice. "What are you waiting for!" she says, pushing the door open. "Let's go!"

Walking to Harker's table is like going to the gallows: I have an apprehensive audience and I know I won't survive. That's okay. I'll do temp work. It won't pay as well, but after this experience, I might actually enjoy it. "Good evening and welcome to Roulette," I say, mouth dry as a shoe. "May I bring you a cocktail?"

Harker peers at me with hard brown eyes. "I certainly hope so."

Oh God. She's mean.

"Two gin martinis," she says. "Up, very cold, two olives apiece."

"Do you prefer a particular brand of gin?"

"Yes. Something not dreadful."

"Of course," I say. "Thank you."

Hunched over his cocktail shaker, Alain mixes the martinis like a nervous chemist. One drop of vermouth too many and kablooey! Game over. His long hands tremble as he spears the olives with the mother-of-pearl toothpicks reserved for VIPs. "Harker is putting together a book of her worst reviews," he says. "It's called *Last Suppers*. She'll put me in there if I don't make these right."

"I'm sure they're perfect."

"I can always go back to Paris," he says somberly. "Or Avignon. No one knows her there."

As he sets the glasses on my tray, Gina comes up behind me. "Well? Does Harker like you?"

"It's too soon to tell. She said ten words and they were all about martinis."

"What's her mood rating?"

If I told Gina the truth, she'd fall apart. "Probably nine when this drink kicks in."

"You go give her the specials now."

"Okay."

"But don't rush her."

"I won't."

"Tell her what she wants to hear."

"I will."

"Don't forget anything," she calls after me. "And smile!"

Heart flailing, I return to the table and place Harker's martini in front of her. "We have several additions to the menu this evening," I begin.

"Which are?" she says, sitting back in her chair.

As soon as the first sentence leaves my mouth, I know I'm done for. I simply can't remember which entrée gets which sauce. I was so stunned by Carl's "breast man" comment that I retained almost nothing of the specials. "Excuse me," I say, flushing. "I've lost my train of thought."

Harker's companion takes a sip of his drink as I try desperately to recall what Carl repeated so many times "you couldn't forget if you were under general anesthesia." Any moment now I'll have to read off my cheat sheet in full view of Gina and Steve, who hover near the podium, watching me.

Think, Erin! Freshwater eels ... bordelaise ... ragoût ... I put on a smile. "For appetizers this evening, we're offering ..." Carl's spirit must temporarily inhabit me, because all of a sudden I'm saying the specials word for word and I'm giving it all I've got. Following Cato's recommendation to act as if I'm describing my first orgasm, I make the fricassee of skate wing with cilantro shoots sound like something everyone should experience before they die. As I finish with a breathless explanation of the black Beluga and lentil-stuffed quail, Harker's companion pulls out a tissue and loudly blows his nose.

Harker unfolds a pair of tortoiseshell reading glasses. "We'd like a chance to study our menus first, if you don't mind."

"Of course. I'll check with you shortly," I say, almost bowing as I back away.

Cato intercepts me on his way out of the kitchen. "Well? How's it going?"

"I'm not sure. I think I just had an out-of-body experience."

He puts his arm around my shoulders. "Been there a thousand times. Now you know what stage fright feels like."

The table of four next to Harker seems oblivious to the food critic in their midst. They have a rousing debate over what to order, finally asking me to intervene and decide between two appetizers "before somebody starts throwing bread." By the time I return to the only somebody who really matters, Harker's martini glass is nearly empty, her menu is closed, and Geoffrey is trotting to and from the table with tastes of every wine we serve by the glass. "What can I bring you this evening?" I ask as she sips a heart-stoppingly expensive Vega Sicilia that Geoffrey refers to as "six ounces of pure, sun-drenched Spain." Though she orders enough food for four, she skips over Carl's favorites and all but one of the specials. I don't dare write anything down.

The moment she's finished speaking, I rush to the computer, my head a jumble of side dishes and appetizers. "Laser-grilled beets en croute," I mutter, tapping the screen as fast as I can. I look up, drawing a post-traumatic blank. "That *is* what she ordered, right?" I see myself at the table again and hear the words leaving Harker's mouth. Yes, definitely. "Jellied foie gras salad..."

I've just hit the "submit" button when Omar comes trotting out of the kitchen. "Chef wants you."

Gina abandons the podium and is right on my heels as I walk through the swinging doors. Carl, wearing safety goggles and holding a gun-shaped instrument to a piece of beef, gives me a baffled shake of the head. "What the hell just happened out there, Erin?"

"What do you mean?"

"What do I *mean*?" He grabs the computer ticket and flaps it around. "I mean this is something I'd expect from a table of six-year-olds! Didn't you push the branzino mousse? And how about the rockfin? I had those spices overnighted from BANGALORE!"

"I told Harker about everything, in detail. She just... wanted the chicken."

"*No*body just wants the chicken! Something's wrong!"

Gina takes the uninspired order as a sign from above. "God is mad at me," she says to the ceiling. "I shop too much this week."

The moment of truth arrives ten minutes later, when Chen gently lays the appetizers on Harker's table. Gina and I watch from the lounge as Harker peers at the plates, confers with her companion, then turns up her palms.

Gina gasps. "*Merda!* She has a problem! Go over there and fix it!"

I fast-fast across the room, skirt flapping around my legs. My tip, my job, the entire fate of the restaurant, hang in the balance. "Is everything to your liking?" I ask a little too shrilly.

Harker points at two of the appetizers. "Can you explain these?"

I stare at her, confused. Is she asking me to repeat the name of each dish to put me through my paces, or did she actually forget what she ordered? Then, with a sudden flash of horror, I understand. Somehow, despite every effort to rise to Gina's expectations, I committed the ultimate blunder. I typed in the wrong order.

"We ordered the foie gras terrine and the roasted tomato salad," she says. "These are . . . beets in some kind of pastry, and this isn't the foie gras I wanted."

I whip the plates off the table. "I'm so sorry. I'll rectify the mistake immediately." I practically fly toward the kitchen while Gina claps her hand to her mouth.

Carl must sense my presence, because he turns from the stove the moment I step up to the line. I set the plates in the window and he inhales sharply. "No, no, *no!* What did you do?"

"I think I ordered the wrong appetizers." Marty, Phil, and José stop working and turn to stare at me. Patrick, dripping lobster tail in hand, slowly shakes his head.

"You think you what?" Carl asks quietly. His pupils are twice their normal size.

"Harker changed her mind a couple of times, and I guess she meant the foie gras terrine instead of the salad. I'm not sure what happened with the beets, except that the menu's been different every day lately, and . . ." I look down at the appetizers expiring under the heat lamps. "I'm really sorry."

Gina bursts in behind me. "I saw everything! It was awful!"

A range of emotions crosses Carl's face: first rage, then

shame, and finally bitter disappointment. A death h
place. His fantasy that the review will be perfect h
to an abrupt and senseless end. "You idiot," he says

"Roulette is over, just like La Caravelle and
Basque," Gina wails. "I want to move back home. I
restaurants, just a little house where I can live by
She runs upstairs to the office, her black dress billov
behind her.

Tears start to sting my eyes. "DON'T cry," C:
mands.

As the rest of the cooks go back to work, h
Harker's appetizers, examines them from every
angle, then sets them in front of me.

"Maybe you don't realize what it took to get whe
he says, looking gray and haggard. "How many
spent sweating in other people's kitchens so I co
one little chance to prove myself to somebody lik
Harker. And you blew it for me. Now what the F
you waiting for? Get these to the table before I th
out of here!"

Despondent, teeth clenched, I take the plates a
I'm told. Luckily, Harker is too absorbed in conver
notice the arrival of her starters. But after a few
bites, she purses her lips and sets down her forl
back to the table, praying the problem isn't my faul

"I'd like more sauce for this terrine, please," she

"Sauce," I repeat, as if making sure I have the ri
dinates. "Of course."

When Carl sees me enter the kitchen, he gets
look. "What now!"

"Harker. More sauce."

"Oh, Jesus!" he cries.

Steve comes downstairs with an empty bottle o
in his hand. "I just found a Web site called stophar

They have a little ticker showing the number of restaurants she's ruined, updated every hour. You can print out a wanted poster of her, but the picture's too fuzzy. All you can make out is her nose."

"Well, the rest of her face is in quarantine if you want to see it," Carl snaps.

"What I want is for everybody to get a grip," Steve says. "Gina's such a wreck, I just had to give her half a Xanax. Even Geoffrey's acting like some starstruck kid. It's ridiculous." He turns his attention to me. "And you," he says, emphasizing every word, "are an absolute embarrassment. You'd better get it together pronto or you're finished here."

chapter 14

Harker lifts the edge of her raspberry gâteau with her fork and peeks underneath as if expecting to find a fly. "More coffee?" I ask timidly. In the last half hour, I've abandoned all pretense of confidence and cheer. I'm scared of her and she can tell.

Her companion gives me a chilly stare. I might as well have offered him a slug of Old Grand-Dad.

"No, thank you," Harker says. "Please just bring our bill."

Walking toward the lounge, I see Carl's face appear at the edge of the dining room. He peeks around the corner for a glimpse of the woman whose review will determine his destiny, but the room is dim and the table too far away. After straining to see past a column and an iris-filled vase, he gives up and goes back to the kitchen.

Fortunately for me, the Xanax has made Gina philosophical and forgiving. "Tonight I start to think," she says, slurring slightly as she reaches across the bar to take a balloon glass of Sangiovese from Alain. "In Italy I have no money but I work hard, grow a garden, and nobody bothers me. Every day is eat, make love, sit outside, and drink home-made wine. Why do I stay in New York just to be unhappy?"

Harker leaves me a hair over fifteen percent, and after

many *good nights* and *thank yous* and *come agains* from Gina, she departs. I stand in the kitchen waiting for Betsy to pipe *Happy Retirement, Neil* on a dessert plate, avoiding eye contact with Carl and imagining how Harker will skewer me in her review. Phil grills fish a few feet away, sweat blooming through the back of his white jacket. He bends down, opens the reach-in refrigerator, and peers inside. After pausing to plate a perfectly browned filet, he says something to Carl and disappears into the basement.

"Sorry, Erin," Betsy says. "I'm a little behind. I'll just be a minute."

I take quick mental stock of my tables. All my guests are on what Cato calls "cruise control," so why not grab this opportunity to make Phil sorry he ever shared my measurements with anything but his diary? I wait until Carl has his back turned, then slip down the unpainted wooden stairs.

I don't see Phil in the humid, sneaker-scented room where the cooks change, and there's nothing in Carl's office but an L-shaped desk and a humming computer. I finally find Phil in the back of the storage room, half-hidden by boxes, a naked lightbulb dangling over his head. At the sound of my footsteps he stuffs something into his pants pocket and starts madly fanning the air. He turns slowly, his face a mask of artificial innocence. "Jesus, Erin," he says, heaving a deep breath. "I thought you were Carl. *Believe* me, he's not in the mood for this kind of thing today."

I sniff the air. "What kind of thing would that be?"

He smiles and pulls out the tiny joint. "It's been a tough sixteen hours. We're supposed to wait until we're off the clock, but I needed a few tokes to help me come down. Want some?"

"Thanks, I'm holding out for my shift drink."

He looks at the joint and puts it back in his pocket. "Hey, about what happened in the kitchen before..."

"Yeah, why don't you explain that? I'd be fascinated to know where Carl got his information."

"Don't be mad, okay? I didn't say anything that private about you. I was talking to Patrick about how cool you were and Carl overheard. He wasn't even near us, and then all of a sudden he starts going on about how cooks shouldn't hook up with waiters and how I should have been home reading Hal McGee instead of...anyway, I swear to God, he has bionic ears."

"Sure. Look, I'd better get back upstairs. I have a cake waiting for me."

Phil reaches out and grabs my arm. "I'm not lying, Erin. I wouldn't do that to you."

"Really," I say doubtfully.

"Really."

"Okay, well, I need to go."

"Just a second," he says, tightening his grip. "Why'd you leave last night?"

"I couldn't sleep with so many people around. I tried to wake you, but—"

He leans in to kiss me, nearly causing me to fall backward onto the shelves of food. "Steady there," he says, laughing.

"Come on. Betsy's probably wondering where I am."

"She can wonder a little longer." He presses himself hard against me.

"Would you stop? You must really want to get fired," I say.

His eyes are half-shut. "No, I just really want you. Come on. I'll make you happy you came to work."

"Nothing can do that. You saw the night I had."

"Poor baby," he says, running a hand over my hair. "Did they beat you up out there?" He seems genuinely concerned and I can't help smiling.

"I hate this job."

He slides his arm around my waist. "Me too, sometimes."

I turn my face toward him and he gives me a smoke-flavored kiss. "Have to check my tables . . ." I mumble.

"Ten more seconds." He paws me through my shirt, and I start to feel overheated and short of breath. The sounds of footsteps and clinking pans become more and more distant, until I hardly hear them at all. As I slide my hands under his chef's jacket, Phil says, "I gotta have you right now."

"You don't mean that."

"Try me."

After another long kiss, the reason-killing effects of desire finally combine with an urge to get back at Carl in his own basement. "If Gina and Steve can do it, why can't we?" I mutter.

"What about Gina?"

"Nothing." I peer outside the doorway to make sure it's safe, then pull down my tights. Phil grins and reaches for his fly while I lift my skirt. I turn my back to him, grab one of the shelves, and try not to bang my forehead on a huge can of olive oil while he pants and moans behind me.

"What the fuck, Phil?" Carl yells down the stairs. "It's bad enough that your station wasn't stocked! How long does it take to find pine nuts? Get up here now!"

"Hurry!" I whisper.

"Coming, Chef!" he screams in my ear. After a violent, your-husband's-coming-home-and-he's-got-a-shotgun jostling, it's over. He closes his zipper and stumbles to the stairs, bag of pine nuts in hand. "That was great. I want to see you later, okay?"

"I'll think about it. I'm not finished being mad yet."

He laughs. "You drive me absolutely fucking crazy."

I trudge toward the changing room at the end of the night, exhausted and ashamed but still carrying the secret thrill of my quickie with Phil. Passing the office, I hear Steve's voice through the door and instinctively know that he's talking about me.

"If I'd had my way, I wouldn't have hired her in the first place." I hesitate in the hallway, not wanting to listen but unable to move.

"She could destroy our reputation," comes Carl's hushed but insistent reply. "Not to *mention* that she's screwing around with Phil. These are the mistakes of a rank amateur. When Cato or Ron put in the wrong order, they catch it before it comes out of the printer."

"Let's not overreact," Steve says. "She bombed tonight, but that was partly Gina's fault. Letting a new waiter handle Harker is one of the dumbest things she's ever done. Of course she won't admit it—you know how stubborn she is. But I'm not going to worry about it too much."

I breathe shallowly and try to keep from shaking.

"All it takes is one little setback and the phone stops ringing," Carl says. "You did everything right at Avenue and you were still eaten alive."

"Avenue was different. The location was rotten, the dining room was dark. . . . Christ, the kitchen wall collapsed on opening night."

"I'm just saying, nobody recovers from that kind of failure twice."

There's a long pause. I hear Steve's chair creaking. "I can't do it. Harold wouldn't like it."

"So the hell what?"

"So, he's brought us too much business. Without the wine tasting, a quarter of our clientele wouldn't exist. He's an old friend of her family's. Loves her to death. If I fire her, I lose

him, no question about it. Not that I'd mind necessarily—
the man irritates me, always has. I can't go five minutes
without getting advice about how to improve the reservation system or the lighting or some such thing. And his
wife, have you seen her? The one with the big ass?"

"Yeah, yeah," Carl says impatiently. "A real talker. Always
coming on to me."

"Gina adores her for some reason. Anyway, the point is,
we have to be careful. Harold could make this ugly for us.
Fruit de Mer switched liquor distributors and it happened
to get out that they'd been cited for health code violations.
That was last year and they're still struggling to bring in
customers. It's always risky when you cut connections in
this industry." Steve pauses. "Besides, Harold knows about
that bill from last year."

"Huh? What bill?"

"For the wine tasting. We used more cases of Pétrus than
we paid for and Harold caught it."

"How many cases?"

Steve clears his throat. "Ten, maybe."

"*Ten?* Jeeesus fucking . . ."

"We've been paying the mortgage on his shitty little
house long enough. He should be cutting us a break anyway.
I acted like it was an oversight, but I'm not sure he bought
it. Oh, he wanted to, and that's the only reason we're still
doing business with him. But he could be a real bastard and
start poking around in our order history if he felt like it."

"Terrific. Just great. So what do we do now? Keep her on?"

"I don't know. Her check average is the lowest of the
group and she still looks terrified half the time. She goes
through the motions, but it's obvious she doesn't belong
here. I think we should just . . . see what happens over the
next couple of weeks. Maybe we'll get lucky and she'll quit."

"Let's make it easy for her."

In the ten seconds it takes me to get from the office to the changing room, I go from shocked to outraged to frantic. Steve's words echo in my head: *Let's see what happens over the next couple of weeks.* I yank off my skirt and toss it over a hanger. Suddenly, temp work doesn't seem like such an attractive option. If I'm going to stay here, I'll have to do better. I need something more, a push to the next level.

I wait for the sound of Carl's clogs on the stairs before switching off the light and going down to the lounge, where the other waiters are ordering shift drinks.

"Looks like you could use a gin injection," Cato says when he sees me.

"Are you kidding? After a shift like this, I'm going straight to bed."

"You sure? Why don't you grab a quick 'tini and meet us at Jane's? We're going to play five-card stud for money. I love taking tips from Ron and Derek."

"Another time, maybe."

On my way past the podium, Kimberly hands me an envelope with my name written on it. "Someone left this for you, Erin."

I stare at the unfamiliar, slanted scrawl. When I tear open the envelope, out drop my earrings and a folded note.

Erin,

Forgot to give these back to you last night. Why don't you wear them to a party I'm having on Friday around 11? 24 East 78th St.

Daniel

Cato appears behind me. "What's going on?" he asks, peering over my shoulder. "Did somebody die?"

I hold up the note. "No, but *I'm* about to."

"Hang on, your hand's trembling so much I can hardly read it." He mumbles the lines quietly, then says, "Holy crap, honey. Are you serious?"

"What do I do?" I say, turning to face him. "I can't really *go*."

"Are you nuts?" Cato grabs my shoulders. "You'll go if I have to dress you myself and drag you by the hair. You're not passing up an opportunity like this."

"What . . . I mean, why would he—he's got a *girlfriend*."

"And you've got hazel eyes like I've never seen. I'm not about to let you waste 'em on a line cook."

chapter 15

I stand in the shower the next morning, rehearsing my upselling tactics ("Would you care for an espresso or glass of Sauternes with your almond granité?") and trying to convince myself that I'm strong and capable. I'm going to prove Carl and Steve wrong. I'm going to turn things around, whatever it takes.

Bang bang bang.

At the sound of my landlord's distinctively loud knock, Rocket immediately starts to bark. Uh-oh. Nick isn't the sort of person who stops by just to chat. "I'm coming!" I shout. So much for decompressing on my day off.

I throw on my bathrobe and run down the hallway with wet feet. Nick is on the other side of the door, wearing paint-spattered jeans and sneakers, his black hair poking out from under a Yankees cap.

"Hi," I say. "How are you?"

"Been better," he says, raising his eyebrows as if I should know what he's talking about.

I respond as if I have no idea. "I'm sorry to hear that. So . . . been doing some painting?"

"Apartment two is for rent," he says. "I got a lot of work to do. The old tenants did something bad to the floor with plants."

Rocket's face appears next to my knee and Nick eyes him warily. "I talked to you about the barking already, Erin," he says, crossing his muscular arms.

"He's still adjusting. But he's quieted down a lot in the last few days."

"Doesn't sound quiet to me. He wakes up Mrs. Sandifer every night when you come home."

I grimace. "She complained?"

"More than once. Why don't you get a cat? Won't bother people and you don't have to walk it."

"Rocket's a wonderful dog. He's just a little high-strung, that's all."

Nick stares at him as if imagining all of his small, future crimes. "The last dog in my building tore out the wiring and bit my wife. My doctor said the stress was no good for me. The only reason I let this one stay is because you've been with me a long time."

"Three years in March."

"I don't need any more complaints. You understand. Your dog behaves and there won't be a problem."

"He will. I promise."

"Okay," he says. "Then I'll try not to worry so much." His creased face relaxes. "If you want to help me paint, I'll be down in apartment two."

✦

My first words when I see Cato on Friday are, "I'm not letting them get rid of me."

He turns from his locker and finishes folding a stick of gum into his mouth. "Did you snort something before you came in? I swear you're paranoid."

But when I tell him about the conversation I overheard between Carl and Steve, his eyes narrow. "Those fuckers don't know a star when they see one. If they fire you, we'll all quit in protest." He pauses, then smiles. "Granted, you have a knack for calling attention to yourself at the worst times, and botching Harker's order was classic."

"Yeah, well, I can't believe they made me wait on her when I didn't—"

He stops me. "Listen to yourself. I can't, I didn't—there's no 'I' in guest, Erin."

"What does *that* mean?"

"Isn't it obvious? You'll never be a great waiter unless you stop focusing on yourself. I got fired from three crappy restaurants before I figured that out."

"You? Fired?"

"Better believe it. I was so self-conscious I couldn't get through the list of mashed-potato flavors without stuttering. They thought I was slow."

I laugh. "That's awful."

"When you've been canned by Ellie's Country Eats in Oklahoma City, there's nowhere to go but up. So there I was, dying to move to New York, no résumé to speak of, and like an idiot I begged for a job at the fanciest place in town. To this day, I can't figure out why they took a chance on me. Anyway, my first table was a sweet older couple, badly dressed, totally out of their element, and about two words into the specials, I realized that I just wanted them to have a good time. It wasn't about how they saw *me* anymore. That's when I stopped being an anxious klutz with a bad memory and started making some real money."

I pull my blouse off the hanger. "So the moral of the story is . . ."

"Forget about yourself. Think of the guests as children with money. They're helpless, so you have to do everything for them. Don't let tantrums throw you off your game. Give them what they want, learn what their cries mean, and never forget who's in charge."

"You make it sound easy."

"It's not," he says, bracing a foot on the edge of a chair and tying his shoelaces. "Taking the high road with obnoxious kids is tough, but that's what you get paid for."

"Okay, I need specifics. I go to the table and . . . what?"

"Empathize. Have some compassion. These people can't get up and feed themselves, you know. Every time you start tripping over your words or worrying about how you look, remember you're talking to big babies in Versace. You're their world. Act with enough authority and they won't even notice little mistakes. They might even surprise you and start behaving like grown-ups."

For the rest of the shift, I try to think of myself as the benevolent ruler of a five-table kingdom. I move from guest to guest, not as an impostor with a stalled marketing career, but as a born server determined to entice, coax, and sweet-talk every guest into dessert and after-dinner drinks. I'm upbeat and patient, responding to absurd demands as if I live to ask Betsy the sugar content of grapefruit gratin, and love nothing more than whipping up a cup of cocoa-dusted cappuccino foam—without the cappuccino.

"This pompano is great, but it would be even better with a sprinkle of chervil and some shallot," says a ponytailed man wearing tiny round glasses. "Would you tell the chef?"

"I'm sure he'll appreciate your advice," I say, though he wouldn't, and I don't dare tell him anything of the kind. "May I bring you a side of our sautéed kohlrabi with watercress? It would be a perfect complement to your meal."

Instead of dodging the Wallers when they ask if I'm seeing anyone special, I tell them I'm working on it and will keep them posted. Mrs. Waller wants to know "what the devil the chef has done to my menu," but she calls me "dear heart," and, when her husband limps to the restroom, quietly confides that his physical therapy sessions are "finally making him a man again."

"That's wonderful," I say. "May I bring you a cheese course this evening? Carl has one serving left of a rare French blue I think you'd love."

"If it's that good, then why not. My cholesterol's up again, but life is short."

Unfortunately, the management is too busy ostracizing me to notice my efforts. Carl is unusually relaxed, snapping Patrick with a towel and calling Derek "Rocco with zits," but he doesn't glance at me all night. Steve gives me every foreign tourist and grouchy customer and barks "Of course not!" when I ask if we take Diners Club.

"Don't expect even results on the first try," Cato says later as we change out of our uniforms. "You made Mrs. Waller happy, and that's a big accomplishment. Now you can go to Daniel's party and let loose."

"I'm not going to stay very long," I say. "I shouldn't be going at all." I tug on the side zipper of my black dress, which gives my ribs a corsetlike squeeze.

Cato whistles. "Look at that. No back and not much of a front, either. Lucky thing I'll be there to protect you."

"You will?"

"Daniel came in yesterday for a drink and told me to stop by."

"And here I thought I was special," I say, only half-joking.

"He invited me to make sure you'd come. It's an old trick."

"I doubt it had anything to do with me."

"Trust me. I'm almost as good at reading men as I am at waiting tables. I know how they think."

We walk through light drizzle to a stately old building on Seventy-eighth Street, and take the elevator to the fourth floor. As we walk down the hallway, I tug at the hem of my dress, which suddenly seems to have gotten a lot shorter. Cato rings the bell and the door opens to reveal a woman with sleek brown hair and small features. Her embroidered jeans and kitten heels look both more expensive and less contrived than my man-killer outfit. "Here for Dan's party?" she chirps.

"If there's any booze left," Cato says with a charming grin.

She smiles. "I think we can scare up something." She shuts the door behind us and leads us down a hallway lined with vintage photographs of New York.

"I'm overdressed," I mutter to Cato.

"You're stunning. Good cover-up job on the hickey."

"I hope Sonia isn't here."

"Oh, I do, for entertainment value," he whispers. "But you know me. I'd rather be horrified than bored."

We walk into a living room lit by flickering votive candles and dimmed wall sconces. Stylish people are everywhere, standing in small groups and scattered across the furniture, holding glasses and listening to blues. There's no Sonia in sight.

Daniel hops up from a dark brown leather sofa. "Hi! Glad you could make it." He gives us each a hard handshake. Though I try to come across as blasé, I can hardly look at him.

"What can I get you?" he asks, gesturing us over to a sideboard crowded with liquor bottles and mismatched glasses. "Erin? Beverage?"

"Vodka tonic?"

"I can manage that."

He pours a double and hands it to me as a huge chocolate

Lab lopes in, his thick tail waving back and forth. Blue metal tags jingle from his collar. "Fritz, I thought I told you to hang out in the bedroom," Daniel says sternly. "You've jumped on enough people tonight."

Cato rubs the dog's ears. "So, he's the one who gets all those prix fixe leftovers."

"When I don't scorch them in the microwave and eat them myself."

Panting loudly, Fritz wags over to me. I hold up my drink, expecting paws on my dress, or worse, my bare thighs. Instead I get a cold, wet nose right between my legs. "Oh... Jesus." My drink nearly sloshes onto the hardwood floor.

"Fritz! Bad dog!" Daniel says, pulling him away by the collar. "He must think you're part of the pack or something. Come here, big dummy. Sit. *Sit.*" He keeps an eye on him while pouring Cato's Scotch. "Stay where you are. Here you go, Cato."

"Thanks. Cheers." Cato surveys the room, then leans close to me. "Lotsa cute guys here," he says. "Time to mingle."

"Don't you dare leave me alone."

"I'm not. I'm leaving you with Daniel."

He moves into the crowd as the dog charges at me again. "Hey, fella," I say, trying to sound like an easygoing animal lover while pushing away his heavy head. "You sure are friendly."

"Fritz, come here." Daniel points to his feet. "So, how's Rocket doing? Settling in okay?"

"He's more than settling in, he's staying for good."

"Really? I had a feeling that might happen."

"Now I just need to work on his barking so I don't get midnight visits from the police."

Daniel pats his dog on the neck. "Good luck. Two rounds of obedience school didn't make a dent with this one. He fetches pretty well. That's about all I got for my money."

"Rocket's too old for school. He'd probably corrupt the other dogs." As I raise the glass to my lips, Fritz lifts a front paw and scrapes it over my shin.

"Ow!" I look down to see two thin bloody scratches.

"Fritz, no..." Daniel pulls him away and drops to his knees to inspect the damage. His breath is warm on my skin. "That must hurt."

"It's not deep," I say, rubbing the blood away. "Honestly, it's nothing."

Daniel stands and snaps his fingers. "Okay, buddy, that's it. Solitary for you."

"Don't lock him up. I feel terrible. He's so sweet."

"He's sweeter with fewer people around. I think somebody gave him ice cream. I'll be right back." He leads Fritz around the perimeter of the living room and disappears through a doorway. I shift painfully on my heels and watch Cato talking to a slender Asian man sporting a tight leather jacket and shaggy, Tokyo-hip hair. Unlike me, they both fit right in.

"Mind if I change the music?" The same woman who answered the door walks up to the nearby stereo and starts flipping through a huge stack of records.

"Not at all," I answer, grateful for someone to talk to. "Anything good in there?"

"I'm sure there is. Dan has amazing taste." She puts out her hand. "I'm Melanie."

"Erin. Nice to meet you."

She takes out an album, glances at it, and sets it aside. "So how do you know our host?"

"Actually..." I stall, wishing I didn't have to answer. "We met at Roulette. The restaurant down the street?"

"Really? At the bar or...?" She waits for me to elaborate, an interested frown on her face.

"Uh, no...I work there."

"Oh! Doing what?"

I take a gulp of my drink. "Just waiting tables at the moment. You?"

"I'm a writer on the show," Melanie says.

"The show," as if *Flashback* were the only program on TV. "That's exciting."

"Yes, it is. Sometimes I think I have the best job in the world." She puts an Ohio Players record on the turntable and turns up the volume. After a few skips it settles into a scratchy R&B groove. "I'd love to go to Roulette with a couple of my girlfriends, but it's absolutely *impossible* to get a rezzie. Do you think you could get us a table?" She looks at me expectantly.

"I'll sure try!" I say, my face frozen in a smile.

"Thanks!"

"Anytime!"

"This wasn't *your* idea, was it?" Daniel comes up beside me and points to the stereo. "I don't want anybody to know I used to like this stuff."

"I'm just a witness," I say.

"It was all my doing," Melanie tells him proudly.

"Okay, Melanie, you stay here and play DJ. I'll show Erin around."

After a trip to Daniel's large modern kitchen ("I don't use it, but I visit occasionally," he says), we leave the party behind and walk down a quiet hallway.

"How long have you lived here?" I ask, noticing the hairline cracks in the plaster ceiling.

"Two years and the only thing I've touched is the kitchen. That's why there's still old wallpaper in some of the rooms. I probably shouldn't buy a vacation house until this place is squared away, but what the hell. I have a hard time waiting for what I want."

We stop at a small, paneled den filled with books and papers. A brass lamp casts a circle of light over the desk and illuminates a worn Persian carpet. Alongside a glass paper-weight sit a Ted Turner bobblehead and an empty can of cashews. "Nice," I say. "Very starving artist, if you don't count the nuts."

"It has an early Hemingway feel, don't you think?"

"Maybe this is where you can start working on those documentaries you told me about."

He smiles. "Someday. Right now, the network owns me."

"I know *that* feeling."

"Yeah, but your situation's different. You'll be out of Roulette as soon as the right position comes along. With my job, I'm really there. Once you have a mortgage and a secretary and people depending on you, it's a whole new level of stuck. Not as stuck as if I'd gone to work for my father's company, but..."

"Do you ever wish you had?"

Daniel laughs. "Not even a little. Dad and I couldn't agree on what time the sun came up in the morning, let alone how to run a business. Anyway, his partners bought him out about five years ago. He moved to Santa Barbara with his second wife."

"So he and your mom are..."

"Divorced since I was in high school. Mom's still here, though, in the same co-op I grew up in. I try to get her out as much as I can, but she's seventy-six, so she'd rather stay in and paint watercolors. She's not half bad."

"That's better than writing horror movies, like my dad."

"But not nearly as much fun to talk about." He reaches out and pushes my hair away from my shoulder. "I see you got the earrings."

"Yes, thank you." I hold my breath as he inspects the beading, the back of his finger touching my neck.

"Nice workmanship. I had some time to look at them up close."

"My brother bought them for me," I almost whisper.

"Dan?" calls a female voice behind us.

Daniel drops his hand. "In here!"

Heels click down the hallway and I turn around into a fog of lemony perfume. It's Sonia, her pale hair swept back, a delicate diamond choker around her neck. Unbelievable. I've gone from overdressed to underdressed and I'm still at the same party. "Hi, babe," she says, kissing Daniel on the mouth. "Sorry I'm late. I hope you didn't worry."

"How was it?" he asks.

"Long," she says, pulling off her cashmere wrap and revealing a slinky lavender dress. "These benefit things are eating up more and more of my time. Not that I don't care about AIDS and the arts, but there's a limit."

He puts his hand on her bare shoulder. "You remember Erin, from Roulette?"

"Should I?" Her head cocks slightly.

"She was at Frank and Patti's a few weeks ago, too."

"Working," I say, covering my embarrassment with the all-purpose smile I've perfected at the restaurant. "You might remember me by my pepper grinder."

"Oh, right. How are you?"

"Fine, thanks," I say, surprised she's asking. "And you?"

"Actually, I could use a drink, so I'm glad you're here. They were serving these sugary cocktails I wanted no part of, so I've had nothing but mineral water all night. I'd love a glass of wine, red or white, it doesn't matter."

"She's not on duty," Daniel says, with a quick laugh.

"She isn't?" Sonia says, as if I'm not standing right in front of her. "Didn't Patti give you the number for the caterer? I thought you were going to hire somebody."

"I decided not to and it's worked out great. I'll get your

wine." He glances at me, his easy demeanor replaced by a stiff coolness. "Erin?" he says, reaching for my empty glass. "Another drink?"

I turn away before he can see my disappointment. "That's all right," I say. "I need to leave soon, anyway. Thanks for the tour."

When I get back to the living room, blues is playing on the stereo again, the room is even more crowded, and someone has opened the French doors that lead to the balcony. Cold air blows in and the long white curtains flutter at the windows.

I pick my way through the crowd, high-stepping over someone's knees and nearly slipping on a cocktail napkin. I finally find Cato sitting on a couch in a dim corner with the same shaggy-haired man he was talking to earlier. He introduces his new friend as Toshio and pulls me onto the couch beside him.

"So, where have you and Daniel been hiding?" Cato asks.

"What do you mean? What's that look about?"

"I think he likes you, that's what it's about."

I snort. "Are you kidding?"

"Dead serious. My intuition is never wrong."

"It is this time. He was just being a good host."

"Yup. Right."

"Come on, Cato. You know who he's going out with. It's obvious we have zero in common, so even if there *were* chemistry, which there isn't, it would be absolutely ridiculous to think—"

"You know what Bill Shakespeare said about protesting too much?"

"I'm not protesting. I'm disagreeing with you."

"You're still wrong." He pulls a cigarette from the pack on

the coffee table and lights it. Toshio takes it from him after one drag.

"Well, it's been a long night," I say, sliding to the edge of the cushion. "I think I'm going to go."

"Because Sonia's here? Don't let her drive you away, sweetie. Stay and fight."

"I don't get involved in fights I can't win. Nice meeting you, Toshio." I smile at him and stand up.

"See you," he says, raising a silver-ringed hand.

"Want me to put you in a cab?" Cato asks.

I watch Daniel and Sonia walk through the room and into the kitchen. What I want more than anything is to escape. "I'm all right, thanks. See you at work tomorrow, okay?"

Cato looks concerned as he studies my face. "Okay. We'll talk then."

Suddenly anxious to leave, I push my way through the crowd and find my coat on the bench in the front hall. I slip out without anyone noticing and shut the door behind me.

chapter 16

I walk through the kitchen doors on Monday afternoon and nearly run into a giant television camera. "Cut!" a man shouts in a frustrated voice. "Joanne, can we keep the waiters out of here, please?"

A woman with round glasses and a Louise Brooks bob appears through a maze of lights, cables, and wheeled tripods. "Excuse us," she says, herding me back into the dining room. "We're in the middle of filming."

"A movie?"

"No. A special for Edible Television. We're on a tight schedule, so if you need to get upstairs, please go outside and in through the back door. No noise. We don't want to have to shoot this again." She puts a finger to her lips. "Shh."

My detour takes me out to the street, around the potted bay trees guarding the entrance, past the gold nameplate on the brick wall, and down the alley. I sneak through the back door into the kitchen, which is lit up like a nighttime construction site. In the center of the room stands Carl, expertly made up in foundation and blush, a puffy black microphone hanging over his head.

Gina watches from the sidelines, her lips moving with Carl's every word. I try to inch behind her, but she snaps out a hand and grabs me by the wrist. "Erin!" she whispers. "Get upstairs and don't come down until everyone leaves."

"Okay. What about sidework?"

"Do it later." She widens her eyes and points to the ceiling. "Go now. I tell you when you can do setup."

In the changing room, Cato is blowing smoke rings out the window while Jane plucks her eyebrows with the help of a compact mirror. Derek sits on a chair under the time clock, phone to his ear.

"If I'd known we were going to kill time, I'd have brought my script," Cato gripes. "I have a brutal audition coming up."

"Is this one I've heard about?" I ask.

"Not yet. My agent must have given somebody a hand job, because it's totally over my head. Off-Off-Broadway, one of the lead roles. Obviously, I enjoy public humiliation."

"Don't be so pessimistic," I say, hanging up my sweater. "This could be your big break."

"I doubt it. Only happens in the movies."

"They're taking forever down there," Jane says. "I should have stayed in bed with Julian."

"There you go, talking about sex again," Cato says. "Good thing I just got some or I'd have to put my hands over my ears and sing." He takes a last drag and flicks his cigarette into the alley. "When's Julian going to make you an honest woman, anyway?"

"He already proposed three times. All I have to do is say yes."

"Three times?" I say, zipping my skirt. "He's persistent."

She shrugs. "I'm not ready to give him an answer yet. I have trouble committing to a hairstyle, let alone a forty-one-year-old man who wants children yesterday. I'm meeting him at Town later, by the way, if anybody wants to come along."

"Can't," Cato says. "Got too many lines to memorize."

"I would, but I'm going out with Phil," I tell her.

She shuts her compact and looks at me. "Aren't you in deep shit with Carl as it is?"

"We're being more discreet now. Or I should say, Phil is."

"I know who she *really* likes," Cato says.

"Daniel?" Jane asks.

"Stop it, Cato," I warn. After last weekend's party fiasco, Daniel is the last person I want to talk about. Mid-service makeout sessions with Phil have been an excellent anesthetic, and in the past few days we've disgraced the wine cellar, the walk-in, and the tiny room under the basement stairs where Carl keeps the root vegetables.

"How's it going with Daniel, by the way?" Jane asks me.

"He's crazy about her," Cato answers. "He just doesn't know it yet."

"He has a girlfriend," I say. "Anyway, I'm seeing Phil."

Cato laughs. "All over the restaurant, from what you told me."

"Cato, one more word and I'll never—"

Ron's shoes squeak in the hallway and he walks in, grinning. "Isn't this wild? Us, on television!"

"Not us, Ron," Jane says. "Carl."

"Roulette's going to be world-famous after this. That means the waitstaff, too."

Cato rubs his eyes. "Hate to break it you, Ronnie, but nobody cares about us. We're as replaceable as the glassware."

"That's not true," Ron says. "This is a specialty field. A lot of us are passionate about what we do."

"Passionate?" Cato laughs.

"I love talking to people about food. That's why I got into this in the first place."

"You love it when they tell you what to do?"

"They don't *have* to tell me what to do," Ron retorts. "I

know what they need before they open their mouths. That takes a lot of skill."

"Would you guys pipe down?" Derek breaks in. "I'm trying to do business over here."

"This is getting boring, anyway," Cato says. "Anybody else want to eavesdrop?"

"Gina said to stay here so that's what I'm doing," Ron says, pulling the *Post* from his bag.

"I wouldn't miss this ego trip for the world," Jane says. "Coming, Erin?"

"Right on your heels."

We creep past the office and sit on the top step, listening while Carl talks about his grandmother, a naturally gifted cook who worked two jobs, fed elderly neighbors, and still found time to teach her grandson about French, Italian, and Japanese food. "The happiest day of her life was when I packed my knives and left for CIA," he says. "She died in her sleep a week later."

"Your new cookbook is getting a lot of advance press," the show's host says. "Is it true that the cover is a photograph of you hand-rolling pasta at age five?"

Carl pauses. "Four."

The minute the shoot wraps, Gina yells up the stairs for us. "Hurry up! We're late! Where are you? Specials in fifteen minutes!"

We scramble to set tables as she hovers around the departing camera crew. "I gave Carl his big break," she brags, trailing the show's host through the dining room. "I give him a nice kitchen and let him make any food he wants."

The host has the look of a man who's at work past quitting time. "Thanks again," he says, giving Gina an obligatory hand pump. "We'll let you know when the show's scheduled to air."

After a frenzy of napkin folding, we gather for the

specials and find Carl in an inflated state of self-worship. An afternoon of televised ass-kissing has left him red-cheeked (or is that leftover makeup?), agitated, and borderline hysterical. Gesturing frenetically, he swaggers in front of us and dissects the rainbow trout with his bare hands. "This is more than a piece of fish," he says, holding out a glistening white filet. "It's the history of a species and a river. It's the story of the American West!"

Just when we think the lecture is over, he glances at his diver's watch and his face contracts with pain. "I'd like a moment of silence, please," he announces. "It's been exactly one hundred and sixty-four weeks since Julia Child passed on."

Jane, Ron, and Cato solemnly bow their heads while I recall the Easter I helped my mother make Julia's beef brisket. All I remember are the five grueling hours we spent putting it together and my mother saying "Crap" when we pulled it from the oven.

After several tense seconds, Carl sighs deeply. "Cuisine will never be the same without her. May my contribution be one-tenth as great."

"Hear, hear," Ron replies.

Carl flashes him an annoyed look. "That's all for today," he says, hanging his clipboard back on the wall. "Now, get your forks and make it quick."

After a nice long float around the ego-sphere, Carl is finally returning to Earth. And he's burning up on reentry.

"Marty! José! *Think!*"

The kitchen has gone from Shangri-La to Shit's Creek in an hour. Carl pours two rare Belgian lagers into a plastic tumbler and swigs from it while growling orders at everyone he sees. "Three minutes, Phil!" he yells. "Cato, come in here to dry-hump Luis one more time and you're out! If you listened during staff meeting, Erin, you wouldn't keep asking so many goddamn questions!"

Ron slinks in, sensing danger. Head low, he writes a mood rating of 7 on the whiteboard, then rubs it out with his thumb and downgrades it to a 6.5.

"Make up your mind, Ron," Carl says. "For fuck's sake, this isn't calculus."

"Sorry, Chef. I know you want us to be accurate."

Carl claps a hand to his damp forehead. "Would you just go away already?" As soon as Ron vanishes out the door, Carl shouts, "Thank you!"

And he's not the only one on edge. His mood must be contagious, because several people in my section seem to have come down with it:

"I'm hypoglycemic, lactose-intolerant, and allergic to salt."

"I've never seen green beans this skinny. Can the chef make me some thicker ones?"

"Would you mind reading me the menu? I forgot my glasses."

By the time I go upstairs to change out of my uniform, my eyes are bloodshot and my hair is bent into a permanent ponytail. But I doubt Phil will even notice. Last time I checked, he was wearing a frayed Red Sox cap backward and had a streak of something brown on his cheek.

We meet at the end of the block and flag a cab. Phil slides in beside me and drops his ragged army surplus backpack onto the floor.

"I'm psyched to see your place," he says as we pull into traffic.

"We're keeping this a secret, right?"

"You think I want to give Carl another reason to rip me a new one? He could do a lot for my career, especially after today."

"How'd you like the show? Didn't he look pretty?"

Phil bristles. "I don't know. I guess."

"What's wrong?"

"I wish you wouldn't knock the guy so much," he says. "I owe him a lot."

"You *work* for him. He takes credit for every dish you cook. Why do you owe him anything?"

"He taught me most of what I know, for one. He's actually pretty cool."

"With his temper? Come on. You can't like him all the time."

Phil turns to face me. "So he goes berserk once in a while. So what? Four years ago, I was doing prep and making some decent sauces. Now I can kick ass behind any line in this city. Kunz, Boulud—I don't care how good their cooks are, I'm as good or better. When I come up with an idea that blows Carl's mind, it's like he saw God or something. He totally *appreciates* what I do for him. Plus, he's bailed me out of a tight spot more than once. Gave me six hundred bucks when I needed to get home and never asked for it back. That's more than I can say for my own family."

"He probably did it on purpose," I say, half-contrite, half-defensive. "That way he can keep you slaving away fifteen hours a day."

"You don't think he went through the same thing when he started out? He prepped for Le Coze for free, just to learn what he could, just to be around him. You don't get it. I guess I shouldn't expect you to."

"I *do* get it," I say, bouncing in my seat as we hit a pothole. "But I still wouldn't let anybody treat me that way for twenty-nine grand a year."

Phil laughs. "Oh, but you'd let him treat you that way for ninety? I've seen you take plenty of crap, and you don't even have anything to shoot for. You're never going to open your own restaurant. You're not trying for Michelin stars. You're either going to leave in a few months or rot in your uniform like Ron."

"What did you say?" I ask, squinting at him.

"Nothing. I'm just making a point."

"Where did you get this idea that I don't understand what you go through? The kitchen is tough, but so is dealing with customers. People treat me like their personal servant, and whatever money they leave isn't enough to make that okay with me. Why don't *you* understand *that*?"

He bites the inside of his cheek, then puts his hand on my knee. "Okay, I hear you. Let's just . . . not do this anymore."

"Great idea."

The driver turns his head to the side. "You want good food? My brother has this place on Canal Street. Best baba ghanoush you ever ate. You both like it and then you won't have to fight."

✦

Phil sets down my alarm clock and rolls onto his back. "Seven thirty already, fuck," he mumbles. "Gotta be at work in an hour."

I stir at the edge of the bed, where I'm sprawled naked with my hair stuck to the side of my face. "It's not even light out."

"Yeah, it is." He sits up and looks around with a dazed expression. He seems to be piecing together the last eight hours. "This is what I mean when I say waiters have it easy. You get to stay here and snooze while I go to the kitchen and figure out two specials that'll give Carl a hard-on."

"Why do you do it, then?" I say into the sheets.

"I don't know."

"There must be a reason."

He pauses. "It's kind of like the army. You join because

you're not sure what else to do, and then after a while it's just who you are. The other guys are depending on you to show up. You learn some new shit and you start being proud of it. The money isn't great and I spend every night sucking in grill smoke and taking heat from Carl, but at least I'm not getting shot at."

I turn onto my back. "I never thought of it that way."

He leans down, kisses my shoulder, and whispers, "I had an amazing time last night."

"I did too," I say, wondering why my knee feels out of joint.

"Is there a coffee place around here?" Phil asks, stepping into his pants. Rocket eyes him from his bed in the corner. "I won't be able to find the subway if I don't wake up."

"I'll make coffee if you want," I offer halfheartedly.

"That's all right. Go back to sleep."

He pulls on his fleece jacket and peers at the gray sky through a crack in the curtains. The sight of his tired face makes me feel guilty and lazy. He's right—while I sleep late in a warm bed, he has to go uptown to brave Carl and the grill.

"There's a coffee place a block and a half away," I say, slipping out from under the blanket. "Give me a minute. I'll walk you there."

A lone raindrop hits the window as I sip my latte and wait for Phil to get his double espresso. "Aren't you a vision," I mutter to my reflection. My hair has been only slightly improved by the wind, and the dark circles under my eyes reach my cheeks. One would think I'd been up all night drinking wine and giving blow jobs. And one would be just about right.

"Wait a sec, where's the sugar in this place?" Phil says.

He's wearing wrap sunglasses and a pilled red wool cap, while all around him, people in suits and trench coats talk on their cell phones or scan newspapers. He stops at the wooden counter, pours a long stream of sugar into his cup, then snaps on the plastic lid. "Okay, let's go."

We walk outside to the lamppost, where a securely-tied Rocket strains toward everyone who passes him. Phil side-steps his muzzle. "One of these days he's going to tear into somebody's leg and you'll get sued," he says.

"He's not dangerous. He's a little hyper around strangers, that's all."

"Okay. As long as he doesn't go after me."

"Hold this," I say, handing him my latte. The wind blows the hood of my jacket against my head as I fumble with the leash.

"Want to take me to the subway? We're almost halfway there."

I loop the end of the leash around my wrist. "I might as well. I'm already awake, more or less."

He hands me my coffee and puts an arm around my shoulders, jostling me as I raise the cup to my lips. A warm rivulet runs down my chin at the exact moment I spot a familiar figure coming straight toward me.

Daniel. Wearing black nylon jogging pants, a windbreaker, and sneakers. In the second before he spots me, I drag my sleeve across my chin, smearing coffee onto my cheek.

"Erin?"

Apparently, I'm still recognizable under my thick layer of ugly. "Daniel! Of all people!" I give him a wide, unbrushed smile. "What are you doing in my neck of the woods?"

He points back down the block. "I've got a friend who lives around the corner. We go running a few times a week."

"Oh! That's great. Good for you. I haven't exercised in months, but then, I've been really busy, so . . ." Help me, I'm rambling.

"You're up awfully early for a woman who works so late."
Daniel takes in my sallow skin and last night's smudged eye
makeup. "Or maybe you're just getting home?"

"No!" I laugh breathlessly. "We've been home for hours."
We. Fuck.

I become aware of Phil standing stiffly at my side. "Oh,
I'm sorry, this is..."

Daniel puts out his hand. "Daniel Fratelli."

"Phil McGregor." His voice is formal in a way I've never
heard before.

"Daniel's one of our regulars," I say, prodding him to be
polite. "At the restaurant."

"Oh, yeah?" Now that he realizes Daniel and I aren't
sleeping together, he brightens. "I'm the grillardin in the
kitchen."

"Grill cook," I jump in.

"Grill cook." Daniel nods, as if he's finally putting everything together. "Well, whatever you are, I'm a big fan of
your cooking." I can see the surprise on his face. This snow-
boarder-type degenerate turns out such spectacular food?

"Thanks. I'm hoping to be sous chef before too long."

I frown at him. "You are? When?"

"Soon. That's my plan, anyway."

"And this must be Rocket," Daniel says, squatting down.
Rocket skitters back and forth with excitement, his claws
scratching against the sidewalk.

"Watch out, he can get feisty," Phil says. "Last night he
went after my foot."

"Not your foot, your *sock*," I say.

"Whatever. My heel's hanging out of the hole he made."

Daniel ruffles Rocket's spotted back. "They say you go a
little nuts sometimes. Is that true?" Rocket wags his tail and
rubs his jaw on Daniel's knee. "I don't know. You seem
pretty friendly to me."

"He is," I say proudly.

"I gotta take off, Erin," Phil says.

"Oh, right. Sorry, Phil has a date with his grill."

"I should get going too. Nice meeting you, Phil. I drop in about once a week, so . . ."

"Yeah, come by the kitchen and say hello. Maybe Carl can show you around."

"I'll take you up on that."

As soon as Daniel walks away, Phil pushes his sunglasses up onto his hat and turns to me. His eyes look almost artificially blue in the weak light. "Do you have the hots for that guy?"

I swallow. "What?"

"You heard me. You like him, don't you?"

I laugh and take his arm. "That espresso's making you hallucinate. Come on. You're going to be late."

chapter 17

At nine o'clock the following night, Kimberly leads my parents, Nate, and the Pancratzes to my section of the dining room. I can't believe my luck. First, Carl hammered me with menu questions at the meeting ("Describe the taste of a hon-shimeji mushroom in five words or less"), then Gina measured my place settings and pronounced them "crooked like a Sicilian mayor." Now, just when the worst seemed to be over, I have to wait on people I've known all my life. And I thought it was horrifying when Rachel stopped in for apps last week.

Steve plays charming host while Cato joins me in the lounge to commiserate. "They've been threatening to do this for a month," I say. "I begged them not to, but they wouldn't listen."

"Don't feel bad," he says. "My mother embarrassed the crap out of me when she visited in May. She ordered the pork chop Cajun-style and asked if Carl could make her some home fries. She might as well have worn her Assembly of Praise T-shirt and parked her double-wide out front."

"You're not making this any better."

"Just preparing you for the joys of Parents' Night."

Steve scoots in Brenda's chair and hands everyone a menu, then passes me on his way back to the podium. "Your mother's a knockout. I'm amazed that she's got a daughter your age."

My stomach turns. "Thanks."

"Why don't you comp their appetizers?"

"Okay. They'll appreciate that."

As I approach the table, Harold raises both arms and grins. "There's our girl!" he calls. "And you thought I only came in to bug Geoffrey and get checks from Steve." The people at the next banquette turn to stare.

"Don't you look *adorable* in that uniform," Brenda says, standing up to kiss me on the cheek. She wears a lime-green cowl-neck sweater and a spiky brooch that threatens to impale her chin.

"Hello, everybody," I say. "How was the play?"

"Wonderful," says my mother, smoothing out her skirt.

"Incredible," says Brenda. "I cried."

"Big yawner," Nate grumbles.

My father puts his glasses on and opens the wine list. "I could write something better. Not that I'm bragging or anything."

My mother snorts. "Your father fell asleep during the second act."

"I was saving my energy for dinner," he says.

Harold leans close, as if divulging a secret. He smells like Old Spice and his royal-blue shirt is open at the neck, revealing a tuft of black chest hair. "I for one am ready for a Rusty Nail. Brenda will have a glass of the Newton chardonnay."

"Excellent choice. How about a beer, Nate? I bet you could use it."

"Just one," he says miserably. "I'm the designated driver."

"Oh, no. Are you serious?"

"We drew straws on the way here. Which means I have to get through this sober."

"Tough break," Harold says, slapping him on the back.

"But if you've never driven a '78 Caddy, you're in for a real treat. I don't even let valets touch her, but I'll give you my keys right now. That's how much I trust you." He reaches into his pocket and hands Nate a key ring. "Here you go. Promise me you won't rev her too high. She's sensitive and she overheats easily. We don't want to end up on the shoulder at midnight waiting for a tow."

My father passes the wine list to my mother. "Having my daughter wait on me hand and foot makes me feel really important."

I smile and point my finger at him. "Watch it. If you give me any trouble I'll sic the sommelier on you."

"God, don't do that. Just bring us something cold and white that won't send me to the poorhouse."

By the time Geoffrey helps me choose a moderately priced bottle and I return to the table with drinks, Gina is regaling everyone with stories of her first chef. Her hair is raked into a severe ponytail and giant gold hoops swing from her ears. The look is 1984 Queens with a hint of present-day Eurotrash. "He steal from us everything and end up at Rikers. I hope they shoot him!" she's saying.

"Oh, how awful," my mother replies. "What a shock that must have been."

"The police find fifty pounds of rib eyes in his apartment. But I never know what happened to all the wine he took, and my pans are disappeared forever."

Brenda smiles her thanks as I set down her wineglass. "He'll burn in hell."

"And he's not the worst," Gina goes on. "We had a manager who sleeps with the waitresses and tells the cooks where they can go. After that I say no more managers. I do everything myself and die early from exhaustion."

"Well, you know what they say," my father tells her. "Sometimes you have to grab the wheel of your own ship!"

Harold slurps his Rusty Nail. "Everybody's a thief if you give them the opportunity. That's why I have security cameras in my storeroom and electric fencing around the parking lot."

Gina wraps a thin arm around me. "Erin will take good care of you tonight." I stand awkwardly beside her, hands locked to my sides.

"We're going to run her around like crazy," my father says.

Forty-five minutes and a glass of Meursault later, my mother still can't decide what to order. "Okay, Mom, let's start narrowing it down," I tell her.

"But everything looks so wonderful."

"Think of the menu as a multiple-choice test," Harold advises. "All of the answers are plausible, but only one is correct."

"You're making it worse!" Mom says, slapping his arm with her napkin. "I'm under enough pressure as it is."

"I got the barramundi last time and it was heaven," Brenda says.

"Why don't you just close your eyes and point?" says my father.

"Remember, shellfish concentrates pollutants," Nate pipes up. "No orange roughy either. It's almost extinct."

"Get the lobster," I say, overruling my brother. "It was flown in from Maine this morning. You'll love it."

"Don't support environmental mismanagement, Mom," Nate says.

"Remember the Nantucket bay scallops we had on our honeymoon?" my father asks, putting his head on my mother's shoulder.

My mother kisses his bald spot. "I remember every minute of that trip. We hardly left the cottage."

"Oh, God. Not again." Nate rolls his eyes.

I feel like a cowgirl who's lost control of her herd. "I'll be back in a minute, Mom," I say over the din of conflicting opinions. "If you're not ready by then, I'll have to choose for you."

As I enter the kitchen to write down their mood rating (nine, on the verge of a riot), Carl gestures me up to the window. "Gina said Harold and his wife are having dinner with your family. Where's the order?"

"I don't have it yet. My mother's still deciding."

"She's had more than enough time to go over the menu. I'd like to see the order in three minutes, max. Cato's ten-top is already seated and we don't want to get slammed back here. Steve staggers large parties for a reason."

Deciding that now isn't the time to make a case for my mother's God-given right to take all night, I go back to the dining room. "Time's up, Mom. The lobster's great. You won't regret it."

She grips her menu as I try to pry it out of her hands. "Would the chef give me a half order each of lobster and salmon? Or an appetizer portion of both? And if I could have a side of the braised leeks with no butter, that would be perfect. Or the pea shoots, extra garlic, depending on which is better."

Oh, Jesus. She's the type of customer waiters dread and damn to hell later. I had no idea.

"Appetizer and entrée, Mom," Nate says, snapping his fingers. "Let's go."

"The microgreens are delicious," Brenda says before draining her chardonnay. "They're grown on Hawaiian fields fertilized with lava."

"Get the Tasmanian trout with fennel gelée," Harold says. "Take a risk."

"Trout and lobster it is," I say. "Now give me the menu."

My mother shakes her head. "Is it too much to ask that I get four things instead of just two? Isn't life limited enough?"

"For pity's sake, Anne," my father says. "I'm ravenous over here."

"Carl will do anything you want," Harold says. "He's not rigid like some of these celebrity ego-jobs."

I raise an eyebrow. "Really?"

"If he has a problem with it, just tell him it's for Harold. He won't care, trust me. Nothing's too much trouble for an old friend. Did you know we go back to his very first job after culinary school? I was supplying this place downtown, fussiest chef you ever met, and here was this kid from Philly turning out brilliant sauces. He flipped that kitchen upside down and made it his own in six months."

Gina squints at me from the podium, obviously wondering why I'm standing around socializing instead of working. "Okay, Mom, I need an answer. Believe it or not, I have other people to wait on tonight." I glance toward the lounge, where Cato stands at the computer, seating chart in hand. *Come on, come on.*

Suddenly, Harold reels off a list of dishes that include words like *split, side, extra,* and *substitute,* all Carl's pet peeves.

"Did I get it right, Anne?" Harold asks.

"Perfect. What a memory you have."

"Mom, I'm not sure if we can take those kinds of liberties with the menu."

"Carl won't mind," Harold says. "I guarantee it."

I flee to the kitchen to ask if these arbitrary changes "are okay, just this once," arriving as Cato's foot-long order spits out of the machine. Carl rips off the ticket and shouts the order to the cooks. He plates two appetizers and gives them to Luis before looking at me. "Another day, another disappointment, Erin."

"I have everything right here. I just need to ask you about some special requests."

"Put it in the computer," he says, waving his hand.

"You don't want to approve them first?"

"What am I going to do, refuse to accommodate a guest? The problem isn't the order, it's your skill as a server!"

Phil glances at me with a combination of fear and pity.

"I tried my best to—"

"Yeah, well, you fell short. An order that takes an hour isn't the guests' failure, it's yours."

"It was fifty minutes. And Harold said you wouldn't mind."

Carl almost smiles. "When Harold becomes a world-class chef instead of a liquor peddler, I'll listen to him. Right now, shut your mouth and put in your order or we'll be sending out their desserts at one in the morning."

As I reach the kitchen doors, Carl asks, "By the way, who are these special requests for?"

"My mother."

He snorts. "Just what I thought. She's an even bigger imbecile than you are."

My heart stops. He didn't really say that, did he? I almost whirl around and . . . what? Hurl an insult of my own? Get fired while my parents sip wine thirty feet away? I raise my chin and command myself to handle the situation maturely—by putting in my order, then running straight to the boss.

After searching the lounge and dining room in vain, I go upstairs to track down Gina. Instead, I find an unsupervised Nino roller-skating the length of the hallway. "Where's your mom, Nino?" I ask over the scraping of plastic wheels. He doesn't even slow down. As he barrels past I grab his shoulders and turn him toward me. "I need to speak to your mother about a crazy man in the kitchen," I say, smiling into his candy-stained face. "Do you know where she is?"

For a moment he seems ready to give me the information I'm after. He opens his mouth, takes a deep breath, and shouts, *"Va' all'inferno!"* before backing out of my grip and skating away down the hall.

Now, I don't speak Italian, but I did take some Spanish in college, and I think a five-year-old just told me to go to hell. "Same to you, sport," I mutter, stomping back downstairs.

"Get ready for table six, Erin," Marty calls. "We've walked on water back here and prepared your order so Mommy and Daddy won't be hanging around all night."

As I help Chen transport the appetizers to my parents, I spot Gina walking out of the lounge, glass of wine in hand. I set down the last plate, grind extra pepper over my father's monkfish with sea vegetables, and approach the podium. "I've been looking for you, Gina," I say.

"I was in the toilet." She purses her garnet lips at me. "You like this color? YSL Red Sin. I just put it on."

"It's very nice. Actually, I was hoping you could help me with something."

She recoils slightly. "Oh. What is it?"

"It's about Carl."

She glances at the reservation book. "The Wallers come in five minutes. Make it quick, please."

"Well..." I put it in terms only an Italian can understand. "He insulted my mother."

Her eyes fly open with horror. "No!"

"Yes," I say, nodding.

"To her face?"

"To me, in the kitchen. He called her an imbecile."

She considers the word for a moment, then shrugs. "We say the same thing in my country. Is not so bad, really."

"It means 'stupid.'"

"I know what it means. I say it myself." She leans over me and frowns at table six, where my mother is laughing at something Nate is saying. "Your family eats, everybody is happy. Carl says something in private because he gets mad. All chefs are a little..." She makes the cuckoo sign at her ear. "Remember that, okay? Is an important day for him. He might win a big cooking award. Peter Archer. They announce the names this morning."

"Good for him," I say. "I'm surprised he's not in a better mood."

"He wins for best chef of New York and Roulette will be in every magazine and all across TV. He does what he wants in his kitchen. You hear me? Don't make trouble with him."

"You must feel like the luckiest gal on earth," Harold says as I help Omar prepare the table for the second course. "Working with Carl is kind of like playing piano for Sinatra, right? It's a privilege to be in the presence of that kind of talent."

"He astonishes me every day," I reply. Omar gives me a barely perceptible smile.

"I had no idea you were serving food of this quality, sweetheart," my mother says. "It's so..."

"Funky?" my father offers.

"Avant-*garde*," my mother gushes. "Lobster in a beaker? Who ever heard of such a thing?"

Harold runs a thumbnail between his front teeth. "I think we all agree that it's brilliant."

"Now tell me if I'm out of line, Erin," my mother says,

"but do you think we could take a peek inside the kitchen, just for a minute?"

"Have you ever seen what goes on behind the scenes at a place like this?" Harold asks her.

"No, never." Her eyes are round and excited.

Harold slaps the table with his hand. "We need to remedy that right now. Erin, when you have a chance, tell Carl we'd like a quick tour. He doesn't have to do anything grand for us, we'll just zip through. In and out. We wouldn't want to get in his way."

"Actually, he's extremely busy tonight, so I'm not sure if this is a good time."

"Oh, he won't care a bit. He's loosey-goosey about that kind of stuff. And while you're talking to him, would you remind him to cook Brenda's steak between medium-rare and medium? Roulette's version of medium-rare might be a little too bloody for her."

"You don't mind, do you, dear?" Brenda says. "I'd hate to have to send it back."

"I'd hate that, too."

"Get Steve over here," Harold booms. "Maybe we can take a peek at the wine cellar after we see the kitchen. I stocked the place, after all, and gave him a darn good deal on it."

I look at Nate, who gives me a helpless shrug. He's dead sober and outnumbered four to one. There's nothing he can do.

As soon as Omar and I clear the main courses, Steve escorts the whole group to the kitchen. He waves my mother ahead of him, then puts a hand lightly on her shoulder blade and follows her inside. I go to the kitchen a few minutes later to ask Betsy which dessert she'd recommend for a man who just had a gastric bypass ("A grape?"), and see Carl laying on the charisma. "Exactly," he's saying to my father. "It isn't about dollars and cents. It's about doing something you love."

"This guy has the most Zen attitude you'll ever find in this business," Harold says. "We could all learn something from him."

Carl slips his arm around Brenda, who practically trembles. "Here's a woman who really enjoys my food," he says, gazing flirtatiously at her.

"I've never *had* such sensual experiences in a restaurant," she answers.

"Don't steal her, Corbett, she's all I've got," Harold jokes.

Steve laughs and leans toward my mother. "Now you know why Gina *really* hired him."

My mother giggles.

"Oh, God," I mutter.

"You know them?" Betsy says, scooping out some easy-on-the-system vanilla–passion fruit ice cream.

"My family."

She sighs. "And you're waiting on them? You poor thing."

"I'm going to fix you a special drink," Alain says during closing sidework. "Something to help you forget so you'll come back again tomorrow."

"Thanks," I say, wiping the T on the computer keyboard with ammonia and a cotton swab. "But I don't think they make alcohol that strong."

"Trust me. One sip and everything will be better. I learned it in France and it works every time."

"What do you put in it?"

He shrugs. "Vodka, rum, lemon juice . . . some other things. I make it a little different for everybody. I drank one myself a few days ago. Was like an instant cure."

"Really? What's it called?"

He smiles and lowers his voice. "Fuck the Boss."

chapter 18

After two weeks of meeting at midnight and parting at dawn, Phil and I decide to take our relationship to the next level. On Sunday at eight, we meet outside of Catch, a restaurant in Chelsea where, Phil has assured me, his CIA buddy and fellow cook, Travis, will "make sure we have the best dinner I'm not cooking myself." I arrive wearing what I hope will be appropriate for both the setting and my perennially casual escort—a low-cut top and jeans. To my surprise, Phil is better dressed than I am.

"Wow," I say as he walks up to me in trousers, a dark green turtleneck, and a black leather coat. "You look . . . amazing."

"Thanks, so do you." He gives me a light kiss. "I didn't want to stick out at Jeremy Rechter's new place."

"Jeremy who?"

"Rechter. He's one of those hotshot, daddy-funded-my-restaurant-and-that's-the-only-reason-I've-got-one guys. He's, like, twenty-eight. Younger than me and he's put in less time, but he's getting a ton of publicity already."

Phil glances around nervously and I find myself feeling sorry for him. "Ready to go in?" I ask.

He puts his arm around me and takes me down a steep

flight of stairs to a blue door. "Drinks and apps should be free, if I know Travis. When he came into Roulette last summer, I blew him and his wife away with this tea-smoked boar I made. They seriously said they'd never eaten anything better."

He opens the door and two couples push out past us and walk up to the street. As we step inside, the entire restaurant, all blond wood and brushed stainless steel, becomes visible at once—a dining room divided into two levels, a partially open kitchen, and a long bar with not one but three bartenders. Standing behind a red desk is a stone-faced Asian hostess. She looks like she's going to interview us to see if we're worthy of dinner.

Phil clears his throat as we approach her. "Good evening," he announces with the self-assurance of a VIP. "McGregor for two."

"McWhat?" she demands, suddenly transformed into an evil customs officer.

Phil leans forward and cups his ear. "Pardon me?"

"I said what was the name?"

"McGregor. Travis Long is expecting us."

Vaguely embarrassed by his attempt to rise above the faceless masses, I pretend to search for something in my handbag.

"He's my friend," Phil adds.

The hostess nods like she's heard it all before and continues to pore over her reservation book. She makes a few scratches with a pencil, gestures to her left, and says, "You wait in the lounge, please."

Phil's cheeks are bright red as we order the house specialty—mango mint margaritas—and find a place to stand in the mobbed bar. "I wonder what Travis is up to," he says, twisting his neck for a glimpse into the kitchen. "I don't see him. Maybe they put him on a different station. He's usually sauté."

"Well, it smells incredible in here. I'm sure dinner will be worth the wait."

He checks his watch. "We should have been seated ten minutes ago. This is bullshit."

"Don't worry about it," I say, rubbing the sleeve of his jacket. "They did a beautiful job on this place, didn't they?"

He studies the dining room. "Little heavy on the granite."

What started as an attempt to introduce some romance into our purely sexual relationship has now become a struggle to keep Phil's ego from collapsing. As long as I keep alive the illusion that everything's going well, the night still has a chance of getting back on track. And considering that it's one of my few nights off, I'm determined to enjoy it.

By the time the hostess comes to rescue us, we're both on our second drink and I'm running out of upbeat remarks about the decorating and the cute multicolored glassware. We follow her upstairs to a corner table, well within view of the open kitchen and the action below. As soon as she sets down our menus and leaves with the mandatory "Enjoy your evening," I lean forward and take Phil's hands.

"This is a perfect table. Aren't you glad we stayed?"

He looks around to make sure we weren't gypped out of a better one. "It could be bigger, but it's okay."

"Just okay? Come on."

He pulls his hands away and squirms out of his jacket. "No, it's fine. I just didn't think it would be so . . . you know, tight in here. I'm not a small guy. I like my space."

Since telling him that he's not as big as he thinks he is will no doubt irritate him more, I sit back and open my menu. "This is twice as long as Roulette's," I say.

"What does that mean? That we should fill ours up with junk like baked mussels and osso bucco?"

"Hello! My name is Amy! How are you tonight?"

Our waitress grins down at us. She has a pixie cut and a skier's tan and oozes confidence, pep, and authority. Rather than putting me at ease, she immediately makes me want to be the perfect guest. "Wonderful!" I say.

Phil skips the formalities and gets right to the point. "Can you tell Travis that Phil is here?"

"Travis?"

"Yeah, he was expecting us at eight thirty."

Amy's perky face falls. "I'm sorry. He's no longer working here."

"You're kidding me. What happened?"

"I'm not exactly sure."

"Was he fired?"

She hesitates. "I don't know. He left this afternoon."

"But why didn't he at least . . ." Phil stares into the distance as his image of free drinks and special treatment is replaced by an anonymous dinner courtesy of the chef who just canned his friend.

"May I refresh your cocktails or would you care for wine this evening?" Amy asks.

Seeing that Phil can no longer speak, I skim the first page of the wine list and decide on a bottle I recall serving at Roulette. "We'll have the 2000 Pur Sang and an ice bucket," I say, clapping the wine list shut. Geoffrey would be proud— or he'd tell me why I should have ordered the 2004 instead.

"Why don't we leave right now?" Phil says when Amy is gone. "I don't want to sit here like some nobody and eat four-day-old fish." He peers over the balcony, disgust on his face.

"We waited a long time for this table and I'm hungry. I'm

sorry about your friend, but can't we just forget about him and have a nice dinner?" I'm using that pleading, motherly tone I usually reserve for Rocket—not a good sign.

Phil leans back in his chair. "Food better be incredible, that's all I can say."

"Did you see the article on the wall downstairs? Three stars from Frank Bruni."

"Big deal. Roulette got the same thing."

Once Amy brings the wine and takes our order, I finally begin to relax. "Did you try the pretzel bread? I could eat it all night."

"There's Rechter," Phil answers, looking into the kitchen. "Not even thirty and he's already a cue ball."

I glance down to see a completely bald man in chef's whites pouring wine into a flaming sauté pan. "Probably from all the stress of running a restaurant."

"Look at him, strutting around. He never even went to cooking school. Didn't have to. His daddy bought him everything."

After forty-five minutes of self-restraint and accentuating the positive, I begin to fold. "You complain a lot, you know that? Why don't you tell me what you think of the wine? Pretty good, huh?"

Phil picks up his glass and takes a sip. "I don't drink a lot of wine, but this isn't bad. Where's the busboy? Omar would have refilled your water by now."

The prompt arrival of our appetizers doesn't improve Phil's mood. He reminds me of Mrs. Waller as he squints at an appealing arrangement of seared bay scallops in citrus vinaigrette. "These aren't legal size. Way too small. They must have paid somebody off."

"Why don't you just shut up and eat them?" I ask with a forced smile.

"No wonder Travis got fired. He probably told Rechter his stuff was starting to slide." Phil reaches across the table and pokes at my tuna with his fork. "Yours looks okay. Not a lot of imagination, but at least he got the temperature right on the fish."

I put down my utensils. "Would you stop criticizing everything?"

He turns his head like I'm talking to somebody behind him, then points to his chest. "Huh? Hey, I'm just making commentary. This is how it *is* when you're a restaurant person. You think I'm bad, you should hear Steve when he goes out. He met me and Carl once at Mary's Fish Camp and went off on it the entire time. I don't think we talked about anything else. He thought the crackers were all right, that was about it."

"I'm a restaurant person, and I don't do that."

"Yeah, but it's not in your blood or anything. You don't have to be critical because you're not in direct competition with every cook in town, like I am." A loud laugh from the next table makes him cringe. "If I'd known it was going to be this noisy, I'd have taken you to Balthazar. You can't hear squat, but at least the food's edible."

"That would have been better. Then we wouldn't have been able to talk at all." I take a bite of tuna, which I dimly register as excellent.

Phil chews with rapt concentration, then turns in his chair and gestures wildly toward the other side of the room. "Do you see our waitress? These scallops need a shot of coarse salt in a big way."

I half-stand and grab his arm out of the air. "You're turning into every waiter's worst nightmare," I hiss, "and if you don't stop it right now, I'm going to get up and walk out."

Unfortunately, he's already managed to get poor Amy's attention. She rushes over with an expression of worry and disdain—I know it well because I feel it on a nightly basis. I do my best to tune out an exchange that begins with Phil saying, "Are we your throwaway table?" and ends with Amy's promise to "make it right." She's barely turned her back when I give Phil a deadly glare. "If you were at Roulette right now, the waiters would be sticking pins in that little voodoo doll we keep at the wait station."

"Gimme a break, it's not like I'm changing the menu." He holds up the salt mill. "All I want is some decent salt instead of this crap out of a can. Is that too much to ask?"

A second bottle of wine doesn't soften Phil's edges as I'd hoped it would, but only magnifies his arrogance and bad manners. He looks up from his striped bass, fork raised. "What is this shit I'm eating?"

I stare at him. "Don't ask me. You ordered it."

"It's got like this"—he pushes the fish with his finger— "Mrs. Paul's breading all over it. I could have gotten this frozen at the supermarket for a lot cheaper."

I force down a bite of skate wing. "This was supposed to be a date, not a bitch session about the food."

"Don't tell me you think it's good."

"Actually, I think it's great. Better than Carl's food, by far." I'm not sure if I mean this or if I've just reached my limit.

"Are you saying . . . I can't believe . . ." Phil grabs his napkin off his lap and throws it on the table. "What do you know about food? You never cooked anything worth two cents in your life."

"So? That doesn't mean I can't tell the difference between terrible and great."

"Of course it does," he says, raising his voice. "You think a master carpenter can't appreciate a nice piece of furniture better than the average guy off the street? When you see what goes into it, you know whether to be impressed or not. And this . . ." He shoves his plate to the center of the table. "Even *you* could cook."

I close my eyes for a second, during which both my appetite and my attraction to Phil fade completely. "Get the check," I say, standing up. "Let's go."

People glance over from neighboring tables as Phil starts backpedaling. "Why are you so pissed off? Come on, there's almost a whole bottle of wine here."

"Sorry, but I've had enough of you for one night. In fact, I've had enough of you forever. Carl was right. We should have kept it professional."

Phil slumps in his chair and gazes at our unfinished dinners. "If you think I'm going to beg, you're wrong."

"It wouldn't matter if you did."

I sit down again while we wait for Amy to bring us the check, which Phil pays with a ceremonious unfolding of large bills. "I'll get the tip," I say.

He shrugs. "Up to you. I wouldn't leave her a lot, though. She was kind of slow taking our order. I hope you're a better waitress than that."

✦

The next afternoon, I almost collide with Phil as he comes down the stairs from the office, paycheck in hand. "Hi," I say, stepping aside.

I'm hoping he'll say something like, "Sorry about last night. Let's put it behind us and be friends, okay?" but he just smirks and rolls his eyes. "Right," he mutters, thumping past me. A few seconds later I hear him say something to Marty and they both laugh.

I continue up to the changing room, determined to handle our fling's messy end as calmly as possible: that is, push it from my mind and act as if it never happened. I put on my uniform, and on my way out I notice the new schedule hanging from a tack on the wall. I scan the list of names until I find mine. *Erin: See Steve.*

I read the words three times before they sink in. See Steve? I check the columns under the other waiters' names, but I'm the only one with instructions to report to the office. I feel a surge of adrenaline. Maybe my connection to Harold and my determined attempts to wait tables like a pro weren't enough to save me. I linger in the changing room for a minute, hoping Cato or Jane will show up and tell me what's going on. When no one comes, I drop my handbag on a chair and walk down the hall.

"Steve?" I knock on the half-closed office door.

"Yup."

"Hi," I say, stepping inside. "You needed to talk to me?"

He looks up from his desk and sticks a pen behind his ear. "Shut the door and take a seat."

I perch on the edge of a straight-backed chair, my hands on my knees.

He clears his throat loudly. "You've been here a couple of months now, is that right?"

"Yes."

"And in that time I've seen some decent work." He smiles and squints with one eye. "Your speed has improved and you seem to have a good grasp of the menu."

"Thank you." I feel myself relax. Maybe this is just an employee evaluation, something every waiter has to go through. I glance down at the desk for evidence of a final check but see only a chipped coffee mug and a scattered pile of what appear to be bills.

"But I've also seen some serious errors. One of those errors might end up in Harker's review and have serious repercussions for this restaurant."

"I'm sorry about that," I say hastily. "I've been very careful with my orders and I haven't made another mistake since then."

"Last Saturday was another example. You spent so much

time chatting with your parents that they took almost an hour to order. It caused a backup in the kitchen that slowed down service for other guests."

"I wasn't chatting with them."

"You were also argumentative with Carl."

"I was explaining the situation."

"See? You're arguing with me right now. Carl and I had a talk and we agreed that we need to see some changes if you're going to continue working here."

I take a deep breath and try to keep my voice steady. "What kinds of changes?"

"More commitment. More discipline. We want evidence that this job is your top priority, not a little side trip on your way to something else."

"Meaning . . ."

He hoists a thick ankle over his knee. "Meaning that you'll go the extra mile. Additional shifts, special events."

"Additional shifts? But I'm already working five nights a week. I don't really have time to do more than that, unless I sleep here." I add a little laugh that he ignores.

"Five nights is nothing in this industry. We don't serve lunch, so you never have doubles, and you rarely log more than forty-five hours a week. You've had it easy here, Erin, and we've been very generous with you. Now we need something in return." He looks at me a second too long and I drop my eyes to my lap.

"We expect you to be at the restaurant six nights, and early on occasion to help out with cleaning. Or late, depending on the task."

"How long will I be on this new schedule?" I ask.

"No idea. I can't give you a time frame right now."

"But I mean, is it . . . *legal* for me to work so much?" I say, smiling slightly. "That's overtime, isn't it?"

Steve stares at me, lips slack, then chuckles. "Take it up with the state if you think you have a case. In the meantime, I'll expect you here at three on Monday unless I call you to come in earlier. Now if you don't mind, I'm up to my eyeballs in invoices."

I grip the arms of the chair. I almost say that I know exactly what's happening—since he can't fire me because of Harold, he's invented a creative way to force me out. I almost tell him to find someone with less self-respect to "go the extra mile," but then I think about the training, the long nights, the laughs with Cato and Jane, the feeling of regular cash coming in. Leave now and it's back to canned beans and classifieds. "Will I have the same day off at least?"

Steve shrugs. "That depends on what needs to be done around here."

"But—"

"Your coworkers could use your help downstairs," he says from behind a sheet of paper. "We have a twelve-top coming in at seven and you're needed on the floor. *Now,* please."

"Don't let them exploit you, Erin," Jane says as we clean silver teapots with polish and old rags. "Stand up for your rights."

"The only right I have left is to quit. Which is exactly what they want."

"Assholes," she mutters. "This is why we need union representation. So they can't get away with working us like pack animals."

"Keep your voice down, Janey," Cato whispers. "You'll wake the management."

Ron looks up from a corner booth, where he's using a

travel iron to steam wrinkles out of a tablecloth. "We're not stirring up trouble with that union business again, are we? All it's going to do is pit us against Steve and Carl and suck dues out of our tips."

"Like I care," Cato says.

"Why should you?" Jane pushes her hair back with her wrist. "Even if we do unionize, you won't be around long enough to join."

"Won't be around?" Ron says. "What do you mean?"

"He got a callback for that play."

"You did, Cato?" I say. "Really?"

He shrugs. "Miracles never cease, huh?"

"See, I told you this would be your big break."

"Slow down, sweetie. The competition's fierce and I stopped getting my hopes up a week after I stepped off the bus from Oklahoma."

"What's the play about?" Ron asks.

"It's a really cool story about an alcoholic who moves back home and ends up falling for one of his mother's friends. It's sort of like *The Lost Weekend* meets *Harold and Maude*. I'm trying out for the lead, so if everything goes well, I'll be onstage groping somebody's grandma by spring."

Ron winces. "Do I have to hear this?"

"I play straight really well," Cato says. "If you didn't know me, you'd think I was as boring as the rest of y'all."

Jane throws her smudged rag at him. "I'm not boring. I licked NyQuil off Julian's neck when he had a cold last week."

Cato gasps. "I *love* NyQuil."

"Shhh," Ron whispers as heels sound in the hallway. "She's coming."

Gina and a pouting Nino enter the dining room, looking remarkably like a mother/son circus team. With her tight gold turtleneck and black leggings, all she needs is a trapeze. "We're going to a birthday party," she explains proudly, stopping in front of us. "Isn't my Nino cute?" She forces him to turn around and model striped parachute pants and a short embroidered jacket.

"That's darling," I say.

"You're dressed just like a little Cossack," Cato says.

"What do you say, Nino?" Gina prompts.

He casts a weary glance toward the bar, as if envisioning a future filled with Frangelico and late nights. "Thank you."

"Don't mention it, kiddo," Cato replies.

Steve blows out of the kitchen with a navy-blue sweater over his shoulders, the auto section of the paper tucked under his arm. "Ready to go?" he asks Gina. "Come on. Let's get this over with." He turns to me. "Erin, Carl's in the basement. He'd like a word with you."

"Right now?"

"Right now."

I sigh and hand my rag to Jane. "I'm on my way."

I feel like I'm reporting to cell block B as I walk downstairs. The door to the storage area is partly open and I hear muffled thuds coming from inside. "Carl?"

The second I step into the doorway, a big brown blur comes flying through the air at me. "Oomf!" I catch a sack of sugar squarely in the chest and stagger backward.

"Put it over there," Carl says, pointing to a metal rack against the wall. "We had a big delivery yesterday and I want this place straightened and organized. It should look like an OR when you're through."

I drop the sack in its appointed place and take stock, literally. Boxes and bags of everything from rice to cornstarch crowd the shelves and every inch of counter space. "Finish before you punch out, but not at the expense of our guests," Carl says. "I don't care if you have one table all night, you need to be upstairs at all times." He turns to go. "Oh, there's a bucket and some rags under the sink by the stairs in case you find any mouse droppings. Borrow Marty's weight belt if you're worried about straining your back. Normally I'd have Enrique take care of this sort of thing, but it's time the people making the money pitched in." He steps past me and creaks up to the kitchen in dark-green clogs.

I've stacked only ten sacks of coffee beans by the time I have to report for the staff meeting. Six hours later, my section is still full, with Kimberly leading tipsy new arrivals to a corner table that's already over capacity. I don't get back to the basement until well after midnight.

"What are they doing to you? You're sweating like crazy," Cato says when I race upstairs to help with closing sidework. "Don't worry, I'll take care of the espresso machine."

I kiss him on the cheek. "Thanks. I'll be back as soon as I can."

When I return to the basement, Carl is already there. He walks from one end of the room to the other like a drill sergeant, his clogs knocking against the cracked cement floor. "Find any droppings?"

"Near the freezer. I cleaned them up with ammonia."

"Good. Insects or spiders?"

"A cricket," I say, rubbing my aching shoulder. "I got rid of it. No spiders, thank God."

Arms crossed, he inspects the storage area before switching off the light and shutting the door. "Looks fine. Have you cleaned under the sink?"

"I haven't gotten to that yet."

"I think there's some spilled lye behind the garbage bags. Better take care of it before you go. If you find anything in the mousetrap, empty it outside in the Dumpster." He slaps his hand against an enormous sack of flour. "You seem to have a real gift for organization, Erin. I might ask for your help more often."

I snap on rubber gloves and spend half an hour with my head under the sink, cursing my existence and disposing of a mummified mouse. I scrub my hands twice and head upstairs for a much-needed shift drink. I'm about to push through the kitchen doors when they open from the other side and clock me hard in the chin. Who the . . . ? Carl on his cell phone.

"The awards ceremony's in three weeks and believe me, I can't wait," he's saying. "I'm finally going to show Holland who owns this town."

chapter 19

HECTOR'S 14TH STREET: Energetic model-types needed for all positions at ultra-chic new Mexican-American restaurant. Hi-intensity, hi-volume. Fine dining experience required, team players only, please. Apply online at chefhector.com. No phone calls.

After a week of helping Geoffrey catalogue Roulette's wine cellar in my free time ("Paulliac, Erin, spelled *au*. Not *o*."), I decide I've had enough. Carl, Steve, you win. I hate to leave Cato and Jane behind, but it's time to send Harold a thank-you note, turn in my uniform, and get the hell out of here.

My first stop is Capers, where the hostess says, "We have two hundred résumés on file, but you're welcome to leave one if you want." I apply instead to three other restaurants that sound like well-paying escapes from my current sentence of hard labor. Hector's 14th Street is the only one to call.

My interview takes place at the showy Brazil Grill, Hector's flagship restaurant in TriBeCa. I sit across from Luke the manager in an office filled with Amazonian artifacts, fielding questions like "What do you love most about serving great food?" ("The guests!") and "Why did you leave your last position?" ("I'm looking for new challenges.") Then I get a quick lowdown on chef Hector Santos, who has become bored with the Portuguese fusion cooking that made him famous and returned to his Mexican-American roots.

"Standbys like nachos and enchiladas are in again," says Luke, who has a mouthful of shiny braces and thin, pale skin. "We opened a month ago and we're already a smashing success."

"Great."

He slides my application into a folder. "Tell you what, let's audition you for a server position later this week. Wear dark jeans and we'll see how you do, okay?"

I decide to squeeze in a shift or two before giving notice at Roulette, just to be safe, and arrive at the warehouse-like Hector's on my precious day off. After serving haute cuisine for the past few months, I can't help feeling a little too good for the place. The furnishings are sparse and the walls what could be called "distressed apricot." Knotted rope, coils of barbed wire, and battered license plates are the only decoration. The effect is one of a sponge-painted ghost town, as I don't see a single human being.

"Hello?" My voice echoes across the dining room. I spend several minutes searching for intelligent life before I discover a man laying tile in a hallway. "Excuse me," I say. "Is the manager here?"

"You mean Luke?" He points down a flight of stairs and I descend into a long, subterranean kitchen. With its low ceilings, narrow passageways, and absence of windows, it feels like Roulette's claustrophobic cousin. Every inch of wall space is taken up by enormous appliances, including an industrial mixer and a brick oven that could double as a crematorium. The cooks are in all stages of preparing for the night's rush, shouting, laughing, and squeezing by each other in the cramped space behind the line. They're rougher than the uptown crew, with nose rings and elaborate tattoos. Seventies punk music pounds through the room. I'm about to ask where I can find Luke, when he comes careening around the corner. "Oh, hi, Susan."

"Actually, I'm Erin."

"Right. Let's get you a T-shirt. Is anybody else here yet?"

"Not unless they're hiding somewhere," I say.

Luke's cheeks turn a blotchy red. "We're going to have to have another meeting. Eddie?" he asks the nearest cook. "When's Hector coming in?"

"His publicist was here this morning," Eddie says without looking up from dicing jalapeños. "That's the last time I seen him."

"All right." Luke leads me to a narrow room lined with lockers. "I'm going to start you out as Lisa's food runner, if she ever shows up. What size are you?" He pulls a garbage bag filled with shirts from a closet and fishes through it.

"Medium. I'm sorry...Did you say food runner? I thought I was training as a waiter."

"Runner is the only position we have open at the moment, but it's a great way to get experience. You just shuttle the plates from the kitchen to the table, help the busboys, and split tips with the front waiter. You'll work your tail off, so you can cancel that gym membership!" he says with a wink. "Medium...let's see. Nope, extra small is all we have. Looks like it'll fit all right." He hands me a T-shirt only a little bigger than a potholder and leaves me to change.

I unbutton my blouse and slither into a scrap of white cotton printed with the words *Eat the Worm*. I can see the outline of my bra and a few ribs. Lovely.

"Are you Erin?" A square-jawed woman in her early twenties stands in the doorway. She wears vivid green contact lenses and an equally tight T-shirt that says *Chinga Tu Madre*.

"Yes. You must be Lisa."

"We're in the dining room setting up. You need to be on the floor right now and not in the locker room."

"I just have to stretch out this shirt so I don't get arrested for indecent exposure," I joke, yanking on the hem.

"It's supposed to fit that way. Come on. We don't have time to fool around."

I follow her upstairs, where at least fifteen rather average-looking "model-types" have materialized out of nowhere and are setting roughly hewn wooden tables with pewter flatware and burlap napkins printed with the Mexican flag. She promptly hands me off to a tall, heavyset food runner named Byron who, despite his poet's name, has the mouth of a parolee.

He glares at me. "Great. Another fucking runner to train."

"Hi," I reply. "How are you today?"

"The bar back called in sick and I need you to bring up tequila from downstairs," Lisa tells him.

"I'm training people who don't know jack shit and you want me to carry up what from where? Do I have six fucking arms? Look at me, do I?" He heads toward the stairs, hitching up the waist of his pants. "Meet me in the kitchen in three minutes, Erin. We have a buttload of work to do."

As I practice the delicate art of balancing a sixty-pound plate-laden tray on my shoulder, a baby-faced man in his mid-thirties enters the kitchen. He wears a brown silk suit, a turquoise necklace, and huaraches. He exudes the sort of slick self-confidence that comes from a large bank account and multiple sex partners.

After greeting the cooks in unaccented English, he puts his fingers into a large silver bowl, tosses what appears to be shredded beef into his mouth, and says to a woman with pink-streaked hair, "What do you think, Molly? More ancho chiles?"

She peers into the bowl. "Maybe you're right, Hector."

"Don't let me confuse you," he says, backing away. "It's your station and you're good at what you do."

I see a blur beside me as Byron ducks. "Holy crap, Erin. Watch the tray, would ya? You almost took me out."

"Meeting in thirty seconds, everybody!" Luke calls down the stairwell.

"Another meeting?" Byron retorts. "Why?"

Luke appears at the bottom of the stairs, his lips drained of color. "Because people aren't getting here on time, that's why."

"I'm usually early."

"I appreciate that, but meetings aren't negotiable."

"I'm not negotiating. I'm telling you, I'm not going to be there. I have too much setup to deal with."

"How would that look to everyone else?" Luke asks.

"I don't care how it looks. It doesn't make sense to bitch at people who follow the rules."

"What makes sense and what's required aren't necessarily the same thing. Everybody upstairs, please."

Waitstaff and cooks alike assemble in a side room that is evidently still under construction. I duck beneath the yellow caution tape and take a seat on a chair swathed in clear plastic. Hector breezes in, catching his sandal on a block of Styrofoam and stumbling as he heads for a dusty booth in the corner.

"Hey, guys," he says. "Thanks to all of you for bearing with us while we get the kinks ironed out. I heard from Luke that we had a groupquit last weekend. Also, a lot of you are coming in late, so I want to hear your thoughts on how we can do better and make this a more exciting place to work."

Lisa raises her hand. "I was here until almost three A.M. last night. When do we start working regular hours?"

Rather than shouting "When I decide you can!" as Carl would, Hector gives her a lopsided grin. "Hang in there, okay, Lisa?" he says with the artful charm of a salesman. "Remember, people have waited a year for us to open. We're all in this together. We need you to give until it hurts for the next couple of weeks."

"I work breakfast somewhere else," says one of the cooks. "I have to leave by one A.M. or I'm shot all day."

"My father worked eighteen hours a day washing dishes when we came to this country in seventy-one," Hector replies. "The restaurant business isn't easy and that's why we love it. We can do six hundred covers at lunch and show up for the dinner shift ready to kick ass and take names. If you're still feeling overextended in a month, let me know and we'll talk then."

After half an hour of listening to Hector's employees express their feelings about everything from the new dishware to the music selection (a show of hands reveals that most of the waiters despise Tex-Mex), Hector sends us off with all-purpose kudos. "Great job, everybody. Appreciate all your hard work. I couldn't ask for a better team." We respond by clapping half-heartedly and getting up before he's finished speaking.

"Who's the boss around here?" I ask Byron.

He snorts. "Depends on who you ask."

I've been busy before, but never like this.

"Where are table fifty-four's chips?" Lisa shouts over the din of the Hector-worshipping crowd.

A staff meal of tamale pie swirls in my stomach as I flip through the computer tickets bulging from the pocket of my short black apron. "I think I just checked on those."

"You *think*? Well, check again!" she commands as the host bumps by me with a group of five.

I sprint down the stairs, which are ski-slope slippery from melted ice and spilled salsa. "Gonna kill myself!" I shriek, voice canceled out by the raucous accordion blaring over the sound system.

The kitchen is mobbed with confused food runners, keyed-up cooks, and one very hoarse expeditor. "That's twenty-three black truffle burritos all day!" he rasps, then coughs into his sleeve. "Anybody got a lozenge?"

The chef de cuisine pushes a spray bottle under the heat lamps. "Here, I made it myself. Eucalyptus, Perrier, and Jack Daniel's. Works like a charm. Listen, have you seen Hector? I'm buried back here."

"He's upstairs having his picture taken with some strippers from Scores," one of the runners replies.

The expeditor shoots the spray into his open mouth and swallows. "Wow."

"I'm waiting on a basket of chips," I say. But I might as well be screaming into a pillow. Fajitas are coming up faster than sewage through a broken pipe and the dishwasher just cut his finger on a cracked bread plate. "I need some super-glue over here!" calls the grill-cook-turned-triage-nurse. "It's bleeding pretty bad!"

A plate of lobster chimichangas appears in the window. "Are those mine by any chance?" I ask the air.

Byron surfs down from the dining room and lands beside me with a thump. "How's it going, Erin?"

I turn to him and wail, "Help me!"

"Wish I could," he wheezes, slamming plates onto a tray. "But I'm already running for two waiters. You're a runner short? Talk to Byron. Need your butt wiped? Byron'll do it. Where's Byron? I want this dead body out of here."

"I'm running food for half the restaurant after an hour of training? Is that what you're telling me?"

Byron nods. "Gets your adrenaline going, doesn't it?"

The autocratic Carl would come in pretty handy right now. I'm about to start crying over corn chips when I see the fry cook drain and salt a basket of the house specialty. "I'll take those," I say, reaching behind the line and plucking the basket out of his hand. *"Gracias."*

He smiles, revealing a gold front tooth. *"De nada,* cutie."

But my contraband and I don't even make it to the stairs. "Get back here and grab a tray, runner number two," calls the chef de cuisine. "The entire left side of your section is being plated as we speak."

After dozens of trips to the dining room, I'm developing tennis elbow, a trick knee, and arthritis in both shoulders. Miraculously, I've limited most of my mistakes to the kitchen, where pandemonium relieves me of any criticism or responsibility.

"I thought I already gave you the beef brisket taquitos," says the chef de cuisine.

"Nope," I say, not telling him that I dropped them on the stairs, where they were first scavenged by passing waitstaff, then trampled, then finally swept to the side by a busboy.

"Okay, just give me five minutes. I'm losing my mind back here. Hector!" he bleats. "Mayday! Mayday!"

Hector, meanwhile, is sitting at one of Lisa's tables with his arms around two women of Social Security age. "Say hello to Hector for me," guests keep saying. "Where's Hector?" "Tell Hector to come over." "We want to see Hector."

But it isn't all Cinco de Mayo. "Excuse me, waitress? What's the story behind this salad? I could get the same thing at Chili's."

Lisa broadsides me with a tray of Dos Equis. "I'll handle it," she tells me. "Go check on table forty-one's desserts."

Ah, table forty-one, where girls in varying stages of undress are forcing the chef to autograph their napkins. "Ladies, ladies, you're getting me excited!" Hector laughs.

By the time I return with a groaning tray of cinnamon flan, sopapillas, and fried gelato, one girl is splayed across Hector's lap while another is attempting to sing the Mexican national anthem. "*Mexicanos, al grito de guerra*—is that right?"

"How would I know?" Hector says. "I don't speak Spanish."

"I need a Vicodin," I tell Byron as we wipe crumbs off still-warm seats. "I've never been so sore in my life."

"Get used to it," he says. "This is your life now. Your name is Erin and you run food. End of story."

The host comes by in his *Border Patrol* T-shirt, peering under tables and retrieving lost jewelry, dropped napkins, and, at table sixty-nine, a shoe. "Must have been the woman they carried out," he says. "That makes two sandals, a boot, and a loafer just this week."

I see a green flash out of the corner of my eye. "Here's your cut," says Lisa, handing me a thin stack of cash. "Minus twenty-three dollars for the grouper taco screwup."

"Thanks," I answer, counting my take. Forty-six dollars. Not much more than I made on my first night at Roulette.

"Erin? A moment of your time?" Luke calls me over to the bar, where the floor is tacky from spilled drinks and

littered with tiny paper sombreros. "Let's review your performance tonight."

He motions for me to sit down. "For your first shift, I'd
say you did pretty well. I'd give you a solid seven—a re-
spectable score with room for improvement." He glances
proudly around the wrecked restaurant. "So, now that
you've experienced our operation for yourself, what do you
think?"

I'm too tired to be tactful. "Truthfully, Luke, the night
was a disaster. People waited twenty minutes for a drink
and an hour for food, and the host crammed them in like
commuters. The computer system crashed twice, nobody
had time to help me, Hector was so busy making friends he
left the kitchen in the weeds all night, the stairs are a recipe
for a broken neck, the shifts are too long, the entrées aren't
worth the money . . ." I stop for breath. "Would you like me
to continue?"

He swallows loudly before nodding.

"Okay, by the time the kitchen figures out where the food
goes and the runners get it to the table, it's cold. And—"

"I mean, no," Luke jumps in. "But thanks for your feed-
back." He finishes a martini garnished with a tiny chile pepper. "We need somebody who can be a little more flexible
while we get up to speed here. From what you've just told
me, Susan, I'm not sure you're a good fit for Hector's."

"It's Erin. And no, I'm not." I follow him to the door and
shake his moist palm.

"Come back and see us," he says, baring his braces.

"By the way, you should give Byron a day off occasionally," I say. "He has a full load of classes and he's failing biol-
ogy. Good night."

"We'll leave as soon as I finish my coffee, okay?"

The next morning, Rocket paws at the front door and whines pitifully. A brief spin around the block at three A.M. wasn't nearly enough exercise. He wants his filthy rubber ball and a real walk, the kind he hasn't had since before I spent twelve hours up to my ankles in flaming tequila shots and crabmeat quesadillas.

"All right." I pour the rest of my coffee into the sink. "Let's go. Just give me a minute to get dressed."

Crossing the kitchen, I hear voices drifting up the stairwell. One I recognize as Nick's, but the other sounds like— my mother? I stop and strain to hear their words. Why would my mother drop by unannounced at ten o'clock on a Friday morning?

Leaning over Rocket, I slide the chain off and turn the deadbolt. As soon as I crack the door, I realize that it's not my mother talking, but a potential tenant looking at apartment two. "When does the lease start?" she asks Nick.

"Two, three days. I just have to fix the dishwasher and then you can move in."

"Come on, Rocket," I whisper. "This isn't the best time to run into Nick. You know how he feels about you."

But Rocket won't budge. After being cooped up all night, he's agitated and he smells freedom. I try to push him back with my leg, but he only squirms around it. "Move it, pal."

My pleading has no effect. I crouch down to haul him away, but as soon as I ease up on the door, he thrusts his head through the crack and forces his way out. I scramble to grab hold of him, just missing the end of his tail as he tears down the hall.

"Rocket, get back here!"

I throw open the door and run after him in my bare feet, pajama bottoms, and baggy T-shirt. By the time I get to the top of the stairs, he's already made it to the second-floor landing. Images of him bursting out of the building and into traffic flash through my mind. If Nick has propped the front door open for people coming to see the apartment, that's exactly what will happen. As I fly down the steps two at a time, I hear Nick's baritone echoing through the empty rooms. "I put a nice new seat on it yesterday."

I see cars zooming along First Avenue through the open front door as Rocket's back paws kick off the last step. He goes airborne over the tile floor of the foyer. "Rocket, stop!"

But my command only makes him go faster. Just when I think I'm about to lose him forever, he veers right and gallops at top speed into apartment two.

I arrive seconds later, panicked and gasping. I race down a hallway that still smells of wet paint and skid into the living room, where Rocket stands by himself, head tilted to one side. Nick's words float in from the kitchen: "That's just the motor. This refrigerator will go another five years at least."

"Come on, before somebody sees us," I whisper, chest heaving. "Let's go."

Rocket eyes me and starts inching toward the bedroom. He's not going to let me cart him upstairs without a fight.

"I already ran your credit and everything looks good," Nick says, his voice getting closer. "All I need is a deposit and the place is yours."

"Great. I'll write you a check."

"Rocket, please," I say, stretching out my arms.

But he isn't in the mood to compromise. As if to show me how long it's been since he went outside, he scratches the floor twice and sniffs the wall.

"No—!" I say, lunging for him.

It's too late. He raises his leg and leaves a long wet stream on the fresh paint just as Nick and his new tenant come around the corner.

"Erin?" Nick says when he sees me, shoeless, hand over my mouth. His thick black eyebrows come together. "You need something?"

The new tenant, a fluffy-haired pregnant woman in her early thirties, is the first to notice the damage. "*Wait* a minute," she says, pen and checkbook in hand. "Did that dog..."

"Yes, he did," I say miserably. "I'm sorry."

"In my new apartment?"

Nick leans forward and peers at Rocket. "What happened here?"

Before I can beg for forgiveness and run off for paper towels and bleach, Nick puts the damp spot and Rocket together. "Get him out!" he shouts.

"I will," I say, trying to grab the petrified Rocket, who takes off toward the safety of the bathroom. He scales the toilet and leaps into the tub.

"I mean forever! Right now!"

"Okay, let me just—" Then his words register. "What?"

"You heard me!" He raises his arm and points at the door.

"You want me to...move out?"

Nick runs a hand over his forehead and struggles to compose himself. "You've lived in my building a long time. You said he wouldn't ruin anything, and I trusted you."

"He didn't! I mean, it's never happened before. It's my fault. I haven't been home much lately and—"

"It doesn't matter. I gave the dog too many chances already. He goes tonight or I put your things on the street."

The new tenant drifts away and pretends to study the bedroom closet.

"*Tonight?* I can't find a place for him that soon."

He shrugs. "You have to."

"Why don't I pay for some new paint? Does a hundred dollars sound okay? I can give you more in case he does it again in the future, which I promise he won't."

He shakes his head. "You have a nice apartment, rent-stabilized and everything. Hard to find these days. That thing wrecking my building is just an animal. You make the choice."

"Please, Nick. Don't put me in this position."

He throws up his hands and stomps into the kitchen, muttering, "Somebody has to clean this before it stains." I hear him rustling around under the sink, and he reappears a few seconds later with a spray bottle and a dry, bent sponge.

"I'll do that," I say, taking them from him. I kneel down and wipe the wall and floor. "See? It's coming out, almost like nothing happened."

"Get the dog out of the shower and go," Nick says.

"Give us one more chance," I say, looking up at him. "I'll do anything."

"Sorry, Erin. I told you to get a cat."

chapter 20

"You have to help me, Rachel! I wouldn't be in this situation if it weren't for you!"

"I'm on a shoot in Staten Island right now," she says in a low voice. "What am I supposed to do?" I hear her excuse herself, then walk into another room and shut the door. "There's a couple out there waiting to pose with their parrot. He's sixty years old and I'm terrified of him."

Exhausted from his trip to the park, Rocket sprawls on the living room floor, gnawing a squeaky rubber hamburger. "So come over when you're finished."

"I can't. I have to deliver prints to a client later and they're not even close to ready."

"Christ! What am I supposed to do?"

"I'm not sure," she says, her cell phone crackling. "Take him to your parents' house?"

"My father's allergic to dogs. The only safe animals are the ones he throws on the grill."

"How about your friends from your old job?"

"I've hardly talked to them since I started waiting tables. I can't just call out of the blue and ask them to take my dog until I find another apartment."

"Jane or Cato?"

"I already tried. Their landlords don't allow pets."

She sighs. "I wish I knew what to say."

I unzip my coat and pull off my shoes. "Great. Now I'm really stuck. Thanks, Rocket."

"Try being a little more forgiving, Erin. He's old. He's doing his best."

"So am I! I spoil him rotten. I hired the most expensive dog-walking service in town. He needs more attention than I can give him."

"Listen, I have to get back to work." I expect her to hang up, but she doesn't. "I'm sorry. You can always take him to a kennel if nothing else works out."

"A kennel! After all he's been through? He won't understand. He'll think I've abandoned him. He'll think he's going to be put down!"

"Relax. I'll call you later, okay? If I come up with any solutions in the meantime, I'll let you know."

As soon as we say good-bye, I start madly flipping through my address book. I call everyone I'd trust to look after Rocket, but they all seem to be out of town, in a meeting, or entertaining in-laws. By twelve thirty it becomes clear that my dog is about to spend at least one long night in a cage surrounded by dozens of other deserted canines.

"Well, this is it," I tell him. "The call I hoped I'd never have to make."

I dial information, then punch in the number. One ring, two rings, three.

"Roulette," Steve answers gruffly.

"Steve?" I begin, adding a rough croak to my voice. "Hi, it's Erin."

He pauses, clearly sensing a problem. "What's going on?"

"Well, I'm feeling just terrible, like I have the flu or something, and I don't think I should come in to work today. I mean, I could if I absolutely had to, but no guest wants a sick server."

"You looked fine the other night."

"Excuse me?"

"I said, you were the picture of health not forty-eight hours ago."

"It came on suddenly."

"Do you have a fever?"

"Yes, 101 to be exact," I say indignantly. I'm starting to believe myself—a good sign, because I think I'm in for a fight.

"My waiters don't get sick," he says. "If they do, they pop a pill to get them through the shift and do their best not to spread anything around. Marty had walking pneumonia last year and still managed to cook for a party of two hundred. I expect that kind of dedication from everybody."

"But . . . I'm dizzy. My doctor said it's not a good idea to walk around." I decide to rouse Steve's mortal fear of getting sued. "I might fall and hurt myself."

He snorts. "You fall when you're *not* sick. I'm sorry, I don't have anybody to replace you. It's Derek's night off, but he works extra shifts at Suburb. So, unless you're going to quit right now and drop off your skirt and blouse, washed and pressed, by noon tomorrow, you'd better be here by three. Make that two thirty. I want you to count the silverware and make sure Enrique hasn't been supporting his relatives with it."

I cough in a last attempt to garner his sympathy. "I don't think this is anything to play around with. It could be something dangerous, something . . . I don't know, from Asia."

"There's not enough staff to cover you while you're pampering yourself for two weeks. Come to think of it, this is probably a good thing. Maybe you can finally learn what it means to give your all to a job."

I take a deep breath. Now is not the time to lose my temper and blow the remaining two percent chance I have of pulling this off. "But I already give my all. I've practically organized the entire restaurant by myself."

"The entire restaurant? We're just getting started. Like I said, be here at two thirty. And gargle with salt water before you come in. Your voice doesn't sound so hot and people hate asking a waiter to repeat things."

I hear the echoing splash of Rocket drinking from the toilet instead of the bowl I filled an hour ago. He walks into the kitchen, muzzle dripping, and looks at me as if to say, "I've had a walk and a drink and all is right with the world."

"Okay," I tell Steve. "I guess I can make it."

"Good, and be prepared to run around. We have a full house tonight and it's going to be busy from seven on."

"Wait . . . Steve? If I can get Derek to cover me, would that be all right?"

"You won't. See you this afternoon."

I hang up and stare out the bedroom window, trying to figure out my next move. Two hours isn't nearly enough time to find a decent kennel, take Rocket there, and get him settled. I riffle through my desk drawers and eventually dig up a list of all the waiters' numbers. I say a prayer that begins with "please" and ends with "or I'll kill myself," and dial the phone.

"Hello?" a man's voice demands.

"Derek?"

"What."

"Hi! This is Erin. From Roulette."

Pause. "Jesus, I can't get away from you people."

I laugh, determined not to let a little rudeness deter me. "I'm calling because—"

"I know why you're calling. And the answer is no."

"Um, pardon?"

"I'm not working for you tonight. I already have two shifts this week at Suburb and four at Roulette. That barely leaves me time to pick my nose."

"I'm sorry about that, Derek, believe me I am. But I'm really sick, just flat on my back. If you could help me out this once..."

"*Sick*, huh? *I* get it."

"And I... need to stay home and rest so it doesn't turn into something worse."

"You're boring me, Erin," he says through a yawn. "Putting me right to sleep."

I realize that shopworn excuses, begging, and tears are not going to work. I'm dealing with a guy who listens to only one thing. "I'll pay you," I blurt. "Fifty dollars."

Derek erupts into a gravelly cackle. "You're pretty funny, you know that? I got a restaurant I'm trying to open and I'm about seventy grand short."

"A hundred."

"Chump change. A down payment on a piece of shit."

"Okay, two hundred."

No answer.

"Two-fifty?"

After a short silence, he says, "I think we might be able to work something out."

◆

"It'll be just like a slumber party," I tell Rocket as we climb out of a taxi at Ninety-third and Lexington. "You're going to love it."

But Rocket isn't listening—he's too busy enjoying his second outing of the day. It's twilight and a bitterly cold wind is picking up. He doesn't strain against his leash as he usually does, but pauses to sniff the air. "You'll have so much fun with the other dogs," I say, petting him through his plaid wool coat. "You'll only be there for a night or two, and . . ." I trail off. "Let's get this over with. They close in a few minutes."

I throw a small duffel bag containing bowls and toys over my shoulder and open the heavy glass door marked "Fur-Lough—A Canine Hotel." I tell myself that, as terrible as I feel, I'm doing the right thing. I'll drop Rocket off, then go home, make some more calls, and get us out of this, somehow.

A bell tinkles as we walk into a small, overheated office that smells of carpet shampoo and old newspapers. There's a small white counter with a neglected fern on one end and a bulletin board covered with animal-themed comic strips and dog-walking ads. High-pitched yapping and deep barks echo behind a caged door. Rocket hesitates and peers around warily. Contrary to what I told him about a night or two, this looks more like twenty years to life. "Please," I whisper, pulling him toward the counter. "Don't make it harder than it already is."

A slope-shouldered older man and his dachshund are signing in. "Stella gets nothing but diet food now," the man says to a young woman running his credit card. Her strawberry blond bun is anchored to her head with a pencil, and she wears baggy scrubs decorated with puppies and kittens. Her name tag says Abby in red Magic Marker.

"I think she's lost weight since we last saw her," she says.

"The vet told us no more cheese. It's made a big difference."

"Did you leave her new feeding instructions on the intake form?"

"Half a cup twice a day," the man says, nodding. "Now, I know this is going to sound paranoid, but I have to ask."

Abby rips the slip from the machine. "Go ahead."

"Stella came home with a cough last time she was here, and I heard there was a dog flu going around. Have you folks had any problems with that?"

I freeze.

"All the kennels did, but it hasn't been as much of an is-sue this season. Stella's young and healthy, so she should be fine. We're stringent about disinfecting everything and we don't let in animals who are obviously sick, so . . ."

The man signs his slip and hands it to her. "That's really all you can do."

"Right. Well, bon voyage. We'll take good care of her." She steps around the counter and takes the leash from Stella's owner, who, after instructing his dog not to binge, walks out.

Abby smiles at me and I force myself up to the counter. "Be right back," she says, disappearing behind the caged door with the whimpering Stella. A minute later, Abby emerges with a can of soda. "Here to check in?" she asks.

"Yes," I answer over a fresh round of barking.

"Are you the one who called a little while ago?"

"That's me."

She leans over and looks down toward the floor. "So this must be Rocket Edwards. How many days would you like to board him?" Abby asks, pushing a clipboard and ballpoint pen toward me.

"Uh, one night, I think."

"Great. Just fill out the first sheet with your vet informa-tion and a local emergency contact."

"Emergency? Okay . . ." I start to write down Rachel's

address, then stop and put down the pen. "I'm sorry. I don't think I can do this."

"First time?"

"Yes."

"Don't worry. He'll be in good hands."

"It isn't that, it's . . . I've changed my mind, that's all."

"I'd be happy to give you a tour," she offers. "I think you'll like our facilities. Most dogs are very comfortable here."

"I'm sure they are. I'm just not ready."

Abby seems almost hurt. "Oh. All right, it's your decision. If you need us, we open again at eight in the morning."

"Thank you. Thanks very much. I'm sorry." I pull Rocket toward the door and onto the dark street, which is now wet with freezing rain. "Fuck," I mutter. "What have I gotten us into?" I walk to the end of the block, then lead Rocket under a fluttering black awning.

I have no idea what to do next.

As I stand, shivering, in front of a shuttered bookstore, I start to wonder if I have everything backward. Maybe I should call Steve right now and quit. How can I find another job and a new place to live when I'm always at work? But if I quit, how can I afford to do anything except give up my dog and move back home? I'm trapped, captive to the money, with no choice but to keep plodding blindly in the same direction.

With a groan of frustration I step out into the squall, toys and bowls jingling in my bag. "I don't know what we'll do when we get there, but let's go home," I tell Rocket as my fleece hat nearly blows off. He licks a patch of ice on the sidewalk while I try without success to hail a cab. Hoping the other side of the street will be better, I cross against the light and raise my arm. Nothing. My fingers are numb and my hope is depleted by the time we start walking down-town.

Why didn't I wear boots instead of sneakers? I stop every few minutes to wave frantically at passing cabs, then swear aloud and keep going. For Rocket, it's all one big adventure—the honking horns, people dashing for shelter, the runaway umbrella that misses us by inches and gets stuck in a tree. I buy a cup of coffee at a convenience store, and when I come out, I realize that I'm not far from Roulette. I wish there were someone nearby who could take in a chilled waitress and a dog with ice-crusted paws, but the only person I know on the Upper East Side is Daniel.

No. I can't.

I don't care how cold and desperate I am. I'll wait here at the curb until a cab comes, even if my feet freeze to the side-walk.

"Please stop trembling, Rocket," I say. "You're making me feel awful."

Just when I think I'll have to stash him under my coat and smuggle him onto the subway, an empty cab rounds the corner and heads straight for us. "Finally," I say, picking up Rocket in my arms. "We're saved."

But the driver isn't slowing down. I glance behind me to see a well-dressed, dogless older man holding out his arm. "Wait, that's mine!" I shout as the cab speeds by, drenching Rocket and me in frigid water. The man hops inside, the roof light switches off, and they disappear into traffic.

Rocket lets out a little cry and shakes violently when I put him down. His soaked dog coat has fallen to one side and his tail hangs between his legs. "Screw pride," I say. "Let's go."

My socks squish in my shoes as I slip along Seventy-eighth Street toward the only person I haven't called for help. From down the block, Daniel's building looks like base camp on Annapurna—bright and warm, with live people and blankets inside. The moment we step under the awning, Rocket shakes again, spraying the doorman with cold droplets. "Sorry," I say.

"Why?" he says, smiling. "I got galoshes and a coat on. That's what they're for."

As he calls up to Daniel's apartment, I have a horrible thought: what if Daniel and Fritz aren't alone? Sonia could be reclining on the couch, reading scripts, deciding who to ruin and who to make rich with the stroke of a pen. I'll stumble in with my dripping dog and mortify the hell out of myself before making some transparent excuse and going back out into the storm.

"You know what, forget it," I tell the doorman as he hangs up the phone and says, "Go right on up."

"Really?"

"Mr. Fratelli's waiting for you."

In the space of four short floors, I comb my hair and attempt to dry Rocket with my scarf, which I stuff into the duffel bag along with my empty coffee cup. When the elevator doors open, Daniel is standing there in worn jeans, a long-sleeved red T-shirt, and wool socks. "What's going on?" he asks, looking concerned.

The smile I'd planned on doesn't come. "I need you to take my dog," I blurt, my voice breaking.

He frowns at me, then at Rocket. "Why? What happened?"

"I . . . my landlord—it's a long story." I shake my head. "This was a mistake. I shouldn't be here."

He reaches out and takes Rocket's leash. "Would you come inside, please? You're blue."

"How about venison and gravy flavor?" Daniel calls from the kitchen. "Does he like that?"

I rub my face with a hand towel. "I don't know. I've never given it to him before."

Rocket yaps loudly. "Well, he's going bonkers, so I must be on the right track. Fritz, you've had enough. Rocket, fight for what's yours."

Daniel returns to the living room as Rocket pushes the bowl around the kitchen with loud, echoing scrapes. "I had no idea Fritz was such a wuss," he says. "A dog half his size shows up and all of a sudden he's the beta male."

"You really don't mind if Rocket stays for a few days?"

"Not at all. Fritz needs to learn to share his toys anyway."

"I can't tell you how much I appreciate this."

"You already did. Four times." He points to my wet clothes. "You should get out of those."

"Oh, well . . . I don't have anything to change into."

"I'm sure I can find you something to wear," he says.

"Thanks, but you've done enough. I should go."

"Not in that condition. Come on."

Wondering if he's going to lend me one of Sonia's blouses, I follow him to a small, carpeted bedroom that overlooks the garden. The down comforter has been pulled up to the rumpled pillows. On the floor are a monogrammed dog bed and a well-chewed scrap of rawhide.

Daniel switches on a lamp and opens the closet. "Size 34 neck sound about right?" He pulls a corduroy button-down off a hanger, then digs around on the top shelf, his T-shirt lifting to reveal an inch of smooth lower back. "I think I've got some old sweatpants somewhere. Here we go." He hands me the clothes and smiles. "They're going to be huge on you. You're so . . . small."

"That's okay. Anything to get warm."

"Getting you warm is my goal."

"Um, where should I change?" I ask in a near whisper.

He stares at me intently. "Wherever you want to. Here would be fine."

"Here?"

He swallows. I can see his chest rising and falling. "Or there's a bathroom around the corner. With a door."

I open my mouth, but several seconds go by before words come out. "Then I guess I'll just—"

He takes my face in his hands. "Shh. Don't say anything."

"What about your girlfriend?"

"What girlfriend?" he whispers.

Looking up at him, I let the clothes slide to the floor. He kisses me, tentatively at first, as if he thinks I might pull away. When I grasp his shoulders he pushes his fingers into my hair and pulls me down onto the carpet. This can't be real. I've frozen to death, and this is my last thought before seeing a bright light and my grandmother Rita, who died when I was eleven. Five minutes more. That's all I ask.

My foot snags the leg of a chair, which bumps noisily away from the wall. I grope at the buttons of Daniel's shirt and feel one pop off as he tries to remove my sweater without taking his mouth from mine. When I open my eyes, I realize that I'm partially under the box spring. Daniel fumbles with my bra while I yank on his belt, and eventually we manage to end up on the comforter with most of our clothes off. He's wearing one sock and pale-blue boxers, while my underwear remains the only thing between me and what I've been trying not to think about for two months. "You're not leaving now," he says. "I won't let you."

"Don't worry," I say breathlessly. "Even if I wanted to, I don't think I could find my pants."

My watch catches on my hair, and when I roll over to take it off, I see Rocket standing in the doorway.

"Hey," Daniel says to him. "Why don't you go chew on something I can't replace? What we're about to do isn't a spectator sport."

chapter 21

I spend the next ten days dashing between work and Daniel's, stopping at my apartment only to change clothes, feed my fish, and water the plants. My days start when Daniel goes to the office at eight and end when we "go to sleep" after I get back from Roulette. Rocket, having claimed his dominance over the laid-back Fritz, shuns his dog bed in the living room and commandeers a suede armchair. "Don't get too comfortable," I tell him. "I'm looking at two more apartments in the morning."

But I'm relieved when neither the Lower East Side loft nor the Soho walk-up is quite right. I'm not even upset when I lose a West Eighties one-bedroom to someone else. I find myself hoping that the perfect apartment won't come along until I'm ready for my pleasant limbo to end. For the first time in months, I'm not agonizing over my future or feeling pressure to find another job. Cato congratulates himself on a matchmaking job well done, and even Steve notices the change in my disposition: "It's about time you smiled," he says.

I spend my mornings hanging around, cleaning up dishes from the previous night's dinner, and letting Fritz and Rocket pull me through the park. "Too expensive," I say when my broker, Carolyn, calls with new listings. "Too small. Too far."

"For someone who needed a place right away, you're awfully picky," she tells me.

On my days off, I grocery shop and buy flowers, planning for the moment when Daniel walks in looking haggard from staying up late so many nights in a row. "I took a five-minute catnap in my office," he assures me. "I feel like I could run a 10K." Whether we're watching old movies, sharing dim sum on a Sunday afternoon, or just talking in bed, tomorrow doesn't matter. I'm homeless and waiting tables for a living. Life is good.

On a Saturday in mid-November, Daniel puts up the canvas top on his car and we head to Long Island to meet Shelley, his real estate agent. With Rocket fidgeting in my lap, I work up the nerve to ask the question that's been nagging me for weeks. "So, what ever happened to Sonia?"

Daniel grins. "I was hoping you'd let that one drop."

"Uh-uh. Not this time."

"Oh, boy." He straightens his elbows and sighs, obviously choosing his words carefully. "It was the classic setup. I'm the single up-and-comer, Sonia is the Porters' niece, and she needs a cushy job to keep her busy. Bang—I'm her boss *and* I'm dating her. I thought she was attractive at first, but I got tired of the spoiled-rich-girl routine in about three days."

"So there was nothing likable about her? Not one thing?"

"If you're asking was I in it for the sex, no, I wasn't. I mean, we've all done that before, but..."

"Hey, speak for yourself."

He reaches over and squeezes my thigh through my jeans. "Come on, tell me the truth."

I squirm away from him. "I don't want to blow your perfect image of me yet. Can't we have a nice infatuation period before we lay it all on the table?"

"The grill cook, Erin. Give me details."

"You're not finished with your Sonia story. I still don't understand how you managed to keep seeing her for two months."

He pulls around an eighteen-wheeler and shifts into high gear. "She wasn't all bad. Okay, she was rude, demanding, and wanted to move in after a week and a half. But she also adored me and gave a *great* foot massage." He laughs and I slap him on the shoulder. "I'm kidding!" he says. "Okay, your turn. Don't tell me you and that Phil kid had scintillating conversations."

"Hey, at least he didn't ask you to fetch him a drink."

Daniel winces. "Sorry about that. You looked like you were about to pour yours over her head."

"I should have. Are you in trouble with the Porters for breaking it off?"

"The word Frank used was *disappointed*. I think he cared more than Sonia did. He was a little frosty to me at first, but he got over it. He found somebody else to mentor her, a smart woman who works her people hard. Poor Sonia's in for a wake-up call."

"So, what do *I* get for going to bed with the producer? Anything?"

"Hmm," he says. "Besides some emergency dog-sitting? I don't know, how about a nice afternoon in the Hamptons?"

We follow Shelley's white Mercedes past city hall and an elementary school to our third house of the day, a clapboard cottage with slanted floors and a flowered curtain hanging under the kitchen sink. While the dogs chase each other across the yard, we walk from room to room, peering into closets and opening cabinets. "Ceilings are a little low, aren't they?" Daniel says, grazing his head on the living room doorway.

"I don't know. You're the six-footer, not me."

"You won't find charming details like that just any- where," Shelley says, trying to flip on the burned-out over- head light. "They really give a house authenticity."

I peer through a wavy picture window at the windswept beach. "The view is amazing."

"Yeah, if I don't knock myself out on the way to look at it," Daniel says.

"You could have the ceilings raised," Shelley jumps in. "Put on an addition, maybe a third floor. This would be a terrific great room if you hired the right architect. You've seen a lot of cottages, Dan. Maybe it's time to think cre- atively."

"Actually, I think it's time for clam chowder and a beer," he says. "Thanks a lot, though. I'll keep this house in mind."

We load up the dogs and trail Shelley down the wind- ing shell driveway. She waves over her shoulder, toots her horn, and turns right; we turn left toward a tiny restaurant Daniel describes as the only place to get great chowder in November.

After parking on a quiet side street, we let Fritz and Rocket take over the front seats and walk into a wood-paneled pub, where just three customers eat lunch from paper-lined bas- kets. We take a table by a brick fireplace piled high with flaming logs. "So, what's good here?" I ask, reading the spe- cials board on the wall.

Daniel opens his laminated menu. "Everything. You can't miss."

"That makes it easy, then. I'll have the steamers."

"Excellent choice. Would you care for shoestring fries with that?"

"Very funny," I say, giving him a smirk.

"I'm just teasing."

"Well...don't."

He takes my hand across the battered wooden table. "Come on. It's not like you serve burgers and shrimp cocktail."

"So?"

"So, Roulette isn't the typical restaurant. And you're not the typical waitress."

"Wouldn't it be great if everybody saw it that way?"

"Half the country thinks I'm shallow because I work in TV. I just don't pay attention to it."

"This is completely different. When I tell people I wait tables, I can see it on their faces. They feel bad for me."

"Nobody felt bad for you at Frank and Patti's."

"That's because they were ignoring me. Didn't you notice?"

"The only thing I noticed was Patti's bad taste in earrings."

He smiles but I have trouble smiling back. "You can afford to think it's funny. You've never been ordered around by someone like Sonia."

"Wanna bet?"

"That's not what I mean. I have to say yes to people, no matter what they ask for or how they treat me. It can be pretty humiliating."

"Isn't every job like that, though? Patti's decorator has been in all the design magazines and she makes him redo the same room every six months. Frank's owned by his shareholders; I have to keep Frank happy..."

"Fine, but those jobs are *interesting*. They take talent. Anybody could do what I do."

He sits back and crosses his arms. "That's ridiculous. Don't tell me you're not using your brain every night. It's the waiters who keep that restaurant running."

"But to Patti and Sonia, we're just there to serve."

"I don't see it that way at all. You make a living and you have as much class and integrity as anybody I know."

"You're ignoring the reality," I insist.

"The reality is that nobody's judging you. One of these days you're going to realize that."

"Maybe if we switched jobs you'd understand," I say, watching the waiter walk toward us.

"Are you kidding? I'd fold after the first night. You, on the other hand...Frank would probably keep you for good."

I manage to laugh. "He'd get a lot for his money. When I wasn't busy producing, I could bring him lunch."

"If more people at the network had that attitude, we'd be number one in the ratings instead of third."

After lunch we put the dogs on leashes and go down the block for coffee. We spend the rest of the afternoon drifting around Bridgehampton, holding hands, looking in shop windows, and commenting on houses. By late afternoon the temperature is dropping and snow is beginning to fall. We drive home in the twilight with the canvas top flapping noisily in the wind, the dogs asleep in the backseat. My cell phone rings as we pass the city limits. It's my broker.

"Great news!" she shouts in her heavy Jersey accent. "Remember that place on the Upper West Side? Well, guess what? The renter backed out, so it's all yours if you still want it."

I pause and glance at Daniel. "Well, actually, I don't. But I'll take it anyway."

✦

I start moving on Sunday and don't finish until the following Thursday. Between shifts at Roulette, I box my clothes and dishes, then spend hours cleaning what is now my former apartment. Rachel helps me wrap lamps and roll up rugs, while Daniel supervises the movers and transports the fish tank across town in his car. I'm so preoccupied with my new, Rocket-friendly space that when Carl asks me to come in early on Friday afternoon, I don't give it a second thought.

"But will it sell?" I hear Steve say as I walk into the restaurant. He and Carl are sitting at the bar with the menu in front of them. Steve wears his terry-cloth robe and plastic slippers and his legs are shiny from massage oil.

"You've seen all the press we've been getting," Carl says. "Of course it'll sell."

"Okay, but olive-oil mousse? Aren't we already pushing it with the liquid nitrogen ice cream? I dropped four grand on a Pacojet that Betsy's used twice."

"We can't be cheap with Holland down the block. Innovating costs money."

"Uh, hi," I break in.

Carl barely turns. "Go punch in and wait for me in the dining room."

"Your time card's been hard to read lately," Steve adds. "Make sure you line it up right."

I respond with the kind of smile only a new boyfriend and a great apartment can bring. "Of course. I'll be more careful from now on."

Ten minutes later, Carl meets me at table one, a yellow-and-black beltlike contraption in his hand. "I have a special job for you, Erin," he says. "Something I couldn't ask Enrique or the night porter to do."

After assignments like scrubbing the grease traps and tightening the hinges on the stall doors in the men's room, I'm convinced I can handle anything. "What job is that?"

"Don't worry, you'll enjoy it. You've seen Broadway shows where the leading lady flies in from offstage suspended by a wire?"

"Yes. So?"

"So, it's time to clean the chandelier."

I almost laugh. "I can't do that."

"Up to you," Steve says from the podium. "I'm sure I can find somebody who'll put on the harness in exchange for three hundred a shift."

Carl shrugs. "He has a point."

"But I'm not very coordinated," I say, suddenly clammy.

"No more negative self-talk. Here, turn around and let's rig you up. You've got a lot of dusting to do before four o'clock."

Eyeing the chandelier far above me, I remind myself that I just signed the lease on eight hundred very expensive square feet. "What if I slip?"

"Don't fight it," Carl says. "Just surrender and you'll be fine."

"Remember, Erin, every piece of that lamp was hand-blown in Murano," Steve calls, slippers slapping the carpet as he walks toward the kitchen. "One scratch and you'll be working here for free until you're fifty."

I step reluctantly into the leg loops, flinching against the feel of Carl's hands as he clips the harness around my waist and tightens the strap. "The ladder's pretty solid, though, isn't it?" I ask.

"As solid as it can be for something that tall and spindly. All right. You're ready to go."

A thin blue rope rises from my waist to the ceiling, where it loops over a metal hook that's the only thing between me and the hereafter. With a brief prayer to whoever's listening, I put my foot on the first rung. "I should have made a will," I whisper. I climb slowly to the top, my damp palms slipping along the ladder's cold metal sides.

"Now take this," Carl calls, poking the hard end of the duster into my leg. My head reels as I grab blindly with one hand, finally making contact and pulling up the long plastic pole. I take a deep breath and get a fix on the chandelier, which is filmy with cobwebs and coated with a layer of gray filth. Reaching out one shaky arm, I guide the duster to its destination and get to work.

"See me when you're finished," Carl says, leaving me to my aerial act. José and Ron arrive five minutes later, followed by Kimberly, so tall in her high heels that if she stretched her arms over her head she could probably touch my toes.

"Top o' the world, Erin!" Ron calls as he sets tables in the lounge. "How's the air up there?"

"Thin." I suck in a lungful of dust and cough. The tinkling chandelier sways dangerously back and forth.

"I hope they fitted you for a body cast this morning," Marty quips when he walks in, gym bag over his shoulder.

"I'm glad someone's enjoying this," I mutter. Geoffrey's rectangular glasses reflect the light as he watches my progress. Soon Alain's favorite pre-service anthem begins floating eerily through the dining room.

Is that all there is? Peggy Lee sings. *If that's all there is, my friends, then let's keep dancing.*

"*Hola*, Erin," Omar says as he wipes down chair legs below me.

"Greetings from the summit," I answer. I try to scratch my cheek with my shoulder. No luck.

"You're safe, right?" he asks.

"I wouldn't go that far." The chandelier is almost finished. One more frosted pink dome and I'll be ready to return to earth. But what's tickling my ear now? I shake back my hair and spot an enormous black spider crawling up my arm.

"*Aah!*" With a short, loud scream, I let go of the ladder and frantically brush off the spider. As soon as I do, I lose my footing and swing out over the dining room.

"Erin!" Alain shouts.

The harness squeezes my hips as I clutch the duster and sail helplessly back and forth. Seconds later, Carl explodes out of the kitchen with Steve on his heels. I see the face of Omar, upturned and amazed, as if witnessing a religious miracle.

"Get me down!" I shout. Just as I'm coming to rest over section three, the front door opens and Jane and Cato walk in. I dangle there, terrified, furious, embarrassed beyond belief as they stare at me open-mouthed. If I survive, I will never live this down. Never.

"I knew you were kinky, Erin," Cato says, shaking his head. "But this time you've gone too far."

Suddenly, Carl begins to laugh. Steve joins in, and then even Alain and Omar can't resist the humor of the situation. "Somebody help her!" Jane shrieks. "For God's sake, we can't just leave her there!"

Carl peels off his chef's whites like he's going in after a drowning victim, displaying a tight gray T-shirt. "Don't move!" he says, inspiring more laughs. Surprisingly agile and athletic, he scrambles to the top of the ladder and slowly reels me in. Before I know how I got there, I'm on the ground with one of his thick arms wrapped around me. "You conquered a fear and eliminated a problem. Now aren't you glad you went up?"

Steve wipes his eyes with a cocktail napkin. "Thanks, Erin. I don't think I've laughed that hard in years."

chapter 22

On Tuesday at eight, Daniel helps me out of a cab near the corner of Seventy-sixth and Madison. "Where are we going?" I ask.

"You'll see," he says. "It's up about half a block."

This is the most information he's given me since he begged me to take the night off. I had to pay Derek two hundred dollars for the privilege, but I have a feeling it's going to be worth it. "Can I have a hint?"

"I already told you to dress festively. Which you knocked out of the park."

"Thank you. Besides that."

"Besides that, you're going to have a great time."

I lower my head against the wind, imagining dinner at a tiny, candlelit restaurant, or maybe champagne in one of the Carlyle's most romantic suites. But the second we turn toward a gray building with gleaming brass doors, I realize he has something else in mind. I've been here before.

"Good evening," says the doorman.

"Daniel Fratelli to see Frank and Patti Porter," Daniel answers.

My stomach drops. He can't be serious.

"Mr. P's birthday today, right?" the doorman asks.

"He's telling everybody it's his forty-ninth, but he can't

fool me," Daniel says. "By my count he's been forty-nine for the last three years."

I give Daniel's arm a deadly squeeze through his black cashmere coat. "Can I talk to you for a second?"

He looks confused as I lead him to a leather settee a few feet away. "What's up?"

"What's *up*?" I hiss. "Why didn't you tell me you were taking me to the Porters'?"

"I was afraid you'd turn me down, that's all. Jesus, you're acting like I got us tickets to a live sex show or something."

"Actually, this is worse."

"We're going to a really nice party. Don't you think you're overreacting a little?"

The logic behind his deception hits me hard. "Oh, I get it. You thought you'd do me a favor and let me hang out with the rich folks for a while."

"What are you talking about?" he says, gaping at me. "I invited you because I like spending time with you. I certainly didn't think you'd get pissed off."

"Pissed off doesn't begin to describe it."

He tips back his head and sighs. "I'm sorry, all right?"

"You don't seem sorry."

"Can we talk about this later?" he says, trying to take my hand. "We're here now and I really don't want to be late."

I jerk away from him. "I am *not* going upstairs."

"Well, I'm not going without you."

The lobby door opens and a blast of frigid wind ruffles my hair. "Look, honey, they'll let anybody into these parties nowadays," says a male voice.

Daniel turns and forces a smile. "Randy, what are you doing here?" he says, sounding strained. "I thought you were in L.A."

"Back in town since last night and damn happy about it."

Daniel touches my shoulder. "Uh, Erin, this is Randy, one of the writers on the show, and his wife, Yvonne . . ."

Trapped, I have no choice but to play along. Yvonne is speaking to me, but I hardly register what she says or even what she looks like. "So nice to meet you," I hear myself say.

"I mean, what do you get for the man who has four of everything?" Yvonne asks Daniel. She holds out a rectangular box wrapped in silver paper.

"A fishing trip on a charter boat."

"You *didn't*."

"It was either that or more golf clubs."

"We bought him some hard-to-find Lafite," Randy says. "Too bad it won't be ready to drink until he's seventy." He stands aside as the elevator door opens. "Shall we?"

"Erin?" Daniel takes my elbow and I find myself getting swept along with the group. I step into the elevator, catching my reflection in the mirrored wall as we start to rise. In my silk cocktail dress and heels, I look the part, but I'm a fraud, a maid in her mistress's clothes. I close my eyes, unable to stand the sight.

"The weather was okay but we just hated the *scene,* you know?" Yvonne says.

I stiffen as Daniel slides his arm around me. "I've heard it takes a couple of months to get underneath all that."

"A couple of months too long," Randy says.

The doors part and the Porters' apartment appears before me, even larger and shinier than I remembered it. Rosalinda mans the foyer in her starched black dress and white apron, hands clasped in front of her. "Welcome," she says.

"Hi, Rosalinda," I say. I expect her to blow my cover with a remark like "Where have you been? Yves is waiting for you in the kitchen," but she just seems surprised, as if she can't understand how a stranger knows her name. She hands our coats to a young woman in uniform and leads us to the drawing room, where guests in suits and sequins stand around in small groups. Patti Porter, wearing an off-the-shoulder taffeta dress, lets out a squeal when she sees us. "Daniel!" she says, kissing his cheek. "How's my favorite producer?"

"Never better. Great to see you."

She immediately turns to me. "So this must be the mystery woman I've been hearing about."

Mystery woman? She doesn't recognize me?

"Hello," I say, with a desperate glance at Daniel. He raises his eyebrows, an expression I take to mean "just go with it."

"I've seen you somewhere, haven't I?" Patti says, studying my face.

"Well . . ."

"Were you at the St. Jude's charity luncheon last week?"

"Uh, no."

"The Fire and Ice Ball?"

"Sorry."

"I know. You're an actress on one of the soap operas. Am I right?"

"I'm afraid not."

"Strange," she says, frowning. "I must have you confused with someone else."

There's a long, awkward moment as Daniel and I adjust to my unexpected anonymity. "So!" he says, rubbing his palms together. "Where's the old man hiding?"

"He's in the wine room with Yves." Patti cups her hand around her mouth. "I think this turning fifty thing is simply a reason to raid the Pomerol. I'd better get him before he misses his own party. Please excuse me." She vanishes into the crowd and a henna-haired waitress appears in her place, holding a tray of fizzing glasses.

"Care for champagne?" she asks in a mechanical voice.

"Damn right, sister," I mutter, grabbing a flute. "And save one for yourself."

Daniel, infuriatingly attractive in a tailored black suit and dark-blue shirt, touches his glass to mine. "That wasn't so hard, was it? Patti didn't even make the connection."

"Just wait," I tell him. "Someone will."

Her timing impeccable, Rosalinda enters the room with the latest addition to the gathering—Sonia. "Believe it or not, that someone just showed up," I say. "What a wonderful evening this is turning out to be."

"For Christ's sake," he replies. "What's she doing back in the city?"

Sonia grabs a glass of champagne from the nearest tray and comes toward us on snakeskin slingbacks. She's wearing a wool dress with a ragged hem that looks as if it got caught in the door of a cab. "Danny," she says, hugging him stiffly. "It seems like months, doesn't it? Maybe it's jet lag. I've been in Europe."

Daniel puts his hand on my upper back. "You remember Erin, don't you?"

I watch Sonia's face go from bored to bewildered as she searches her memory and finally places me. "I heard you were dating somebody," she says, "but I had no idea you were seeing . . . *her*."

I clench my jaw and glance at Daniel, whose face is drained and pale. "Well, I am."

Not to be upstaged, Sonia says, "I've met someone, too. Oh . . . here he is." She looks past my head and waves. "Roberto!"

Daniel and I both turn toward the door. Patti is leading in a man who appears, from his blond streaks and copper skin, to have logged too many hours under the St. Moritz sun. He saunters over, filterless cigarette in hand. "This is my boyfriend, Roberto," Sonia tells us. "He's from Madrid, but he's living here now. With me."

"How's it going?" he says in studied American slang, then excuses himself to go track down a "real" drink.

"Moved him in already, huh?" Daniel says.

"I've known him for three weeks and four days," Sonia retorts. "We really connect."

"Here comes the birthday boy!" cries Patti, mercifully cutting the conversation short. Everyone applauds as Frank walks in carrying a magnum of wine in each hand.

"Sorry, I didn't think Sonia would be back so soon," Daniel whispers to me. "Come on, I've got some more interesting people I'd like you to talk to."

"I'm not talking to anybody."

"What are you going to do? Stand here?"

"Why not?"

"Please, Erin. I realize I screwed up, but can we at least *try* to be sociable?"

As much as I'd like to drive home my point, I can't take any more humiliation. Withdrawing to a corner would only attract attention, and it's too late to storm out. "Fine. Let's get this out of the way."

A live jazz quartet plays Stan Getz as Daniel introduces me to a young entertainment lawyer and her husband, a real estate developer who "owns midtown," and several emaciated, shiny-skinned women over forty, all of whom have two last names. Everyone is smashingly dressed and delighted to meet me. No one asks what I do for a living, either because they don't care or because they assume I don't do anything. By the time people start wandering into the dining room for dinner, I have the beginnings of a very nasty headache.

Daniel searches for our place cards on one of three china-laden tables. "Okay, I'm over here . . ." he says, pointing to a chair beside Frank. "And you're . . . right here." He brings me to a seat on the far side of a table by the window. I'm like Pluto—banished, frozen, forgotten.

He checks the other names. "You're between Sonia's boyfriend and Edie. That's not bad."

"Who's Edie?"

"Frank and Patti's daughter."

The bratty underage drinker? Unaware that I've experienced her for myself, Daniel gives me a brief character description. "Smart kid but a real handful. She came along late in life, so they indulge her sometimes. Hopefully she'll go to bed early."

"I'll say a little prayer."

He stoops down and looks at me with round eyes. "This hasn't been too awful so far, has it?"

I turn my head in the other direction. "It's worse than awful. I can't believe you lied to me."

"What do you mean? Sonia's the only person who even knows who you are."

"That's one person too many," I grumble to the view of Central Park. "A real sweetheart she is, too."

Frank Porter takes his seat, cueing the other guests to sit down. "I'd better go," Daniel says. "Try to have fun, okay?"

"It's too late for that."

He shoots me a regretful backward glance and pulls out his chair as I stand alone, seething. Roberto comes up behind me and squints at his place card. "In Spain, you sit with who you like."

"Maybe I should move there," I say. As the guests sit down, I hear footsteps in the hall. I've heard of fashionably late, but this is absurd.

"*Buona sera!*" a woman calls from the doorway.

Patti claps her hands together. "Gina and Steve! I'm so glad you could make it!"

I almost drop my glass. Daniel turns and our eyes meet. Sorry! he mouths. I glare at him and crumple my place card into a ball.

"Italians," sneers Roberto. "They're so vulgar."

Suddenly, like the little sister I'm glad I never had, Edie appears in a gauzy blue dress and ankle-wrap sandals. "What's this, the kids' table?"

I try to think of a clever retort, but none comes. I'm struck speechless by the sight of my bosses exchanging air-kisses with Patti while spouting various transparent apologies. "We were so *busy,* we have to pull ourselves away like this!" Gina yanks at her own arm, feigning dismemberment.

"Don't listen to her," Steve jokes. "She couldn't decide what to wear."

Patti laughs lightly. "*Pas de problème,* we were just sitting down. Steve, you're across from the man of honor. And Gina, I'm sure you and Mr. Roberto Basura will have lots to talk about, both being from the Mediterranean."

I slump into my chair. Gina. At this very table.

"I remember you," Edie says. "You're the maid who worked at our last party."

"Mmm," I murmur. You're the least of my worries, twerp. Here comes Gina, her heels steep, her face fallen. She looks at the hawk-nosed garden designer across from me and the elderly writer of presidential biographies on Roberto's left and visibly shivers. She knows it as well as I do. This is the worst table in the house.

"Hello, Gina," I say. "What a coincidence."

She stares at me, her red mouth open. "You. But how . . . ?"

"My date is right over there." I lift my chin toward Daniel, who is half-standing and shaking Steve's hand.

Gina tosses her head in disgust. "I don't talk to you." Steve shoots me a puzzled frown from across the room as Gina throws off her jacket, revealing a black lace-trimmed bustier.

"Señora, good evening," Roberto says, jumping up and pulling out her chair. I guess Italians with cleavage aren't quite as vulgar.

"*Gracias,*" she says, smiling at him.

He sits and leans close to her. "You speak Spanish."

"*Sí,*" she says.

Oh, really? Then why does she scold the Mexican bus-boys in Italian?

Patti floats over, beaming as always. "I see you've all found your places."

"We certainly have," I answer.

Clearly thinking that Patti recognizes me, Gina rushes in to grab the spotlight. "*Tu casa es bonita* this evening, Patti."

"Oh!" she says with a laugh. "Well, *mi casa es su casa!*"

"Cut the crap, Mother," Edie says, picking at the rim of her hand-painted plate with a thumbnail.

Patti's expression doesn't change. "Would you like me to talk to Dr. Berger about increasing your dosage?" she asks sweetly. "Because I'll call him tomorrow. Well, enjoy your-selves, everyone."

I press a hand to my throbbing temple while Gina jabbers on in Spanglish. "Mexico *es* dirty! *Malo!*" she exclaims to Roberto. "I go to *la playa* in Acapulco and get sick from breathing the air!"

"*Sí, sí,*" he says to her breasts.

After several agonizing minutes, the waiters bring out snow crab salad, and with a cry of "*Bon appétit!*" from Patti, dinner gets under way. Unfortunately, I left my *appétit* downstairs in the lobby. I've got Gina's voice in one ear, Edie's exasperated sighs in the other, and, since deep breathing isn't helping my head, I start throwing Bordeaux at the problem. After two glasses, I only feel worse.

"Pardon me," I say, pushing back my chair and grabbing my handbag. I ignore Daniel's worried expression and walk down the hall past the kitchen, where Yves is probably whipping up something to match the napkins. Once in the bathroom, I shut the door, lean against the wall, and relish the silence for a minute. I'm rummaging through my purse for aspirin, when the knob turns and in comes Patti.

She gasps and steps back. "Forgive me! How embarrassing. I *must* have this lock fixed."

"That's okay," I say, relieved I wasn't caught scouring the medicine cabinet. "Actually, do you have something for a headache?"

She touches my arm. "A headache? Of course. Come with me."

I follow her through the library to the master suite, an all-white sanctuary of soundproof windows and heavy brocade drapes. "Well, there's a bit of everything here," she says, pulling open a drawer in the night table. "Valium, Seconal . . ."

"Aspirin?"

Patti smiles. "Of course." She takes out a bottle and drops three tablets into my palm.

"Thank you. This is a wonderful party, by the way."

She leads me to a master bath the size of my apartment, runs water into a small crystal glass, and hands it to me. "I'm glad you're having a nice evening. I can't tell you how much I worry about every detail. I hardly slept last night." She catches sight of herself in the mirror. "Sometimes I wonder if anyone even notices my effort." Her high white forehead wrinkles. "Is your table all right?"

"Absolutely. My dinner companions are—fascinating."

"I'm so glad. I knew you'd all get along beautifully." She tilts her head. "It's just driving me crazy how familiar you seem. Oh, well. You must have one of those faces."

As I follow her back down the hall, I try to match the demanding woman I worked for only weeks ago to the kindly, vulnerable person in the bathroom. It's not just that we're treating each other differently—we're different people. Without my uniform, I'm someone who understands a hostess's travails, someone she looks to for approval. She's interested in my happiness and my headache, and she'll happily share her pills with me. All I have to do is ask.

When I return to the dining room, the waiters are clearing the plates and Gina and Roberto are in the early stages of an argument. Edie, listening intently, appears to be enjoying herself for the first time all night.

"Modigliani," sighs Roberto, crossing his arms over his chest, "is big crap."

"My Nino paint better than your Picasso!" hisses Gina.

Daniel spins around in his chair. You okay? he mouths.

I smile. Just dandy.

Before he can turn back to face his table, Sonia leans over and says something to Patti. Patti purses her lips with concentration, then her eyes dart across the room and settle on me. Her mouth is open, her expression a sickening blend of confusion, disappointment, and gossipy fascination. She's solved the mystery at last.

I duck my head and sip my wine as if I have no clue I'm the object of scrutiny. When I gather the nerve to look again, I see that Daniel has joined the conversation. His face is flushed and he smiles nervously as Sonia and Patti listen with rapt concentration. Apparently, they want to know what Henry James–like turn of events dropped a common

waitress into the middle of their exclusive shindig. He gestures more dramatically than usual as he throws out an excuse. "...works so many parties, she just forgot, and so did
I, if you can imagine that!" He laughs.

I'm amazed that Patti seems to buy this convoluted story.
"...tell her she doesn't have a *thing* to be embarrassed about
in my house."

"That's almost as funny as the way Roberto and I met,"
Sonia breaks in. "I was in a shop in Barcelona when this *bird*
flew in—"

"Oh, Daniel," Patti interrupts. "You'll have to tell Yves
about it before you go. He'll think it's hysterical. You know
the French. They have that wry sense of humor."

"I'm sure Erin and I will be laughing about it for a long
time to come," he says.

By the time I pick at a slice of coconut cream cake, decline
Daniel's offer to dance, and bid Patti and Frank a mortified
good night, it's almost one in the morning. Daniel and I
crowd into the elevator with several tipsy revelers, but
don't speak until we get outside. "Coming?" he says, opening the door of a waiting cab.

"I'll find my own way home, thanks."

"Stop being ridiculous. It's cold and late. I'm not leaving
you here."

I look down the dark, nearly deserted street. A fine mist
falls and clings to my hair. "Fine," I say, getting in and sliding toward the window.

After Daniel gives the driver his address, I lean over the
front seat. "If you could make a second stop at Sixty-third
and Columbus, that would be great."

"Why don't we go there first," Daniel adds quickly.

The driver turns on his meter. "Okay. Sixty-third and Columbus."

I sit back and close my eyes as we leave the Porters behind. After fighting the urge to cry for the past three hours, I feel strangely empty. All I want now is to go home and see my dog.

Daniel touches my knee. "Look, Erin . . ."

"Don't." My voice is cold and flat.

He takes his hand away and we sit in awkward silence until the driver pulls up to my corner. I start taking money from my bag, but Daniel stops me. "I've got this."

"I can afford it," I say sharply, pushing a ten at the driver.

"Wait for me, will you, please?" Daniel asks him.

I step onto the sidewalk and Daniel climbs out after me. "Bye," I say over my shoulder. "Thanks for a terrific time."

"Hold on." He grabs my arm, forcing me to turn around. "Listen, I know I was an asshole tonight, but I never meant to embarrass you. I had this stupid idea that you'd realize your job didn't matter to anybody and then you'd . . . feel better about it. Or something."

"You just wanted a date to a fucking party."

"That too, but . . ." He sighs. "I wanted you to see that you're the same as everyone else. I knew you'd be surprised when we got there, but I figured you'd have a great time anyway. Don't you understand my side at all?"

"You should have told me up front. I had a right to decide for myself."

"I agree. Absolutely. I wouldn't have put you in that situation if I'd thought it was going to backfire."

A cold gust flattens my dress against my legs. "You can't imagine what it's like, knowing that Patti and your ex-girlfriend look down on me," I say, my voice catching.

"They don't look down on you. They just can't relate to anything outside their sheltered little existence."

"Can *you*?"

He frowns. "Huh?"

"Growing up insulated, choosing between television and a cushy position at your father's company?"

"Now you're being unfair," he says, his tone hard.

"Was this just a little adventure for you, slumming it with me? Do you feel closer to the common man, less guilty for having so much money that you can blow it on a house you don't need?"

He stares at me. "I really care about you, Erin, but this is bullshit. Don't push me away because of one mistake."

"A mistake? Is that what you call it?"

"I brought you to my boss's house without asking you first. Christ, if your job's such a problem, why don't I talk to Andrea in the marketing department at the station? I'm sure you could work there temporarily."

"I don't need your help," I snap. The cabdriver gives his horn two quick taps. "Time for you to go."

"We're not done talking about this," Daniel insists. "I'm coming inside."

"Sorry. Your feel-good social experiment is over."

"My *what*?" He throws his arms up in frustration. "I didn't think ahead. Okay, Erin? Goddamn it— Give me something here."

The tears come as soon as I open my mouth. "You don't understand who I am, Daniel. You can't. It's not possible."

"Maybe not. But at least let me try."

"Try to what? Be the kind of person who won't trick me to prove a point? You saw Patti's face tonight. It was obvious what she thought. I told you that day in the Hamptons, but you didn't believe me. Why didn't you believe me?"

"I wanted you to feel comfortable with the people I

know, and I thought I could make it happen. I guess I botched it." He reaches for me. "Can't we put it behind us?"

"No," I say, stepping back. "I have nothing more to say."

"Come on . . ."

I wave my hand to show I'm not listening, then turn and head toward my apartment. I'm half-hoping that he'll follow me, that we'll stay up all night hashing things out and fighting our way back to where we were. But when I get to my building and look back, he's closing the cab door behind him.

chapter 23

Sleepless, eyes swollen, I drag myself to the subway the next afternoon while mentally replaying my fight with Daniel.

Was the whole thing my fault? Will he ever come in for dinner again? With each thought, I vacillate between outrage and regret, finally settling on sick numbness. I lean my head against the window and stare at the dark tunnel. No longer caring what anyone thinks, I've worn my ugly black shoes and my uniform under my coat. All I have left are a scrap of dignity and an old terrier.

I trudge through the restaurant and up the stairs, responding half-heartedly to Betsy's hello. From down the hall, I hear the hushed voices of Cato and Jane and the snorting sound of Ron laughing. I round the doorway of the changing room to see them sitting by the window. As soon as they sense my presence, they scramble to hide something under the table.

"What's going on?" I ask.

Ron claps his hand to his chest. "You almost gave me a heart attack," he says, pulling a bottle of champagne from the floor at his feet. "I thought for sure you were Gina."

Jane takes a stack of plastic cups out of her lap. "You're just in time. We almost started without you."

"What's the occasion?"

"This is more than an occasion. It's an act of God." She points to Cato, whose eyes are bright and glassy.

"Why? What happened?"

"Remember that callback I told you about?" he asks.

I instantly know what he's going to say, and conflicting feelings rush through me: excitement, sadness, envy, pride. A tiny, shameful piece of me wishes he'd been passed over, at least until I could escape with him. More than anything, I just don't want him to go. Between Daniel and Cato, I've lost a lot in the past twelve hours.

"I'm so happy for you," I say, bending down to hug him.

"Thanks. I already gave my notice."

Jane passes me a bubbling cup. "When's your last shift?" I ask.

"Next Friday. Rehearsals start the week after that. Rehearsals!" He fans his face with his hand. "Here I go again. Panic attack."

"I can't believe you're leaving," I say, sitting next to him. "This is happening way too fast."

Ron raises his cup. "To Cato Poole, a talented waiter and a great guy. We haven't always gotten along, but I'll miss fighting with you over private parties. May you burn up Broadway."

"Off-Off," Cato says.

"Close enough." We tap plastic.

While Cato tells us about his new role (which entails three costume changes and pulling an audience member onto the stage every night), I envision life without him. Left behind like widows, Jane and I are grouchy and depressed. Nights are long, hectic, and humorless. Derek, now dealing amphetamines to fund his restaurant dream, becomes our de facto leader. Gina appoints Ron "master of sidework," a move that results in an eighty-page manual and wineglasses that crack from over-polishing. Before I know it, the critics are raving about Cato's performance, Jane is graduating and moving on to a neonatal unit somewhere, and I'm consoling myself with a shift drink, a busy Thursday, and memories of a man who used to be a regular customer.

"Okay, drink up," Ron says, passing around a tin of mints. "We'd better start sidework before somebody comes looking for us."

Jane takes a swig from the champagne bottle, then stashes the evidence in a locker and follows Ron downstairs. A few seconds later, I hear the office door creak open down the hall. "Erin," Gina calls. "I need to talk to you."

"Uh-oh," I tell Cato. "I knew this was coming."

"Knew *what* was coming?"

"You're not going to believe the night I had," I say with an empty laugh. "Remember Frank and Patti Porter?" I give him a quick summary of the worst date of my life, including excruciating highlights from my argument with Daniel. "Everything was going so well. Now it's a mess."

"Come here." Cato puts his long arms around me. "You poor thing. No wonder you look like you woke up on a bench in Hunts Point."

I shake my head against his shoulder. "I wish I'd never walked into this place."

"And gone your whole life without meeting me? Bite your tongue."

"Erin!" Gina yells. "I wait for you."

Cato pulls back. "Okay, sweetie. Time to face the music."

"I hope she fires me."

"She won't. That's too quick and humane for Gina."

I drop two pens into my skirt pocket and go down the hall to the office. "Hi," I say, stepping around the half-open

door. Gina wears a white mock turtleneck and a cross necklace draped with a limp gold Jesus.

"Come and sit down," she says, waving me inside from
behind the desk. Nino is kneeling on the floor, playing with
a sauceboat, a violet crayon, and some liquor minis.

"How are you, Nino?" I ask.

"Okay," he replies, not looking up.

"He gets bored easy, like all boys," Gina says. She gives
me a just-between-us-girls smile. "You go to the party last
night with a man you meet at my restaurant?"

"Yes."

"He's a handsome one. All the women look at him when
he comes to Roulette. They turn in their seats." She pauses
and her face grows serious. "Patti Porter is my friend."

"I know."

"New York is a big city, but really is a small town. You understand what that means."

"Not exactly," I say.

Nino makes loud *vroom-vroom* sounds and starts working
his crayon between the floorboards. "We don't run around
in the same circles, you and me," Gina says. "You are a
young girl with no money. No experience."

The blood pounds in my ears. "What are you getting at,
Gina?"

"You must remember one thing: you are a waitress. Daniel
is in another world and there's no place for you."

"Are you telling me not to date him?"

"I see you wonder about it too."

That she's right inflames me even more. "I appreciate
your concern, but I can look after myself."

"Can you? When I meet Stevie, I was manager in a little
trattoria near Rome. I was working hard and I still have
nothing. But all my life my mama says I am special, so inside

my head I'm never poor. And when I marry Stevie and get rich for the first time in my life, I know the way to act. But you, you don't think the same like Daniel. Everybody sees last night you're not one of them."

I grip the edge of the chair. "Daniel wouldn't have brought me if that were true."

"It makes you feel better, okay. You believe that."

"I wasn't always a waitress," I blurt without thinking. "I had people working under me for almost five years. I have a closet full of expensive suits."

She nods slowly. "Harold says something different."

Trapped, I try another approach. "Who I see outside of Roulette is my business."

"Yes, but when you sit at a table with me and my friends, is my business too. It bothers Patti to find out the girl she once hires comes to her home and acts like somebody she is not. This is how you behave?"

"I don't have to announce where I work."

She puts on a sympathetic expression. "But when people think they meet you before and you say nothing, you look like *una fessacchiona*. An idiot."

I stare at her in shocked silence.

"I just ask you to be careful, Erin. My waiters are my children. I hate to see a man hurt you because he has a little fun."

"He wasn't just having fun," I say, willing my voice not to shake. "You don't know him the way I do."

"Ah, but I know his kind. I have lived longer than you and I can read a man. He takes you on a little ride, and when he is through he finds someone else. I see it many times. In every country is the same."

If I don't leave now, I'll say something that will guarantee I never work in another New York restaurant, even if I want to. I stand abruptly. "Are we finished here? Because I have a dining room to set up."

"Yes," she says, pulling a magazine from under a stack of papers and flipping it open to the first page. "You go on and get to work. But please don't forget what I say. I think only of your best interests."

✦

Ring Ring Ring.

I lie awake, listening to the answering machine switch on for the third time in an hour. The caller hesitates, then hangs up.

"Please leave me alone, Daniel," I mutter. After a rambling message in which he promised to kill his inner goodwill ambassador and told me again how sorry he was, he left two more messages begging me to call, no matter how late it was. But after a hellish shift at Roulette, all I can think about is escaping into sleep. It seems pointless to talk to Daniel now, and his voice, once so exciting, makes me wince.

Ring Ring Ring.

"Would you stop?" I groan, heaving myself out of bed. It's almost two in the morning and my head is reeling from lack of sleep. I get to the cold kitchen just as the machine records a quiet *click*. I stand for a minute in my nightshirt, too exhausted to shiver, staring out at the bare trees and the quiet, rain-slicked street. Then I reach behind the phone and unplug the line.

I suffer through another restless night filled with dreams starring Daniel, Gina, and half of New York society. Waking just after dawn, I sit at my computer and find a surprise e-mail from the HR director of Design Refined Furniture.

She thanks me for submitting my résumé in September, and asks me to come to their midtown office for an interview with the VP of marketing. Hopeful for the first time in months, I type out a reply, telling her to expect me the following day at eleven thirty sharp. After twelve weeks of character-building, I'm going to nail this job. I can feel it.

Unfortunately, my positive mood is soon destroyed by a shift filled with demanding guests, special orders, and cringe-worthy flashbacks to the Porters' party. The night is so busy and some of my tips so paltry, that when Daniel walks into the lounge at ten thirty, it almost seems scripted. Though he wears a crisply ironed button-down and blue slacks, his eyes are ringed with dark circles. The moment I see him, my blood pressure soars.

"Hi," he says.

I brush past him, seating chart in hand. "Hello."

"I've been trying to reach you," he says, following me to the computer.

"I know. And you've been keeping me awake in the process."

"I'm sorry about that, but . . . why haven't you returned my calls?"

"Please, Daniel," I say, eyes on the screen. "I don't have time for this right now."

His dark hair appears in my peripheral vision. "We have to talk."

"I can't. I'm working."

"When you're finished, then."

I finally glance up. "What are you doing? Are you trying to make things even harder for me?"

"Of course not."

"Well, this doesn't look good." I tilt my head toward the podium, where Steve stands with his eyebrows raised, giving me a warning glare.

"I'll just sit at the bar until you're done. But I'm not going away until we figure this out."

For a moment I feel pulled toward him, sucked in by the thought of being happy again and pretending nothing happened. Then I remember Sonia's arrogant face and Gina's words, and the humiliation and anger come back in a nauseating rush.

"Please don't bother me anymore," I say, tapping the screen forcefully. "I don't think we should see each other. I thought I made that clear."

"Listen, Erin—"

"I already have. Now, if you'd like to order something, I'll be happy to get it for you. Otherwise, good night."

If I thought sending Daniel away would make me feel better, I was dead wrong. I'm depressed and brokenhearted for the rest of the shift, and it takes every ounce of effort not to let it show. When a woman at my last table orders persimmon white tea, I flee to the waiter's station in the kitchen, grateful for a few minutes when I can look as drained as I feel. It wouldn't have worked with Daniel anyway, I tell myself. It was brief, wonderful, and doomed.

I'm digging around in the cabinet by the lowboy refrigerator when I hear shouts echoing up the stairs. "Holland, of all people!" Carl yells.

"Don't take it personally," Marty replies. "Remember when you were Mike's sous chef? He taught you a lot and you respected the guy, but you jumped at the first chance to—"

"This isn't ABOUT Mike Butler! I took you with me because I recognized your talent. I gave you a shot and I trusted you, and now you betray me to the ONE person who wants to see me fail!"

"What was I supposed to do, tell him no? I can finally be boss of my own kitchen. That means a hell of a lot more money and exposure than I'm getting here!"

Carl laughs. "On a cruise ship? Boats are where hairnet flunkies go to die."

"It's an upscale operation, Chef. Caribbean routes, big marketing budget, tricked-out kitchen. And I'm getting in on the ground floor."

" 'It's an upscale operation, Chef,' " Carl mimics in a whiny voice. " 'I'm getting in on the ground floor.' "

"Give me a break," Marty pleads. "My wife's pregnant and she hates living in the city. I need the money. Opportunities like this come along, what, once every ten years if you're lucky?"

"I haven't given you pay hikes? I haven't gone to bat for you with Steve so you could pull in more than ninety percent of the sous chefs in town? The second you walk out of here, your career is over. I'll make sure of it. And if you pull a Doug Psaltis and slander this restaurant, so help me God they'll find you in the East River."

There's a long silence, then Marty says, "Come on. We've been buddies for years. No hard feelings, all right? I told Holland I was giving you two weeks' notice."

"What? Fuck notice! You're gone tonight!"

"To*night?*" Marty says. "Are you serious?"

"Better believe it."

"Screw you, then! Send me my last paycheck." I hear a door slam.

Carl thunders up the stairs, marches past me, then stops and turns around. His breath wheezes in and out. "Who's closing?" he barks.

"Ron and I are," I answer.

"He can go, but you'll have to stay late. The Archer

Awards are tomorrow and the walk-in needs a complete overhaul."

"The walk-in?"

"That's right. Every corner of this kitchen needs to be taken apart, bleached, organized, and put back together again before morning. There's a good chance the press will be coming, and we need to be ready. Phil!"

"Yes, Chef?" Phil turns, his face heatstroke pink from scraping the grill.

"You, Patrick, and Enrique will be staying too. Call your mommies or whoever's waiting up for you and tell them you won't be home for a while. It's going to be a long night for all of us."

Any fantasy I had of being rested and prepared for my interview evaporates just after midnight, when Carl leads me to the walk-in.

"I want you to clean the floor, the walls, every shelf," he says, opening the enormous steel door. "Then alphabetize the produce."

"Alphabetize the . . . why?"

"Because I need to be able to find things, that's why. We had twenty crates of vegetables delivered this afternoon and they're all over the place."

"But . . . do I have to finish it all tonight? I've got something important to do in the morning and I was hoping to get home at a decent hour."

He rolls his eyes. "You and Marty have a lot in common, you know that? Both of you came here to grab what you could and then you complain when things get hairy. You don't see Phil and Enrique bitching, do you?" I follow his gaze to one of the stoves, which Phil has pulled away from the wall. He scrubs the floor on his hands and knees, bottle of beer beside him, radio blaring on the counter above his head. Enrique appears to be dismantling the dishwasher using nothing but a wrench and assorted Spanish obscenities.

I look at a case of celery root and let the idea of alphabetizing at thirty-four degrees sink in. I don't have to do this. I can quit and leave by the alley door, just like Marty did. But isn't that what Carl wants? To see me wither under pressure and break into tears? If I go home, I'll only lie awake agonizing over Daniel anyway. And, interview or no interview, the thought of proving Carl right is more than I can bear.

"I just need to run to the changing room to get my coat," I tell him. "It's cold in there."

"Good," he says, sounding surprised. "If you have any questions, I'll be out here working with everybody else."

Forty-five minutes later, I'm still on a search-and-destroy mission for anything that's leaking, past its expiration date, or on the wrong shelf. The door pops open and Carl's head appears through the shredded plastic curtain. He smells like at least two cocktails. "You look half-dead, Erin."

"I've never felt stronger in my life," I say, wringing out a bleach-soaked rag with numb fingers.

"Patrick got through the freezer downstairs in half the time it's taken you just to clean in here. You'd better get a move on or I'll lock up the restaurant with you in it." The door bumps shut behind him.

Contrary to what Carl promised, my first neatly organized shelf does not make me glow with pride. It just shows me how much time and energy it's going to take to finish the job. Whistling gaily, he comes in every few cases of produce to check on my progress and give me some discouraging words. "At this rate, you'll be here until Memorial Day."

"That's okay. I don't have anything planned." No matter how many veggies he brings me to file ("Found some more carrots!"), I take them without complaint, determined to outlast him, stay positive, and never let him see how close I am to stoning him to death with Mattamuskeet sweet onions.

By two in the morning I'm fighting frostbite, but outside the door, the air is balmy and there's a party in progress. Every time I chuck out empty crates, I'm treated to another glimpse—Carl chasing Kimberly through the kitchen, Enrique announcing that he's the best dishwasher in New York, Patrick sitting at the prep table, wine bottle in hand, declaring his love for Carl and Carl's food. "Let's go get a tattoo right now, all of us," he slurs. "I mean it. 'Roulette' in big letters, right on my ass."

There's a toast to black truffles, to François Vatel and Bernard Loiseau, and to Carl himself for fearlessly leading cuisine away from the ordinary stove and toward the centrifuge and the industrial heat gun. They wish Marty a permanently seasick journey on the high seas, culminating in death by shark bite. Eventually they drop their bottles into the recycling bin and their voices die away, leaving the kitchen unnaturally silent.

I push open the door and step into what feels like a floodlit kiln. There's a chef's jacket on the floor and the radio is now playing static, giving the room a desolate, postapocalyptic vibe.

"Well, if it isn't the girl who pissed on my heart," Phil says, making me jump. He's leaning against the prep table, one arm crossed over his white-jacketed chest, a joint in his hand. "Want some? It's Carl's. He always styles us when we work late."

"No, thanks."

"You should. Might make you nicer."

"Come on. You're not still mad at me."

Frowning, he rubs his chin with his thumb. "You mean,

because you dumped me in public? Because you're banging that Daniel guy?"

"Why do you care who I go out with?"

He takes a drag, holds in the smoke, then lets it curl out of his nose. "Carl's got a thing about being professional, remember? It's bad enough screwing me, but screwing a guest? He's going to freak when I tell him."

"Go ahead. I'm sure he'd like to know what we did in the basement during service."

Phil's eyes narrow when he realizes he's been cornered. "You think you can just show up and change all the rules around? You didn't belong here to begin with. We even took bets to see how long you'd last."

"Oh, really? Who won?"

He smirks. "Nobody. We never thought you'd make it past the first week."

chapter 24

Carl inspects the walk-in from floor to ceiling before finally letting me go, twelve and a half hours after I punched in. "Tomorrow you can clean out the reach-in," he says, unlocking the front door and holding it open. "There's chicken blood in there that goes back weeks."

I fall asleep in the cab on the way home, snatching a few minutes of much-needed rest before preparing for my interview. Once I get to my apartment, I plow through dozens of Internet hits and articles about Design Refined Furniture before nodding off at my desk around dawn. I wake with my cheek on my mouse pad and the sun in my face, furious at Carl for keeping me up all night.

Dizzy from lack of sleep, I turn on loud music, wedge a mug of French roast next to the shampoo bottle, and take a long shower. Eye shadow, lipstick, and several slaps to the cheeks make me appear brighter but not necessarily conscious. After trying on and rejecting four different outfits, I settle on gray wool pants and heels, toss back a nutritious breakfast of smoked almonds and Camembert, and grab my coat.

Look out, world.

I take a cab to East Fifty-seventh Street and ride a paneled elevator up to the offices of Design Refined. As I approach the thirty-first floor, I smooth my French twist and anxiously rehearse Cato's serving tips. "Get into character and see what happens. Act with enough authority and they won't even notice little mistakes."

I enter the sparsely decorated, cream-toned lobby and give my name to the receptionist. Sitting on a boxy white leather couch with no legs, I begin to get a feel for the product. Hip. Very hip. And very uncomfortable. A minute later, a small, lively man with blue eyes and prematurely graying hair walks into the room. "Hello," he says, forcefully shaking my hand. "I'm Gary. Let's go have a talk and get to know each other."

He leads me to a conference room with floor-to-ceiling windows and a stunning view of midtown. After introducing me to Robin, his dimpled, big-boned assistant, we sit at a gray glass table. "Would you like some water?" he asks.

"Yes, please."

He fills a goblet and hands it to me.

"Thank you." There's a moment of silence as he flips through my résumé. Robin smiles at me. I smile back. Gary takes off his glasses and sets them on top of my trumped-up work history.

"So, Erin," he says.

I clear my throat. "Yes, Gary?"

"Tell us a little about yourself."

"Well, I was born on Long Island . . ." I hear myself talking, rattling on about my years in the industry, my lifelong interest in building brands, and how I've blazed new trails at every job I've held. I sound a little manic. A little, well, not together.

"So, most of your work was pretty close to home," Gary says. "Local corporate accounts."

"Right." I nod, wondering if I should have said, "Not exactly," and detailed our one national account even though it was a condom company and I knew nothing about it. Christ, don't let me blow it this early.

"But you have an interest in the international furniture trade?"

"Absolutely. Very much so."

Gary pours more water into my empty glass. "We're looking for a person with energy and original ideas, a self-starter with solid experience who can carve out their own niche. That's why your résumé intrigues us."

I lift the glass to my lips and take a sip.

"How did your previous position prepare you for Design Refined?" Robin asks.

"Well," I say with the confidence that comes from having memorized my answer over crates of designer lettuce. "For the past five years I've helped to develop creative products for a young, upwardly mobile market." Imagining myself tableside, I go on to sell Erin Edwards like *le poisson du jour,* leaving out the bad points (been around for a while, nobody else wants me) and talking up the good (cheap, only one left). After a draining half-hour question-and-answer session, Robin swivels on her black suede cube and says, "Well, you've certainly done your research. It shows."

"Very impressive," Gary agrees. "When would you be available to start?"

"This afternoon, if you're ready for me." We all laugh.

They're going to offer me the job, I think. I can't wait to walk into Roulette this afternoon and break the news to anyone who will listen.

"I'm curious," Gary says, sketching a 3-D box along the edge of his legal pad. "How have you been keeping yourself busy since you left Hillerton-Jones last spring?"

I look at his kind, interested face, and suddenly, three months of high-stress service with a smile are nothing to be ashamed of. "I've been waiting tables."

"Oh? Where?"

"Roulette, on Madison Avenue."

"I see."

The room goes quiet and the atmosphere turns tense. Robin shuffles her papers. "And what made you decide to work in a restaurant?"

"To be honest, I had a little trouble finding the right marketing position and I had expenses to meet, so . . ." I trail off. Why the hell did I tell the truth? I should have said I was taking a class, traveling, *anything* but waiting tables.

"So, you've been out of the marketing world for nearly a year now, if we include your period of unemployment," Gary says. "That's a lifetime in this industry."

"Yes," Robin agrees. "I don't see how service work is relevant to the position we're trying to fill."

Shit. Now what? I can't let this job slip away because of one blunder. "Actually, it's very relevant," I say, raising my chin.

"Really?" Gary replies. "How?"

"Well . . ."

They both lean forward, waiting for my response. My heart bangs against my rib cage. "Uh, Design Refined isn't that different from a restaurant, if you think about it."

Getting only blank stares, I plow forward, hardly knowing what I'll say until it comes out of my mouth. "Whether you sell high-end furniture or Ossetra caviar, you have to understand your target audience. I've learned more about customers during three months of waiting tables than I did in five years of marketing. When guests sit down, I immediately have to find out who they are and what they want. It's like"—I sweep my hand through the air—"creating a new marketing campaign ten times every night."

Gary rubs the back of his neck. "I'm not sure I follow."

Desperate for time to think, I take another swallow of water. "As in any business, it's all about relationships. I don't write slogans for faceless consumers anymore. I know their names, what they wear, and what they talk about with their spouses. If they don't like what they ordered, I can't use market research and focus groups to find out what went wrong. I have to know them well enough to promote another product on the spot."

"Then aren't you more of a salesperson than a marketer?" Robin asks, crossing her legs.

"I'm both," I say proudly. My voice gets clearer and more confident as I realize that I actually believe what I'm saying. "So I have a perspective most of your applicants won't have. More than anything, I'm part of a team. We share knowledge about guests, food, wine . . . and we help each other. I couldn't succeed without the support of other waiters, who are as much a part of my success as I am. I'll bring that kind of devotion to teamwork to your company if you offer me the chance."

After a long silence, Gary speaks up. "Interesting, Erin. You've certainly given us something to think about."

"We'll be in touch," Robin says. "Lunchtime, right?" She glances at her thin silver watch and exchanges a look with Gary, who gets to his feet and shakes my hand.

"It's been great talking with you," he says, leading me to the door. "We have several more applicants to talk to, but we'll call you as soon as we make a decision."

What happened in there?

Leaning against the wall of the empty elevator, I close my eyes and put my hands over my face. If I weren't in a public place, I'd cry. I won't be hearing from Gary and Robin again, that's for sure. No matter how hard I tried to save the interview, it was over the second those two words—waiting tables—left my mouth.

Why does their reaction surprise me? Until a few minutes ago, I looked at restaurant work exactly the way they did—as an embarrassing blemish on an otherwise impressive résumé, a waste of time that couldn't possibly teach me anything valuable. Only when I had to defend it did I realize how wrong I was.

It's as much your hang-up as it is theirs. Daniel's words come back to me as the doors open and I step into the marble lobby. Hurt and angry as I still am, I have to admit that he had a point. Wasn't I the one who used to sit in nice restaurants, just a little smug with my career ambitions and my platinum card? I judged everybody I met by where they worked, went to college, and went out at night, and when it was time for me to stand on the other side of the table, I turned the same harsh eye on myself.

I walk through the revolving doors and onto the crowded street, but instead of hailing a cab, I pull my cell phone from my bag and dial. "Daniel Fratelli, please," I say when a receptionist answers. "This is Erin Edwards calling."

"Just a moment."

Nervously pacing, I pretend to window-shop while I wait. Maybe I should have talked to him last night and at least heard what he had to say. Maybe he really *is* sorry, maybe now we'll understand each other and—

"Ms. Edwards?" The receptionist comes back on the line.

"Yes?"

"I'm sorry, but Mr. Fratelli is in a meeting. Would you like to leave a message?"

I hesitate. "Actually, do you have any idea when he'll be free?"

"I'm sorry, I don't. He's tied up most of the afternoon and then he's going out of town for the weekend."

"I see." Is that it? Has he given up on me already? "Okay. Well, thanks. I'll just . . . try again some other time."

◆

"They gave the statue to the wrong person!" Gina wails the next day.

"I know," Alain says soothingly. "It's unfair. They're fools, these silly judges. They have no taste."

I sneak into the lounge, hoping to set tables while avoiding any discussion of the Peter Archer Awards. After the week I've had, another one of Gina's dramas is more than I can take.

"I feel like I'm going to fall down," she says, holding out her empty glass. "Give me more Campari."

"Are you sure?" Alain says. "It's only four o'clock."

"So? You French people drink like you go to the electric chair."

"Okay, but we're good at it."

"Erin!" Gina calls, spotting me. "There's been a tragedy. Carl lost last night. All of New York is crying."

"I'm sorry to hear that," I say, barely able to contain my glee. "So, who was the winner? Rick Holland?"

Alain sets Gina's drink on a cocktail napkin and she belts back half of it. "Some dumb woman who doesn't cook her food. No meat, no nothing. Completely raw. I never see such ugliness. Her husband is rich, so she buys a little hobby and takes awards from people who need them."

"He'll probably be nominated again next year."

"Next year?" Gina scoffs. "I'll be an old woman then. Too

old to care." She finishes her drink, checks her face in the mirror behind the bar, then yanks her quilted Chanel bag off the stool. "I'm going to go buy something. You have to be manager tonight, Alain. I can't face it."

Service has just begun when Alain gestures me over to the bar, his characteristic smile absent. "Steve called down from the office. He wants to see you."

"Did he say why?"

"No, but I can hear he's in a bad mood."

"The award thing?"

"Not only that. Gina's mother is moving to America."

"To *stay*? Oh, God."

He nods. "I know. Not good for any of us. They think I can manage the dining room from behind the bar because Gina is unhappy? It makes no sense."

Though Carl put on a cocky smile during the staff meeting and called the awards "rigged bullshit that don't affect me or this restaurant one iota," there's no telling how Steve's taking it. I head upstairs and knock softly on the office door. "Come in," Steve calls. He sits at the desk with a beer and the *Times*.

"Alain said you wanted to see me?"

"Yes. I'd like to get some dinner."

"Oh! All right."

"What are the specials tonight?"

Christ, I have four tables downstairs. "Well, we have an appetizer of flourless dumplings with root vegetable gel—"

He glances around the room as if he isn't the least bit interested. "Forget the bells and whistles. I don't want to think that hard right now. Just bring me a mesclun salad and the rabbit loin, extra crispy." He looks down at his newspaper.

"Here?"

His head snaps up. "What?"

"Should I bring it to you here?"

"I suppose you could bring it to the wine cellar, but that wouldn't do me much good, would it?"

"No, I suppose not." I turn to go.

"I need a place setting," Steve says from behind me. "And another Moretti, immediately."

I put in the order, open wine for a considerably more appreciative customer, then run back upstairs with Steve's place setting, salad, and beer. I rap on the office door, feeling like a beleaguered room service drone. "Yurgh," Steve grunts.

I walk in and lay down the plate between his flatware and napkin. "Pepper?" I ask, raising the stainless steel mill over his head.

He gives me an annoyed smile. "You've waited on me three times now. When have I asked for pepper?"

I envision my neglected guests rioting from lack of food while Steve cross-examines me. "To be honest, I can't remember. I wait on a lot of people."

He leans forward and jabs at the salad with his fork. "It's your job to remember my preferences," he says through a mouthful of leaves. "Now please bring me a glass of Duckhorn cabernet. Is Dr. Benitz here yet?"

"He and his wife are sitting in Ron's section."

"Have Ron tell him I won't be in until later. I'm not going to spend all night jawing with guests about this awards nonsense."

"Got it." I pivot on my heel and run down to the kitchen.

"Omar already cleared table eight and you haven't fired the second course!" Carl shouts when he sees me. "It's a good thing you weren't this brain-dead in the walk-in the other night or you'd be chilling on a shelf with the lamb kidneys. Where the hell have you been?"

"Waiting on Steve upstairs."

"Where's Gina?"

"Shopping."

"Who's watching the dining room?"

"Alain. Kimberly is working the door."

He yanks down a pan from the rack overhead. "That's nice. Gina takes an Italian holiday and turns everything over to the bartender and a woman who thinks foie gras grows on trees." He points his skillet at me. "You'd better get up to speed. I don't want the guests suffering while you take breaks on the stairs."

"I'm doing everything I can."

"Well, it's not enough. You need to start being in two places at once."

"What?"

"You can't fire the second course by arguing with me," he says, turning his back. "If I don't get a ticket in thirty seconds, I'll give the table to Ron."

As I speed-type at the computer in the lounge, I see Jane heading toward me, her eyes wide. "I hate to do this, Erin. I'm sure you're looking forward to getting off early for once, and God knows, you deserve it."

"What's going on?"

"I got a voice mail from Julian and—"

"You need me to close for you tonight."

"How could you tell?"

I smile. "Just a sense."

"He's been dropping hints all week. He asked me to meet him at the bar where we had our first drink together. I think he might be getting ready to propose again, and I *can't* screw it up this time."

Not wanting to blow the wedding of the century, I give in. "Say no more. But you'd better send me an invitation."

"Of course," she says, hugging me.

"Let me know what happened, okay? I'll be dying of curiosity."

"You'll be the first person I call," she says. "After my mother!"

Gina, wiped out from a Fifth Avenue bender, slumps on the office chair usually reserved for errant employees. I step around a mountain of colorful bags and deliver the rabbit, roasted past recognition and garnished with rosemary, to Steve.

"May I bring you something, Gina?" I ask.

She puts a hand to her forehead. "Hot water and lemon. I can't eat. I just find out Evelyn Harker's review comes out Thursday."

Steve rolls his eyes. "You're going to starve until then? What good's that going to do?"

"How can I think about food?" she asks, dropping her hand. "Carl's award was robbed by that woman, the blond half-wit with the lousy restaurant in the country! The review is my only hope. If is not good, I don't ever eat again. I lose my joy for living."

"Aw, cripes," Steve says, wincing. "Here we go."

"To you, is not so important. To me, a bad review is like shit from God."

"I should send Harker a bill for all that junk you just bought." Steve looks at me. "Bring her a plain steak."

"I'm not hungry," Gina says from the corner.

"Rare," Steve says. "With truffled mashed potatoes, if we still have anything that simple lying around."

"You like peasant food, move to Yugoslavia," Gina says.

"Carl doesn't cook for pig farmers. His menu is for smart people."

"If wanting to eat something I recognize makes me stupid, so be it," Steve says. "You're wasting away. You've got to have more than whipped oxygen and sea urchin consommé."

"You Americans eat too much."

"Go get her steak, Erin. *Now.*"

Lord help Gina's mother if this is how things are at home. I hardly have time to drop off two cocktail orders before the controversial filet mignon is ready. I place hot water, lemon, and the steak on a tray and bring it to the office. Gina sits on the edge of her chair, wearing new suede pumps and cutting off price tags with Nino's child-size scissors.

"Take this away, please," Steve says, pointing to his empty plate.

Gina spies the steak and potatoes and cries, "Why is everybody trying to make me eat?"

"Maybe if you did, your mood would improve," Steve says. "You've been a bitch since your mother showed up."

"Is not her fault. She is wonderful and makes Nino happy."

Steve laughs. "He's afraid of her."

"He is not! He is all the time following her around!"

Steve swallows and sets down his empty wineglass. "At least you got her saying hello in English. It's a miracle she talks at all, she's so damn cranky."

"She's seventy years old! What do you want?"

"Some peace."

"Uh, where shall I put this?" I ask.

Steve sweeps an armful of tissue paper and empty bags off the desk and onto the floor. "Here," he says, tapping the blotter. "And bring the bottle of Duckhorn with you on your next trip."

As I transfer the hot water and lemon to the desk, a tiny droplet falls from the edge of the saucer onto the toe of Gina's pump. She sucks in a breath. "My shoe! Do something! Hurry up!"

I hesitate, then set down the tray and pull an extra napkin from my skirt pocket.

"I love these more than anybody," Gina says, kicking out a foot. "If there is a spot, I'll die." I bend down and carefully dab at the suede.

She cocks her head and appraises the damage. "Maybe it will be okay. I have to see. I let you know."

"Would you care for anything else?" I ask through gritted teeth.

"Nope," Steve answers.

"A crème brulée," Gina says. "Nice and hard on top."

I fetch the dessert and race back to the dining room just in time to see a six-top sitting down in my section. So far, trying to be in two places at once isn't working out too well.

"We thought you weren't coming back," snaps a woman in a strapless dress when I bring her martini. "For what you charge, we should have our own waiter."

"I'm terribly sorry. I'll do everything I can to speed things up for you." I watch as Omar fills the six-top's water glasses, fostering the illusion that someone is taking care of them. That buys me a few more minutes during which I have to type in two orders, explain the desserts to a Carl-obsessed group of amateur cooks, and learn to fly so I can get an aerial view of my tables.

By the time I wind-sprint to and from the computer, a corner deuce is waving for the check and the six-top, no longer fooled by full water glasses and a basket of fennel seed brioche, is peering around with craned necks. "They've been sitting forever!" Kimberly whispers as she walks by with an armful of menus.

Answering would take precious seconds I can't spare. I'm rushing toward my neglected party at top speed, when Alain motions to me from the bar, which is wall-to-wall collagen and highlighted hair. "The boss wants you," he says, hanging up the house phone.

"Right now?"

"He says he just needs you for a minute."

"Goddamn it." Cato, Ron, and Jane are too swamped to save me, and Derek wouldn't give me the Heimlich unless we'd agreed on a price in advance. Ignoring my six-top's frantic gesturing, I duck into the kitchen and fast-fast my way up the stairs. "You called?" I pant, leaning into the office.

Gina, wearing a completely different outfit than the fuchsia satin pantsuit she had on ten minutes ago, says, "I need help."

No kidding. "With what?"

Steve twirls a toothpick in his mouth and points to the floor. "Carry these bags out to the car, please."

"Now?"

"Of course now."

"But I have a busy section and a six-top waiting."

"Why didn't you tell that to Alain?"

"I didn't have time."

He rolls his eyes. "Well, you're here now, so you might as well help my wife on your way down."

Gina picks up a shoebox while I loop a dozen giant bag handles over my arms. "Don't forget this," Steve says, tossing Gina's discarded pantsuit over my shoulder.

The smell of Poison wafts around me as I stagger downstairs. The door to the alleyway is open and Steve's black Hummer hulks in the darkness. "Put them on the passenger seat," Gina says, lighting a cigarette.

I maneuver my way around the back and wait for her to open the door for me. Instead, she climbs inside, starts the engine, and turns on the radio full blast. "What?" she yells, finally noticing me through a haze of smoke. "It's open!"

As I hook the door handle with my free pinkie, the outfit over my shoulder slips. I twist to catch it on my arm, but it's too late. Fuchsia satin slithers to the dirty, ice-crusted pavement.

"No!" she screams from inside the car. Only now does she open the door for me, hitting me squarely in the hip. "My la Renta! Pick it up!"

I heave the bags onto the sofa-sized passenger seat and snatch the pantsuit off the asphalt. "No harm done," I say, laying it gingerly over the back of the seat.

"You hope!" She reaches over, slams the door shut, and peels out of the alley with a screech.

I run back to the dining room, smile and apology ready, but my six-top is gone. The only things left are crumpled napkins and crooked chairs. "Shit!" I whisper.

The kitchen doors swing open behind me and Steve comes striding out. He looks at the suspiciously empty table, then at me. "What happened here?"

"I don't know. I guess . . . they left."

"They *left*?"

"I was helping Gina out to the car and . . ."

"And what?"

"By the time I got back they were gone."

"You're blaming this on my wife?" Steve says, narrowing his eyes.

"I couldn't carry shopping bags and take care of my tables at the same time."

"You've always been slow," he snaps. "Slow and

argumentative. Do you have any idea how much money you just cost me?"

The people who need their own waiter glare at me from across the room. "I'm not a valet, Steve. I said I was busy, but you—"

Steve holds up a finger. "Go do your job. I want to see you in the office before you leave tonight."

chapter 25

When Carl sends Chen looking for me, I know I'm in trouble.

"What does he want?" I ask, eyes on the computer screen. My section is finally clearing out and the last thing I need is another ridiculous request.

Chen shrugs and says cryptically, "What no one tells me I don't need to know."

"Oh. Tell him I'll be right there, then. Thanks."

Carl gestures me over to the heat lamps as soon as I enter the kitchen. "What's this about you closing? I thought it was Jane's turn."

"We switched because she has something to do."

"Great," he mutters. "Isn't that beautiful. All right, tell Omar to set table fifteen. A couple of producers from Edible Television just called. We'll be having the five-course tasting menu and I'll need you to stick around."

We? "I'm sorry, how many people again?"

"Three! Two producers and myself."

The night that couldn't get any worse just did. "How long do you think I'll be here?"

"No idea, and don't ask any more questions or you'll be begging Marty for a job in his floating cafeteria. Maybe you should worry less about your beauty sleep and more about the tip you'll get if you don't screw this up royally. Ask Phil for details about the tasting menu and make sure table fifteen is set properly. Tell Geoffrey to stay too. Oh, and Luis told me about your six-top. If you drive away any more business from my restaurant, I'll personally call that jackass Harold to come pick you up."

I look over at Luis, who is helping Enrique stack ramekins on the metal shelves under the pickup window. Our eyes meet, but his face stays placid and blank. He knows who signs his checks and sends him home with free end pieces of Kobe beef, and it isn't Carl's least favorite waitress.

I'm fresh out of reasons to smile when the front door opens five minutes before midnight. At the sound of customers in the foyer, Steve straightens from his usual slump and makes the long journey across the lounge. It can't be the producers arriving. There are way too many voices.

A man with wavy salt-and-pepper hair leads a crowd of at least ten up to the podium.

"Evening!" Steve says, looking slightly confused.

"Hello, I'm Ira Bloom from Edible Television," the man answers. "I realize Carl wasn't expecting such a horde, but a bunch of us were working late, and before I knew it, I was heading uptown with two of our lawyers and half the marketing department. Is that all right?"

I feel the blood drain from my face.

"That's fine, Mr. Bloom," Steve says. Behind his frosty smile, he seems to be calculating how many thousands of dollars this little comp is going to cost him, and how it might pay off in publicity. "If you wouldn't mind having a seat in the lounge, we'll set a larger table for you."

"Great. Thanks for being so accommodating."

Omar, having read the situation from across the room, is

already pulling two long tables together. "Twelve, right?" he asks me.

"Right. I'll be back in a minute to help."

I find a freshened-up Carl pacing the length of the kitchen. A large rosemary branch sprouts stiffly from his button-hole, giving him a look that's two parts hick, one part Greek myth. He's nervous—I can tell by the rash spreading over his neck. "Are they here yet?" he demands, smoothing his hair back from his forehead.

"They sure are."

He pounces on the ominous tone in my voice. "What does that mean?"

"It means there are twelve of them."

"*Twelve?* For dinner?"

"It looks that way."

"But you can't—it'll never—" He stomps through the kitchen, yanks open the walk-in door, and steps inside. As soon as the door closes behind him, I hear a muted "FUCK!"

He emerges a few seconds later and immediately shouts, "Start the amuse bouche!" to the cooks, who scatter across the kitchen like rats. Broad chest heaving, he moves close to me. "This entire night depends on you. You realize that."

I can't possibly bluff my way through, so why try? "I don't have much experience with large parties, Carl. None, actually. Steve never gives me more than six people at once."

"Believe me, I'm not expecting great things from you, especially after what happened earlier. Just try not to make a complete ass of yourself out there. And later, after everyone's gone, we're going to talk about your future at this restaurant."

By the time I wish Carl dead ten times over and return to the dining room, everyone is taking their seats. How the hell am

I going to wait on a group this size? I have trouble with a polite five-top, let alone a boisterous table of twelve.

"I hope it's not too late to talk business," Ira is saying as Steve lays down menus. "We're all very excited about the concept for Carl's show. I'd like to wrap up the final details tonight if we can."

Carl's show. God save us, the man is trying to inflict himself on the rest of the nation. And he wants me to help him do it.

"Stay until dawn if you like," Steve tells Ira, then guffaws while giving me a glare that says, "Hurry up and get these people some alcohol so they're easier to snow."

It takes me several round-trips to the bar to deliver the equivalent of four quarts of vodka to various producers and chicly-dressed marketers. I duck into the wait station and, using Cato's "octopus" method, draw my largest seating chart to date. Though it looks disturbingly like a map of Brooklyn, it's better than relying on my exhausted memory. If only it could describe the tasting menu for me.

I stand beside Ira's chair, every episode of public speaking (from chairing meetings to making a toast at my mother's fiftieth-birthday dinner) rushing back with disturbing clarity. When Cato said, "Large parties are more fun," he was lying.

Ira turns to me with an asymmetrical face that appears to have been assembled out of spare parts. "I know that look," he says, grinning. "You're about to pitch a product, and a very impressive one at that."

I'm so nervous that I actually giggle. Ira kindly instructs his chattering tablemates to be quiet. "Listen up, ladies and gents, or we'll never eat."

With twelve pairs of candlelit eyes on me, I begin describing the evening's—make that the morning's—menu in vivid detail just as Carl enters the room. I expect to lose concentration and stumble, but a combination of knowledge, practice, and nothing left to lose has resulted in a courage I didn't realize I had. I'm amazed to hear myself continue without stuttering or transposing words as Carl nods at the group and takes his chair next to Ira. I skim smoothly through the main courses, round out my recitation with a preview of the desserts, then beam warmly at Carl. "It looks like you're the only one without a cocktail," I say, as if he were a guest at my own dinner party. "What can I bring you?"

He stares at me silently for a second. "Bombay on the rocks. Please."

"Let's tape the show at six A.M.," Carl blusters as Omar and Geoffrey (breaking a rare sweat) help me carry the first course to the table. "I have a full schedule here at the restaurant, but I've always liked pushing myself to the limit."

Ira takes a sip of his Barolo. "Unfortunately, the studio doesn't open until eight, and that slot is booked for Bobby Flay."

"Oh, I understand," Carl says too quickly. "No problem. As long as I don't have to share a dressing room with Rick Holland!" He bursts into laughter.

Ira eyes Carl over his fork. "I've heard there's a little friendly competition between you and Rick. Any truth to the rumors?"

"No, no, not at all. Are you kidding? We've been friends forever. His food knocks me out."

"That's good, because we're hoping to have him as a guest on one of the episodes. Kind of a co-chef, as it were."

Carl forces a smile. "Absolutely. I'm all for it."

"Of course we'll want your input on this, but I'm leaning toward a show with a soundtrack and lots of close-ups, very *Nigella* but with a macho edge."

"Works for me."

"We're looking at several chefs, but right now, you're first on our list. Whoever we choose has to connect with our viewers, whether you're heading up your own show, judging an episode of Cook Wars, or traveling around Asia eating raw horsemeat and drinking schnapps. Build an audience and we'll give you a lot of freedom."

When I lean over to refill Ira's wineglass, Carl gives me a quick, meaningful glance. This would not be a good time for me to detail his daily schedule of abuses and tirades. "There's a lot of theater in this business," he says, his teeth blue from Barolo. "A lot of grandstanding and self-promotion. But for me, the food comes first."

"And so does your staff, from what I've seen." Ira winks at me as I start collecting empty martini glasses. "Almost one in the morning and still smiling. How do you do it?"

I take a few seconds to decide which response would startle Carl the most. "Smiling is easy when you're serving food of this caliber. Are you enjoying the five foams?"

"Is that what you call them? Yes, they're out of this world," Ira says, though he's hardly touched the pale dollops of lather (or as Jane would say, "pond scum") that sit in a circle on his plate. A sheen of sweat rims his hairline. "Whew! Are those chile peppers I'm tasting?"

Carl's expression switches from blatant pride to concern in an instant. "Bird's-eye chiles grown especially for me in a little mountain village in Thailand," he says, as if this alone will convince Ira he likes it. "I grind the skin and then aerate it with a special titanium tool developed at Los Alamos. I like to put it between the garlic and kelp foams to wake up the palate."

Ira reaches for his water glass. "Oh, it's awake, all right! Terrific flavor, though. Really unusual."

"It's very popular with our guests," I lie, tossing the

clearly uncomfortable Carl a life raft. "People are surprised by it at first, but they end up requesting double portions on their next visit."

"Is that right?" Ira says.

"Ten years ago, putting a raw course on a menu was a risk," Carl says. "Now it's commonplace. Same with foams. Pretty soon you'll be able to walk into a deli and ask for some roasted onion froth."

"I'm not sure I see any construction workers going for that," Ira says, "but I suppose you never know."

As I leave the table with my loaded tray, I hear Carl excuse himself. He catches up with me and steers me toward the wait station by my shoulder blade. "Message for Phil," he hisses. "Get your head out of your ass."

"In those exact words?"

"That presentation was a disaster. There was twice as much foam as there should have been and the plate was too warm. The stuff was spreading all over the place. Tell him this isn't the time to fold. If he wants a shot at replacing Marty, he'd better focus. He's got Lorenzo and José to help him, so there's no excuse for bullshit work."

"But I did it the way I always do!" Phil cries a minute later. "It's not my fault the guy doesn't like it!"

"Sorry. I'm just the messenger here."

Lorenzo and José scramble around in a panic, their culinary futures hanging in the balance. "What's going on with that pear relish?" Phil yelps.

"Don't ask me," Lorenzo says. "I thought José was taking care of it."

José frantically checks his station, then opens his mouth wide and screams silently. "My mistake," he says, managing to calm himself. "I forgot to make it. Erin, you'll have to wait on the next course."

Not what I wanted to hear. "How long?"

"Ten minutes?"

"Okay." Just as I reach the kitchen doors, I hatch an idea that could make the upcoming delay less noticeable for our most important guest. This is what Cato would call turning a screwup into a twenty-five-percent tip. "Hey, Lorenzo, do you have any of those fruit foams on hand? One of the producers wants to try them. And get out Carl's cookbook. We're going to need another amuse bouche."

Steve sits between two of Edible Television's attorneys, slathering Betsy's warm walnut oil bread with butter and telling lawyer jokes. "Why does California have the most lawyers, and New Jersey the most toxic waste dumps? Because New Jersey got to choose!" He laughs loudly. Surprisingly, everybody joins in.

At the other end of the table, Carl's foot jerks back and forth as he regales Ira with tales of dedicated waitstaff, reliable vendors, and committed cooks. "We're like family. We count on each other."

"That's a refreshing attitude," Ira says. "I don't mean to sound jaded, but I've seen too many chefs mow down anyone in their path to get from point A to point B."

"Excuse me," I say, laying a chilled plate containing three peaks of pastel fluff in front of Ira. "I thought you might like to sample a few more interesting tastes. Nothing spicy here—just tart and lively." I point to each. "Macintosh apple, heirloom tomato, and lemon with lavender sugar."

"What a nice idea," Ira says, nodding. "That's very kind of you."

Carl gapes at me as if I were wearing antlers. As he swirls the wine slowly in his glass, I can see him wondering when I transformed from inept to invaluable. I wish I could pinpoint the moment myself, but I don't remember exactly when it happened. I only know that I feel competent, relaxed, even comfortable. Having been driven to the brink of giving up, I've finally found my footing.

Ira takes his first spoonful of lemon foam and his eyes roll back in his head. "Div*ine*."

By the time I bring out miniature parsnip and honey soup shots with sweet potato crisps, Carl seems to be wondering how he ever made it this far without me. I glide back to the kitchen, as calm and drained as if I'd just finished a marathon. It took three months, a botched interview, a lost six-top, and a table of twelve for me to realize that Steve, Carl, and Harold aren't doing me a favor anymore. Which is exactly why, after Ira and the others leave tonight, I'm going to say what I've wanted to say for a long time.

It's nearly three in the morning when the party finally breaks up. "Good-bye, Erin, thank you," Ira says, slipping me two hundred-dollar bills.

"It's been a pleasure," I tell him. "Please visit us again soon."

Steve pumps his hand and pushes one of Carl's cookbooks on him. "Hot off the presses," he says. "Doesn't come out for a week, but it's already in the top fifty on Amazon. It's going to be a blockbuster."

"My wife's been begging me for a copy. I only hope she starts with something simple!"

Carl walks Ira to the foyer, chattering all the way. "... glad I got to meet everybody ... sure we'll have a mutually beneficial relationship ... at the lawyer's office on Tuesday ... Good night!"

As Steve clomps toward the kitchen, Omar and I undertake the monumental task of clearing dishes.

"Erin?" Carl calls from the lounge. He waves me over to a

little round table, where he slouches with a snifter of cognac. "Sit down," he says.

As soon as I do, my legs start to tingle. I've never been so happy to be off my feet. Carl waits a few seconds before speaking. "I witnessed something incredible tonight."

Oh, no, he's going to wax poetic about his own food. "Really?"

He looks at me intently. "I saw another side of Erin."

"You what?"

"I'd almost given up on you," he says, breaking into a tipsy smile. "And then all of a sudden, here's this hot-shot who helps me seal the deal. You were inconspicuous, knowledgeable, and your instincts were right on. You charmed Ira, covered the kitchen's mistakes, and . . . Oh— bringing out the soup shots from my cookbook was first-class."

He laughs, and I shift uncomfortably. I'd have given anything to hear these words a few weeks ago, but now I'm just embarrassed. Embarrassed and completely unmoved.

"Thank Lorenzo," I say. "He's the one who made them."

"But it was your idea, wasn't it?"

"I suppose so."

"You know, I love it when my employees surprise me. It means I can coax something exceptional from even the most average person."

I frown. "Average?"

Carl reaches across the table and puts a warm, damp hand over mine. "Now you understand why I've been so hard on you."

"Actually, I'm not sure I do."

"Look at you, Erin. You're still screwing up, but now you're *inspired*," he says, holding up a fist. "A few more months and you'll be unstoppable."

Did he really just say that?

"I saw it in you the first day, when you walked into my kitchen late and tried to bullshit your way through. You had guts and heart and that's the only reason I let you stay. If I hadn't kicked your ass and pushed you to the limit, you wouldn't be where you are right now."

I want to argue and tell him I succeeded in spite of him, not because of him. But I can't. Because he's right.

"I won't be where I am for long," I say.

"Of course you won't, because your career is just beginning. You took a while to blossom, but now it's time I asked more of you. Much more."

I give Omar an apologetic smile as he carries a rack of clean stemware to the bar. He shakes his head—he knows I'm trapped. "I don't have anything more to give, frankly."

"Oh, yes, you do. I'm convinced of it. We have a lot of interesting times ahead of us. The first thing I'm going to do is talk to Steve about increasing the size of your parties."

I pull my hand away and stand up. "I should help Omar. It's late."

"Or early, depending on how you look at it. Alain! Grab a glass and join me. I can't celebrate by myself."

Omar and I roll up the tablecloths, put the chairs on the tables, and turn out the lights in the dining room. "See you," he says, heading toward the back door of the kitchen.

"Thanks for all your help," I call after him.

Now it's time for that long-awaited chat with Steve. I walk upstairs, feeling every minute of the last three months in my back. Taking out my hair clip, I stop at the open door of the office. "Steve?"

"Yup." He sits with his boots up on the desk, kingpin-style, tallying the night's winnings on the adding machine.

"You asked to see me?"

"Uh-huh. My wife called. It seems you're paying for some shoe repair and dry cleaning. Also, you owe me eleven hundred and forty dollars for that table you lost. I looked up the check average of every six-top over the past year and that's the figure I got. Those people were bankers from Chicago, people with pull."

"If you'd allowed me to wait on them, they wouldn't have left."

"Don't even try it, Erin. I'm not in the mood for your excuses."

I lean my shoulder against the wall and look at him. "You're a lucky man, Steve."

He glares at me from under his wispy eyebrows. "What are you talking about?"

"To have this restaurant, in this city. To have people like Omar, Ron, and Jane working for you. And me. People who come in day after day and give you everything they have. The cooks worked their hearts out tonight. I hope you appreciate that."

"You're bringing tears to my eyes, Erin, but I don't need to be reminded of my good fortune. I want you here at three tomorrow to clean the wait station, inside and out. It's been a shambles for months."

"Sorry, but I won't be able to."

"Oh? Why's that?"

"Because I'm not coming in tomorrow. I quit."

"You quit?" He throws back his head and laughs. "Where are you going to go?"

"I'm sure there are other restaurants in this city that would hire a waiter with my skills."

He turns off the adding machine and rips the tape. "On second thought, forget what you owe me. It's worth a thousand dollars just to be rid of somebody who skated in here and pretended to be a professional. You think I'm so gullible that I didn't realize who you were?"

"I've had my difficulties, but I'm as good as any waiter here. Even Carl said so."

"Did he, now?" Steve suppresses a grin. "Well, if you think you're going to pull the same stunt someplace else, think again. I know a lot of people, Erin. By tomorrow, your little charade will be common knowledge with every manager at every decent restaurant in Manhattan. You'll have to move to Buffalo to find work."

I almost lose my composure. I almost crack and let anger and weariness finally take over. But instead, I turn and go down the hall to the changing room. I feel strangely numb as I take off my uniform and hang it in my locker. I'd always imagined my last night at Roulette as a happy one—I'd have a great new job and the worst would be over. But the worst is still ahead. If I'm lucky, the money I've saved will last until January. That doesn't give me much time to concoct a new life.

After pulling on my jeans and sweater, I punch out and drop my time card in the slot. I pause at the door, take one last look around, then turn off the light.

chapter 26

The weekend passes in a catatonic haze. I go out only to walk Rocket and pick up Chinese food, then slide back under the covers with chopsticks, Kung Pao chicken, and the remote. When I'm not sleeping or flipping through channels, I'm staring at the ceiling I won't be able to afford if I don't find another job before my savings run out. Cato, having heard the news from Omar, leaves a voice mail message trying to confirm rumors ("Alain said Patrick told him you threw a cocktail tray at Carl. Is that true? Where are you? Call me!") and assuring me that even the best waiters can't change the mood rating of someone like Steve.

Rachel drops by on Monday afternoon. "I brought something to cheer you up," she says through the intercom.

"Don't be shocked by my appearance," I warn.

"Am I ever?"

I leave the door open and flop down on the couch in my robe. Glancing through a gap in the curtains, I find that not only is the sun shining but the world has gone on without me.

Rachel walks in and strains to see me in the dim room. "Oh my God. You look terminal."

"I am. I have no reason to go on."

She puts her bag next to the couch and sits down. "You're

in a grieving period, that's all. I give it a week, two at the most. Now let's talk about your contingency plan."

"Roulette *was* my contingency plan."

"Oh. Right."

"See? I never should have quit. I can't even get another waiting job, thanks to Steve. I mean, I guess I could work at a bar somewhere . . ."

"He's bluffing."

"I know Steve. He doesn't bluff."

"You had to leave," she says, putting her hand on my arm. "It's time to get back to what you like doing, anyway."

"Are you kidding? I tried that with Design Refined. They practically laughed me out of the office."

"So? You're too talented to give up. Remember those marketing ideas you gave me last summer? When I complained about being broke?"

"Yeah. Back when I still used my brain for higher ideas."

"Well, guess what? I've been so busy I hardly have time to talk about being busy."

I pause, forgetting for a second that the world revolves around me. "Really?"

"Last month I finally did what you said and went into hock getting a Web site designed by these guys downtown. I put the address on my flyers and I've already gotten three shoots from it."

"No kidding. You mean I'm still good for something?"

"And your animal shelter idea was fantastic. Pet Parade wants me to take the April picture for their charity calendar."

"Wow," I say, managing to summon a little enthusiasm. "That's great."

She reaches out and pulls back the curtains. "This is just an idea, and you can take it or leave it, but maybe you should try consulting for a while. There have to be other people like me out there, small-business types who need help."

"Uh-uh. I'm not an entrepreneur."

"You could be if you tried."

"Something like that takes money to launch and years to build. My father's had his own business for years and it's still a struggle. I mean, how would I start?"

"Do what you told me to do," she says. "Get a Web site, work your connections, sacrifice."

"What about finding clients?"

"You did it at your last job. What's the difference?"

"Money. Time."

"Welcome to the real world."

"I only have enough savings for two months. You're acting like this would be easy."

"It wouldn't be. Photographing people's mutts isn't, but it's the path I chose. All I needed was a little boost, and look what happened."

I quickly imagine my future according to Rachel. In between sending out résumés and mulling over the idea of another service job, I research consulting and actually start a business. I turn down the thermostat, stop taking cabs, and subsist on pasta and jug wine. I set up a cozy home office and enjoy complete freedom, followed shortly by bankruptcy and a year-long stint as a runner at Hector's.

"It'll never work," I tell her.

"Just *think* about it. Oh . . . I almost forgot." She reaches into her bag and pulls out a black-and-white photograph. "Here," she says, handing it to me.

I stare at the picture of Rocket sitting on the grass, head turned to the side, whiskers blowing back in the wind. A cloudy sky shows through the branches of an oak tree in the background. "When did you take this? It's incredible."

"Remember that little trip we took to the park when I was trying to convince you to give him a home?"

"*Then?* Why didn't you show it to me before?"

She smiles. "I was waiting for the right time."

◆

After Rachel leaves, I put my waitressing shoes in a bag for the thrift store and decide to find out what I'm really up against. Sitting at the kitchen table with my laptop, I type *how to start a consulting business* into Google and get pages and pages of hits. I'm just beginning to scan them when I hear the phone ring in the living room. "Don't let it be Daniel," I mutter. "Oh, hell. *Please* let it be Daniel." It's probably my father again, wanting to discuss how to tell Harold I quit. "Sorry, Dad, you'll have to wait until later," I say as the machine picks up. But it isn't my father, or Daniel.

"Hello, Erin, this is Robin Howe from Design Refined. Gary and I enjoyed talking with you last week and were hoping you could come in for a second interview on Wednesday if you're available. Just call or e-mail me when you have a chance and we'll set up a time. Looking forward to talking to you. Bye."

◆

I sit at the conference table on Wednesday morning, more relaxed than I've been in months. I'm rested, informed, and secure in the knowledge that, this time, Robin and Gary really want me. We touch on salary ("How does something in the hundred range sound to start?" Gary asks), then discuss future projects ("I hear pony hair is making a comeback," I find myself saying). Taking in the dazzling view of midtown, I realize that things are finally working out for me. Roulette, Carl, the Porters—they're all in the past. I survived a rough ride through the restaurant business and an agonizing affair. I'm a different person now, and my future is just beginning.

So what's missing?

"You'll have the office next to Deborah, one of our graphic designers," Gary says. "But you won't be seeing much of each other. Everyone's putting in seventy-hour weeks so we can hit the deadline for the spring catalog. Better warn your boyfriend!" He laughs.

I chuckle back, wondering how Rocket will take it when I disappear again. Strange dog walkers. Lonely hours filled with barking and chewing through electrical cords.

"What do you think?" Robin asks.

"I think it...sounds great!" I say, smiling broadly. What's the matter with me? Here's the perfect opportunity—they even embrace my dark waitressing past—and I'm hesitating?

"We assume you need to give notice at Roulette," Gary says.

"What? Oh, yes. A week should be plenty."

Robin picks up her BlackBerry. "That would bring us to...December second. Can you be here on Monday the fifth?"

"Sure..."

"Good," she says, pressing a few keys. "We have a breakfast meeting at seven that morning, then I'm flying to Atlanta on Thursday for a trade show. I'd like you to come along."

"Me?"

"That way, you can get familiar with our company *and* our competition. When we get back, we'll be going full-steam on the catalog, but keep your bags packed because we head to Panama in February to check out the new manufacturing facilities."

"Panama?" I feel like the perfect man just asked me to marry him and I'm scrambling for reasons to back out.

Everything I wanted is right in front of me, but somehow, without my noticing it, what I want has changed.

"You seem a little overwhelmed," Gary says. "Are we throwing too much at you at once?"

"Not at all!" I say, snapping to attention. You're almost out of money, Erin. For God's sake, take the job.

"Bonuses are based on company profits," Gary begins. He talks insurance and benefits while I picture the path ahead, the decisions I'll have little or no say in, the work I may or may not get credit for, the structure that, from here, looks more like a trap. This isn't why I quit Roulette. For most of my life I've been the perfect cog—doing whatever was required of me and going where the boss told me to go. Now I'm out of sync with the world I knew. Three months of faking it and reinventing myself have left me braver, smarter, almost reckless.

"... which vests after you spend ten years with the company," Gary finishes. "Am I leaving anything out, Robin?"

"I don't think so. Erin? Any questions?"

"Actually . . ."

Robin and Gary look at me.

"I don't . . . I mean, I'm sorry." I grab my portfolio and stand up.

"Is something wrong?" Gary asks.

"Not at all," I say, shaking their hands. "I appreciate your offer very much."

"Is this a question of salary?" Gary asks. "Because if so . . ."

I walk around the head of the table. "The salary's fine."

"We could add one more week of paid vacation," Robin offers.

"That's very generous. But a friend of mine told me about another opportunity and, well . . ." I smile and open the door. "I just realized I'd be crazy to pass it up."

chapter 27

With Rachel's help I draw up a business plan. I create a budget and e-mail everyone I lost contact with when I started at Roulette. A college friend refers me to her stepmother, who sits on the board of a small charity. "Our donations this year are pitiful," the woman tells me when she returns my third phone call. "We need somebody who can turn that around." When she agrees to meet with me and read over my marketing proposal, I finally allow myself to believe that this could work. If I ace the meeting and use everything Cato taught me about reading and adapting to customers, I might be helping a group of wealthy women protect the Hudson River by this time next week.

I get up early on Friday, anxious to finish my proposal and do as much research as I can before tomorrow's appointment. I haven't even put on my robe before Rocket starts barking and scratching at the door. After a quick cup of coffee, I get dressed and we head down to the chilly, sun-drenched street. We pass the bagel shop, Rocket's favorite tree, and the newsstand on the corner. As we wait for the light to change, I spot the new issue of *Manhattan Today* hanging between *W* and *Metropolitan Home*. Next to a cover photo of Tory Burch in a Santa hat are the words *Evelyn Harker Sounds Off.*

I pluck it off the rack, pay, then lead Rocket into the park. With the words, "Stay where I can see you," I let him off his leash, sit on a bench, and flip through the pages until I find the Roulette review.

This week, Manhattan's most elusive mystery woman revisits a favorite Madison Avenue eatery and finds that someone has rearranged the cupboards . . .

ROULETTE—WHERE SHE STOPS, NOBODY KNOWS
by Evelyn Harker

If you eat out in New York, you've heard the buzz about Carl Corbett. With a just-published cookbook and twenty half-hour shows in the works for Edible Television, the chef of Madison Avenue's Roulette is on the brink of the sort of fame that turns perfectly good cooks into faces on soup cans. When I last reviewed his restaurant, the menu was clever but restrained, offering dishes that wowed the senses while avoiding the pretense common in so many Manhattan kitchens. Since then, innovation has bred unchecked, spawning bizarre recipes (laser-seared calves' brains, anyone?) and kitchen gadgets better suited to a trauma unit.

The dining room is still a glitzy retreat from the outside world, though triple-paned glass would have helped with the street noise my companions and I heard from our window table.

I stop reading and look up. Window table? Companions? So the woman we thought was Harker wasn't her at all. I think back to that night, to the blonde sitting with three other people at the window table in my section. The woman who asked a thousand questions, argued over what to order, and ate from everyone else's plate. She was actually Harker in disguise.

The menu, however, is unrecognizable. The appetizers have been pared down to focus on a few simple elements, painstakingly prepared. It's an interesting idea, reducing food to its essence so that diners aren't distracted by, say, flour or spices. But the daikon "opera ticket" with balsamic ink, while fun to look at ("Le Nozze di Figaro, Seat C3"), is really only a square of radish with a bit of vinegar. A single Olympia oyster "cooked" over lemon-infused gravel makes me long for such quaint techniques as throwing ingredients together and introducing them to a hot stove.

In contrast to the service on my last visit, our waitress is attentive, energetic, and informed enough to explain the starters, which include Inverted Philly Cheesesteak (the cheese is on the inside!) and Freeze-Dried Arugula Rolls (wrapped in rice paper grown on reclaimed battlefields outside Hanoi). The cheesesteak, grilled filet mignon slices injected with crunchy panko and Mull of Kintyre cheddar, would be delicious in any arrangement, but dehydrated arugula reminds me of the state of dim sum in Las Vegas circa 1974. Ligurian olive oil comes in a one-ounce jigger like cheap whiskey, and would benefit from something to put it on—guzzling oil is for Chevy Novas, not someone dropping three hundred dollars on dinner.

After a disappointing start, I hold out high hopes for the main courses, particularly the slow-baked whole rockfin. Though many chefs have stopped serving rockfin, Corbett isn't ready to abandon this threatened species. "Given a choice between my patrons and the future of the planet," he says, "I'll choose my patrons every time." Fair enough, but anything wrapped in chili skin "cellophane" and served on a vertical skewer should come with a warning label. If I wanted a mouthful of mace, I'd attend an anti-WTO rally. Fortunately, I can still taste the spit-roasted pigeon legs, which are rich and tender and accompanied by a bracing blue spruce jelly.

Fizzy champagne "relish" overwhelms crab meat stuffed into metal cylinders that give off smoke when you touch them. I keep expecting to find David Blaine hiding behind my wineglass.

Pastry chef Betsy Lowe is the sole steadying influence in the kitchen, whether she's dazzling diners with smoked ginger mille crêpes or turning a classic American flavor on its head with cherry Popsicle ice cream. Her pear cake with caramelized ricotta is my current favorite dessert—anywhere. No matter what she puts her hand to, she demonstrates the sort of imaginative discipline Corbett lost somewhere between the sous vide chamber and the dry ice machine.

Molecular gastronomy is the new tightrope for daring chefs, but not all manage to create culinary spectacles without becoming spectacles themselves. Once capable of producing a near-perfect dining experience, Corbett seems to have been led astray by a desire to outshine his contemporaries, or maybe by Cirque du Soleil. Whatever the cause, he's mislaid his own style in the process. If he can just step back and let the food speak for itself, Roulette may once again be a safe bet.

When I finally raise my head again, Rocket is gone.

"Rocket?"

I put the magazine on the bench and stand up, looking for his white ears in a row of bushes along the path. He was here just two minutes ago. I call him again, hoping he'll run out from behind a tree or down the leaf-strewn hill. But he's vanished.

Worry rising in my chest, I start down the paved path, then reverse course and trot across an open field. If I know Rocket, he's off-road and digging for rodents. "Come here, kiddo!" My voice sounds shrill and frantic, and a few passersby turn to watch me.

"Have you seen a Jack Russell in a blue fleece coat?" I ask an unshaven man dragging a malamute away from an old rubber ball.

"I think so. Couple of minutes ago, right?"

"Right."

"He went that way," the man says, pointing in the direction of the half-frozen lake.

"Thanks." I take off at a jog, clutching Rocket's retractable leash and listening for his bark. He couldn't have made it to the street yet. No, I won't even consider that. I stop at the edge of the water, heart beating wildly. I'm contemplating diving in to search for him, when I hear high-pitched yelps coming from a clump of trees several yards away. A moment later Rocket comes racing across the grass, ears back, with another, much larger dog on his tail. Fritz.

The ground seems to tilt under my feet. Then Fritz is jumping up and leaving muddy paw prints on my jacket while Rocket wades foreleg deep into the lake to bark at a duck. "How did you find us, Fritz?" I ask, rubbing his head. When I glance back toward the trees, I see Daniel in his black coat and suit, walking toward me with a red ball thrower in his hand. I don't care that I'm wearing old sneakers and pajama bottoms under my ripped jeans, or that my hair is stuffed into a knitted hat with a tassel on top. I'm too happy to see him.

He starts a little at the sight of me. "Hi there."

"Hi."

"Is my dog bothering you?"

"No more than usual."

"He's being pretty friendly. He must think he's seen you before."

"I wonder why."

We look at each other, our smiles fading. He chucks a ball

across the field and Fritz tears after it, kicking up clouds of dirt.

"I stopped by Roulette last night," he says. "Alain said you don't work there anymore."

"I quit a few weeks ago."

"I thought maybe you were trying to avoid me."

"No, it was just time to go."

"So . . . what are you doing now?"

"I got a good job offer, but I decided to do some consulting instead. We'll see where it leads."

"That's fantastic, Erin. I'm really happy for you."

"Thanks."

He fiddles with his gray cashmere scarf. I swallow, my throat dry.

"Listen," he says. "I've been thinking a lot about what happened with us, obsessing over it, actually—"

"So have I."

"I've been kicking myself ever since I took you to that party. I was an insensitive ass. I realize that."

"You're not going to get an argument from me."

He takes the ball from Fritz's mouth and throws it again. "The way Patti and Sonia acted that night . . . I should have known it would happen. Maybe I did know and I couldn't admit it. Anyway, I just wish I hadn't lost you before I figured things out."

Lost you. Though I've spent weeks nursing my anger, the words sound too sad, too final. Is this what I want? To never see Daniel again unless our dogs find each other in the park? To always wonder how things might have turned out if we'd made it past Roulette?

"Why did you stonewall me like that?" he asks. "Why couldn't we hash it out together?"

I squint against the sun. "Because I felt duped, Daniel.

It was like . . . you weren't who I thought you were. Some other guy stepped into your place."

"It kills me to hear you say that."

"It's the truth."

"Then I guess I understand why you cut me off," he says. "I really put you in a bad spot, didn't I?"

"The worst."

After a long silence, he says, "I'm sorry. I hope you believe that."

He bends over to pet Rocket and I try unsuccessfully to conjure up the hurt I thought I'd never let go. Until now, I didn't *want* to let it go. It was easier to blame Daniel for everything than to think that our biggest obstacle might be me. "I called your office a few weeks ago," I say.

"Really?" His face brightens. "If I'd known that, I'd have come to your apartment and camped on the doorstep until you let me in."

"I just needed to talk, I guess. Maybe yell at you a little more."

"I wish you had," he says. "I can take yelling. But not seeing you . . ."

"It's been hell," I admit.

"For you too?" he says, stepping closer. "Jesus, I miss you. Not having you in my life anymore—it isn't right."

"I don't like it either."

"So . . . what does that mean?"

I smile up at him. "What do you want it to mean?"

He lets the ball thrower fall to the ground and grabs me. A busy Tuesday morning goes on around us: sirens wail in the distance, people jog by, the page of a newspaper blows across the grass and catches on my shoe. But we just stand there by the lake with our arms around each other.

✦

One month later . . .

"I'll get another show," Cato says, pouring sugar into his coffee. "I wasn't that crazy about the script, anyway."

It's a week before Christmas and we're sitting in a diner on Lexington Avenue. Cato's shirt is open at the collar and he has on the same charcoal-gray pants and rubber-soled shoes he wore every night at Roulette.

"I don't get it," I say. "How does a play just lose funding?"

He shrugs and looks out at the sidewalk, which is lined with gray, recently plowed snow. "Crummy producers. No interest from anybody else. Same thing happened to my friend Lee, except he had four months of rehearsals behind him. At least I didn't put in that much time. It was great, though. Just standing onstage in front of all those empty seats, I felt like I was finally starting to live."

"I'm sorry it didn't work out," I say. "But I'm sure you won't be away from the spotlight for long."

"Believe me, I'm doing everything I can to stay visible." He blows on his steaming coffee and takes a sip. "It could have been worse, I guess. My friend tried to get his bartending job back and they acted like they'd never seen him before. At least Carl went to bat for me with Steve. Weird, huh? Carl was *nice*. Anyway, he probably just enjoys having me around so he can give me shit about falling flat on my face."

"You mean, the way *he* did in Harker's review?"

Cato winces. "Everybody knows you waited on her, too. Talk about adding insult to injury. Jane said Carl flipped when he saw the article. Got chest pains and had to go to Lenox Hill for a shot of downers."

"How'd Gina react?"

"She drank like a Big Ten freshman and passed out in the private dining room. Steve wouldn't talk to anybody for about a week, but now he's his bitter self again. Just like old times."

We laugh. "Except for the menu," I say. "Daniel told me it's different."

Cato leans against the wall and stretches his legs over the seat of the booth. "Yeah, you should have heard the blow-up between Steve and Carl. Carl wanted to keep it edgy, but Steve's pushing him to ditch the foams and go back to crowd-pleasers. Carl spends half his time at the TV studio anyway, which means Phil's strutting around the kitchen playing head honcho."

"He's the *sous* chef?"

"For the moment, but he's barely keeping it together back there. It's only a matter of time before he goes after José with something sharp and about yay long." He holds his palms far apart.

I squeeze out my tea bag and set it on my napkin. "I bet Jane's glad you're back."

"Yeah, but she'll be moving on to bedpans and IVs pretty soon. You heard she finally said yes to Julian, right?"

"She left me a message the next morning. Is Derek still around?"

"He's trying to find investors to help him open a place in Brooklyn. Last I heard it was looking pretty promising."

"Uh-oh. Derek's going to be in charge of something?"

"Scary, huh? God help the poor bastards who live in Williamsburg. He doesn't have a clue. Oh, and guess who's moving on in search of better money? I'll give you a hint. He knows absolutely everything about waiting tables."

I think for a few seconds. "Ron?"

"Yup. He's starting at Vong next week."

"You're not serious."

"It takes a lot of guts to start at the bottom when you're a member of the Viagra set. He's actually going to work some *lunch* shifts until he moves up the ranks. That's why I'm staying put. I'm not going to be the new guy who gets stuck working Christmas. Besides, I won't be in this business much longer. It's gotta be my turn again soon, right?"

"With your talent?" I say. "Of course."

He stares into the distance for a minute before smiling and looking back at me. "So, what's happening with you? You're going out on your own, huh?"

"Yeah. I already have a few clients—a charity, and a spa that just opened in Chelsea. I got offered that job I told you about, but I turned it down."

"No shit? Good benefits and everything? I could tell you were crazy from the moment I met you."

"I'm definitely taking a risk. Things are tight right now and I'm learning as I go along, but working for somebody else . . . I don't know, it's time I did things my way."

"You're going to be big in this town," Cato says. "You made an impact at Roulette that's shaking the place to this day."

I raise my arm for the check. "Better than going out with a whimper, I guess."

"My motto is, it doesn't matter what they say as long as they're still talking about you after you're gone." He pulls his wallet from his backpack. "I'm getting this one, sweetie. You're trying to build an empire and I'm head waiter at the money tree. It isn't booming like it was, but it's still a decent living." He lays a twenty on the table, more than twice the amount of the bill. "I really thought I'd said good-bye to that world."

"You did before, you will again."

We put on our coats and walk arm in arm to Roulette. It's only mid-afternoon, but the sky is already darkening and the streetlights have switched on. "I'd go in, but I'm not quite ready to see Gina yet," I say.

Cato pulls his backpack off his shoulder. "This might sound strange, but I think she was fond of you in her own way. Italians love a challenge."

"So do Americans. I guess that's why I didn't leave the first day."

He takes my shoulder and shakes it gently. "Sure you won't come in and say hi to the old gang? Things are always different after you leave a place. The people get nicer when they realize they've got nothing over you."

"I'll come in with Daniel some night. How's that?"

"Just don't forget to ask for me. I may be close to hanging up my tie, but I'm still the best in the city."

I reach up and kiss him on the cheek. "Yes, you are, and I don't know how I'd have made it without you."

He smiles. "Now it's *your* turn to show *me* how it's done."

"Okay. I promise I won't quit this time."

"I'm counting on you." He steps past the potted bay trees and pulls open the front door. "Well, here I go. Best acting job I'll never get famous for."

I wave while walking backward up the street. "Knock 'em dead."

He bows and disappears inside.

Acknowledgments

Enormous thanks to our agent, Kim Witherspoon, and our editor, Susan Kamil, who helped us turn our mishmash of autobiographical ingredients into a story. Thanks also to Kerri Buckley, for her creative wisdom and insight, and to Barb Burg, Theresa Zoro, Alexis Hurley, Julie Schilder, Noah Eaker, and Peggy McPartland. Margo Lipschultz offered encouragement and guidance in the early stages, and Beth Aretsky made sure we got the details right. Without the keen eye of Eleanor Jackson, this book might never have been published. Many thanks to Carlos Llaguno of Brasserie Les Halles and Andrew Carmellini of A Voce Restaurant, and to Mimi Sheraton, Jeffrey Steingarten, Amanda Hesser, and Frank Bruni, whose writings make us love to read about food and restaurants. Finally, we're grateful to Paul, Jack, and our parents, for their love and support.